Body Brace

Everything can change ... except murder.

A body brace is a kind of holder that secures the TV camera and helps stabilize footage. That comes in handy when reporter Elizabeth Danniher takes on an assignment for KWMT involving a kids' camp and a Cottonwood County historic reenactment. The assignment takes unexpected turns, leaving triple mysteries to unravel. But a body brace can also be metaphorical, providing support as Elizabeth and friends negotiate changing futures ... with some surprises.

5-Star Praise for *Body Brace*

"These books always make me think about my own life relationships and the mysteries make me exercise my brain in a different way. I'm always left curious and wanting more. Not because of cliffhangers, but because I care about the characters and how they make me look at myself."

Caught Dead in Wyoming series

Sign Off

Left Hanging

Shoot First

Last Ditch

Look Live

Back Story

Cold Open

Hot Roll

Reaction Shot

Body Brace

Cross Talk

"While the mystery itself is twisty-turny and thoroughly engaging, it's the smart and witty writing that I loved the best."

—*Diane Chamberlain, New York Times bestselling author*

More cozy mystery

Secret Sleuth series

Death on the Diversion

Death on Torrid Avenue

Death on Beguiling Way

Death on Covert Circle

Death on Shady Bridge

Death on Carrion Lane

Death on ZigZag Trail

Mystery with romance

The Innocence Trilogy

Proof of Innocence

Price of Innocence

Premise of Innocence

BODY BRACE

Caught Dead in Wyoming, Book 10

Patricia McLinn

DAY ONE

THURSDAY

Chapter One

THURSTON FINE'S VOICE hit me as I walked into the newsroom of KWMT-TV.

Mornings aren't my favorite in the best of circumstances. Morning and Thurston Fine are a deadly combination.

Then add on the fact that they stood beside the widening in the hallway that served as the break room.

In other words, they were between me and my next hit of coffee.

"Children playing at cowboys and Indians? Absolutely not. That is beneath my dignity." Thurston's lofty tone was worthy of someone who'd endured a slanderous affront to his journalist ethics.

For the anchor of KWMT-TV of Sherman, Wyoming, that meant it was play-acting. He has no journalistic ethics. Some—including me—would say he's not a journalist, period. As for his dignity, he had the touchy spun-glass external kind, involving clothes, cars, and hair gel, but none of the deeper than the bones-into-the-soul kind.

"It's not—" began the station's News Director.

Fine cut him off. "I don't do that kind of story. I'm not going out to that God-forsaken dust bowl and report on a bunch of screaming kids."

As I discreetly slid past them to reach the coffeemaker, I mentally noted that it was not the first time he'd refused an assignment. And not the first time I'd wondered how he got away with talking to a News Director that way, even though this News Director was Les

Haeburn, who possessed a temper but no spine. Not a pretty combination.

So how did Fine get away with dictating to Haeburn? Tempting to say Fine knew where Haeburn's bodies were buried?

As much as I liked to figure out puzzles, did I truly care about this one? Nope. Trying to work out the Haeburn-Fine dynamic felt like the worst possible use of my time. Well below scrubbing toilets.

At that moment, the best use of my time was pouring a lot of coffee into a big mug.

In a few of the stations I've worked at, the News Director did the dictating. At the good ones it was a collaborative relationship among News Director, anchors, reporters, editors, camera people, and more. Those were the gems.

KWMT-TV was a lump of coal.

Over the twenty-some months since I'd arrived, I was pleased to observe it developing into a somewhat more refined lump of coal, but coal nonetheless, at this rate it would require millennia multiplied by millennia to aspire to diamond status.

Mind you, I don't take direction from this News Director the way I did at other stations on my climb up to the No. 1 TV news market. The pinnacle from which I'd plummeted to KWMT.

If you don't like being ruled by numbers, don't get into TV news. Every TV news market is ranked, based on "TV households," because a household and its residents don't count if they don't have a TV. From the top, those rankings go from New York, through LA and Chicago, past Washington, D.C.—which considers itself a big deal, but c'mon, it barely slips into the top ten at No. 9, so in TV land it's barely into the world of the big boys—right down to the bottom of the triple-digits where KWMT-TV resides.

"It's a news story." Haeburn almost pleaded with Fine. "The angle's the brand-new location this year."

"That is another reason I won't do it. There are important people who are totally against this event."

My interest picked up. If Fine's idea of *important* people were against it, I might be all for it.

"Like who?" I asked Thurston.

"I'm not telling you."

"You should be telling our viewers. It's what journalists do."

Before Thurston responded, Haeburn, with the unsettling air of a predator sensing a nearby prey, turned to me.

"*You* could do the story."

Had he picked up on that fleeting thought about my interest picking up?

Contractually, Haeburn wasn't in a position to assign me stories willy-nilly. I had the consumer affairs beat with the "Helping Out! with Elizabeth Margaret Danniher" segment and "special projects" of my choosing. That didn't mean he couldn't ask, but he seldom did. The one area we seemed to agree on was minimizing our contact.

"Me?"

"*Her?*"

Haeburn turned on Fine. "Why not? You won't and it's a news story."

That gave me an instant to recognize that Haeburn wasn't asking me solely to put Thurston's nose out of joint. Nor to get at me. It was to get himself out of something.

If he *had* picked up on that tick up in my interest, it was from somewhere deep in his self-serving lizard brain that knew how to manipulate reporters.

That landed on the negative side of whether to take the assignment. Getting Les Haeburn out of a predicament, especially by being manipulated did not appeal.

"It wouldn't kill you," Haeburn said to me.

"I'll think about it."

I saw my response discomfited Haeburn. Not my intention, but it didn't break my heart, either.

He hoped I'd say yes, because not having this story covered put him in some sort of pickle. At the same time, he hated that hope, because it meant relying on me. And he absolutely didn't want to be grateful to me.

He also didn't want Fine chewing his tail.

Snares in every direction.

"*She* won't do it either," Fine said to Haeburn, as if I weren't standing right in front of him. "There's no dead body involved, her little buddy's no longer here, and it's not *Pulitzer* material."

My *little buddy* was ex-NFL player Michael Paycik, formerly KWMT-TV's Eye on Sports, and now at a network affiliate in Chicago taking his rightful spot in the big leagues.

Watching how Mike's advancement ate at Thurston provided solace for missing Mike.

"Thurston, you do know there's no category for TV news in the Pulitzers, don't you?" I asked.

He scoffed, as if I'd made a faux pas.

Then he turned and marched into Haeburn's office. Time to get started on that tail-chewing.

Haeburn leaned toward me and said in a low voice, "I'll give you Diana as much as you want if you take—"

"Les!" Thurston demanded from the News Director's office.

Our News Director scurried in and closed the office door.

Immediately commenced the tail chewing.

Amazing they still hadn't figured out that most of what was said in that office could be heard in the newsroom bullpen—especially when it was said loudly by Thurston Fine.

The thrust of his comments repeated that the story shouldn't be covered.

The promise of having Diana Stendahl at my disposal as the assigned cameraperson might otherwise be a nudge toward doing the story.

She was the best shooter at KWMT-TV and my favorite co-worker—hands down since Michael Paycik left Sherman for the heady climes of the Number Three market in the country. Diana also was my good friend.

But Haeburn so rarely involved himself in daily decisions that assignment editors—occasionally bullied by Thurston—determined most reporter-shooter pairings. For him to meddle now could turn the assignment board into chaos.

Boy, I hoped Haeburn wasn't starting to show interest in day-to-day operations—the downside was so steep, I wouldn't risk it.

Especially since Diana and I generally wrangled the schedule to our liking without Haeburn's blessing.

On the other hand, if Thurston's idea of *important people* didn't want it covered, it became more tempting.

Decisions, decisions.

✧ ✧ ✧ ✧

I WENT INTO the station's library to research.

It was dusty, windowless, cramped, and entirely devoid of allure. That meant it provided privacy not available in the newsroom bullpen of decrepit desks and chairs ... and nosy eyes and ears.

Usually, the nosiness didn't bother me much. It had increased significantly over the past year and a half, which I considered a sign of progress from apathy toward being a normal newsroom. In this case, though, until I decided about this assignment, I'd keep it to myself.

With hints supplied by Haeburn and Fine, I deduced the assignment involved coverage of a week-long camp for children, followed on Saturday by a reenactment by adults of a Cottonwood County historical event called the Miners' Camp Fight.

Both events had been held on a specific property in the county for as far back as I spot-checked the clips—at least a couple decades.

But this year's was in a new location.

That was Haeburn's hot angle.

Not.

The change of venue might involve Thurston's *important people,* but I wasn't picking up anything tangible from the *Sherman Independence* archive. Under owner and editor Needham Bender, if there'd been anything tangible, it would have been reported.

The name Nadine Hulte, cropped up frequently as the source for unrelentingly upbeat quotes. The woman ran the Two Rivers Camp and organized the reenactment. I hadn't encountered her before.

However, familiar names showed as being on the committee—the same names on most of the civic committees in the county. Also, the

Sherman Western Frontier Life Museum supported both the reenactment and the camp. Clara Atwood was, essentially, the museum and
we'd crossed paths before. I'd consider us amicable professional
acquaintances.

After my first pass at research, it was clear this wasn't a story that
would have the Emmy Awards clamoring and the Pulitzers sure
wouldn't be moved to add a broadcast prize to honor it. But its biggest
downside remained setting a precedent of doing anything Les Haeburn
asked me to do.

I went outside. Not to escape the dust, because the wind-swept
empty space around KWMT-TV's building and parking lot generated
plenty of that, but for fresh air.

Considering calling Needham Bender to see if he knew anything
interesting not in the *Independence*, I took out my phone.

It immediately indicated an incoming video call.

Mike Paycik.

Chapter Two

WITH THE RECENT encounter with Thurston fresh in my mind, I flashed back to the day Mike gave his notice at KWMT-TV.

It was splendid to see his colleagues—almost all his colleagues—genuinely wished Mike the very best and were hugely pleased for him moving on to bigger and better things.

The exceptions were Les Haeburn, Thurston Fine, and a handful of acolytes. If there'd been a bucket of nails to chew, they'd have finished them off in no time.

Then came the day Mike left for Chicago.

Not such a splendid day.

Except it was what he was meant to do. A job he deserved. A place he knew and had friends.

There was absolutely no downside to this huge career advance for him ... except for leaving his friends behind in Cottonwood County.

But he still had his house and his ranch and his roots here.

He'd be back, he insisted. For visits.

At the moment, however, the visiting was going the opposite direction.

Jennifer Lawton, a KWMT-TV news aide and computer whiz, was in Chicago, visiting Mike.

Not only was Jennifer gone, but with her there, Mike hadn't called as frequently.

He was occupied with his guest, which I understood. Really. I just felt like the kid in the class not invited to the birthday party.

"Mike!" I answered with extra enthusiasm.

"Hey, Elizabeth. How are you?" He looked and sounded tired.

"Good. How are you and Jennifer doing as neighbors?"

Mike had a small apartment in Evanston, the first suburb north of Chicago along Lake Michigan. Jennifer's parents wouldn't have approved of her staying with him. But Mike solved it beautifully. His neighbor was in Europe and gave permission for Jennifer to stay in her apartment for the week, with Mike thoroughly big-brothering her from across the hall.

Her own space. From Jennifer's viewpoint that made the trip a success right there.

He exhaled. "I thought we'd go to a few ballgames, have great meals, that kind of thing."

"Jennifer doesn't want to do that?"

"Oh, yeah, we did that. *And* the Field Museum and Shedd Aquarium and the Museum of Science and Industry. And then she went back to Science and Industry—twice—and a library because she can work with 3D printing and a laser something-or-other and other stuff I thought was only in Star Trek movies. And I think she's ready to move into this robotics workshop place she discovered in the Near North. Or maybe they're trying to get her to move in, because from what I can tell they're real interested in a couple of her ideas.

"Jennifer's wearing me into the ground, Elizabeth. She wants to see everything. Right now. I did have one brilliant idea. Got her on one of those architecture tours on a boat and got to rest my feet and my eyes—"

"And fell sound asleep. I heard."

"Well, I was tired."

Trying not to laugh—but not trying too hard—I crooned, "Poor baby."

"You mean me, right? Because my head is past exploding, but for Jennifer it's like super-charged fuel."

Now I did laugh. "Just promise me you'll do two things. Get her to the Art Institute and some live theater." I counted Chicago as my home base, having grown up at the fringes of the metro area.

He groaned. "And Mrs. P made me promise to take her to the

Chicago Historical Society. I'll need a vacation to recover from Jennifer's vacation."

Mrs. Parens was a retired teacher and principal who had Michael Paycik's number so thoroughly that a neutral look from the woman standing more than a foot shorter than him made the former NFL player quake in his proverbial boots.

And now I knew she could accomplish that from twelve-hundred miles away.

"Only a few more days before Jennifer leaves Sunday and you can rest up."

"Yeah." Before I probed this uncharacteristically down tone, he asked, "What's new there? Anything cooking?"

By that second question, he meant along the lines of murder investigations several of us—including him and Jennifer—pursued together.

"Pretty quiet, except a historic reenactment this weekend."

"Oh, the Miners' Camp Massacre."

"Miners' Camp Fight," I corrected.

"Right, right. Keep forgetting they changed that. Don't tell Mrs. P."

I related my encounter with Thurston and Les, including my thoughts on dignity.

"He doesn't have the spun-glass or the soul kind," Mike said. It was no great sacrifice to let him win that argument. "But what about Two Rivers Camp? That should be part of the coverage."

"Yeah, that, too. Did you attend? Why Two Rivers? Doesn't look like it's near any rivers."

"Sure, I went. The rivers are the communities. The—Gotta go. Call coming in from a source. I miss you guys. Really miss you, Elizabeth."

And he was gone.

The mirage of remembered Chicago moments called up by his accounts faded into the view I most associated with Cottonwood County—fence line, sage brush, distant cattle, against climbing mountains and a sky so big and blue it reminded me of infinity even more forcefully than star-studded night skies did.

✧ ✧ ✧ ✧

I STOPPED AT the Sherman Supermarket on the way home from the station.

Not for my regular shopping, but a quick pick-up.

This is one difference between Cottonwood County and Manhattan, where I previously lived ... along with the whole matter of significantly fewer people, no tall buildings, lots more cattle, and way bigger skies. In Manhattan, much of the population shopped frequently, even daily, for that night's dinner. In Cottonwood County, a fair percentage of shoppers are in the supermarket for this month's staples, because a trip into town takes some doing.

Me? I was there for dessert.

Not for my favorite Pepperidge Farm Double Dark Chocolate Milano cookies, because I had a more than adequate supply at home. Also at work. And a few backup packages at friends' houses.

But for something to serve for dessert tonight, because Diana was coming over. Actually, she was bringing dinner. The best kind of dinner guest.

I picked up a sea salt caramel pie. They also had sheepherders bread made fresh that day. It couldn't possibly be as good as my next-door neighbor Iris Undlin made—especially when she brought it over warm from the oven—but it would do in a pinch.

Iris told me it was an old recipe from the border region where France and Spain met, brought to the American West by Basque sheepherders and now made mostly in Dutch ovens—how's that for international?

On the way from the bakery to the front of the store to check out, I visited the cookie aisle and picked up a couple more packages of cookies. I'm a strong believer in backups of backups when it comes to cookies.

Two checkers were working. I chose the one with the longer line— mind you, in Sherman that's three people instead of two. The reason for opting for the longer line was the checker.

All branches of the Cottonwood County grapevine passed through

Penny Czylinski's checkout stand at the Sherman Supermarket.

I wasn't in the market for news or gossip at the moment, but it would have felt like I was using her to only go to Penny when I wanted information.

Besides, she might not share when I was looking for info if I didn't stay in her good graces.

"Bye now, Loraine. Well, hi there, Elizabeth. Iris and Zeb gone another week, I see. And no steaks with that handsome Mike Paycik off to Chicago." Her sigh was shorter than most people's breaths—no sense wasting time on non-words. "Hear you're covering the Two Rivers Camp and reenactment?"

"I haven't—"

"Emmaline Parens will be happy to hear that. She was not pleased with Thurston Fine year before last. Standing out there like a stick, getting—"

Mrs. Parens was among the familiar names on the committee I'd read about.

"—every other word wrong and as miserable as a turkey on Thanksgiving. She's been involved from the start. Least after a group of them made a hash of it the first year. Changed the history all up, as if everybody didn't know the Indians won that fight. Didn't even include Indians that first year, which made it a downright lopsided affair. That's when Emmaline Parens took hold of the reenactment. Then she started the camp—"

"About the reenactment—"

"—a year after that. Practically had to hogtie kids—from the reservation and the others. But after a bit, the word started spreading and there hasn't been an empty spot for a couple decades now. Why, the greatest battle in Cottonwood County, of—"

A reference to the history being reenacted? Or when Mrs. Parens took hold of the event?

"—course. Bye now, Elizabeth. Hello there, Bella."

Spit out of Penny's aisle like a gumball from a gumball machine, I gathered my shopping bag and headed out, wrestling with a difficult concept.

If he knew about Mrs. Parens' involvement and he knew about my connection to her, Les Haeburn might be sneakier than I'd given him credit for.

Chapter Three

I CALLED DIANA from the parking lot. She was all for extending the dinner invitation to Mrs. Parens and Gisella Decker—otherwise known to us as Aunt Gee, because of that familial tie to Mike.

We might have included Aunt Gee regardless, since her knowledge of the county, while not as deep in history as Mrs. P's, included a mental database from decades as a sheriff's department dispatcher. Add in that she provided transportation for Mrs. P from the town of O'Hara Hill—second-largest in the county and therefore barely a hamlet—and it was a given.

But when I called Mrs. P, it turned out she and Aunt Gee were in the car, driving to Sherman for a dinner connected to the reenactment and camp. After a quick consultation, they accepted an invitation to stop by for dessert.

After a moment's internal debate, I went back in the store for a second pie.

Leftovers are always better than coming up short.

As I pulled out of the parking lot, my phone rang.

With no hello, Mike said, "Hey, did you hear Russell Teague's in a hospital here? I forgot to ask when I called before."

Russell Teague was an uber rich, uber strange, and uber reclusive sometimes-resident of Cottonwood County.

He'd inherited a ranch from his father that adjoined the ranch of Tom Burrell. One of the other familiar names on the committee involved with the historic reenactment and this kid's camp. But unlike Tom's ranch—often referred to as a real nice spread in the local vernacular—the Teague place was considered a ranching disgrace.

Russell left the county as a youngster, tied himself to his rich maternal grandfather's purse strings, then made a dubious name for himself with expensive quirks and quests, including flying hot air balloons over tall mountains. After inheriting the ranch from a father who'd searched for treasure instead of ranching, Russell carried on that tradition while also compiling a private Old West town.

Among the historic buildings he'd snapped up and moved to his ranch, he seemed to particularly like saloons.

He also was one of two remaining contenders in an ongoing legal action to sort out the future of a stash of historic gold coins.

"What's wrong with him? And why is he in Chicago?"

"What's wrong is he's dying. Word is it's multiple organ failure. He tried to buy a couple, but—"

"A couple organs?"

"Yup. That's the rumor. But it appears that with a bunch of them going, even Teague can't manage it. It's some syndrome his mother died of, too. The top specialist is here at Northwestern."

"Wow. There was nothing about it on the rundowns for tonight's newscasts."

"Tribune had a story this morning. I'd think AP would have picked it up."

AP—the Associated Press—definitely would have picked up a story on Russell Teague from the *Chicago Tribune*. Especially a story about him dying.

I pulled over and started texting. "I can't believe Audrey would miss that on the wires, unless—"

In unison, we groaned, "Thurston."

Our esteemed anchor had a habit of turning off the police scanner because the noise penetrated his private office—the best one in the building—interrupting his afternoon naps. Most of the time someone remembered to check, but not always.

Recently, he'd started disabling AP alerts. Because, naturally, he didn't want to be interrupted by anything like *news*.

Problem was, he was so inept, he frequently disabled alerts for the entire newsroom.

And with Jennifer away for the week, our best defense against his tech ineptitude was absent.

"Messaged Audrey to find the story," I told him. "Warned her to check alerts, too. Tell Jennifer she might get a call about how to turn them back on."

"Will do."

"So, how's the job? Tougher than KWMT?"

"Not really. You prepared me well. Besides, I've got a lot more help and the equipment's a dream—once you learn it. Jennifer came in with me one morning and—after she stopped drooling—gave me tips and shortcuts. Despite her wearing me into the ground, we're having a great time. Wish the rest of you were here, too."

"What? And miss my big potential assignment this weekend?"

To my surprise, he said, "You should do it."

"To save Les' unworthy derriere?"

"No. To give it good coverage. It's an interesting event. Lots of history. Tom could tell you—"

"Mrs. P and your aunt are coming for dessert and to fill me in enough to decide."

"What's for dessert?" Nice to know I still knew how to distract him.

"Sea salt caramel pie."

"Mmm. I wonder if—"

"I am not sending you pie. There's plenty of great pie in Chicago. Now, don't you need to be working?"

"Nah, done for the day. But Jennifer just got here and we're going to dinner."

"Tough life."

"Yeah." He had a grin in his voice. "Take that assignment, and give it the full E.M. Danniher touch."

Chapter Four

TRUTH BE TOLD, I might welcome an assignment—not that I'd let Fine and Haeburn know that.

Though the reason was open to debate, as Diana and I proved over dinner by debating it.

Diana had dropped her kids—Jessica and Gary Junior—at separate activities. Then she picked up takeout from Hamburger Heaven for our dinner.

"How're the kids?" I asked as I made salad from ingredients in my fridge so we'd feel noble before finishing with the sea salt caramel pie when Mrs. P and Aunt Gee joined us.

"Fine."

I turned at something in her voice. "Diana—?"

"I heard something about a big story and Thurston turning off the wire notifications. Fill me in."

Okay. So, she didn't want to talk about whatever that was in her voice.

I relayed Mike's news about Russell Teague, Thurston's turning off the alerts, and the update since.

Audrey had messaged that Thurston balked at *disrupting* the Five to add anything more than the bare statement that one of the county's wealthiest residents was in serious condition.

And even then, Fine made it sound like Teague was hospitalized in Chicago with a bad sniffle.

That segued to the topic of the assignment, telling her specifics of the exchange with Thurston and Les, then mentioning I might welcome the assignment, thus leading to our disagreement on the possible cause of that welcoming.

"You're lonely," Diana said.

"I'm bored," I disputed.

"And your boredom happens to coincide with Mike leaving town and Tom leaving the playing field?"

"That is an inaccurate description of what was an adult and reasoned discussion that concluded with the decision to put the welfare of his young daughter before anything else."

"Tell it to the Marines."

"Diana Stendahl. I'm shocked at your imputation that I am not being truthful." From that lofty tone, I descended to normal. "Did you know that's only half of the original phrase? *Tell it to the Marines, because the sailors won't believe it.* Can't imagine the Marines are happy at the implication they're more gullible. Although—"

I was aware of Diana turning her head toward me, but chose not to assess her reaction. I was busy cutting my hamburger in half.

"—there was a movie with Cary Grant and Ginger Rogers that my mother dug up where Grant's a World War II newsman caught in an area Nazis are flooding into and forced to read this piece on the radio saying the Nazis can't be beat. At the end he tells his listeners to tell the Army and Navy they might as well give up and—above all—to tell it to the Marines. Pretty clever, huh? Because the Nazis take it at face value, but American listeners know everything he said was hooey."

"Hooey?"

"It's a strange movie. Part romantic comedy, part war movie. It's called *Once Upon a Honeymoon.* The war movie part is a reminder that nobody knew how it would turn out, since it was made in the early—"

"Elizabeth."

"—Forties. Oh. And Ginger Rogers doesn't sing or dance."

"Any more?"

"About the movie? I don't think so. I could look it up and—"

"No."

"Oh, wait. There is one more thing. John Banner's in it. Sgt. Schultz from *Hogan's Heroes.* He fled his native Austria when it unified with Germany because he was Jewish. Family members were murdered in the Holocaust. And he joined the U.S. Armed Forces during the war."

"That's both sad and interesting. But it's even more indicative you've been watching and reading too much about old movies and TV shows. Elizabeth, you've got to snap out of it."

"There's nothing to snap out of. I'm fine. It's just been quiet with Mike gone, Jennifer visiting him, Iris and Zeb on vacation, and Mrs. P, Aunt Gee, and Linda—" My friend, Linda Caswell. "—wrapped up in what I now realize is the committee for this reenactment, while you and—"

"You could have volunteered to help."

"Me? Recreating Cottonwood County's history from more than a century ago when I need to look up what happened two years back? Mrs. P would laugh me out of the committee. And—yes—Diana, I did notice you cut off my saying anything about what you and Sheriff Russ Conrad have been up to."

She smiled.

The smile of a woman having a really good time with the right man.

I simultaneously felt happy for her and like I wanted to go see what old movie was on TV.

Maybe I *was* a little down.

But then Diana's smile faded.

"What's wrong?" I asked.

"Jess has been demonstrating her full teenager-hood lately. Nothing major," she added quickly. "Talking back. Viewing me as a cross between a certifiable dolt and a dictator. That sort of thing."

"Huh. She seemed fine last time I saw her."

"That was almost two weeks ago, when your nephew was still here."

My brother Bill and his wife Anna, along with their four kids, visited on their way to and from Yellowstone Park—along with my parents, who already made the trip earlier in the summer.

Bill and Anna's oldest, James Robert, but always called J.R., was a year older than Jessica. They *had* seemed to hit it off…

"You mean Jess and J.R.—?"

"The greatest love story ever, at least in her mind."

"Are they in touch?"

"All day, every day. I can't decide if I'm dreading or looking forward to when nature and distance take their toll. But to get back to the assignment, you should take it, Elizabeth. I've been scheduled for them for a month. I've shot them most years since I started."

"That sneaky beast." I told her Haeburn dangled her out as an enticement.

"How about not thinking about whether *he* wants you to do stories, but about whether *you* want to do them."

"Not factor in irritating Thurston versus helping out Les? What an odd concept."

"Embrace it," she ordered. "Start from the top. What do you know?"

I told her what Penny said about the reenactment, adding, "This isn't the same as the Battle of Cottonwood County, is it? Mrs. P didn't seem convinced when that professor aired his theories last winter."

"That's because this has nothing to do with the Battle of Cottonwood County, which—if it happened at all—would have been in 1876. The Miners' Camp Fight—"

"Previously known as the Miners' Camp Massacre, according to Mike."

"—was about the Bozeman Trail and happened in 1867. Mrs. P would say about the Bozeman Trail and broken treaties. She'd be the one to tell you details."

"I don't know why there was a fight here over people going to Bozeman, but I do know one thing."

Diana raised *Oh, do you?* eyebrows.

"The Native Americans won, because it was once called a massacre. Would've been called a battle if the other side won, right?"

She chuckled. "You're darned near a graduate of the School of Mrs. P."

Chapter Five

AFTER MRS. PARENS and Aunt Gee arrived, the conversation centered on the ongoing kids' camp and the upcoming reenactment. Right after we dealt with the topic of sea salt caramel pie.

Initially saying they were too full for dessert, both Mrs. Parens and Aunt Gee decided to accept a sliver when they saw Diana and me indulging.

I indulged unimpeded, while Diana explained why her kids weren't attending the camp this time around.

"We got caught by the every-other-year schedule. By the time it came back on my radar, they'd committed to other things."

"Why is it held every other year?" Diana could thank me later for the redirect. "And why the move when it seemed to have been at its previous site forever?"

I knew what the *Independence* said. I wanted to hear what they said.

"The schedule of every other year remains a topic of discussion amongst the committee. Another proposal would be to have the camp annually while the reenactment continues in alternate years."

"It will continue to be discussed forevermore," Aunt Gee grumbled.

"As for the site—" Mrs. Parens loftily ignored her neighbor's insertion. "—it moved after the heirs of the property where the events originated sold it to Palmer Rennant three years ago. The next reenactment and camp were grandfathered into the sales agreement. We asked him at the time of the sale as well as multiple times subsequently about continuing at that site. He persisted in delaying giving us an answer. The fact that he did not attend or demonstrate support for the events two years ago increased our uneasiness. Our lawyer drew up an agreement for moving forward. We had numerous meetings with Palmer Rennant without, however, a conclusion."

"Stood us up, too, more than once," Aunt Gee said with indignation. She seemed to be in a particularly feisty mood, which was saying something.

"In the end it was only last September that we received an informal indication that he would bar our activities from his property and it was not until the end of the year that he officially informed us of that decision." Palmer Rennant was in serious trouble with the teacher.

"We were fortunate to have that earlier indication," she resumed, "because, based on that, we sought other venues. We were further fortunate that this other landowner allowed the use of our new location.

"And, finally, we have been most fortunate to have Nadine Hulte running both the week-long Two Rivers Camp and the reenactment. Her experience over the past decade and a half, as well as her impressive organizational skills have allowed the events to proceed as smoothly as ever, despite changing locations."

"Well, I don't see Nadine as being so perfectly organized," Gee objected. "Coming out of the meeting tonight, the light showed inside the back of her SUV and it was a mess. Piles of magazines and newspapers and bags and bags of stuff. Old clothes, water bottles, pill bottles, and I swear enough shoes to start a store—if anybody wanted old, used shoes. You didn't see it, going around the other way, but it was a mess."

"No doubt that is from her job with Paige Schmidt involving estate sales and therefore temporary. She is more than organized and competent with the camp and reenactment." Short and to the point from Mrs. P … Aunt Gee definitely got under her skin this time.

Distracting the combatants, I asked, "Who's Palmer Rennant? I haven't come across him."

"He and his family moved here ten years ago. To all appearances they are upstanding citizens," Aunt Gee said.

Which meant they had not been subjects of sheriff's department dispatch calls, but she didn't know them personally, so there was no telling what they were truly up to.

"Newcomers, huh?" My question drew a grin from Diana, not from either of the other two. "Ranchers?"

"They bought a ranch, but, no."

"What's he doing with the land he wouldn't let the camp and reenactment use again?"

"Nothing. Doesn't matter what anyone says about property rights, it's a disgrace." Aunt Gee cast a disapproving look toward Mrs. P. "Could have been the end of both those Cottonwood County institutions if not for this other property."

"Who's the owner of the new property?"

"That's another excellent question." Aunt Gee paused to give her next words additional weight. "Because we don't know."

"Really? An anonymous landowner?"

Mrs. Parens remained unfazed by the concept. "Our lawyer, naturally, checked that the signatory permitting our activities was legitimate and legal. If the owner remained anonymous behind a holding company or another construct, that person is not obligated to reveal himself or herself to us."

Emmaline Parens never would have made it as a journalist. Not only allowing other people to keep secrets, but not sharing the secrets she did know. And I had the distinct feeling she knew more than she was telling. Which made me want to know.

"Do you think Rennant dragged it out before telling you no on purpose? To mess up your arrangements for this year?"

"I cannot speculate on the man's reasons. However, it is unimportant, since Two Rivers Camp is already a success and the reenactment will be as well in the new venue," Mrs. Parens said.

Aunt Gee was having none of that—thank heavens. "I can speculate all right. Power. He was sitting back with his mind made up, laughing up his sleeve at the yokels jumping through hoops, hoping and hoping he'd say we could use his property when it belonged more to us than him, no matter what the deed said."

"I never observed any indication that he felt he was superior in that way to his fellow residents." I noted Mrs. Parens' usual precision and spotted an opening in it.

"That way? What about in another way?"

"I could not say."

I kept trying. She kept blocking me.

In the end, I tried opening another door. "He's not a native?" Aunt Gee shook her head. "So not a matter of someone coming back to where he grew up. Why did he move here? Do you know more about him?"

"They moved here when their elder child, their daughter, was a freshman in high school. She was an excellent all-around student and now has graduated from college and is working at a hospital in Boston. Their son is starting his sophomore year in college, studying computer technology. In that area he excelled, as well as in athletics. However, he did not apply himself in other areas."

If anyone ever committed a crime in this county over an academic record, Emmaline Parens would solve it in a heartbeat.

"Anything else?"

"I do understand that the parents divorced a year ago after thirty years of marriage."

A wife cast aside after thirty years? Now we had conflict. Wouldn't help this story any, though, since Rennant was out of the picture. But questioning habits are hard to break, especially with Mrs. P clamming up.

"Know any details? Other parties involved?"

Mrs. Parens' mouth pursed as she held silent. Aunt Gee glanced from me to her, then brightened.

She thought she knew more about Palmer Rennant than her neighbor did. At the very least, she was willing to tell more. That worked for me.

"No *known* other parties," Aunt Gee said.

"Gisella," Mrs. P admonished.

Aunt Gee was having none of it. She focused on me and I returned the favor. Mrs. Parens had scruples? Fine. She could sit in the corner—

figuratively—with them while Aunt Gee and I dished.

Diana, apparently realizing my hostess instincts came in a distant second behind my question-asking instincts, did a pantomime, lifting her dessert plate, gesturing toward the fridge, and nodding to the other plates on the table.

"Please, help yourself and anyone else who wants one, Diana." I wanted a second slice, too.

"Both Rennants worked in some sort of tech, very high earners. And he—maybe both of them—were entrepreneurs. They did that fire. Well, yes, Diana, thank you, I will have just another sliver."

"Fire? Oh. F-I-R-E? Financial Independence, Retire Early?"

"That's it. They socked away money to be able to leave their jobs. He sold a company, too, which is how they bought the property."

"Sounds like a dream," Diana said.

She had takers all around for a second slice. Good thing I'd gone back for the second pie. We weren't likely to run out tonight, but I wouldn't have had leftovers.

Gee swallowed a mouthful. "Understand it was a dream they worked real hard to make come true. Don't know much more than that. Oh, except he dated Clara Atwood from the museum not long after the divorce became final."

Gee could say *the* museum, because the county had only one. The Sherman Western Frontier Life Museum. Which, to my knowledge, had one full-time employee, Clara, the curator.

"Oh, did he?"

"Uh-huh," Aunt Gee confirmed with significance.

"Not long after the divorce, which happened a year ago, which was when informal word came through that Palmer Rennant would not welcome back the Miners' Camp Fight reenactment and Two Rivers Camp on his property. That's interesting timing."

"It is," Aunt Gee agreed.

Both of us looked toward Mrs. P. She pressed her lips together.

Others might think that was an *Mmm* of appreciation for the pie. I knew better. We weren't getting any confirmation from her.

"Anything else?"

Aunt Gee shook her head with regret.

Time to wheedle my way back into Mrs. P's good graces.

"Such a shame Palmer Rennant interfered with the reenactment. How far back does the tradition go?"

Mrs. Parens spoke precisely, "The reenactment began in the early 1950s as an effort to draw more tourists on their way to Yellowstone Park to Cottonwood County."

And away from Cody was the unspoken element of that statement. Sherman and Cottonwood County often tried to lure the financial boon of tourists heading for Yellowstone away from Cody and Park County. It was a difficult sell, since there was a direct route from Cody to the Park's Eastern Entrance. Coming to Sherman required a deliberate detour north that only a small percentage were willing to make.

Cottonwood County didn't quit trying.

"Initially," Mrs. Parens continued, "it was held every year. However, that became a strain on the resources of the county and the participants. By the early 1960s, it was being held every other year, and by the end of that decade it ceased as a regular event. It was, however, revived sporadically, generally in conjunction with anniversaries of events. The quasquicentennial was a turning point."

"The what?"

"The quasquicentennial is the one hundred and twenty-fifth anniversary." Mrs. Parens' expression remained solemn, but in her eyes glimmered either satisfaction at pulling out a word I didn't know or mischief at pulling my leg.

No telling which.

"I've heard of sesquicentennial for a hundred and fifty years—"

She nodded approvingly.

"—but never quasquicentennial."

"Then it is a shame you were not here for the celebration in 1992 of that anniversary of the Miners' Camp Fight. It was quite a success, being a cooperative effort of the miner reenactors, the tribal reenactors, and a broad group of organizers. That became the beginning point of holding the reenactment and Two Rivers Camp every other year. In many ways the camp has been more influential than the reenactment, though not as lucrative," she said, "and therefore not of as much interest to a segment of the county's leadership.

"The marked exception to that lack of interest stems from those who attended the camp themselves and now are in a position of leadership. Friendships have been forged at that camp that have lasted ever since, and friendships continue to be forged there. We are particularly pleased by attendees who now send their children or are otherwise involved, connecting new generations."

"That could be an interesting angle, to talk to two people who met at the camp and now have their children at it. Do you or Clara have names of people to contact? If I decide to take the assignment," I added far too belatedly.

"Nadine Hulte would be the best person to contact as I am certain she has such names in her records, if not from her memory of running the event over the past decade. Though with such short notice, I'm not certain..." Mrs. Parens trailed off in entirely uncharacteristic uncertainty.

That triggered my suspicions.

"There is one pair of former camp attendees who would be the optimal choices to contact in the interests of time and because I am certain they would willingly help you. Davon Everett and—"

That name rang a vague bell, but didn't explain her trailing off.

"—Tom Burrell."

That name rang a city's worth of bells, all clanging an alarm together, explained her pause, and more than justified my suspicions.

She looked at me with limpid innocence.

I wouldn't say Emmaline Parens looked like a sweet, elderly lady— she was too upright, too intelligent, too exacting for that—but I hadn't expected such perfidy from her.

And, in this case, not all aimed at me, either.

Tom Burrell would *not* be happy if Mrs. P pushed me into interviewing him.

Which I was not going to do.

"Huh. Is Davon Everett, related to O.D. Everett?" I asked.

"He is his son. You remember O.D. Everett?"

"Yes, from the museum committee dinner last winter. I try to remember men of good judgment, which he demonstrated by watching 'Helping Out'." As soon as we were introduced, he'd brought up the feature that represented my regular beat as consumer affairs reporter for KWMT. "And he wasn't just saying it, he knew details of specific pieces."

Mrs. Parens gave me the half patient, half chiding look that said she thought I was avoiding a topic.

I dove in. To prove I wasn't.

"And Tom Burrell, huh? I suppose that means Tamantha is involved in the camp now?"

"Tamantha is, indeed, involved and has been for several years. O.D.'s grandson is also involved in—"

I interrupted first with sorrowful headshakes, then words. "Such a shame there's no time to delve into that aspect. If only I'd known about this assignment last week—if I take it. Actually, there's a funny story about that."

I regaled her with the account of Thurston Fine not wanting the assignment—gleefully throwing him under the bus of her ire—and of Les Haeburn's uncharacteristic begging that I take it.

Her half patient, half chiding look returned.

Okay, she wasn't buying my change of subject to KWMT-TV's inner workings? I'd dangle a topic she couldn't resist.

"The history of the reenactment's interesting, but what about the original event? There must be something important, since they've chosen to reenact it."

With a glint of a challenge to Mrs. Parens, Aunt Gee said, "Some will tell you that's because Cottonwood County doesn't have a great deal of choice of events from its history. Suppose they could reenact Rupert Caswell's arrival at the end of the first cattle drive here, but since that would be a bunch of dusty cowboys bringing along a half-starved herd after traveling all the way from Texas, and bedding down—exhausted—for the night, that wouldn't be too inspiring."

We waited for Mrs. P to respond to the deliberate provocation in that dismissal of the county's history.

I used the time to memorize it word for word to share with Rupert's great-granddaughter. Linda Caswell would love it.

"I cannot disagree with that assessment." Mrs. Parens' calmness didn't falter even at three jaws dropping. "I believe this event was selected for reenactment based on its action, rather than its specific historical significance. Still, it is a small part of a larger whole that is significant. If it helps to elucidate that larger history, it can be viewed as worthy."

She turned to me. "I should be pleased if you choose to take this assignment. If you do, I hope to talk to you at the site about the history of the fight here and how it fit into events occurring elsewhere in what became the state of Wyoming. I will be there both Friday for the wrap-up of Two Rivers Camp and Saturday for the reenactment. However, I believe it is time now for Gisella and I to take our leave."

She'd resisted the invitation to stand up for Cottonwood County history. What the heck was going on?

AFTER MRS. PARENS, Aunt Gee, and Diana left, I watched the Ten— the newscast at that hour.

With more than five hours to prepare since the Five, Thurston worked more than a sentence of the breaking news of Russell Teague's condition into his spiel.

This time he made it sound like an on-air get-well card, delivered to someone he was trying to curry favor with. Even if Russell were well enough to watch TV news, he wasn't getting KWMT-TV in a Chicago hospital.

I brushed my teeth twice to try to get the bad taste out of my mouth.

DAY TWO

FRIDAY

Chapter Six

I **TOOK THE** assignment.

First, I told Audrey, who was working as assignment editor this week. I told her not to put it on the board yet.

She half rolled her eyes at me, because I was making her job a bit more difficult, though she knew everything would turn out fine. And she gave away that she would enjoy some of the trip to that happy ending with a dry smile.

I needed to hit the ground running. First, I checked if I'd missed anything from KWMT-TV library resources, then the *Independence's* far better database of articles for information on Nadine Hulte. She showed up in a flurry of mentions every other year with a spattering in between. All about the camp for kids associated with the reenactment.

Palmer Rennant didn't show up at all, except for one cutline under a photo of him and his son, Palmer Junior, after a track meet. Which told me Rennant was a man in his late forties, neither handsome nor not. Make it mildly attractive.

When I broadened the search to national news resources, Nadine and Palmer disappeared.

Remembering Aunt Gee's comment about Rennant selling a company he'd started on his road to financial independence, I checked business resources. On the fourth, there he was. Owner of a company with one of those names that sounds like an insurance company but could be anything from rockets to an under-eye-puffiness cure. He sold it to a company that was part of a third company that was held by a fourth—all with eminently forgettable names. The sale price wasn't mentioned. And his name didn't show up after that.

The company he'd sold to—before adding those degrees of separation—was in Maryland. I took a shot and called Baltimore news outlets, then governmental agencies. But a buyout of a company more than a decade ago wasn't on anyone's radar. Nor did KWMT-TV in Sherman, Wyoming, motivate any feats of memory.

With Maryland splitting the geographic difference, I called reporters Matt Lester in Philadelphia and Wardell Yardley in Washington, D.C. Neither covered business, but they knew people who did.

No big surprise I didn't reach either. I left messages saying what I was after and hoped they could help, but it was for background, no more. In other words, I wasn't calling in favors.

Twirling a pencil through my fingers—if I'd been that good with a baton as a little kid my path in life might have been far more glamorous—I debated.

Calling a source with such scant background went against the grain. On the other hand, Palmer Rennant wasn't the subject of a story, much less an inquiry. At most, he was on the periphery of this story. Plus, the story had very short legs—after the reenactment tomorrow, there'd be minimal interest until two more years rolled around. And at that point who would care this guy kicked them off the long-standing site? They barely cared now, having found a new home.

I called.

After my mostly futile efforts to get background and all that debating, the guy didn't answer. I left a message, dangling KWMT-TV out there—hoping it carried more oomph in Cottonwood County than in Maryland—and deliberately vague references to a story.

Les Haeburn and Thurston Fine wouldn't be in the office for a while yet, but it was still time for me to leave.

Specifically, it was time to corner a real, live person I'd called earlier.

Also to get a good brownie.

✧ ✧ ✧ ✧

THE MOST POPULAR item sold in the gift shop of the Sherman Western Frontier Life Museum were brownies made and brought in fresh each day by Vicky Upton, who worked behind the counter.

Vicky hated me for a good portion of my first year in Sherman.

The first time I'd eaten one of those brownies, I hadn't known Vicky made it until halfway through. I'd had an immediate image of Vicky poisoning it. Yeah, not rational. How could she predict I'd come in on any particular day, right?

Or that I'd buy a brownie.

Okay, that she might have been able to predict.

But, with the brownies known for their freshness, she couldn't hold onto a poisoned one for any extended period of time on the off-chance I'd come in. And making a poisoned one each day to try to catch me would really cut into her profit margin.

So, I'd kept eating her brownies.

Mind you, I wouldn't take this chance—even as calculated a chance as it was—for broccoli or oatmeal or granola. But they were good brownies.

Still, I increased the odds in my favor by always stopping at the shop first. Just in case she kept a poisoned brownie in reserve, she wouldn't have time to swap it out while I was otherwise occupied in the museum and then catch me on my way out.

I spotted her through the glass door into the shop at nearly the same time she spotted me.

She didn't snarl at me.

A few months back we had a moment of near bonding over pursuing someone who'd tried to run down a young woman, but I hadn't counted on that doing permanent good.

But now, I'd actually go as far as saying we'd advanced to the bottom edge of neutral.

That was good. It made it less likely she'd try to poison me.

We each said hello—not pushing it with any *how are yous*—and I purchased a brownie. I said, "Thank you." She said, "You're welcome."

It was the kind of détente moment that gets mentioned in This Week in History features.

Buoyed by that progress in reducing the apparent chances of me dying while feeding my chocolate addiction, I went into the main part of the museum and told Sandy, a volunteer at the front desk, that I was here to see Clara Atwood, the curator.

Sandy smiled, which I especially appreciated now that she no longer hoped each time I came in that I was a paying customer.

She called Clara, then hung up and said, "Clara said to go on back to her office. Have a good day."

Past a door labeled Staff Only, a corridor led alongside cubicles. The curator's was the last one on the left. It certainly didn't raise questions about Clara Atwood wasting museum resources on her professional digs.

I stepped into Clara's space to find it already crowded with one other person there.

Chapter Seven

SHE INTRODUCED ME to Nadine Hulte, describing her as the coordinator of Two Rivers Camp and onsite coordinator for the reenactment.

"Nadine came into town to pick up supplies. It's rare we see her here during the week of the camp. This should save you both time."

I noticed Clara didn't bother with the *I hope you don't mind* rubric. That was typical of her. She was a take-charge kind of person. In this case, I didn't mind. Because she was right, this came as an unexpected bonus.

"We're so glad you're coming to the camp." Nadine's smile seemed genuine, though frazzled at the edges. Who could blame her after four days of corralling a bunch of kids and with two more days to go on these events? "We've been trying to get Thurston Fine or *someone* to come out all week."

"I told you that was a long shot," Clara said.

That didn't appear to cut any ice with Nadine Hulte. Probably in her late thirties, she was short, with her dark hair in a frothy chin length bob—the froth thanks to the wind. Lighter skin around and above her brown eyes made me guess at large sunglasses worn for long days.

She wore utilitarian jeans, t-shirt, and front-zip hoodie, with what looked like intermittent smudges of charcoal dotted down the right side of her front.

"I don't understand why it would be such a long shot when he did a story on us before—"

Clara winced.

That reaction reminded me she'd once dated Thurston, which she now regretted. Had he been vehement about not doing the story this year because of its association with Clara?

Heartburn at seeing his former love? That sounded far too human for Thurston. Remembered dismay at having his on-air hair mussed by being outdoors? More likely.

Not privy to any of my thoughts, Nadine stuck to her course.

"It's a great event—two great events—and absolutely worth covering for KWMT-TV."

She was one of those people so devoted to a story she wanted told that she kept selling it even after we'd agreed to do it.

"It's such a shame you didn't come out earlier to see the activities the kids participate in. Not that you won't get good material today. You'll see when you come out. We work hard to give the kids the best experience possible, while leaving them the freedom to also discover opportunities to learn on their own. Not too much structure, but plenty of safety. It lets them grow in their own way."

Before she got too carried away, I hit practical issues. "Safety must be a concern. Kids around campfires, running around? Knowing first aid, for instance."

Did the charcoal on her clothes suggest campfires to me, which suggested safety issues?

"Oh yes, all our volunteers are trained in first aid, including the older kids who help with the younger ones. We have never had any major mishaps. But we do have all the required equipment on hand."

"Fortunate and well-prepared," Clara said. "Nadine has taken many advanced first aid courses. She knows her stuff."

Nadine smiled at her.

My mind followed unfortunate possibilities—mishaps, injuries, lawsuits. "I suppose you have to have insurance. Not only accidents, but event insurance for the weather around here?"

"Of *course*. With kids around and being outdoors, plus doing crafts, and cooking. And then the reenactment—the participants and even the spectators. Beyond that, there's protection in case weather or an emergency or a hundred other things force partial or complete cancelation, and we had to refund tickets when we'd already paid or committed to pay expenses. That could wipe us out. We get special event insurance that bundles coverage for the camp and reenactment, that way we save a little on the premium."

"Smart."

"Wherever we can save a penny to spend it on the events instead, that's a win."

"Wish we could get it cheaper, but with only two people offering it in the county, it's hard to comparison shop. The weather's never shut us down, but that and all the other disasters are in play every time," Clara said darkly. "Plus, this year we've got complications with the camp and reenactment being in a new location. It made a lot more work and a lot more headaches for Nadine, among other things."

"I heard about the involuntary move," I said. "That must have been difficult."

"That's all past," Clara said. "The new location's turned out great. There's a sort of natural staging area for the camp and the reenactment. More room, too, so we drew in a second group of reenactors who hadn't participated before."

The *Independence* used that angle for an advance story, talking about reenactors from two tribes coming together for the first time.

"The creek still has water," Clara continued, "while the other one was dry, which made it hard to tell the story about the miners stopping for water. Also, we're closer to where the fight actually happened. It's a more inspiring backdrop."

"Still, Elizabeth should talk to Palmer Rennant for the other side of the story. That's what journalists do, right? I'm sure if you called him or went out to his place—I understand it's not that far out of town—he would give you that angle. Both should be repre—"

Clara cut her off. "Rennant? She doesn't want to talk to him. Talk about old news. We've moved to bigger and better. He has nothing to do with the events anymore. Forget him."

She did not appear enthusiastic about KWMT devoting coverage to the location change. That made sense when she could sell the event with cute kids and a historic reenactment. Those were the moneymakers, not dry administrative matters.

I smiled neutrally. "I understand neither place is the original site? Why not use where it really happened?"

"Landfill." Clara grimaced. "The site was used as a dump when the town started. By the time people became interested in the history, it was hard to backtrack from that."

"But as Clara said, this new location is great," Nadine said with determined, but tired, enthusiasm. "I can't wait for you to see it. And to talk with the kids. Please join us for lunch."

"My cameraperson and I won't be out until two today to see the camp, before coming back tomorrow for the reenactment. But that should be plenty of time. The kids are there each day until five, right?"

Her face fell. "Yes, we're there until five. But we help set up for the reenactment, so there's little true camp activity this afternoon."

Kids can be difficult to interview but video gold. "Let me see if we can move the time up."

"That would be great. If you can make it by noon, we'll be having our last lunch celebration before the arranging in the afternoon." She rallied. "But no matter when you come, we'll have plenty to show you and kids for you to talk to."

Chapter Eight

DIANA, BLESS HER, did all the rearranging, because she had the schedule to keep.

With a backlog of "Helping Out!" episodes, I didn't worry about fulfilling that obligation unless something good came along. So, I was free to head out to where Two Rivers Camp was held this week and where the reenactment would take place tomorrow.

After a couple phone calls.

First, to Audrey. She told me Les and Thurston left for lunch.

She'd described Les as frantic and Thurston as smug.

After a moment's consideration, I had her transfer me to Les' office line. I left a voice mail saying I was on the assignment, working with Diana.

The main reason was that, although I had Les' cell number, he didn't know that and this didn't seem the moment to break it to him.

Also, it couldn't hurt Les to stay frantic a little longer and it might help Thurston to have a deeper fall from his extended period of smugness.

I drove farther north than Diana's or Mike's ranches and somewhat east of town. Following the directions, I left the paved road for well-maintained gravel, seeing a line of buttes extending in a long, easy sweep, somewhat closer to me on my left and farther away on my right. The road curved around next to a creek, then ended in a final curve, putting the face of the closest butte directly in front of my SUV's windshield.

Pulling in beside a dozen or more vehicles, I brought my focus down from the butte.

It took a moment to realize there was more area between me and the butte than I'd thought. It formed a lopsided V, with the steeper of the two rising sides progressing to the sheer uplift of that impressive butte, with more ranged behind it.

The creek formed the point of the V, with the gentler slope on the near side of the creek.

Knots of kids in varied colored t-shirts dotted the slope just across the creek from where I'd parked. Nadine Hulte and four teenagers set up a square of picnic tables in the middle of the groups. And well to the east of the kids' activity, a series of blue tarps were strung in a semicircle, blocking the view of what was behind them.

Between the kids and the tarps, a simple plank bridge crossed the creek, a few lighter boards attesting to repairs made this season.

I crossed the bridge. Turn left for the kids? Turn right for the tarps?

I chose left, and started toward Nadine.

She waved, but there was more a sense of waving me off than welcoming. I gestured toward the kids beyond where she was and she nodded.

Pretty brave of me, volunteering to wade into the kid zone on my own. Nobody could say I hadn't picked up new skills since coming to Wyoming.

The sun felt good after an overnight temperature drop. The sun didn't rebound the temperature, but at least it was brighter.

I listened to one girl telling a group about how the Crow tribe used rabbitbrush for cough syrup, yellow dye, and wove its branches into baskets.

At another group, the name Fort Phil Kearny caught my attention. I'd swear I'd heard that name from Mrs. P.

Amid urgings to "oh, oh, listen to this," half the group shared with the other half what they'd learned about how soldiers and a few of their families lived there, including an account of tents not securely set up, letting snow come in and settle on sleeping faces. But also picnics that included tinned salmon, pineapples, and plum cakes.

I might have lingered there longer, but I recognized a voice from the next group up the slope.

Tamantha Burrell.

I smiled. Tom had kept up the new haircut a group of us got her during a "girl's" day out weeks ago. Good for him.

In answer to something she'd said, I heard a smaller girl ask, as I neared their circle, "But when did they play?"

"Kids didn't play much back then. Everybody helped with stuff—getting water and taking care of the animals and cooking and washing clothes. Think how hard it was to get that bucket of water in the stream and get it back up here today and then how much water you'd need every single day."

Standing behind Tamantha, I saw eyes widen in her audience of kids younger than her.

"So they had a lot of work to do. But they also did smart things. Who tried the butter churn?" Most hands shot up. "Pretty hard work, huh?" Nods agreed with her assessment. "But they were pretty smart then, too, so when they were on a wagon train, the people who had a cow would put the milk in a bucket under the wagon and it would get bounced around all day because what they called roads were mostly ruts. And what do you think happened to that milk?"

A little girl with pigtails mouthed a word.

As if she'd heard it, Tamantha said, "That's right, Lia, it became butter."

Amid chatter about how much easier that would be than the churn—without consideration of what else might get included in butter made by the under-the-wagon method—one of the boys pointed at me and said loudly, "Who's she?"

Tamantha twisted her head around. "Hi, Elizabeth." Then she turned back to the others. "This is E.M. Danniher from the TV station. I know her so I can call her Elizabeth. You all call her Ms. Danniher."

That order given, she returned her attention to me.

"Are you here to do a story?"

"Yes. I'm waiting for Diana—Ms. Stendahl," I added to stay within her rules of deportment. "Looks like you're a teacher here."

"I supervise little kids because I've been coming for years and years," she said modestly.

"A veteran, huh?"

The finger-pointing boy—Tamantha needed to work on him about that—did it again, while objecting with a mocking, "*She's* never been in the Army."

"It also means someone experienced at something."

I admired the way Tamantha responded. Not a hint of a sneer. Matter-of-fact, not lording her superior knowledge of the word over him.

He took it the way Tamantha delivered it, with an interested, "Huh."

Someday, I hope to grow up into Tamantha Burrell.

"This is my group," she told me.

"Hi, group."

Several giggled, a few looked at me with solemn confusion.

"We were talking about making butter," Tamantha told me. "Now I'm going to tell them how people used to put it on Sheepherder's bread, like we're having at lunch."

"Oh, I like that."

"Yum."

"That's my favorite."

Majestically acknowledging the enthusiasm with an inclination of her head, Tamantha continued, "To be really authentic you have to dig a hole in the ground and bake it there. Some people use yeast, but I read up on it and a sourdough starter's more authentic."

"You know how to make bread? From a sourdough starter?" Tom Burrell knew a lot, but I doubted that included bread-making. And I'd bet Tamantha's mother hadn't taught her daughter to make bread before her death. Both because she didn't know how and she didn't teach Tamantha much.

"We learn here." Aha. Tamantha returned her attention to the gathered kids. "Everybody will have some today at lunch and when you come back next time, you'll be old enough to learn how to make it yourselves."

Judging by the expressions of the younger kids in her circle, Tamantha should be on Nadine's payroll for drumming up repeat business.

In a more conversational tone, she added, "I love fry bread, too, but they don't let us make it here because of the hot oil and the fires and the littler kids."

"Gabubu bread doesn't use as much oil," one of the younger girls said.

Tamantha perked up. "It doesn't? Maybe we can make that next time."

"It's real good with fruit stew. Or with chili."

Tamantha frowned. "I'm not sure if chili would be authentic. We'll have to look that up."

They became fully occupied in discussing whether the miners would have had chili. One boy suggested that if they did, the tribes could have taken it after routing the miners—he announced proudly his older brother was going to be a warrior tomorrow—and that way it could have been introduced early to the tribes ... and thus historically accurate to eat now.

Happy to leave Tamantha to field the delicate issue of historic accuracy without crushing impressive creative thinking, I wound my way among the groups and back down to the picnic tables.

Chapter Nine

NADINE HULTE PUSHED her hair back with both hands and, now that I saw her close up, appeared significantly less well-rested than yesterday.

"As you can see, it is not cowboys and Indians as your colleague said."

I raised one open-fingered hand, disavowing connection to Thurston Fine. "The kids seem to be fully engaged."

The defensiveness dropped from her voice. "I hope so. It's a struggle sometimes to present the full history, the history of *all* the people. Around here, the mountain men, their rendezvous, and the battles—always the battles—are the most popular. But those represent such a small view of the lives in this area at that time."

"Not a lot of women involved?"

"Precisely. Nor children, nor family life, nor daily life. For the children who participate, we prefer to offer an immersive experience in real life of that period."

"How do you do that?"

"We pair each child from a Native American background with a child not from a Native American background. First, they create a name for their pairing and wear the same color t-shirt, reinforcing they are a team and—" She smiled faintly. "—easing our task of organizing them, since we deal with them two at a time. Each pairing spends two days experiencing aspects of daily life from the 1860s as a Native American would have, then two days experiencing aspects as a settler would have at that time. With half in the opposite order and all material tailored to the age group."

"That must require a great deal of supervision with so many kids across all ages and from different backgrounds."

"We have a thriving mentoring structure in place. We select children who have experienced our program, who have shown leadership and responsibility. It really helps having the older kids teaching the younger ones. It seems less like school, more like they're picking up things naturally."

"And getting the inside scoop from older and cool kids," I said. "I saw it at work."

She grinned fleetingly. "Exactly. On the fifth day, we spend the morning having them share what they have learned, as well as what they have taught each other. That's what we've done this morning.

"For me, this is always the best part. To see their recognition that they have taught each other so much—that they had so much knowledge to share."

In my direct line of sight, Clara Atwood emerged from between two blue tarps, looked around, spotted Nadine and me, and started in our direction.

"How do you organize the mentoring?"

"The fifth-graders have two pairs of younger children to guide. The eighth-graders oversee two of the fifth-graders and their groups. Then the older high schoolers supervise three of the eighth-graders' groups. Of course," she added hurriedly, "we have the required number of adults, each with thorough first aid training, and thoroughly vetted through background checks."

"When my cameraperson arrives, we'll get you on camera with background on what the camp covers and we'd like to talk to kids. A variety of ages."

"The girl you were talking to—Tamantha Burrell would be an excellent choice."

"Mmm. My cameraperson has a personal relationship with the Burrells. Better to talk to other kids." It was true. It just wasn't the whole truth.

Clara, who'd arrived in time to hear that, gave me a look that combined skeptical eyebrows with a sympathetic grimace.

Great.

She'd heard … *something.* Heaven only knew what.

Redirecting to a topic I knew would interest her, I said, "Did you hear about Russell Teague, Clara?"

"That he's sick? Yeah. Heard that last night on the news."

"It's more serious than Thurston might have made it sound."

"Oh?" She didn't cross the line of good taste, but she was interested. Teague and the museum were the final major parties left in the legal dispute over historic gold coins found the year before. "How serious?"

"He's not expected to live much longer."

In harmony, she and Nadine sucked in a breath.

"I had no idea. I wouldn't have wished that on him, but I won't pretend I'm not thinking how good this could be for the museum." Clara pressed her lips closed. Likely to keep speculations about those gold coins from spilling out.

Nadine, on the other hand, had moved on. Or, should I say, she moved back—to the topic closest to her heart, our coverage of her events.

"Whichever kids you'd like to talk to who are willing to talk to you would be fine. There are a few who might be shy, but most will be happy to be on camera. You know, the more I think of it, the more I feel that, out of fairness, you really should talk to Palmer Rennant."

"No, she shouldn't," Clara said emphatically. "Have that colossal jerk get airtime—which could otherwise be devoted to the camp and reenactment? No way."

Peacemaker that I am, I said, "In this case it's moot. That angle could have worked when the shift to the new location wasn't settled or even for an upcoming-events type story, but now that's been what we call overrun by events. We'd be backtracking on the story. We want to stay with what's fresh—and that's the camp and the reenactment."

"I still think—"

"Oops, there's Mrs. Parens, telling me I'm taking too long." Clara tipped her head toward the tarps. I saw the familiar small, erect figure appear, then disappear between two tarps. "She asked to talk with you, Elizabeth, if you have time. I was sent to get you. If you don't mind, I'll stay here."

"I don't mind, but I see my cameraperson arriving and need to get with her. When I get to talk to Mrs. Parens, I'm telling her you never said a word."

Nadine smiled and so did I, as I left to meet Diana. Clara did not.

Chapter Ten

MRS. PARENS SPOTTED me immediately when I eventually entered the tarped off area.

Diana had shot four groups sharing what they'd learned during the week. Now she was picking up background of the buttes, then planned to catch the kids at lunch. After lunch, we'd pull out a few from their reenactment prep duties for one-on-one interviews, plus get Nadine on camera with background.

That gave me lunchtime to check in with Mrs. P.

She was talking with another woman and an older man. I recognized Anna Price-Fox and O.D. Everett from meeting them last winter at an event I attended as a command performance—with Mrs. P doing the commanding. They were among the area's most influential tribal representatives.

We all said hello. I would have been fine continuing our conversation with them, but they excused themselves and left the tarped area. Perhaps for lunch.

I not only resisted the temptation to blame Clara for my tardiness, I invited Mrs. Parens' censure when I said, "I'm glad to have a chance to talk to you before I do any recording about tomorrow. Should I call the event being commemorated a battle or a massacre?"

She gave me a severe look. "I believe you intend to draw a reaction from me with that provocative question, Elizabeth. However, I am fully aware that you are aware that neither term is appropriate to these circumstances. Both *battle* and *massacre* are overstatements. The more neutral terminology of *fight* is more balanced and thus acceptable, yet, far more accurate would be to term it a *skirmish*."

She had my number. I had tried to provoke her ... in hopes of getting more information than she'd shared last night.

"That doesn't have the same ring to it. Why did it happen at all?"

"Ah, why is a complicated question."

Showing off a bit, I said, "I know it involves people going to Bozeman." That sounded significantly thinner aloud than it had in my head, so I added, "On the Bozeman Trail. And broken treaties had a big impact."

She looked at me expectantly. But I'd shot my wad. *Shot my wad*— how was that for a nice reenacting term, since it's based on how muskets operated, with wad and musket ball, and *not* on male sexual habits, as my tittering nephew J.R. tried to tell me when they visited earlier in the month.

Yes, I am getting old.

Besides, more accurately, I'd shot Diana's wad, since she was my source for this information.

Mrs. P emitted a soft sigh—more in sorrow than in anger, but disappointment outstripped both. I really wished Diana was with me, instead of safely out there with the campers. I missed Mike and Jennifer, too, and wished they were here. Or Tom.

No. I took that back. *Not* Tom.

No regrets on his absence. In fact, I was positively *glad* he wasn't here.

Not for the reason some might think, because of any lingering awkwardness between us since he'd declared *no mas* on ... well, whatever *mas* there'd been between us. There *was* awkwardness. Probably no way there couldn't be. But that would go away. Eventually.

And it wasn't the factor now.

The reason I didn't want him here was because he would know *everything* about these historical events and I would look even worse in contrast than I did being ignorant on my own.

"In the period we're discussing, it was not referred to as the Bozeman Trail, but rather as the Montana Road. The purpose was to shorten the trip from the Oregon Trail to the region around current Bozeman, where gold had been discovered."

"Ah, gold," I said wisely.

She eyed me. Then she gestured to a map spread out on a table beside her.

In her home, she had a considerable collection of historical artifacts, including maps and photographs that stretched up the walls. She used a pointer to compel attention to specifics there. I now realized her finger served as well, as it traced up the east side of the Big Horn Mountains.

"This portion of the route traveled largely through Crow territory, as delineated by the Fort Laramie Treaty of 1851. However, by the time of the discovery of gold in Montana and the use of the trail, the Crow had been largely pushed out.

"That occurred as a result of the United States failing to enforce the treaty, with ongoing incursions from miners, emigrants, and others, as well as disputes among the tribes. The disputes among tribes were exacerbated by the depletion of the buffalo herds they relied upon.

"By the time the Montana Road was being traveled in 1864, the map of the 1851 treaty was largely mythical. With attacks on wagon trains increasing into 1866, the U.S. Army moved to erect forts to protect Montana Road travelers. Yet the Army ordered the forts be built on the west side of the Powder River, under the delusion the territory, per the 1851 treaty, was controlled by the Crows when, in fact, the Lakota, Arapaho, and Cheyenne considered that their territory.

"That meant the forts—especially Fort Phil Kearny, south of what is now Buffalo—were under constant pressure, if not attack. Fort Reno was built closer to the Oregon Trail and Fort C.F. Smith just north of the modern-day Wyoming border. That north-south stretch was the most dangerous of the Montana Road.

"A small group of travelers cited that as their reason for trying to sweep west of the Big Horn Mountains, up through the Big Horn Basin. However, the basin is semi-arid. That is why it remained uncultivated until the spread of irrigation through the ditch systems with which you became familiar last year, Elizabeth. The travelers—gold miners—who tried this different route, had traversed most of the dry expanse before reaching an area now part of Cottonwood County.

"By the time they found water here, they were desperate. However, so was a small band of Lakota, who had ventured this far west to scout buffalo herds and other game.

"The account of the survivors among the miners is that the Lakota raced down an incline toward them and overran the camp. This terrain suits that scenario far better than our previous location."

She gestured toward the butte.

I squinted toward it. "Wouldn't the raiders be spotted?"

"In the accounts of the event, they came from a clump of trees and bushes farther along the creek the miners had camped beside. In their desire for water, they had not scouted the area sufficiently. In our scenario, the riders will start from a cut in the butte that is more than sufficient to mask their presence before they begin their descent."

A call came that lunch was ready for the older kids—which I suppose included us.

I said no thank you to joining Mrs. Parens and, instead, asked the teenagers if I could join them for the two stews—meat and fruit—the Sheepherders bread and baked pudding in individual cups drizzled with honey and cinnamon. They filled me in on their week's activities and pointed out which of the younger kids they thought would be comfortable on camera.

Diana didn't get much to eat, but she got good footage of the kids' animated connections. Not to mention their delight in the dessert.

After that, we did short interviews of a dozen kids, one by one. While the others "broke camp," removing the stations where they'd had their activities and setting out stones that indicated where tomorrow's spectators were supposed to stay on the opposite side of the creek from the butte.

Diana added a lovely panorama shot from the creek, up to the butte that seemed to shimmer in the afternoon sun.

With that one in the can, we headed back to the station, to edit pieces for the Five and Ten o'clock newscasts.

We could have done three times as many with all the good stuff the kids gave us, even without Tamantha.

She'd been so busy with the other kids we'd only waved good-bye to each other before I left. Once again proving she was a better grown-up than most who qualified for the title chronologically, she showed no evidence of disappointment to not be one of those interviewed.

The packages for the Five and Ten went together easily. So, we also roughed out a recap piece for Sunday night.

And even so, we got out at a decent time.

I asked Diana if she wanted to come over for a glass of wine, but she said she'd better get home and check on her kids.

I hadn't imagined the tension in her voice last night. It was there again.

But I wasn't going to push.

Not yet.

I tried Rennant again—no answer to my earlier message, so I wasn't hopeful, but sometimes if you catch people on the fly, they accidentally answer and don't have time to think up a reason to say no.

No fly catching this time. He didn't answer. I left another message.

I went home to indulge in some Shadow therapy.

At this time of year, that consisted of sitting in a chair in my back-yard—blooming after my parents tended to it earlier in the season—with my dog and a glass of wine. Wearing a jacket. In August.

The sky was mostly clear, though Warren Fisk had told me rain was expected overnight.

Poor Warren's weather segment had been sliced so short that he'd taken to disseminating the weather by telling everyone he met what was coming up.

Watching Shadow's ears as he listened to the sounds of approaching night was enough to make me Zen even about what Thurston Fine had done and would do to the intros to tonight's packages.

Though maybe I was also just a tiny bit lonely.

On that note, and with the wine glass empty and rain clouds beginning to slide in to wink out the stars, I went inside.

I'd be around plenty of people tomorrow.

DAY THREE

SATURDAY

Chapter Eleven

WARREN FISK WAS right. It rained hard overnight. But now it was bright and warmer than the past couple days. Back to summer after the visit to autumn.

The place was buzzing when I arrived with Diana in the Newsmobile, an indestructible vehicle of KWMT-TV lore, including having no shock absorbers or springs in the seat. The Newsmobile could get anywhere … and its occupants felt every inch of the journey.

The recreation of the miners' camp sat low on the slope opposite the spectators, with a wagon, several tethered horses, a campfire coming to life, and props placed around, such as bedrolls, cooking pots, panning supplies, a wooden water bucket, ropes, and more.

The blue tarps remained, stirring more today under the remaining influence of last night's rain. Thanks to periodic gusts displacing the bottoms and edges of this outdoor version of a stage curtain, we saw miner and Native American reenactors mingling, chatting, and tending to horses.

Spectators already occupied the gentler slope, with the creek between the two sides.

The spectators included a clump of the camp-goers in their themed t-shirts, discreetly herded by adults.

One of those adults was Thomas David Burrell.

As I've said, we have a history.

No future, based on his view that our indeterminate status was confusing and detrimental to his daughter, but definitely a history. Of some sort.

I suspected Tamantha was a heck of a lot better equipped to deal with uncertainty than either he or I was, but she's his daughter and I respect his looking out for her welfare, even if the consequence is a distance between us that makes me sad.

"Ahem." Diana cleared her throat.

"I saw him."

At that moment he also saw me.

After a slight pause, he nodded.

You have not been nodded at until you've been nodded at by a tall man standing in strong sunlight wearing a cowboy hat. The shade of that brim is like a shutter coming down over his face. It's a greeting and a door closed in your face.

In this instance, a fine metaphor for the situation.

I raised a hand and produced a brief smile, then faced Diana.

"Okay, we go to work now. You need anything from me?"

"Nope," she said cheerfully, but her eyes said she was concerned about me.

I was glad that all my eyes said to her at the moment was *sunglasses*.

"I'm off to find the powers that be for any updates. We'll meet back here right after the reenactment." I checked my phone. "Good. We have connection, so we can call to stay in touch."

Diana immediately went to work with her camera, getting scene coverage of the audience. Without discussion, I knew she'd get set-ups of the miners' camp and preparations behind the tarps.

She'd also shoot the actual reenactment. We'd finish with comments from participants and watchers.

I sighed and surveyed the scene, assessing where to start.

Mrs. P, of course.

My path toward the blue-tarp enclosed area took me past knots of people, a number of whom I'd met over the past months.

I successfully kept moving while saying hello to Jean Chalmers from Chalmers Travel, Viv Eckhart, a neighbor of Jennifer's family, and Mrs. George, a neighbor of Tom's and sometimes babysitter for

Tamantha. Then I waved to Linda Caswell and Connie Walterston, both friends and seated together in prime spots. That broke my on-a-mission concentration long enough that I was caught for more than a hello.

The catcher was Verona Fuller, an insurance agent who'd done a no-holds-barred on-air interview for a "Helping Out!" segment on insurance fraud inflicted on customers by unscrupulous insurance sellers. It remained one of my favorites.

"…and this is Paige Schmidt," she added after our hellos. "She now owns the estate sale business near the Haber House Hotel and I've persuaded her to join our women in business group."

"Paige and I have met," I said with a smile and a handshake. She was a lot less jumpy than when I'd met her before. Maybe being the boss did that for her. "What brings you to today's event?"

"Nadine Hulte works for the business now."

"Works for *you*," Verona urged in an undertone. "Your business."

Paige ducked her head in a combination of acceptance and avoidance. "The business needs more than one person—there's so much to do—and she knows a lot about history. Not that we're specialists in antiques or—"

"You handle antiques. In the rare instance when you might need to consult a specialist, you have a roster of helpful contacts," Verona amended.

If Verona had taken Paige under her wing for business coaching, the younger woman would surely learn a lot … if she wasn't smothered.

"I suppose. Anyway, Nadine helps with the clean-out and setting up. Not full-time—"

"Yet. But when the business expands…"

"—but she's real helpful. You were totally right about her, Verona."

"I was certain she was the right person for you. Though I haven't seen her in a while, when I'd have expected to a few weeks ago. I was chatting a couple days ago about that to a new client who came in to see if damage to his new truck was covered. He was lucky it was so little," she confided to me. "Hitting animals can cause *so* much damage."

"Oh, dear. I've been keeping her so busy," Paige said. "Although maybe she got insurance from Kamden Graf. I saw her Thursday with him and your new client outside the Ferguson house. I couldn't believe that even with all she's doing she was picking up things needing to be disposed of and—"

She broke off at Verona's outraged glare. Remembering Clara saying only two people offered the insurance they needed, I deduced Kamden Graf was Verona's rival in that market, and she would not take well to Nadine switching to him.

"I, uh, I hope I haven't taken advantage of her," Paige faltered with an anxious look toward her mentor. "She's such a hard worker—"

"You have not taken advantage of her," the older woman relented. "Don't apologize for giving someone employment. It's great that you've had so much business, mostly brought in by word of mouth."

"Uh-huh. And for the past few weeks we were doing that big old house I told you about where the woman kept everything for fifty years and then her husband continued on since she died."

"Oh, yes. The Fergusons," Verona said.

The name sounded familiar, but the elusive memory of why hadn't surfaced before Paige continued.

"And I do mean she kept everything. There were newspapers and bottles of pills and calendars and magazines from decades and decades ago. Why, it took Nadine a full day to get through that woman's bathroom. Thank heavens there weren't any dead, uh, rodents. But even so, I couldn't have done that without Nadine. I was so worried we wouldn't finish before all this takes up every second of her day, but we did because some of her time opened up, and she worked so hard. So, of course, I came here to support her."

She shot a look toward Verona, looked guilty, and added in a totally different voice, "I would have come anyway, because it's an important part of Cottonwood County's history and as a woman business owner, I support all of our culture and history."

After farewells, I left them with Verona beaming at the other woman.

"Good day, Elizabeth."

I turned to find that Mrs. Parens, accompanied by Aunt Gee, had approached from my blind spot. I greeted them both, then asked, "What do you think of this new site for the reenactment?"

"Nice," Aunt Gee said.

Mrs. Parens gave me a little more. "This setting provides twin benefits in being more accurate and offering more scope for the actions of the reenactments, this year and in the future."

"I thought I'd ask people how they like the change." And hope the people I talked to were more sound-bitable than either of these ladies have proven themselves to be.

"Look behind the scenes at the preparations." Aunt Gee nodded toward the blue tarps. Their flutterings revealed vignettes of people— all men, reinforcing Nadine Hulte's point of little about women and kids—in Nineteenth Century miner or Native American garb, mixed with those in modern day t-shirts and jeans, with the horses in the background. Among the modern-day folks, I recognized O.D. Everett and Anna Price-Fox directing the painting of symbols on the faces and bodies of the riders in red, white, blue, yellow. Clara Atwood and Nadine also had clusters around them, asking for guidance, decisions, help, or all three.

"No, thank you. I don't want to ruin the illusion. For my first time, I want to see it strictly as a spectator."

"You could stay down here for the usual spectator view and talk with those who have watched the events many times before." Mrs. Parens did not approve of that idea.

"Or I could…?"

"If you are willing to take on a bit of a climb, you could gain a broader view."

"One from the Native Americans' viewpoint?"

"Oh, not that, precisely, because then you would need to be on horseback, in fact, bareback, as well as flouting historical accuracy of having a woman—"

"Much less a white woman," Aunt Gee interposed.

"—in the attacking group."

Discussion of my participating on horseback was academic.

Tamantha had gotten me into a saddle, I'd made progress from the most placid of horses to very placid, and didn't make a fool of myself. I'd come to truly enjoy our rides. But not even Mrs. Parens was getting me out of a saddle on horseback.

"Short of me ruining the historical accuracy by joining in with the Native American group, how would I gain this broader view?"

"The reenactors representing the tribes will come from that opening."

She pointed up.

The butte looked as if an ancient river had coursed along it, carving out designs in its striated surface. From here, what Mrs. P pointed at appeared to be simply a shadow in the irregular surface. I'd take her word for it there was an opening.

"That," she continued, "will allow them to swoop down on the camp. You would gain a view from behind the Native American riders, seeing events from their point of view though not as a member of the party, if you loop to the left and climb up even with where they will emerge, while remaining back enough that you do not impinge on their movement."

"Or get trampled," Aunt Gee said.

"Nonsense, Elizabeth will not get trampled. However, you should not dally. The reenactment does not have a specific time to start, but it should be soon. You want to be in place and visible to the riders."

With the image of trampling in my head, I did not dally.

At least at the start.

Chapter Twelve

I SWUNG WELL left of the shadow I associated with Mrs. P's *opening.* Then began the climb.

From this angle, I saw that the ancient river I imagined forming this landscape had, in one place, carved a channel between the main formation and a rock cluster the size of a two-story house. The area between was the opening Mrs. P referred to. Actually, it had two openings, one toward me, another toward the miners' camp, tarps, and audience below. I suspected the openings connected behind the rock formation, but didn't know for sure.

It felt solitary here. Quiet, except for the wind rushing to its next endeavor and the sweetly piercing whistle of the meadowlarks that cut through it.

The climb became hard enough that I used my hands to balance at times. Never for handholds, because the ground was covered in skittery stones and dirt that offered no handhold.

I'd like to say that was also when I began panting. But I'd started that much earlier.

Finally, I reached a spot that gave me a view of the opening on my side behind the house-sized rock and seemed far enough away from the opening closer to the audience to ensure I was out of trampling territory.

I was taking video with my phone—not with any thought to air it, but as a memory aid—when nine riders came out from behind the tarps below and started a leisurely diagonal route across the slope, heading toward the other opening, the one closer to them.

All male, all riding bareback. A couple appeared to have leggings on, the others wore loin cloths, and nothing else except the paint I'd seen them acquiring on body and face.

I thought of some of the spots of my anatomy that got sore when I rode and winced vicariously for them.

But it didn't seem to bother them at all. They rode farther forward than someone in a saddle, more on the horse's withers than the middle of the back.

With a quarter of the distance left to go, three riders pulled to a stop for a brief discussion. With that completed, they used their heels to urge their horses to catch up.

Either the other horses or their riders weren't prepared to cede the lead. They leapt forward, racing to be the first to the opening cluster. As they came closer, I saw the paint formed designs and picked out a symbol here and there, despite their speed.

The smallest rider, who'd been closest when the rush started, disappeared from my view behind the rock cluster first.

A sound came, distorted by echoes to the point that I couldn't tell absolutely if it came from rider or horse.

The others were right after him, the ones from behind catching up, then overtaking the main group, and all of them thundering into the gap that took them out of my view.

More sounds registered, and now I knew they were human. Most cut short, but feeling even more urgent because of that. And not in keeping with the apparent good nature of the race to reach the opening on their side of the rock formation.

Were they practicing in preparation to turning around and descending on the miners with whoops? What I heard didn't sound war-whoopy to me, although my expectations might be deluded from movies and TV.

Some sort of ceremonial preparation?

But the miners weren't all in place yet, with most still behind the tarps, as I saw from this height. The riders would be able to see the same thing.

And these sounds didn't fit a ceremonial preparation, either. They gave me an impression of confusion. Or worse.

Then a rider emerged from the opening nearer me. He was in his late teens or early twenties, one of the three who'd pulled up for the consultation, and he rode the horse I'd picked out as the fastest in the dash to the rock formation, outstripping most of the group, despite the others' lead.

His horse shied and sidestepped. The rider handled that with easy confidence.

But his body language and expression conveyed neither ease nor confidence.

He made eye contact with me and jerked his head back toward the opening.

I started toward him as fast as I could.

He disappeared into the opening, which obviously did extend all the way behind the rock formation.

As I followed, I pulled out my phone. Don't know who I meant to call, but no connection made that question moot.

Rounding the near edge of the large formation, I saw that the opening between it and the curve of the main butte widened back here into a fat crescent moon with enough room for eight times as many horses and riders as occupied it now.

A couple of the riders were still astride. They held the reins of the other horses, up against the wall formed by the butte.

The rest, including the rider who'd summoned me, were on foot, in a semicircle halfway to the front wall. They parted as I neared.

A body was on the ground.

Chapter Thirteen

THE BODY WAS curled over on itself. As if someone in the fetal position had turned from his side to mostly on his front, with the crown of his head in the dirt and his face toward his chest. That chest was presumably as bare as the rounded back that presented itself to the sky.

No, not directly to the sky, because the rock formation was cupped, leaving an overhang protruding fifteen feet off the ground, as if half of a deck umbrella extended out of the rock. A small bush sprung up along the rock, as if it, too, protected the body.

A flash of red caught my eye.

Blood?

No.

On the one shoulder visible, marks in red and yellow resembled what I'd seen on the warriors on horseback.

One cowboy boot was mostly tucked under the body, the other was turned out, a dusty, partial hoof print showing on the darker surface. As I neared, I saw a tear in the bottom of the jeans. Higher, the bare back bore impressions of blows. Nothing as perfect as a hoofprint, but the general shape was right. The upper back, neck, and head were close to the base of the rock wall, hampering my view of it.

Yet the jeans, the boots, and the apparent age of the body did not match any of these riders.

I shifted my weight, leaning to the side for a better view.

The red and yellow colors I saw on that shoulder were matched on the upper back. All were faded, some eroded, with rivulets of flesh revealed. And now, lower, I saw faint remnants that indicated more marks had once been there.

No blood.

I scanned the body and the dirt around it again.

Definitely, no blood.

One of the reenactors crouched beside the body. The summoner was behind me, to my right. The others retreated another step.

Pitching my voice to the crouched guy, I said, "If he's dead, you shouldn't—"

"Aleek's checking," the summoner said. "He's training as a paramedic."

I was confident I knew the answer, but the paramedic-in-training was already next to the body, his footprints clear, no sense making an issue of it now.

"Not a paramedic yet," he mumbled.

Putting two fingers below the jaw, under the ear, he shook his head. But he also tried the strangely slanted wrist. And shook his head again.

I pulled out my phone, taking pictures and video.

Less of the victim than of the marks in the dirt.

They looked like all horse's hoofs except for the pulse taker's single track in. That might be significant. It meant the reenactors—smartly— had mostly stayed back.

"What are you doing?" A paunchy guy who appeared to be the oldest of the nine riders asked me suspiciously.

"Documenting the scene as we found it. At least as I found it. Could be important to prove that none of you went near the body, except to check for signs of life. So stay back, the rest of you." By now I'd moved around for photos of the other side, using zoom and staying back myself. "Someone should call the authorities. Right away."

The guy who'd summoned me said, "We don't have phones here. They're down with our stuff."

No place to keep them, with no saddle and wearing so few clothes.

I stopped taking photos long enough to try the phone.

"No connection."

"That's the other reason not to bother with phones up here," the summoner said.

"Anybody know who he is?"

My question received a couple negative grunts and otherwise silence.

Paunchy said, "Who's going to ride down and get one of the organizers?"

"No riding, either." I looked over the horses. "They'll want to look at your horses for, uh, evidence. They shouldn't be ridden until that's done. It would be best if you keep them quiet and calm so they don't move around a lot, too."

The reenactors looked back at me with varying degrees of comprehension.

I exhaled. "I'll go."

I was the logical choice, since I'd be of little use in keeping the horses calm.

"You sure?" This was the summoner again. He was far from the oldest, yet seemed to be the unofficial leader. "It's a hard climb on foot for uh..."

An old lady danced on the end of his tongue. He's fortunate it didn't fall off the edge.

"I made it here."

"Yeah," said the youngest rider. "And it's downhill."

He made it sound like curling up and rolling down wasn't past even me. He skidded right off my list for favorite reenactor.

"I might get connection without going all the way down. I'll check as I go."

I went back the way I'd come.

Sergeant Wayne Shelton of the Cottonwood County Sheriff's Department probably wouldn't thank me for it, even though he should, because I was really thinking of him. If I'd taken the other way, going down in full view of the recreated miners' camp and shouting to the audience that someone needed to call the sheriff's department, what were the chances his crime scene would be left as it was now?

I'd intended to check for phone connection sooner, but those loose stones and dirt kept me occupied with keeping my balance on the first, skidding descent.

No connection here, either. And this, too, came under the heading of probably a good thing, because nobody would have understood my words amid the huffing and puffing.

I continued down. Two more times I tried. I swear one time it had negative bars.

Finally, more than halfway down with the butte no longer looming over me as much, I had connection.

Okay, maybe Shelton still wouldn't thank me.

Because my first call was to Diana.

"Can you see me?"

"Yeah."

"You need to get up here right away. Drive the Newsmobile as far up as you can, then we'll have to climb."

In true Diana style, she said, "Okay." And hung up.

My second call also wasn't to Shelton.

So, he *really* wouldn't thank me.

"Mrs. Parens? It's Elizabeth. Don't make an announcement, but something's happened up at the butte. Can you get a ride up here? Can you see me? If you catch Diana and—"

"I will be there shortly."

Even ending the call immediately, she wasn't in time to catch Diana, because I saw the four-wheel drive Newsmobile chugging away from the parking area.

My third call... Nope, not Shelton, either.

I called the station and asked for Audrey. I really, really wished Jennifer was around. I could send her the video and she'd squirrel it away someplace Shelton would never think of, along with digging up information.

As Audrey answered, I did a mental head *thunk*. But before I could act on it, I needed to give her the heads-up that a body had been found before the reenactment could start, but that was all I knew. With her speaking phrases that could not be put together on her end as there being breaking news—at least not by Thurston—we'd postpone his tantrum over my working this story.

Not that Thurston would have come out here anyway. Wind, dust, sun. No way he'd subject his coif to that triple threat.

I kept the conversation short, promised more as soon as I knew it, and called Jennifer in Chicago. That was my head-*thunk*. Just because she wasn't here, didn't mean she couldn't do her magic. I got her voicemail. Confident she'd read between the lines, especially since this wasn't our first rodeo, I said I was sending her an attached video and would she please deal with it as she thought best to be sure it was preserved.

With the Newsmobile now approaching, I called Shelton directly, rather than 911.

"How did you get this number?" he growled. He was in a vehicle, moving fast.

"I have my sources. Do you want to know why I called?"

"No, but you're going to tell me anyway."

"Because it's my civic duty."

"It was your civic duty before you started making other calls."

"How—? Do you have spies here?" Had to be Mrs. Parens. Diana wouldn't have called him.

"I have my sources," he echoed back with a growl. "What's going on?"

I told him.

"You sure he's dead?"

"Someone took his pulse. They said the guy who did was training as a paramedic, so he should know." Also, there'd been no bleeding from the horse's hoofs. Shelton didn't need me telling him that. He'd see for himself when he got here. Including that some of the hoofs had shoes on them, which surely would have caused bleeding if there'd still been blood pumping.

"Identity?"

"I have no idea. No one else mentioned a name."

He started asking more questions, but Diana had passed me in the Newsmobile. The vehicle was part mountain goat to be able to take on this angle. That might explain some of the noises it made. I started back up the incline.

"You're breaking up. Sergeant? ... Are you there? Can you hear me? I can't hear anything. We must have gotten disconnected."

"I can hear you and you can hear me, Danniher. Do not—"

I clicked off to the music of his swearing.

Diana had turned the Newsmobile sideways to the slope. I supposed on this gradient, the wheel-turning tricks I'd learned for Illinois wouldn't cut it.

I joined her at the back of the Newsmobile as she pulled out gear.

"What's up, Elizabeth?"

"There's a body." I jerked my head to the rock formation. "Up there. Where the reenactors were supposed to gather for the attack on the camp."

"Of course there's a body," she muttered. "One of the reenactors?"

"No, I don't think so." I reviewed my take on how he was dressed and how the riders reacted, and repeated more strongly, "No."

For the trek up to the butte, Diana donned a padded body brace for the camera, hitching the shoulder straps in place first, leading more straps over her chest, then buckling another set around her waist.

Her torso supported the camera this way, rather than only her arms.

Having the camera on her shoulder, while using a shoulder brace, was fine for level ground—on the rare occasions she found some in Cottonwood County—but this was best under these circumstances. She'd be ready to shoot at any moment and what she captured would be steadier.

"Want me to carry anything?"

I often asked that. She always said, as she did now, "Nope. This way I know where everything is if I need something fast." Then she added, "Let's go."

As we started up, I saw a utility vehicle start from among several others parked on the far side of the tarps. It pointed toward the butte.

We climbed.

Chapter Fourteen

THE HORSES HAD been moved, revealing the dark opening into a cave in the butte. It was as wide as a pickup truck is long and a person-and-a-half tall at the center. A bushy plant grew near the left side of the opening. The reenactors had moved the horses well to the left of this. Most important, the new position distanced the horses more from the body.

Someone—I suspected the young man I'd identified as being in charge—had drawn a large semicircle around the body with his foot. Other than those handling the horses, all the reenactors stood in a group safely behind that approximation of a police line.

Whatever low conversation there was stopped when Diana and I entered the channel between the butte and the rock formation.

"The sheriff's department is on the way, but it will take a while," I announced generally. I probably hadn't needed to add the last phrase, since they knew about driving distances and times around here. An approaching sound prompted me to add, "I think some of the organizers will be here much sooner."

As I turned to consider the body, I noticed only the in-charge reenactor and the would-be paramedic didn't look the opposite direction.

Sure wished I could see the face of the dead man, possibly recognize him, at least take a photo for later identification.

No bulge of a wallet in either back pocket of his jeans. Some men carried a wallet in the front pocket.

Or he could be without ID.

I squinted at the yellow and red marks on his back. Something was different about them from the reenactors'.

I tucked that detail away and kept cataloguing. The jeans with no belt and the boots were unremarkable. The bare back was pale.

He had been older and less fit than the riders, even the paunchy one, who, other than that paunch, had a tautness of muscle.

The utility vehicle arrived in the entrance to the channel nearer the reenactment. It paralleled the back wall formed by the butte, avoiding the flow of horse tracks that came in close to the rock formation.

I went to the passenger side of the utility vehicle, where Mrs. P sat. The driver was O.D. Everett, the tribal leader I'd met at an event last winter and been re-introduced to yesterday. Shooting footage all the while, Diana headed the same direction, but by a different route and stayed far enough away that few would realize she was in listening distance.

O.D. Everett moved as if to get out of the vehicle.

"You probably should both stay where you are, at least until Sergeant Shelton and his team get here," I said. "The fewer people's tracks there are, the less unhappy he'll be."

Everett gave a grunt that accepted the advice with a dry hint of amusement that indicated he'd encountered Shelton.

With no hint of amusement, but absolute calm, Mrs. Parens said, "Elizabeth, I asked Tom to call the sheriff's department to say there had been a … mishap that required their attention."

"I called Shelton, too," I said. "They're on their way."

At that moment, the young reenactor who'd summoned me went to the driver's side, exchanging a look with Everett that likely had lots of substance known to them, but impenetrable by me.

"Grandfather. Mrs. Parens."

He seemed to view that as the end of what he was going to say.

"I'm Elizabeth Margaret Danniher with KWMT-TV in Sherman." When that didn't elicit a response, I went for blunt, "What's your name?"

It was O.D. Everett who responded. "He is my grandson, Paytah Everett."

The young man declined his head in acknowledgment.

"It was smart to keep people back, Paytah. Are you sure you don't know the man?"

"Not one of ours," he said under his breath, directed solely to his grandfather.

When he saw I'd heard him, he clammed up.

I raised an eyebrow to young Paytah. He pretended not to see it.

So I spoke the question.

"I'd understood a couple different groups are participating. Are you sure or are you concluding he wasn't part of the Native American contingent because you don't know him? Could he be a member of another group?"

He looked at Everett, who looked at Mrs. Parens, who looked at me. I returned her look with open, guileless honesty and integrity.

She frowned.

Then she sent the round-robin back the other way, looking at Everett, who held her regard for an uncomfortable amount of time, before turning to Paytah.

This outgoing message from Everett was shorter. But after Paytah collected it, he took his time and didn't complete the circle by looking at me. But he did speak.

"All the reenactor riders met here last week to practice. All rode up from the staging area. Then down. He was not among us last week. He was not among us today."

I accepted the information and the logic with a nod. "Anything else?"

"None of ours wore jeans. Authenticity," Paytah said.

"The painting," muttered O.D. Everett, who had good eyes to have spotted that. Though the body was visible to both occupants of the utility vehicle.

"Yeah," Paytah agreed. "That, too. Also not ours. Don't mean anything."

Was that what registered about the marks? That they were just marks and not symbols? Maybe.

No, there was something else.

Even where the paint on the dead man remained, the edges of the marks looked smudged, indistinct compared to the reenactors' painted symbols. Plus, those areas where little paint remained.

"When did you put your paint on?" I asked Paytah. Again, the round robin of him to Everett to Mrs. P to me, then back.

"About an hour ago."

"Do you make your own paint?"

"Most don't for this kind of thing. The traditional stuff has a lot of—" He started a gaze toward Mrs. Parens, stopping short of the destination. "—uh, stuff in it. We use tempera. Comes off after."

"Even this paint should not be used this way," said O.D. "Disrespectful."

"Did you bring the paint this morning?"

This round robin moved faster. That was progress.

"Some. We had told the organizers we had little red or yellow. It was there when we came."

"Did you use paint last week for the practice?"

Apparently, he considered that question not worthy of checking with anyone else, because he just said, "No."

"And none of you know who he is?"

Paytah shook his head. O.D. Everett simply looked back at me. Mrs. Parens said, "It would be exceedingly difficult to identify anyone under these circumstances."

Good point.

I took out my phone and zoomed in the camera to see if I could get a view of the dead man's face from this angle.

Nope.

However, I did see an expensive watch with a dial that looked like it had come off the instrument panel of a classic sports car.

I snapped a couple pictures of that. Then showed the photo to my panel of three.

"Do any of you recognize this watch? Associate it with someone you know, perhaps?"

Paytah shook his head. O.D. Everett did more of the silently looking at me. Mrs. Parens said, "I cannot claim any expertise at identifying watches."

Before I pursued that with any of them, Paytah turned toward his grandfather, possibly intending to shut Mrs. Parens and me out. If so, he hadn't dealt with journalists at a death scene before.

"Grandfather, can you talk to Jeremiah? He is upset. He was the first—Others of our horses landed blows, but his horse was first."

"Even as an accident, he must accept it if his horse caused this man's death and—"

"He didn't."

Paytah said it at the same time I did.

He jerked his head around to me. "Why do you say that?"

"You first."

Before he answered, if he'd intended to, one of the reenactors called to Paytah. "Deputies."

Chapter Fifteen

SHELTON'S FIRST PRIORITY was having deputies back us all up behind police tape.

I made a tactical decision to stay closer to the reenactors than to the utility vehicle and against the butte. Diana stayed with me.

The deputies enclosed the utility vehicle inside the tape, leaving Mrs. Parens, O.D. Everett, and Paytah outside it and on the far side of the utility vehicle, well away from the other reenactors.

They continued the police tape in a big semicircle with either end connected to the rock formation.

It enclosed the body, of course, adding considerable territory to the impromptu line Paytah had drawn with his foot.

With a jerk of his head to the unfamiliar deputy stringing police tape, Shelton indicated a desired extension. Following the direction of that head-jerk, I saw why.

Needham Bender, owner and editor of the *Sherman Independence* had arrived, along with Cagen, one of his reporters. Usually, they split up to cover more territory, but Shelton had blocked that move with that added tape.

For once I appreciated the sergeant's sneakiness.

I greatly respected Needham. That didn't mean I wanted him to get a story before me. Before KWMT-TV.

Shelton started young Deputy Richard Alvaro into the group of reenactors, gathering names and details. And sent a Sherman Police Department officer named Hollister into the cave behind us.

I watched that with interest. I suppose it was possible someone had hidden in the cave. I should have thought of that.

Then Shelton strode to near where Diana and I stood.

He gestured for us to come to him.

I gestured for him to come to us.

Diana shoved me in the back.

My stumble forward cut the distance in half. He angled slightly, cutting it more, without appearing to.

"What did you see? Briefly."

I told him.

As I finished up, Needham caught my eye and raised a hand to me. I reciprocated.

Shelton looked over his shoulder, then back to me.

"From the time I left Mrs. Parens down below where they were getting ready, I didn't see anyone around—coming out or going in this channel from either side until the reenactors arrived. I didn't have my eyes on it every second, but I was gauging distance as I came up, so I checked pretty regularly. Plus, it's open on either side. No place for someone to duck into.

"None of the reenactors did it—at least not when they went charging in there. They were one right after the other," I said of the riders. "None entered this area far enough ahead of the others to have time to arrange anything. No time at all."

Shelton grunted.

"Not to mention he was already dead."

He slitted his eyes. "You're a Medical Examiner now?"

"Common sense. He didn't bleed when however many of those horses ran over him. So he was already dead. Not to mention the body staying in that position."

"You keep that off the air, Danniher."

"No promises."

"You ever want anything more from me—"

"Hah. When have I ever gotten anything from you?"

"I can see to it you get less. Blocked, stonewalled, banned from the department."

"And I can see to it that that's reported all over KWMT-TV."

"All right, you two," Diana said. "We won't report it unless we get confirmation from a non-law enforcement source. And we'll let you know before we put it on-air. In turn, the sheriff's department will give us the okay to have it as an exclusive when it can release the information."

"Fine." I pretended not to be at my most gracious. Though, since I counted as a non-law enforcement source, we could use it any time.

Shelton gave a sharp nod.

In truth, we both knew it was likely moot. Even if no one else recognized the significance, Needham Bender would. And I strongly suspected O.D. Everett and Mrs. P had, along with half of the reenactors.

On the other hand, the next edition of the *Independence* wouldn't be out until Tuesday, so we could afford to hold off a bit.

Shelton left us without even a word of farewell. Someday, that man will hurt my feelings.

"Why did you ask that young reenactor about when they put their paint on?" Diana asked.

"Theirs looked sharper than the victim's. More deliberate. His looked … worn, weathered. Possible his were made from a different substance. If it was the same stuff, it might help with the timeline of how long he was out here."

"Huh. I'm sure I got good shots of that, but can't hurt to be sure…"

She stepped right up to the tape, adjusting the camera as she went, zeroing in on the body.

And Shelton zeroed in on her.

"Sampson. Move the circle back on that side. All the way to the wall."

He glared at me as he said it, which was entirely unwarranted, since I hadn't moved.

Deputy Lloyd Sampson looked at us apologetically, but he picked up the tape in his gloved hands and used it to gently herd Diana back to me.

"To the wall," Shelton repeated.

Sampson kept us moving back, looping the tape over the bushy plant at the base of the wall, near the entrance to the cave, leaving the reenactors and their horses on one side and us on the other, but both groups outside the investigative circle.

The reenactors had considerably more space. In contrast, with the tape on the other side of us also touching the butte wall, we were forced into the cave's opening.

Needham Bender grinned at us from the opposite side of the taped off crime scene, because he was now a good ten feet closer to the action than we were.

How to make one journalist happy and another grumpy in one stroke.

"It would serve Shelton right if it turned out the murderer hid in the cave and there's all sorts of evidence here," I grumbled.

"We checked it out earlier in case," Sampson assured us earnestly. "No footprints or any tracks going in or out except coyotes."

"Coyotes?" I looked over my shoulder into the cave. Its darkness could hide interminable depths.

"Lots of 'em."

If it had been Shelton or Sheriff Russ Conrad or even Richard Alvaro, I would have scoffed. But Lloyd, bless his literal heart, did not say things to get a rise out of people. I turned on my phone's flashlight and scanned deliberately into the dark for multiple pairs of yellow eyes.

What I saw were rocks and dark space.

A good start, but it was a quick and dirty approach that covered only a small portion of the area.

I came back to my left and methodically scanned, working my way toward the right. I deliberately kept the scan low.

I'd been in caves before when small eyes glowed at me.

Bats.

Not my favorite, swirling around my head. On the other hand, they weren't likely to take a chunk out of one of my legs. Or both legs.

But this cave stayed nicely dark, until I reached the far right-hand side.

It wasn't a pair of eyes that dully showed in the flashlight's beam. It was a slightly curved string of at least five evenly spaced dots. Like a gap-toothed Cheshire Cat keeping a secret while lying on its side.

"Diana?"

She did not interrupt shooting to respond, "Hmm."

"When you get to a good spot to stop, come look at something back here."

"Uh-huh."

With Diana still shooting what was available to her of the crime scene, I edged inside the cave, keeping my flashlight fixed on the dots.

I kept my light on the area for maybe ten minutes.

Or at least thirty seconds.

Barring my Cheshire Cat theory, the pattern didn't make sense to me.

I moved farther to the right to get a new angle. The dots maintained their spacing from each other, though now they looked more vertical.

"Okay, what have you got?" Diana came inside the cave, standing on my left side.

"See the line of dots?"

"Not very well." She flipped a light on. Nowhere near the power of even the smallest of the standalone lights she used if we had a nighttime set-up, yet significantly more powerful than my flashlight app. "Move more to the right."

With our lights hitting from different angles, she turned on the camera without a word.

Unless she had a better view than I did, she still wasn't sure, but she followed the cameraperson's instinct to shoot now and decide later.

She moved in closer, and I followed, keeping the same angle between our lights.

Then I swung further right, but closer to the dots.

We sucked in a breath simultaneously. A sound that echoed away into the cave.

"Can't do much more, Elizabeth. Not without better light. I've got decent footage, considering the circumstances. But you know we can't use it on-air."

"Yeah. I know. It would break the dead body rule."

Chapter Sixteen

"WE WON'T GET it on-air because KWMT-TV, like most stations, won't let our viewers be exposed to the direct sight of a dead body, though if it's covered or in a body bag, that's fine. Like nobody knows what inside those bags."

She made a sound.

"Okay, okay, you're right. I'm not really lobbying to have dead bodies on-air. I agree with the rule. And the cable stations have gone way too far the other way. But when we see what you got, we might consider arguing that this is more like showing a mummy and those have been on-air. Plus, a shot of the back of the belt with the studs helps humanize it, without showing the rest of the body."

The studs were what had caught my attention. From where I stood now, the belt appeared roughly vertical on a likely male body on its side, with its back to us.

At some point a rockslide had covered most of it, leaving visible that span of belt, a scrap of checked fabric above it and denim below it.

Another opening in the flow of rocks was roughly where one might expect to see a head. Or a skull.

"See if you can get anything in that gap a little higher up. If there's anything visible in there."

She grunted acknowledgement. "Probably not enough light, but I'll try. Anyway, that's not a bad argument about maybe getting something of this on-air, though I wasn't thinking of journalistic standards. I was thinking of Shelton. Because he's on his way over here. And he's not going to want us to use the footage—and before you say we can use it anyway, do you want to torch that particular bridge."

"Bridge? One made out of fraying rope, swinging over an abyss, and only going one way, from us to them without reciprocating. What's the use of that?"

"They could have kicked us out completely, sent us back to the vehicles."

"What are you two doing in there?" Shelton asked.

"We might get sent a lot farther away than that," I said to her grimly. I turned to him. "Sergeant Shelton. We were just coming to get you. There's something here you need to see."

DIANA AND I were pushed back out of the cave, but they couldn't push us too much without letting us into the crime scene. The other crime scene.

At some point, they'd figure out they needed to open an alleyway for us to leave, but for now, we were stuck on the fringes of each of the scenes.

The only good news was we still had hours until airtime to get this story back to the station.

Thurston would have a hissy fit because this breaking story would intrude on his litany of *churnalism* stories—reports churned out from news releases and, in Fine's case, called-in "exclusives" his cronies wanted on-air.

The additional footage and detail on discovery of the body in the cave multiplied the news value of what we had on the body found during the reenactment.

Especially since all other news outlets—in other words Needham—had been consigned to the far side of the main crime scene and could only gather what was happening in the cave from eavesdropping on bits and pieces law enforcement blabbed when they wandered his way.

I saw him take out his phone and try to make a call. To us? Or to his staff at the paper?

Didn't matter, because there was no connection up here.

Diana kept shooting, inside and outside the cave. I tried to edge closer to pick up words from law enforcement.

I hoped she was having better luck with her camera than I was with my ears.

The light had improved in the cave because law enforcement brought in major illumination. It showed the cave wasn't very deep, with no apparent outlet.

The downside was all the law enforcement figures standing between us and the body. We couldn't see past them except in snatches as they shifted positions. But that meant there were far fewer bodies between us and the original crime scene. Diana was happy with a sequence of a sheriff's deputy from a neighboring county taking photographs while crime scene techs continued with the first body.

Shelton turned and came directly toward me, lifting the police tape out of his way. This time, no messing around with gesturing for me to come to him.

As soon as he passed Diana, she slid toward the cave and aimed her camera into the gap he'd left.

Focused on me, he didn't appear to notice.

"How'd you spot this guy?" he demanded.

"I told you, Sergeant. I was surveying the cave with the flashlight on my phone. And—"

"Why?"

"Does it matter why?" That was a mistake.

A dry glint of amusement at my expense came into his eyes. "Afraid of critters?"

"It's always wise to know what's behind you." I might have had my own glint of amusement at his expense as I said that, since, at the moment, what was behind him was Diana getting footage.

"Uh-huh. You were waving your phone around and—"

"Methodically scanning the area."

"—what caught your eye?"

"The studs on the belt. Not bright, but enough to form a pattern. A sort of vertical line, which didn't match anything I could think of."

"Yeah, snakes don't often have spots that shine in the dark."

Snakes. I hadn't thought of that. Wasn't about to let him see that. "Or go straight up walls of rock."

"Oh, they can do that. But not many around here glow in the dark even a little bit."

He was trying to rattle me—pun intended—and I refused to give him that pleasure. Bridge or no bridge to the sheriff's department.

"I went closer to examine the pattern, then Diana joined me with a better light and we saw it was a belt and the belt was still on what was left of a body."

"Did you have reason to suspect a body was here? Is that why you came up here in the first place?"

"What? No. My coming up here was Mrs. Parens' idea. So, if you're going in for conspiracy theories, try her. But why on earth would I suspect there'd be a body here?"

"No telling with you," he grumbled.

But his tone was slightly less hostile, which generally passed as friendly for Shelton.

While keeping it conversational, I lowered my voice slightly, hoping to encourage him to spill. "It looks like quite an old body."

He grunted.

"That could complicate identification."

"Hmmm."

"The University of Wyoming must have an anthropologist who could help with a forensic examination."

"Imagine so."

His mildness raised my suspicions.

I probed more. "And if not, there's the University of North Texas Center for Human Identification, which is excellent."

He stuck his hands in his pants pockets and rocked front to back on the soles of his boots. "That so?"

"That's so. They've helped resolve many missing, unidentified, and unclaimed cases."

"That's real interesting," I didn't recall Sergeant Shelton ever describing anything I'd ever said that way. "Me? First thing I'd do is check out the wallet, see if there's identification there."

"*Wallet?*"

I pivoted my head toward the inside of the cave, and what I'd taken as a century-or-more-old mummy. I couldn't see much through the thicket of law enforcement.

"Yup. Wallet. In his back pocket. In his jeans. From Sears Roebuck."

"It's a recent body?" I heard my voice climb in surprise. That rock slide sure didn't look recent.

"Didn't say that."

"You said recent enough to have a wallet."

When did men start carrying those in a back pocket? And jeans from Sears. When had the catalog started? I'd have to look that up, but almost certainly more recently than I'd been thinking.

The denim, checked shirt, and the location had seemed to my reenactment-primed mind to indicate someone from that same late 1860s period.

Shelton was—gleefully—saying I was wrong.

Did that mean—?

"Is there a connection to the death of—?" I jerked my head toward the body behind me.

"Didn't say anything like that. Don't go jumping to another wild conclusion and putting it all over TV for everyone to start calling us with leads that waste our time."

"Who is it? Wait—Don't answer that yet. Do you know who the first body is? The one out here."

"The Cottonwood County Sheriff's Department is not releasing an identification at this time. If there's a news conference, you'll be notified."

I scoffed at that. "But you do have an inkling about this body."

"Didn't say that."

"But you said—"

"We can see there's a wallet. We're not fooling with the evidence until the experts get here. Since we're professionals."

He was slipping if he thought that dig would get to me. "How long ago did he die? How long has he been here?"

"Don't know."

"But you have an idea."

"Maybe."

I narrowed my eyes at him. "You think you know who it is."

"Might have a thought or two based on knowledge and observation, but that's all the more reason not to blab to you. It will take the experts some considerable time to get here, examine the remains, take them back to where they can do their science, then get us the report."

"You could take a peek at the wallet."

His brows clamped down in a mighty scowl that I liked to think was necessary to conceal a temptation to grin.

"Interfering with evidence. We don't operate that way in the Cottonwood County Sheriff's Department."

His *harumph* served as a good-bye.

"Don't go away angry, Sergeant," I said a little louder than necessary.

He pivoted toward the cave, taking a second to glare at Diana, who had stepped back from where she'd bowed the police tape into the cave just in time.

She looked back at him blandly.

He grunted, ducked under the tape, and returned to his spot in the semicircle of law enforcement types.

As Diana adjusted the body brace, she curled her fingers around a strap with her thumb pointing skyward.

She'd gotten something.

Chapter Seventeen

"**WE'LL HAVE TO** see how well the body brace worked and what the camera picked up," Diana said, when we were in the Newsmobile and, finally, away from prying ears. "But with all that light it should be better than what I got to start."

After our descent, we'd debated doing a quick setup on site, with the butte as my backdrop, but decided against it. Shelton had left a couple deputies down at the Newsmobile's level with hand-held radios that allowed him to issue orders from up above.

Say, an order about changing his mind and not letting the media depart.

We opted to do our departing while the departing was good, ensuring we'd be able to pull together a story, even if it didn't have the perfect set-up.

"With those lights in the cave," she continued, "I saw a skull among the rock. Pieces of a skull. Looked like there was a good-sized hole, but the missing chunk could have been out of sight."

I called the station while Diana drove with her usual disregard for the physics of staying in one piece. At least telling Audrey the news distracted me.

After Audrey made the first slash and burn through the scheduled story blocks, she called back to fill me in. I heard Thurston bellowing in the background.

A sweet sound that warmed my heart.

"Start working the sheriff's department desk officer for an ID on the first victim—first victim we found today," I told Audrey.

"Will do." She ended the call.

There was something niggling at me...

"You're doing the story, right?" Diana asked.

That brought my attention back to the matter at hand.

"Uh-huh. Thurston can't claim it when he refused to go out there or have anything to do with the event."

"Oh, he can try."

"He won't succeed."

We quickly outlined the story, as well as tactics to keep Thurston's hands off it. Then we looked beyond tonight's newscasts.

"We need to figure out if these two deaths are related. And to do that, we need to know who the victims are," I said.

"Could either one be natural?"

I chewed on that a moment. "It would really stretch my imagination for the first guy to be natural causes. No way to know about the guy in the cave at this point. But, for sure, the sheriff's department will treat both as suspicious at the very least. And we will, too."

"You don't think the guy in the cave is from way, way back?"

"I *thought* I thought that, but Shelton changed my thinking, or at least opened up the possibilities. If he wasn't kidding about the wallet—"

"Shelton's so well known as a big kidder."

"—and the jeans being from Sears, that makes our mystery man far more recent than I was originally thinking."

"Why are you grimacing?"

"Shelton. Sure wish he'd looked in that wallet. No, what I really wish is *we* had. We'd be a lot farther—" My phone rang. "—along."

I checked caller ID.

It was Mike.

"Hello. I have you on speaker with Diana in the Newsmobile."

"You found a body while I wasn't there?"

Correction. It was Jennifer.

"While we weren't there."

And Mike.

"You have no claim to expect to be involved in investigations anymore because you moved away," Jennifer said. "But I still live there."

"Well, you're not there now, so—"

"You two don't need Diana or me for this dispute and we can use the time to put together a Thurston-proof package, so I'll hang up and—"

"No, no, don't hang up," Jennifer said. "I got your message. The video's backed up multiple places, including with some buddies Sergeant Shelton would never find. But who is the dead guy? How did you find him? What's going on?"

I explained, with a few contributions from Diana, starting with the body they knew about ... before expanding to the one they didn't.

Chapter Eighteen

"…**AND THEN I** realized it was a belt that was still on a body, though from what we could tell there wasn't a whole lot left. It—"

"*Another* one and totally by accident?" Jennifer's voice climbed.

"You tripped over two dead bodies in *one* day?" Mike demanded at the same time. "I said to give the coverage the E.M. Danniher treatment, but I didn't mean *that.*"

"Very funny. I didn't trip over anything. You could say the horses did with the first body, but not me. And the second one was found thanks to thorough and careful examination of my surroundings."

"She was looking for coyotes," Diana said for the benefit of the speaker. "Lloyd Sampson put the thought in her head."

"I wasn't—" The challenge of her look changed my verbal course. Not from guilt but from self-preservation. At the speeds she maintained, a blink took her attention from the road too long for me. Keeping her pacified was essential to self-preservation. "—only looking for coyotes. Also bats."

Mike spluttered over a chuckle. "Only you would be looking for coyotes and bats and find a dead body from who knows when. I can't believe you found two bodies. Shelton must be apoplectic."

"You don't have to make it sound like I'm going for a high-volume discount, Paycik."

"Well, when you start finding them in pairs again—"

"Again?" Jennifer interrupted.

"Red Sail Ditch," Mike said.

"This is different," Diana said. "The other time they were contemporaneous. These two are from different times."

"Technicality," Mike argued.

"Plus, she didn't find the first one then," Jennifer said.

"Thank you, Jennifer. And it wasn't like I wanted to find any of them—coyotes, bats, or a dead body—this time. Although, now that the body in the cave's been found, we obviously have to look into it."

"Why? If the second one you found's from way back, what possible connection could they have?"

"See, that's what I thought, too. You hear a body was found in a cave and you think ancient." Maybe, just maybe I was still smarting from Shelton's riff off my thoughts on IDing the body through anthropology. "But there was the belt."

Mike kept going, "Native American from way back? Or someone from early arrival of the pan-European type? Someone else from history?"

"Has to be from when someone would be wearing jeans from Sears and with a wallet in his back pocket," Diana said.

"The body had a wallet? What was in it?"

"We don't know yet. Shelton doesn't, either. He's having the experts deal with it. Listen, guys, we need to go. We can talk tonight, after the Ten if you want."

"We want," Mike said firmly. "Call when you're home and can talk."

As soon as the call ended, Diana asked, "Why give them the bum's rush? We aren't at the station yet."

"Couple things to work out before we get there. It's bothering me that Shelton told me about the wallet and didn't even try to tell me not to use it."

"He wants you to put it on-air. Are you going to?"

Her question clarified my thinking. "As much as I'm tempted to thwart Shelton, hell, yes, we'll put the wallet on-air. But ... not the belt. Let's hold that back, at least for a while. We'll give Shelton what he wants on the wallet—not that he'll appreciate it. But it's great detail. It might help someone identify the body before the experts do. If it tells someone their dirty laundry has been found and is about to be spread out for all to see, that doesn't hurt."

"That's what Shelton's after," she muttered.

"Yep. But the owner of the dirty laundry might come to us before him."

"Ever the optimist."

"Yeah, but…" I added a sharp, "*Darn.*"

Or words to that effect.

"What?"

"Jennifer asked it straight out and I rolled past it. Got so tied up in the second victim—well, probably the first one killed, but the one we found second—that I haven't focused on the identity of that first victim, the one who was—"

"I know. Found first. Let's keep them in the order we found them. Until we have names. But you did tell Audrey to work the sheriff's department for the ID."

"Yeah. Knew something was off when I told her to do it and didn't listen to my own conscience. Shame on me. A total Thurston move on my part. Wait for the news release. And there was something…" I ran back the events from when Paytah Everett led me to the first body.

"Something from Shelton?"

"Nope. It was Mrs. P. She said, *It would be exceedingly difficult to identify anyone under these circumstances.* Not that she didn't know who it was, not that she couldn't identify him, but that the circumstances made it difficult. And I let that slide right by."

I had my phone out and hit speed dial.

"You think you can get her to tell you when she chose not to earlier?" Diana wasn't only asking, she was warning that I was setting myself up for major disappointment.

"No." A voice answered on the other end. "Hi, Aunt Gee. I have a quick question for you. Two, actually."

I'd bet all the leftover sea salt caramel pie that she knew up-to-the-minute details on the sheriff's department investigation.

"Just a minute."

I heard an identifiable voice in the background, then a door opening and closing, followed by birds chirping, and a solitary car passing.

The voice belonged to Ferrante, the desk deputy at the sheriff's department. The rest of the sounds matched Gee getting up from a waiting room seat and walking out to the patch of grass in front of the building.

My questions might be quick—once I got to ask them.

Because first she told me how she should have been on the scene, as someone involved in organizing the event and associated with law enforcement. She never should have opted to remain at the main site when it became clear something was wrong at the starting point for the Native American reenactors.

"You were in the right place," I told her. "You kept people calm at the main site and made sure they stayed until they could be asked if they'd seen anything. Did anyone?"

"Not a thing. But now Emmaline is at the sheriff's department, giving a statement, acting downright peculiar, and I can't do anything useful or—"

"I know, Aunt Gee, but you couldn't be two places at once and what you did was vital. My second question's about the spelling of the victim's name. I want to be sure to get it right. That's B as in boy?"

There was a long pause.

A long uncomfortable pause while I tried to prepare an answer for when she asked me what the heck I thought I was doing trying to get her to divulge department business with such a weak ploy.

"Did I mention that Emmaline has been acting peculiar?" she asked slowly.

Feeling my way, I said, "You did. A crime scene can have that effect—"

"Before today. Wound up. That report about Russell Teague being ill … Wouldn't talk about it, but definitely something there. But you're right. Worse since the body… Sorry. What was that you were asking? Oh, if the spelling of the victim's name starts with a B as in boy. No. It's P, as in Paul, A-L-M-E-R."

I repeated the name for Diana's benefit. She frowned. A voice in my head jumped up and down screaming to forget that was a common last name and leap to the conclusion it was the first name I'd heard multiple times recently. Trouble was, was the voice in my head an angel or a devil?

"And the last name, is that T as in Tom—tomorrow?"

Diana shot me a look. I ignored it.

"No, no, no. R like renter, not T like tenant. R-E-N-N-A-N-T." I followed her connections—Rennant, which rhymed with tenant and segued to renter.

Palmer Rennant.

That went a long way to confirming Mrs. P *had* dodged with her *It would be exceedingly difficult to identify anyone under these circumstances.*

Another of her answers floated back into my memory. *I cannot claim any expertise at identifying watches.*

She'd tangled with Palmer Rennant over permission to continue the events on his land. She'd met him. She'd, no doubt, seen that watch.

And Aunt Gee said she'd been acting peculiarly…

"Thanks, Aunt Gee. The body in the cave—?"

"No idea."

That was the crisp Gisella Decker I knew.

"Understand. Can't believe I had the first and last names spelled wrong on the other one." My self-disgusted sigh was a prizewinner, especially considering how distracted I was. "You saved me. May I take you and Mrs. Parens out for lunch tomorrow? I know you usually cook, but—"

"Not cooking tomorrow. I'm working the middle shift, so, yes, I'd like that. I'm sure Emmaline will join us."

Whether she wanted to or not, judging by Gee's tone.

"Great. I'll call you in the morning. Have to go now."

We were flying into the KWMT-TV parking lot as I ended the call.

"I can't believe Aunt Gee told you the victim's name." Diana sounded half pleased, half not. "Since the changes in the sheriff's department—"

"In other words, your sweetie Sheriff Conrad taking over." Her loyalty to Conrad was why she was half not pleased.

"—Gee's been reticent about sharing with us."

Us was why she was half pleased.

"Reticent? She's been darned near a vault. As soon as you land this thing, I'll share all."

Only with the Newsmobile engine off did I repeat Aunt Gee's concerns about Mrs. Parens, along with my own thoughts.

Diana stared at me. "You can't think—And you can't *possibly* think Gee thinks—"

I interrupted her firmly, "I believe Gee and I are of one mind in thinking Emmaline Parens is keeping things from us that connect to the death of Palmer Rennant and those things are making her uneasy and the faster the case is solved, the better for Mrs. Parens. Where Gee and I likely diverge is that she thought giving us the ID couldn't hurt and I'm certain it can help."

Chapter Nineteen

WITH ONLY A few minutes to spare, I supplemented my earlier research on Palmer Rennant, noting his address and phone number had not changed in eight years. I found a number for Willa Rennant, who had previously lived at Palmer's address and now had a different one. Must be the ex-wife.

With that first name, I found a photo of her in the *Independence*.

Diana called me to join her in the second-largest editing bay.

We weren't using the identification on air—not only wouldn't I risk exposing Aunt Gee as the source, but it ran far too great a risk of broadcasting it before the family was notified. But knowing it subtly steered the story.

Especially since the dead man was the landowner who'd forced Two Rivers Camp and the Miners' Camp Fight reenactment to move.

"You're thinking that's a motive?" Diana asked as I squeezed in next to her. "But they found someplace better."

"True. But for there to be no connection…? Anyway, that has to wait. What've you got?"

"Before we get to that… First, I sent the footage to Mike and Jennifer. Second, Needham's putting out a one-page special for tomorrow, going to his home delivery customers and a limited number will be available around town—mostly at restaurants."

"Darn him for being so smart. Sneaky and smart. All right. That means tonight's packages have to be even better to take advantage of our lead."

"I've set aside most of what I shot before going up to where the body was," she said.

"Shame about that."

"Might be able to use some for advance coverage next time. Also thought I'd slide a release form past Les, to share some with the organizers. Crowd shots, the camp set-up, anticipation, stuff like that."

"Nice. I bet they'd love that."

"Not bad for the station, either, if it's used with a credit."

"Would you mind not offering right off? It might be a goodwill gesture that gets us in for a conversation at some point."

"Sure thing. Now, here are a couple establishing shots up to the butte." They captured the slightly grim grandeur, providing great mood-setters. "Okay, now we start."

As always, she had great footage. Including a shot that caught the profiles of most of the reenactors looking appropriately solemn and mysterious with their painted faces, and a shadowed presence on the ground beyond them that hinted at a body without showing it.

"Body brace did well. Kept it steady. Absorbed a lot of motion."

I snorted. "You did well."

She also had a terrific section where she panned down toward the reenactment site and the audience, but my favorite was a moody view of the area from before the official vehicles arrived. Plus, she covered all the bases with views of the authorities at work.

The early footage inside the cave pretty much looked like it had been shot in a cave. There was only so much even Diana and a body brace could do in the dark.

Her shots of the back of the law enforcement figures semi-circled around the site worked great, with the intensity of their interest conveying the mood.

The well-lit, detailed footage she got at the end of the remains amid tumbled and stacked rocks wasn't good for on-air. But was good for us.

The position of the body and, I suspected, the rocks, held the belt in the position we'd seen, with the shirt and jeans tailing away.

Just below that high point, the outlines of a wallet showed as faded lines in the now-slack fabric of the jeans' back pocket.

Too bad the lights didn't let me see right through to the content.

Especially to the name of this victim.

The only compensation was Sergeant Wayne Shelton must be nearly as antsy about getting his hands on that wallet as I was.

"What?" Diana demanded when I abruptly straightened.

"He wasn't."

"Who wasn't what?"

"Shelton wasn't as antsy about the contents of the wallet as I was—or as he should have been." I'd wondered earlier, but now I *really* wondered.

"You think he knows who the body in the cave is?" Her voice skidded up with surprise laced with skepticism. "But he didn't know it was there until we found it and there wasn't enough to see to identify without the wallet. Unless you think… You can't think…"

"That Shelton's responsible for the body in the cave? No. I might have blown it with thinking he'd need a forensic anthropologist to hit the century of the departed, but I still think it's old enough to make Shelton being responsible an impossibility."

"Is that the only reason? You don't think that knowing him—"

"As far as he'll ever know that's the sole reason," I said firmly. "My suspicious mind's the only reason he gives me a shred of respect. If I went all maudlin, thinking he wasn't capable of such a thing—of *anything*—he'd kick me to the curb completely. But he wasn't antsy enough about getting into that wallet and that means only one thing—he thinks he knows who it is."

She frowned. "How could he?"

"Does the county have famous missing-person cases?"

"Not that come to mind. But if it's from a long time ago, I wouldn't know."

"Good point." I exhaled deeply, feeling oddly unsettled. "And our best source for all things involving Cottonwood County history isn't blabbing."

She tipped her head and raised one eyebrow, eyeing me with lopsided intensity. "If Mrs. Parens knows, Tom might."

"Next time I talk to him—" Which was sure to happen, but didn't mean I'd rush it. "—I'm telling him you think he's prehistoric. In the meantime, since we know the identity of the other victim, Diana, will you—?"

"Ask around for gossip on Palmer Rennant and all who knew him."

"Diana—"

"I'm not complaining. Not really. I know that face, Elizabeth. So, I knew what was coming."

"You mean the face that hopes you'll use your excellent skills in talking to people and making them so at ease that they tell you things, combined with your stature in this county and far-reaching connections among its citizens?"

"That's the one. I'll see what I can find out."

My lips parted to say something about wishing she'd be as open about what was bothering her, but the moment passed when she turned to the screen.

"Let's wrap this up," she said. "Sooner it's finalized, sooner I can get busy asking around."

Chapter Twenty

"WHAT IS THIS?" Thurston Fine bellowed in his best overly emphatic voice—less an anchor's than a late-night TV pitchman's voice that woke you from a doze on the couch.

His hand fisted around the sheet with one line of copy I'd left on the anchor desk.

I was already set up in front of Warren Fisk's blue screen with the weatherman's blessing, so Diana's footage would start behind me as I introduced the video package.

"It's your intro to the lead story. It's on the teleprompter."

Since all it said was, *We have an important breaking news story for you now from KWMT-TV reporter E.M. Danniher*, the teleprompter was overkill. Except this was Thurston.

"I will not permit your story about cowboys and Indians—"

"Miners, not cowboys. And if you'd left the scanner on, you'd know there were two dead bodies found out there. *That's* the story."

"I will not—"

"Three minutes to air, Thurston, and you haven't done sound checks," came from the booth.

He scrambled behind the desk, put on his mic, and earpiece. His sound check was mostly declaring to me that he should have the story.

I was half-tempted to say, *Want it? You can have it. Right now.* And walk out.

No chance on earth he'd swim. He'd sink to the bottom. Trouble was, he'd take the story and KWMT-TV with him.

And I hated to see the increased pride in their work shown by a number of people at the station go down the drain, too.

So, I metaphorically bit my lip.

Until just before the countdown.

"Read the intro, Thurston," I said firmly, then gave him the carrot I hoped would get him past his snit. "After this one story, the rest of the newscast is yours."

Jerry—the sole camera operator and de facto floor manager—did the countdown.

The camera came in on Thurston's face. His expression reminded me of a toddler nephew when he was denied ice cream.

"Good evening, I'm Thurston Fine, *the* news anchor here at KWMT-TV."

He didn't usually add that description. Anyone watching would pick up that fact, but I supposed it worked as self-smoothing of his ruffled feathers.

"We have a story for you now."

Caught by the short intro being cut to a third of its length, there was a slight gap before even the fleet Jerry could get the camera on me.

After that, everything went perfectly.

While the video package with my voiceover played, I kept my focus on that, not looking toward the anchor desk. A trick I'd learned with said ice cream-deprived nephew, who only cried when someone looked at him.

Don't look at him, no meltdown.

With the camera back to me, I said into the lens, "We will bring you more on this important story in the days ahead. I'm E.M. Danniher of KWMT-TV. Back to you, Thurston."

"You shouldn't promise the viewers you will have any more on this story, E.M."

Shock started my eyes toward him, but as he continued, I was back to the camera.

"You can only say KWMT-TV will follow the story. But there's no guarantee we'll find out anything."

"KWMT-TV *does* promise our viewers that we will *pursue* this story with vigor and I will personally promise them that *I* will pursue it to the fullest extent of my ability."

I left the studio at the first commercial break with a brief wave to the control room and without making eye contact with Thurston, who cooperated by keeping his head down as if reading his script.

My jaw throbbed from clenching my teeth.

No inclination to chuckle at Thurston Fine's foibles now.

Heading for the exterior door to walk off my mad in the parking lot, still wearing my studio jacket and top, which was not a good idea because of how dusty the lot was, but too angry to care at the moment, I was stopped by the news aide on duty.

"We've gotten calls." Dale said that without much enthusiasm, which could indicate the calls were negative. Or his listlessness could be because Jennifer was out of town.

"What did they say?"

Dale looked up at the overhead TV screen, where Thurston was back on the air, repeating a news release from his country club verbatim. In the B block. As if it were news.

"Pretty much everybody said they appreciate you pursuing the story and you'll figure it out and tell them all about it in the end. One caller said, *You go, girl. Tell that stuffed—*" The phone rang. "You get the gist."

I stifled a grin. "Thanks, Dale."

It was a good enough lift that I U-turned and changed out of my studio clothes before heading for dinner—alone. I really missed Mike's company for between-newscasts meals. And more.

Back at the station, I tried to drag an official ID out of the sheriff's department, the second time on-set just before I went on. No luck.

With the Ten finished, I could really think through what came next.

Chapter Twenty-One

HOME, WITH SHADOW curled around—and on—my feet, drinking a glass of wine on the front porch, looking out on the dark street, half of me filled with great content at the quiet, the calm, and the foot-warming presence of my dog.

He appeared wholly filled with content.

I liked to think some of that was my presence. I knew a lot of it was the teenage girl from down the street pinch-hitting for my vacationing next-door neighbors Iris and Zeb Undlin, my usual Shadow-care backup. Thanks to the neighbor girl, he'd eaten at his regular time and that added a whole lot of contentment and security for a dog who'd once nearly starved scrounging for himself.

As for the half of me not filled with content, it was occupied with missing my usual cohorts in these inquiries.

I missed Diana, gone home to her kids, like a normal person. I missed Mike and Jennifer, in Chicago, having adventures. And, yes. I missed Tom, even more out of reach.

My phone rang. I jumped, the sound as loud as a siren in the stillness.

Mike.

Or Mike and Jennifer.

As I answered, I grabbed the wine glass and opened the door for Shadow and me. The topic of the upcoming conversation had the potential to disturb my street's nighttime peacefulness more than the ring had.

"Know more about the dead bodies yet?" Mike's question confirmed my perspicacity in not answering with speakerphone.

"Give me a second to get inside."

"What's the first step to find the murderer?" Jennifer asked.

"Gotta know who's dead," Mike said.

"If you saw somebody kill somebody else, you'd know who the murderer was, even if you didn't know who was killed."

"Yeah, but that didn't happen in this case, so—"

I didn't try to intrude on their squabble until I was on the couch, the half-empty wine glass on the coffee table, and Shadow in the gap between the two.

"Hey," I said loudly. "Why bother to call when you two can go along on your own for hours?"

"Sorry, Elizabeth," Jennifer said.

"We call because we want the news. The news behind the news you gave on the Five and Ten. All the news that putz declared you'd never get for KWMT—as if you haven't done that a bunch of times already."

"*We* have," I amended. "At least he didn't repeat that on the Ten."

"He didn't dare," Jennifer said. "Dale messaged about the calls supporting you." He had to be the source for their seeing the newscasts, too.

"Thanks, guys. I have a tentative ID on the first victim. The guy run over by the horses."

Jennifer shuddered. "Ever since I was a little girl, I've had nightmares about that."

"Well, this time you don't have to worry because he was probably already dead. You can see on the video that with the amount he was hit by the hoofs, there'd have been blood if he was still alive. That should make you feel better."

"A little sensitivity, Mike," I urged. "Now, want to hear the ID?"

This time they were unified. "Yes."

"The name's Palmer Rennant."

Mike said, "There was a kid who played basketball and ran track at Cottonwood County High—"

"His father."

"That's rough. Good kid. Don't think I met the father, but the mother's nice."

"Her name's Willa."

"She's got to be a prime suspect," Jennifer said promptly. "Spouse and girlfriend or boyfriend always are."

Mike grunted, conceding.

"Diana's checking with her friends and connections to see who knows what about Palmer Rennant and his family. Apparently, he and Willa were divorced a year ago, finalized about the time the son left for college. And remember, this ID isn't a hundred percent."

"How did you get it?"

I told them.

Mike whistled. "Aunt Gee must be really worried about Mrs. P. How strange is she acting?"

"She's so contained, it's hard to say. But with Aunt Gee thinking that…"

"Agreed," Mike said. "As for the ID, even with Aunt Gee being able to hold onto plausible deniability, I'd say it's pretty darned close to one hundred percent."

"Not until it's an official."

Jennifer came down on the side of Aunt Gee's identification being one hundred percent accurate when she said, "I'll do a background check on Palmer Rennant."

"Can you do that from there?"

"Couldn't have when I got here, but I can now. I've beefed up Mike's system."

"You have? I only gave you the Wi-Fi password."

She scoffed with a click of her tongue.

With that topic dealt with, I said, "The other thing we know is he bought the property the camp and reenactment had been held on for decades three years ago. After they used the land two years ago, he strung them along, then said they couldn't."

"You think it's significant his body was found at the new loca-tion?" Mike asked.

"Possibly. No, I'll go stronger than that. I don't see how it's not significant in *some* way."

"People in Cottonwood County know the events are held every other year," Jennifer said.

"So we should, what? line up all newcomers as suspects? We'd have to start with Elizabeth."

Jennifer retorted, "Hey, you're the one not around there anymore."

"You're not either right now. Besides, I'm still *from* there and I knew where the massacre was being reenacted."

"Skirmish," I corrected him. "Besides, I'd have checked before I dumped a body, and then I'd have found out."

"You're thinking that unless the killer wasn't from here *and* wasn't aware of Cottonwood County traditions *and* wasn't smart enough to check, which led to them dumping the body where it would be found fast, then the killer *wanted* the body found fast."

"Yes. And nice recap, Jennifer. Otherwise, think of how many places the body could have been put in Cottonwood County and not found for a long, long time. Like—"

"—that cave," Mike and I ended together.

"Could Rennant have been left there so the cave body would be found?"

"Interesting question, Jennifer," I said.

"If that was the purpose—or a purpose—of leaving the body there, wouldn't the killer have done a better job? It sounds like it was pretty much a fluke that you found the one in the cave." Arguing with her own point—the girl truly was learning.

"There might be an argument that it was a foreseeable outcome, considering the dynamics between Shelton and me, but that would rely on the certainty that I'd stand where I stood and he'd corral us toward the cave... I'd say pretty much a fluke. Still, having Palmer Rennant's body there certainly increased the chances of the body in the cave being discovered."

"We keep saying the body was found there," Mike said. "*Was* Palmer Rennant also killed there?"

"That's a good question," Jennifer said.

"I have another one. Since it wasn't the horses, what *did* kill him?" Mike asked.

Chapter Twenty-Two

"I'LL SEE IF I can access the postmortem," Jennifer said.

"That's going to be tough, but if you got it, that would be amazing. And we'll pursue other sources here."

From Chicago, Mike chuckled. "Penny, I suppose. And Diana's contacts in the county. You know," he mused, "if it's shooting or stabbing, we can be pretty sure he wasn't killed there. Same theory as the horse's hoofs—no blood on the ground around him."

"True, but that's a big if. He could have been strangled or poisoned or—"

"Electrocuted," Jennifer said.

"You have that on the brain. Besides, that's accidental." To me, Mike said, "She was impressed by a lightning storm over Lake Michigan earlier in the week."

"It was amazing."

Reining them in, I said, "Unless and until we know a cause of death, we're going to have a hard time knowing for sure if he was killed there or the body was left there."

"What about how long the body was there?"

"Another one law enforcement won't know for sure until they get all their forensics reports."

"But?"

"But what?" I asked Mike.

"That's what I'm asking you. There was a definite buildup to a *but* in that answer about law enforcement and forensics, especially with that *know for sure*."

"Mmm," I conceded. "We have more to go on with how long the body was there than whether he was killed there or dumped there."

"Like what?" Jennifer asked.

"First, I asked the reenactors if they'd ever been to that spot before. They said they'd had a quick run-through with the miner reenactors last Sunday, before the Two Rivers Camp started. No body then. I need to check if any of the organizers were up there during the week. Didn't have time to ask Mrs. P before Shelton and his buddies showed up."

I continued, "The second major element is what Diana and I saw at the scene. Starting with the body. The paint on his back wasn't nearly as fresh as the reenactors'—the edges were blurred, which could be from rain last night. Or, *possibly*, from being there longer. But I don't think so."

"Why don't you think so?" Mike asked.

"Shelton got us out of there before they moved the body, so I can't be sure, but I didn't see decomposition to indicate more than a couple days."

Jennifer half-swallowed an *eww* sound.

"Besides, from his position and holding it after the horses, I'd think rigor mortis had to be in effect. That's roughly twelve to twenty-four hours after death. But that's not firm with conditions like cooler temperatures—like from last night's rain."

"You're saying twelve to twenty-four hours give or take—but how much give or take? Another twenty-four?" Mike asked.

"I'll check with a source tomorrow."

Jennifer asked, "How does this even help us?"

"Narrows the window of how long he was there, which helps with when he could have been killed, and that ties in with alibis—if we're lucky. We did catch one break."

"What's that?" Mike asked.

"Something to do with the body?" Jennifer asked with markedly less enthusiasm than he'd shown.

"No. It has to do with the weather and tracks in the area. It rained most of last night."

"That's why the paint was worn off," Jennifer said.

"Probably some. Although the body was sort of protected under an overhang of rock. Did you see it in the video?"

"Yeah," Mike said.

"So, I don't know how much the rain would have affected the paint. But it did affect tracks. There were none on the east side as I climbed up. I can't be as sure on the west side. But I can say I didn't see anything that looked like vehicle tracks except the utility vehicle O.D. Everett and Mrs. P came in. Which I'd think I would, even under the hoofprints. Unless the reenactor riders worked really hard to obliterate them, which I don't believe. When they went charging in there, they definitely were not organized. Plus, the hoofprints behind the rock formation weren't dense enough to wipe out vehicle tracks except in a couple places—"

"Like around the body," Jennifer said morosely.

"Yup, which was situated where most of the riders curved around the edge of the rock formation—a blind curve. They were on the body before they saw it."

"Listen to you—figuring all that out from tracks. Elizabeth Margaret Danniher, a regular mountain man—mountain woman."

Modesty and accuracy demanded I demur with, "Common sense."

"You couldn't have started with this information and skipped the stuff about the body decomposing?" Jennifer asked.

Chapter Twenty-Three

"BOTH ARE IMPORTANT. Another question is how would somebody get a body up there? Horseback from the west side, like the reenactors did, but carrying a body? Especially if it was already in that position. And if it wasn't, the killer posed him that way. Though how or why… Besides it's even steeper on the east approach. I don't see how a horse, much less a vehicle—"

"Horses could get up there easy, whether with a body tied on or the victim riding in alive, killing him, then leading out the dead guy's horse. So can a truck or other vehicle get up there. All you do is start farther away than where the camp was held. That way—"

I remembered the utility vehicle swinging east before it started the climb to the butte, but had been too occupied to follow its entire track.

"—you're not trying to go straight up. You go on a wide diagonal. It's easier on the west side, but either direction, if you come in from the side and angle your way in, you can do it. Heck, I've seen a passenger car do it by starting far enough away."

"You drove up there?"

"Yeah. But not a passenger car."

"Why? Not why didn't you drive a passenger car, but why you drove there at all."

"We were kids. Horsing around. Looking for a place we wouldn't be bothered."

"Where deputies or parents wouldn't see the vehicles, wouldn't realize a bunch of us were together," Jennifer added.

"You, too?"

"Sure. It was a hangout spot."

"Did anyone ever go into that cave?"

"Yeah," Mike said.

"Some did," Jennifer said.

"Nobody saw anything?"

"Not that I ever heard and we would have heard about a body for sure. We never stayed long. That cave's known for rock slides. Would've been dangerous."

"Saw evidence of slides," I said. "Looks like some covered up the body, but more recent ones might be what exposed it enough to be spotted."

"Took eagle-eyed Elizabeth Margaret Danniher." Mike chuckled.

"Lucky me."

"How are you going to figure out who it is?"

"The sheriff's department has a huge advantage on us. They'll likely have an ID from the wallet long before we'd get something. Best idea I've had so far is to try to narrow the time period the body might be from to have a better idea if it might be connected to the recent disappearance."

"Could be from really long ago and the new dead guy could have been killed in a feud over an archaeological find," Jennifer proposed.

"Archaeological find wearing blue jeans from Sears?" Mike asked.

"Still could be really, really old," she protested. "Didn't they have that catalog forever? I remember Mrs. P talking about it."

"Checking dates for Sears jeans is on my list. I'll try to get more insight from Aunt Gee and Mrs. Parens at lunch tomorrow. I'm taking them to Ernie's."

"Aunt Gee is letting you take her *out* for Sunday lunch?"

"Practically insisted on it. Especially Mrs. P's participation. Gee's covering the afternoon shift, so she wouldn't have been doing one of her Sunday extravaganzas no matter what."

Mike sighed. "I sure do miss those."

"Putting aside your stomach, let's get back to the dead guy we're thinking is Palmer Rennant. Jennifer, that's great that you can run a background check from there. If you run into any issues—"

"No problem. My guys can help and Dale will research for me if I need local information."

"Be careful how much and what you ask of him." Her fellow news aide would do anything for her and wasn't as adept at avoiding detection as she was. "Don't want him to lose his job."

She perked up. "Hey, you didn't say don't hack."

"That, either. Another big factor to tackle is when Rennant was last seen. Along with rigor mortis, knowing his movements might narrow the possible time of death a lot. Diana and I will work on that, but law enforcement is far better equipped for it."

"Then we weasel it out of them," Jennifer said with full confidence.

"When you come back tomorrow, you can be in charge of weaseling."

"You've a far better weaseler than I am—" She meant it as a compliment. "—but about tomorrow ... I'm staying a couple extra days."

"Oh?"

"Yeah. I talked to Mom and Dad and... I'm going to Northwestern Monday. It's right here in Evanston, so it's not a big deal."

"Oh." That came out in an entirely different tone.

Jennifer had shown no interest that I knew of in a four-year degree. Although she had shown interest in the journalism tenets I'd shared with her. And Northwestern's Medill School of Journalism was one of the top, if not *the* top journalism program.

"They have this program I heard about from a guy at the robotic place," she added.

Oh. Gone was the heady momentary thought that she wanted to follow in the Danniher footsteps.

"It's a great school," Mike chimed in. "A degree from there—"

"I don't know about the whole degree thing. I'm not a kid like the freshmen."

A whole year, maybe two, older.

"You have a lot of interests. Northwestern has a great journalism program, too." Yes, I slid it in there like a pushy parent trying not to be overtly pushy.

"Maybe a combo program." That came from Mike.

"It's just talking. I pushed back my return flight before I knew you'd find two dead bodies. And we're going to a play and the Art Institute tomorrow, so I can't do as much as usual until I get back."

I fought off a defensive urge to say I hadn't found Palmer Rennant—the riders had. "Doing the background check would be great, but don't let that stop you from enjoying the rest of your time."

After we ended the call, I covered Shadow's nighttime routine, which included a special treat. I gave it to him once and forevermore it was part of his routine. Which made it part of mine, unless I wanted to be stared at reproachfully into the wee hours.

Upstairs, I got ready and settled into bed, breaking that rule about not looking at screens before sleeping by checking my phone.

I had a message I hadn't noticed while talking with Mike and Jennifer.

You okay? asked Tom Burrell.

A stampede of replies about being a hard-bitten journalist on the trail of a story, about looking for murderers before, about taking care of myself streamed through my head, competing with striving for at least neutral to preserve my connection with his daughter.

I wrote back, *Just fine. Tamantha?*

Unruffled.

Of course. Tell her chili was sold in stands in San Antonio, Texas in the mid-1800s, but recipes could be a century older.

I'd taken a moment for a little non-murder-related research.

Will tell her. Explanation?

Ask Tamantha.

Good night.

I didn't respond.

It was too … *something* … messaging him good night from between the sheets.

DAY FOUR

SUNDAY

Chapter Twenty-Four

I WOKE TO a nightmare—Thurston from the night before.

Thurston Fine had ambitions to move up and out, but he also had the ineffable look of an anchor aging in place.

It's as if they'd become molded to the anchor chair, caught in a time period just in the rearview mirror. Not notably dated, but ever so lightly shellacked.

It happens in any size market, this aging in place. Sometimes with those who are in or have adopted a hometown. Or who have found their level, know it, accept it, are satisfied with it.

Thurston Fine did not know he was aging in place. Oblivious, as to many things.

For the first time, it struck me that I, too, might have acquired that lightly shellacked appearance. Or soon would.

After all, I'd told my stand-in agent—the friend of the family who'd stepped in when my divorce claimed an agent as well as a husband, career, and a few other items—to stop looking for new positions, in addition to telling Mike no thanks when he said his Chicago station expressed interest in my work.

I looked at the clock and got out of bed.

No time for meandering thoughts. Even before my lunch with the ladies of O'Hara Hill, I had questions to ask.

The first was answered by checking the sheriff's department website. They'd made the identification official.

Next, to read Needham Bender's special edition of the *Independence*.

No ID there. At least the sheriff's department hadn't played favorites with the media.

"DEX, I NEED information on rigor mortis."

Not the conversational opener you might use with most people, especially on a Sunday morning, but it was perfect for Dex, who doesn't believe in chit-chat or much else having to do with social interaction, and does believe in science. Especially science having to do with the murdered and tracking down who murdered them.

That helps make him a whiz in the FBI's lab. It's also taught prosecutors not to use him as a witness if they can help it. He's too interested in the science. Not only does he not favor the prosecution—or the defense—but he can make jurors' eyes roll back in their heads.

He's done that a time or two to me in the years he's been a source—"unnamed" or background—starting when I was working my way up through the ranks of national reporters. I had him call me Danny then to throw off eavesdroppers or supervisors who might connect him with my reports. He still calls me that, as do others in my circle, who picked it up then.

Since my fall from the Number One market dropped me here, he's continued to offer me insight.

"There is a great deal to be said regarding rigor mortis." Note that Dex didn't exclaim over my interest in the subject. To him it was weird when people weren't interested. "It is a fascinating chemical change. With death, the human body ceases to produce Adenosine Triphosphate, which is necessary for muscles to relax. It is a misnomer to term it as a process that positively stiffens the muscles of the deceased. It is, rather, one that no longer allows them to relax, so that in that absence, they stiffen by default. An entirely different matter, and one which should be fully explained to laymen, especially those in a position where their knowledge of such matters is vital, as I attempted to recently."

"Prosecutor wouldn't let you explain it to a jury?"

"No. Although the defense attorney did and I thoroughly explained the elegancies of the processes taking place in the body of the deceased."

Oh, Dex. I hoped the jury righted their rolled-back eyes and took in the gist of what Dex said, along with his abiding truthfulness, and did not reward the defense attorney's cleverness in egging Dex on.

I wasted no sympathy on the prosecutor. He or she was almost certainly a new, hotshot, overconfident jackass, who'd been tempted by the impressive degrees and accolades in Dex's bio and thought they could handle his testimony when so many before failed.

I hoped justice had been done, despite cleverness, egos, and earnest scientists.

"Can you give me a basic timeline—the most basic you've ever given—for rigor mortis?"

"I cannot give you a timeline that would be useful, Danny, without knowing the details of the body and the environment, preferably from being there myself and doing my own examination. Age, weight, percentage of fat, state of fitness, whether the individual had recently completed exercise, disease—each of those greatly affects the timeline of rigor mortis."

A lot more variables than I'd thought.

"And then environmental factors come into play. Heat, cold, whether the body is moved during the process of rigor in such a way as to break the rigor, all alter what is laughingly called the *normal* timeline."

He wasn't laughing.

"Let's start with that normal timeline, Dex. Then we can layer on factors."

"Its accuracy is not reliable or—"

"It gives me a place to start. Please?"

"Very well. The effects generally show first in the eyelids and are observed to advance to the muscles of the neck and jaw, since smaller muscles demonstrate the cessation of ATP—"

"ATP?"

"Adenosine triphosphate, as I said." He didn't miss a beat in picking up. "—more quickly than larger muscles."

I've never understood why medicine insists on speaking Latin when you're sick. You feel bad enough as it is.

Or, in this case, dead.

"Couldn't see any of that, Dex. The body was face down. In that rough timeline people talk about under normal circumstances—"

"*Normal* circumstances," he scoffed.

"Isn't rigor mortis mostly set after twelve hours and remains that way for—?"

"At least start before twelve hours. From the first ten or so minutes after death, the body begins to cool and rigor is barely noticeable as it gradually affects smaller muscles first, as I said. From approximately—" He said it like a dirty word. "—eight hours to twelve hours after death, the rigor of muscles, including the large ones, becomes advanced. That state remains for an additional period of— again—approximately twelve hours. After that, is a period when the stiffness of the muscles gradually passes off, most often completing that process by thirty-six hours, with that figure shortened or extended by circumstances."

"That helps. Thank you for—"

"However, the grossest assessment that I find helpful—" He did not mean *gross* as in Jennifer's *eww*, but in the sense of undetailed. "—is death came less than three hours earlier if the body feels warm and there is no rigor, death came three to eight hours earlier if the body feels warm and there is stiffness, death came eight to thirty-six hours earlier if the body feels cold and is stiff, death came more than thirty-six hours earlier if the body is cold and not stiff."

Rennant's body had retained enough stiffness to hold that facedown fetal position. That put death most likely eight to thirty-six hours before I saw it. The lower end not as likely, because of the big muscles involved in the position.

I closed my eyes and saw the paramedic-in-training touching under the chin. Had he started to shake his head then, even before he could have hoped to find a pulse? I was pretty sure he had. Because the skin was cool?

That would also push the death toward the longer period.

I needed to talk to him.

Something Dex said earlier triggered another thought—could Palmer Rennant have climbed up to where he died? I knew first hand that it qualified as vigorous exercise. How would that tie into a timeline?

"Dex, go back to what you said about exercise and disease. How do they affect the timeline?"

"Exercise depletes the body of oxygen, which ATP requires, thus advancing the effect of rigor mortis. Drugs that increase body temperature can do that. A disease such as pneumonia, however, generally retards rigor mortis, while Huntington's disease generally accelerates it."

I needed to find out about Rennant's health and fitness.

"...and if the rigor is broken during that period, say a limb is moved, the rigor does not return."

"Wait. Say that again."

He did.

I described the body as I'd seen it, then backed up and described the horses running over it. Finishing with, "Do I understand you correctly, the horses couldn't have trampled him and still have the body in that position?"

"Trampled, with their full weight coming down on him, no. Striking glancing blows here and there could affect rigor where the blow fell, while the general position held. The factors I mentioned, as well as the solidity of the surface under the body—"

Before he took this off in another listing of factors, I said, "That's very helpful, Dex. Thank you."

"Rigor mortis is complex, Danny. The interactions of the factors—"

"I'm beginning to recognize that, but until I know more so I can ask specific questions, I don't want to waste your time."

"Very well."

"Wait," I called out before he hung up.

Not in a snit. He just wasn't wasting his time or mine. That was Dex.

"Dex, do you have a forensic anthropologist who could look at video of a ... a body and give me some information."

"Where?"

"In a cave in Wyoming."

"I doubt they'd go to Wyoming."

"No, I meant—" Rather than get involved in those details, I shifted. "I'd send the video and talk to them on the phone, wherever they are."

"I'll call you when I have a name."

And then he did hang up.

Chapter Twenty-Five

MRS. PARENS AND Aunt Gee were both amenable to having lunch out, which we finalized when I called, to coincide with their return home from church.

Under the theory of being prepared to strike while the iron was hot, I called on my way to O'Hara Hill, which was north of Sherman and far enough west to cozy up to the mountains.

An Army might or might not travel on its stomach, but secrets in Cottonwood County definitely transmitted through food, whether from the Sherman Supermarket or Ernie's in O'Hara Hill.

In the evening, the small restaurant/bar with the history of O'Hara Hill tacked up on its walls was usually packed, but not for Sunday lunch. Ernie, the owner, was sitting at the bar, reading the special edition of the *Independence*. It was a solid report of Saturday's events, with background on Two Rivers Camp, the Miners' Camp Fight reenactment, and the buttes. But it didn't advance the story past what we'd had on-air last night.

I asked Ernie for a quiet table. He looked at the three of us so knowingly I half expected him to wink.

After seating us, I heard him tell the server to take our orders quickly and not to seat anyone near us.

Perfect.

With a firm end time on this conversation when Aunt Gee needed to be at the sheriff's department substation for dispatching duties, I did not waste time after our orders were taken.

"Do you—either of you—know of people who've been missing

from around here for a long time?"

"You are pursuing the corpse found in the cave?" Mrs. Parens asked.

I didn't have to answer that I was taking them one at a time, because Aunt Gee said, "There are a number of missing persons. Merry Melville from four years ago, though most everyone thinks she took off for Florida, going after a guy she'd worked with. And Joanie—"

"More likely a man. And I think it's someone from a while ago."

"That cuts the number of possibilities. More women go missing and too high a percentage of them are, in fact, victims of foul play." Gee shook off her grimness. "How long a while?"

"Some time after men started keeping their wallets in the back pocket of their jeans. Oh, and wearing jeans and a checked shirt."

The two women exchanged a look.

"What?"

"Cowboys and other workingmen have been wearing denim pants and checked shirts for nearly a century and a half in this region," Mrs. Parens said. "In the earliest days, veterans of the Civil War continued to wear varied pieces of their uniforms, since that did not entail added expenditure. The Union shirts were particularly well-regarded for durability. In subsequent decades, mass-produced material became available, especially in checks."

"I thought cowboys wore plaid if they weren't in solid colors." Or maybe I was thinking of a specific rancher.

Mrs. Parens said, "Plaid came along as a widely available pattern workingmen could afford early in the Twentieth Century."

I sighed. "Too bad it wasn't a plaid shirt, then. Would have limited when this guy could have ended up dead in that cave and—Oh, wait. Sergeant Shelton said the jeans were from Sears. No, he said Sears Roebuck."

"I'm afraid that won't help you greatly, either," Aunt Gee said. "People around here started ordering from the catalog when it started—what? right at the turn of the century?—so that doesn't—"

"The catalog began in the mid-1890s," Mrs. Parens corrected quietly, pretending not to notice she'd irked Gee.

"—narrow your time period much."

"No, I'm afraid it doesn't. Mrs. Parens, you said cowboys and other workingmen. Would that include miners?"

"The images I associate with miners more often included solid color jackets or outer shirts or coveralls, although that is merely an impression. I would not be comfortable making a positive statement on the issue without researching extensively."

"Thank you, but that's not necessary." I mentally added a *yet.*

"Are you thinking the remains might be of a miner?" Aunt Gee asked.

"Even saying *might be* is too strong. Although, obviously, the site is pretty much on the route the miners took trying a Bozeman Trail—Montana Road—" I slid in the correction. "—shortcut. I know the cave is east of their route, but..."

"It is not beyond reason that one might have gone astray as the group angled north and west, although accounts of the survivors do not mention that and one would think they would have included such an event. However," continued Mrs. Parens, "another possibility might have come later. There was gold found in 1870, south and slightly west of Cody, in a place they called Kirwin. The original miners were forced to leave, since that was Shoshone territory according to the 1868 treaty that, in essence, closed the Montana Road. In that instance, the military did enforce the treaty. A decade later, the miners were back. The instances of those miners in that location, combined with the cave where you found the remains being along a natural route from Kirwin to Bozeman does raise that additional possibility."

Hah. I'd bet Mrs. P went home last night and refreshed her recall of where and when gold was found in the region. I wasn't asking and risking irking her and potentially damming her information river for that detail.

Though I'd love to know if she'd raised the possibility to Sergeant Shelton.

"You would need to tell us more details for us to provide useful information," Gee said.

"I'm afraid I don't know many more details at this point. Someone who wore jeans, a checked shirt, and a studded belt. With a wallet in the back pocket," I said.

Mrs. Parens' gaze sharpened. "A studded belt," she repeated.

Had Shelton mentioned the wallet to her? Was that why she focused on the studded belt instead?

"Does that mean something to you?"

"I am sorry to disappoint you, Elizabeth, but I cannot say that it does."

Our orders arrived.

As we ate, I switched to Palmer Rennant.

They added little to what they'd already told me about him and his family.

The Rennants belonged to the country club and socialized with people there—so said Gee, quoting Penny.

That might explain Thurston Fine's *important people* commentary. He belonged to the country club, too, and considered all his fellow members important people. Was that the extent of it? Or did Fine have a more personal connection to Palmer Rennant?

They didn't know.

Watching Aunt Gee, I said to Mrs. Parens as casually as possible, "I'm surprised you didn't recognize that watch of Rennant's. It's memorable and sitting across tables at those meetings last year…"

"What watch?" Gee asked.

I described it. She shook her head. "Don't remember anything like that."

Mrs. P looked the slightest big smug.

As for the conflict over Rennant kicking the Cottonwood County events off his land, Aunt Gee indicated she'd told me Thursday night what she knew and Mrs. Parens wasn't talking.

I shifted to a new angle. "Tell me what was going on behind the tarps during preparations for the reenactment."

"Organized chaos," Gee said. "The reenactors who were going to be miners running one way trying to put together their clothes and props for the camp. The attacking reenactors—with their horses—stripping down to remarkably scant clothing and having the symbols painted on them."

My phone vibrated with an incoming message. I ignored it. I could feel time running out and I'd gotten so little.

"One of the miners," Gee continued, "split out the seam on his pants and a group was trying to fix them well enough so he didn't moon the audience, while others were looking for a replacement pair of pants. And another one swearing someone stole his Army shirt. All this with Nadine Hulte—to give credit where credit is due—keeping everything from descending into complete chaos."

Another vibration, another message.

"She is remarkable in those circumstances," Mrs. Parens said. "She has blossomed into a capable and responsible person from the shy, uncertain girl she was when she began to volunteer. It has been most gratifying to watch her development."

"You have done far more than help her. She would not have *blossomed* without you."

Gee supporting her neighbor did not alter their rivalry one iota. It was that kind of relationship.

"Nadine has worked extremely hard to build her confidence by acquiring skills and expanding her abilities and her willingness to take on additional responsibilities. She has become invaluable to Paige Schmidt in the estate sale business."

Somebody was not giving up on sending me messages. They'd just have to wait.

I still had questions. "Was she or Clara Atwood painting the symbols on the reenactors?"

"Nadine? Clara?" Gee said in surprise.

Mrs. Parens, though, was less surprised, because she'd heard me asking Paytah about paint yesterday. She likely hadn't seen the detail of the markings on Palmer Rennant's back, but could she see they were red and yellow?

"Members of the tribe perform that service, using the opportunity for the elders to teach the younger generation," she said.

If these messages didn't stop coming in and this phone vibrating...

Chapter Twenty-Six

"**WHAT ABOUT THE** paint Paytah said the reenactors didn't bring? Who provided that?"

"The red and yellow?" Gee asked. "The committee approved that purchase Wednesday. It was used for the campers, too."

"Nadine bought it?"

My phone rang.

"You should answer your phone," Mrs. Parens said.

"Or turn it off, Elizabeth," Gee said. "I always do before a meal."

Another ring.

"Did Nadine buy the paint?"

Mrs. P wasn't answering.

Gee looked from me to her and back. "No. There's no mystery. Clara Atwood bought it and took it out to the site Thursday morning."

Third ring.

I broke down and looked at my phone.

The screen said the call was from Tom Burrell. The messages, too.

He barely waited for my hello.

"Elizabeth, are you with Mrs. Parens and Gee Decker?"

"Yes." It came out breathless, because fear that flashed into my head that he'd only call me if something happened to Tamantha evaporated with his question ... taking my oxygen with it.

"I've been trying to get hold of them. Sally Tipton's had a serious stroke. She's in the hospital. She listed Mrs. Parens as her emergency contact. When they couldn't reach her, they tried me."

I'd first encountered Sally a year ago. She was somewhere in age between Mrs. P and Aunt Gee, but an entirely different personality. They were smart, strong, competent, generous, tart women. She was not.

"I'll put her on the phone—"

"No, wait. Where are you?" he asked.

"Ernie's."

"Okay. Will you ask Gee to drive Mrs. Parens to my place and—?"

"I'll drive her to the hospital. Gee has to work."

"No. Bring her here, if you don't mind. I'll take her the rest of the way."

"Okay."

I waited a beat. He said nothing.

I held out my phone to Mrs. Parens. "It's Tom—Tom Burrell. He needs to talk to you."

Aunt Gee had her phone out, checking messages. "Sally Tipton. Stroke," she said.

"Yes."

She clucked her tongue and kept reading.

Mrs. Parens listened silently to Tom.

At the end, her expression unchanged, she said, "Yes. Thank you."

Apparently attuned to the changed mood at the table—or already aware of the news through the Cottonwood County grapevine—Ernie brought us our bill, asked if we wanted anything wrapped to go, and patted Mrs. Parens lightly on the shoulder. She nodded briefly, occupied with her purse. More occupied than she needed to be.

I paid, quashing protests from Gee.

Outside, Gee said, "I wish I hadn't agreed to cover this shift for Donald."

"Nonsense, Gisella," Mrs. Parens said briskly. "You are generously helping him and you can rest assured Tom and Elizabeth have my transportation covered."

During the short trip to their street, Gee read aloud a few of the messages she'd received, which gave no real added information.

I asked Mrs. P if she wanted to get anything from her house, she said no, so we dropped off Gee, and headed south toward Sherman.

"Did you know Sally listed you as her emergency contact?" I asked.

"No, I did not." She looked straight ahead.

"Are you surprised?"

"No, I am not."

Because Sally had no one else? Or because nothing Sally did surprised Mrs. Parens?

At least I got to have a *not surprised* of my own—at Mrs. P immediately going to Sally Tipton's side at the hospital.

But I was surprised at her closed-off silence.

Or maybe I wasn't entirely surprised.

Mrs. Parens had gone to bat for the woman before, even though there was something odd in their interactions. Not friction, exactly, because Sally mostly presented a sweet, flighty front that fended off friction.

Mrs. Parens' attitude to Sally was hard to pin down. Less patient, more stiff than with others. And yet an element of protectiveness.

I had questions for Emmaline Parens.

It would be exceedingly difficult to identify anyone under these circumstances.

But this didn't seem a fair time to ask.

We reached the entrance to the Circle B Ranch.

I drove the rising and twisting ranch road to its final curve. As we crossed the wood bridge, we spotted Tom and Tamantha coming out the front door, onto the wide porch, looking like a family portrait.

I parked and we all met between my SUV and Tom's truck.

Tamantha gave me a big smile. Tom didn't.

"Thank you, Elizabeth."

"Glad to help." To Mrs. P, I said, "Let me know if there's anything I can do—for you or for Sally."

Chapter Twenty-Seven

LEFT ON MY own, I called the Widow Rennant.

If an ex qualifies as a widow.

Ex-widow? That didn't work. Widow-ex?

"Willa Rennant? This is Elizabeth Margaret Danniher from KWMT-TV. I'm—"

"Oh, yes, I've seen your reports on murder cases."

"—the 'Helping Out' consumer affairs reporter."

"That, too. Though you're probably not calling me about that."

I liked her directness. "I'm not. I'd like to talk to you about Palmer Rennant."

"You'd need to come here. Now."

I'd expected to need to persuade her, overcome reluctance.

This went beyond directness.

"Your house? That's fine—"

"Not my house. Palmer's."

She rattled off the address fast enough that it was a good thing I already had it and hung up.

How ex was she if she was at Palmer Rennant's house this soon after his death?

SHE WAS NOT alone.

The large house, in fact, appeared to be well occupied by members of the Cottonwood County Sheriff's Department, judging by the number of official vehicles outside.

I'd figured they'd be here ahead of us, but being reminded of it didn't improve my mood any.

In contrast to the house, the corrals and neat barn appeared deserted. A red truck, new, but with the mandatory spray pattern of Wyoming dust mimicking custom flame paint along the sides, was parked on the left, beside the porch.

A smaller SUV in pale blue was off to the right side. I'd bet that was Willa Rennant's.

The double front doors were mostly glass, with the wood frames around them painted bright red. Where the doors met, both had scratch marks at my mid-thigh level. Looked like animal claws to me. Not like I'd imagine a wild animal would make, certainly not a big one. More like a short dog or a tall cat.

Willa Rennant swung open the left-hand door.

I identified her both from the *Independence* photo I'd seen at the station and because she wasn't wearing a uniform, while the people in the background were.

"Hello, Ms. Danniher. Come in."

"Hello, Ms. Rennant. Thank—"

"Elizabeth, what are you doing here?"

Even if I hadn't recognized the voice, I would have known immediately that the law enforcement officer addressing me wasn't Shelton. Calling me by my first name and not growling. Couldn't possibly be my favorite sergeant.

I turned to Deputy Richard Alvaro.

"You can't be here," he said before I said a word. "You have to leave."

He still looked young, but he was becoming old in the way of law enforcement—say no first and ask questions later.

"I invited her," Willa Rennant said calmly. "You said I could have someone here with me if I chose and I choose Ms. Danniher."

I liked this woman.

"A lawyer. Somebody like that."

"I don't want a lawyer."

"Then you'll both have to leave."

"I am here as the representative of my children, who inherit this house from their father. I am not impeding your search in any way. You already said I could sit in the music room while your team searches the rest. Ms. Danniher will join me there."

She gestured toward a room to the right of the front door with a grand piano. Good guess for the music room. There also were couches set at right angles to each other under windows. So we didn't have to share the piano bench.

I didn't look toward Alvaro as I followed Willa Rennant's gesture into that room.

It's best not to put up the backs of young law enforcement by seeming to gloat. Even a little.

Besides, there wasn't time to waste.

He'd call Shelton immediately. And if Shelton decreed I had to go, Willa Rennant would need that lawyerly presence to get me to stay, which would interfere with me asking questions.

Far better to get my questions in now.

Before I had a chance to ask any, though, she asked one of her own as she closed double doors behind us.

"I take it you are looking into Palmer's death as you have other cases?"

"I'm part of a group that's done that in the past. We hope to look into this situation, too." Though, as I said it, I felt a twinge. My *group* felt sadly depleted of late.

"Good. What do you want to ask me?"

Genuine approval of an inquiry into her ex's death? Or an effort to deflect my suspicion?

At this point, did I care?

I looked over at the piano, topped by a forest of family photos, mostly of young people who had to be her children.

That, as well as other impressions of the house, had me thinking Palmer kept the marital home in the split. Not unheard of, but it did raise the question of how well Willa Rennant did in the divorce. Can you say motive?

"When did you last see your ex-husband?"

"I would not ordinarily be able to tell you with precision, but the instances are fresh in my mind after speaking with the sheriff's department, as are the distinctions."

"Distinctions?"

"I last saw him Thursday morning, entering the pharmacy on Cottonwood Avenue, near the courthouse. I last saw him face-to-face and had a conversation with him the week before at the country club. I had played a round of golf with friends and he was waiting for members of his foursome. We had a drink—water," she specified with a faint, wry smile.

"Was he sick? Was that why he was going to the pharmacy?"

"You would need to check with someone else about that. Someone who saw him frequently. I wouldn't know."

An ever-so-subtle edge to that prompted me to ask, "Do you have someone specific in mind?"

She shrugged. Quite convincingly, actually. "The most recent rumors I have heard say he switched to seeing a woman named Jolie. I'm not acquainted with her, nor did I see him with any one woman enough times to make me think a particular person is the Jolie of rumor."

Her mouth and the lines at the corners of her eyes relaxed.

I felt myself relaxing, too.

Not because she did, but because if Shelton had told Alvaro to kick me out, I'd be gone by now.

"You heard about other women he'd dated?"

"My dear, I heard about other women he'd said hello to. Some people feel it is their duty—or their privilege—to keep the ex-wife informed of the ex-husband's romantic status at all times. However, if I had to guess why he was going into the pharmacy, I would suspect it was in search of candy corn."

"In August?" That slipped out unintended. Not one of my better questions, since I'd seen Halloween stuff creeping out earlier and earlier.

Willa Rennant's slight smile reappeared. "All year round. The man loves it. He has been known to order it at astronomical prices online during the offseason, despite my telling him it is almost certainly old … and then be crushed that it was stale. I know he's begged the supermarket to get it in early, but he has not budged the manager—or should I say Penny? He has been more hopeful of persuading the pharmacy."

The man's craving for pre-season Halloween sugar made him more human than anything else I'd heard about him.

And his ex-wife's slipping into present tense when she spoke about it had the same effect for my view of her.

But I wasn't here to like either one of them.

"To your knowledge, did he have any ongoing diseases?"

She slowly and somewhat tentatively shook her head.

"Anything like pneumonia or Huntington's disease?" I pursued.

Her eyebrows rose. Most people would have asked why I was asking. She tried to figure it out herself.

"Not as of a year ago. The last I knew of his medical situation was that he had slightly elevated cholesterol and seasonal allergies. I do believe he would have told me if he'd had a serious diagnosis. We have remained… I was going to say cordial and that might not be entirely accurate. It is—was—"

If she faked that slight wince, she did it well. On the other hand, someone who killed an ex then regretted it might well wince.

Chapter Twenty-Eight

WILLA PULLED IN a slow breath and restarted.

"It was more distant than that. More like someone you spent time with on a long cruise. Have you ever done that? And it's a true friendship for the time you are in it, but when the time comes to go your separate ways, nothing remains of the feelings, except the memories. The difference with Palmer and me was that we still were and always would be connected to an extent through our children. We retained a polite, even friendly distance."

"Did he exercise vigorously?"

She smiled slightly. "Seldom."

"Did he ride horses?"

Back to bemusement. "Was he ever on a horse? Yes. But my children and I ride far more than he did. The horses came with me in the divorce and there was no dispute over that. He far preferred mechanized transport."

"That's his red truck out front?"

"It is." She made a sound between a sob and chuckle. "For once not parked to block the middle of the stairs. I was after him all the time about parking there because it was convenient for him, but blocked everyone else trying to come in that way. And now, the one time he didn't park there…"

She pushed at tears in her eyes. Not rubbing, which would have disturbed perfect eye makeup, but using the side of a finger below each eye to dam the moisture.

"Did he like to explore in areas of the county unfamiliar to him?"

She clearly made the connection to where his body was found. "You mean hiking?"

"Or in a vehicle?"

"He hiked at times with the family, but on his own? Not that I was aware of. As much as he loved vehicles of all sorts, he also respected nature. He was not one of those people who went off-roading across wildernesses. Not at all." She caught herself up. "At least he was not when we were married. I cannot vouch for what changes he might have had in attitudes and actions while in the company of other people over the past year."

Ah, back to Jolie.

"Did he have an interest in Cottonwood County history?"

A glaze of caution slid into place. "No. He viewed himself as an iconoclast in that area. He said fads, trends, and self-interests of modern populations keep monetizing it, changing it, reinterpreting it to suit agendas, making it a constantly moving target, and therefore false."

She shot the words out like she'd memorized them from hearing them so often.

Curious at her reaction, I asked, "Do you agree?"

"Oh. Agree? ... Well, he had a point about it changing, especially about self-interests of people applying their biased filter. But that doesn't negate history's importance. It means you need to work harder to find the truth."

"Did his view on history come into play in his decision to not allow the Miners' Camp Fight reenactment to take place on the property he purchased?"

She shifted in her chair, bringing her left hip farther forward, giving me a better view of her left shoulder and less of her face.

Body language 101 said she wasn't comfortable, likely wasn't going to be forthright.

Maybe that glaze wasn't caution. Maybe it was something else.

"I'm sure his views did play into that."

Talk about an anticlimax...

"Did you agree with his move to stop letting them use that property?"

"It wasn't my property when he made the decision, which made it also not my decision."

There was something else there.

I wanted to dig more.

But that risked alienating her. Better to leave the door open. I could always alienate her later.

"What kind of man was he?"

Her shoulders relaxed.

"Flawed—as we all are. More good than bad in him. And not even *bad*. Mostly oblivious." She paused a moment before adding, "Self-centered, which caused the obliviousness. Like parking where it was convenient for him, but inconvenient for others. Waking him up to the reaction of other people or the impact his actions had on them... Not easy."

Although she smiled, she looked older and more tired.

"And this association with Jolie...?"

"Truly, I know only the rumors. I *can* say that after our divorce, there were rumors of other *associations*. They were none of my business." The glint of amusement was back. "During our marriage, his infidelity was not marital. It was occupational. In addition to moving from job to job, with considerable compensation increases each time, he consistently had side-gigs. He liked to move from one endeavor to another. That was his particular brand of wanderlust. Two of those became promising businesses, which he sold profitably."

Was that a hint of dissatisfaction I heard? Because he'd sold them, rather than holding on to reap larger rewards? Or something else?

A direct question wasn't likely to take us where I wanted.

"How about you? I understand—" Always a gentler way to introduce what I knew, rather than saying, *I dug as deeply into what of your past is available online as I could in the limited time I had.* "—you had an impressive career in tech."

"Not really. I stayed with the same company, which is seldom the way to advance by leaps and bounds in those companies—"

Or a lot of other companies that value the new and shiny employee over the reliable and proven one.

"—which are often run by people with very short attention spans. However, I did advance some and that offered stability in benefits that allowed Palmer to move around. Well, I say allowed. He would have done it regardless. I should say it allowed our family stability in benefits it would not otherwise have had."

Definitely some dissatisfaction. How deep and how sharp?

"Did you have side gigs, too?"

She chuckled. Genuinely amused, but with more than a dash of dryness.

"Me? My side gig was having and raising our children. A business I never intend to sell off."

Her gesture to the photos landed somewhere between a command and an invitation to comment. Invitation would have done for me, since I wanted to keep her talking. I suppressed the urge to reject the command. Keep her talking, that was the priority.

"I can see why. Your kids are impressive. I heard about your son running track here from Michael Paycik, who was KWMT-TV's sports anchor."

"Track as well as cross country and playing basketball."

"Ah." I hoped that sounded impressed. "Your daughter must have already been in college when I arrived here, but clearly she cornered the market in county accolades."

"After initial resistance, they loved growing up here. That is one thing their father did for them."

I left a beat of silence, to see if she'd say more. She didn't.

"It must be hard for them with all this."

"Yes." That didn't carry much conviction. "They're flying into Denver and driving up Tuesday night. I told them there was no need to rush home, since the funeral cannot happen until the sheriff's department releases Palmer's body. Still, it will be good for them to have time together to process their father's death before…"

Her phone dinged a notification. She looked at it and seemed to brighten.

One of her kids … or did someone else make her happy?

"If you'll excuse me, I need to take this call."

"Of course. We can talk again another time." That prepped her for the inevitable revisit. "I'll see myself out."

What accompanied me out of Palmer Rennant's house were layers of questions, most of which would not be answered until we dug deeper, some of which would never be answered. The question on the top layer came from that final, trailed off word.

Before what?

Before encountering the reality of an investigation into his murder?

Before encountering a mother not plunged into deep mourning over their father's death?

Either way, she deserved some points for recognizing whatever that *what* was and trying to make it easier on her kids.

Chapter Twenty-Nine

ON MY WAY back into town, I stopped at the station on the eastern edge of Sherman.

I put together a follow-up story on yesterday's events in the near isolation of a Sunday afternoon at KWMT.

The substitute assignments editor said there was no news from the sheriff's department.

I focused the package mostly on recapping the finding of the two bodies, wrapping up the camp and the fact that the reenactment hadn't happened, and KWMT was working the story. It let us use more of Diana's great stuff.

Then I sat at my desk, searching for more on the members of the Rennant family. And letting my mind drift a bit so it sorted priorities in the background.

I hadn't been at that long when Diana came in.

"Saw your vehicle in the lot as I went by," she said to me. "Something up?"

"With the case? Nope. Did you hear about Sally?"

"Yeah. That's not why you're here, is it?"

"No. Did the recap story for tonight." I explained about the call cutting short lunch—and conversation—with Mrs. P and Aunt Gee. "Not that I was making much headway. Then I met the ex-Mrs. Rennant at Palmer's house. Oh. Mike messaged and said he and Jennifer would call about ten our time to share updates. Want to come over?"

He wouldn't have much to share. He was covering a Cubs game.

Ah, to be at Wrigley Field on a sunny Sunday afternoon. Especially if they won.

"Can't. Kids. But I have time for you to fill me in on your conversation with the ex-wife."

"Of course."

Yet I didn't start right away. Something felt off. Odd…

"Me, too," she said.

"You, too what?"

"I miss the rest of them, too—Mike, Jennifer… and Tom."

"That's not—"

"Yes, it is."

I wouldn't win this stare-off—not with the mother of two.

"Do you want to hear this or not?"

"I want."

"The ex-wife's attitude interested me. Outwardly, she seemed fine with the divorce… But is she really? Can anybody be that okay with a divorce? And she had a definite edge about a couple things—him refusing to let the reenactment continue on the property he bought and a possible other woman."

"I want to ask you about the possible other woman, but in the interests of saving the best for last, I'll ask about the property first."

"She said he had a hate on for history, but that didn't explain her edginess. I figured I'd try to get more information before I tackle her again on that topic."

"Good. Then we can skip to the other woman. Did she seem jealous?"

"Mildly irked. She was more willing to talk about that than Rennant kicking the reenactment and camp off that property."

"That is weird. Did she say who the other woman is?"

"She said all she knew was the first name—Jolie."

"Oh."

My head came up. "You know her?"

"Assuming there's not more than one Jolie in Cottonwood County, yes. But only a little. More like I know *of* her, especially after hearing her name today in connection with Palmer Rennant." Diana paused, then gave me a significant look. "She's married."

"That sure tosses her spouse into the suspect circle. What's his name?"

"Kamden. Kamden and Jolie Graf."

Something niggled at me, but I put it aside to listen to Diana.

"There's also lots of talk about Kamden Graf having affairs. In fact, I'd say he's notorious. They've been married a while. They belong to the country club, but live in town. He's in insurance."

Insurance... Now I had the niggle. Something from Verona and Paige about Kamden Graf and insurance and taking a client.

I waited for Diana to expand. She didn't. Instead, she said, "Huh."

"Huh, what?"

"You're back to playing Free Cell. I wondered if last night was an aberration."

"Last night? I didn't play—"

"Yes, you did. While we were in the editing bay, talking about follow-ups."

I wanted to deny it. Her expression didn't let me. "Habit, I guess. Calming. Lots better than smoking."

"No arguing that. Apparently, a habit you're not aware of." She tipped her head for a new angle as she studied me. It was unnerving. "You used to do it all the time and especially when we started working on these inquiries. The habit faded away. And now you're back to it."

"I can tell you think that's significant, but I have no idea why."

"Your fade-out of Free Cell-playing coincided with Tom being a more willing participant. Now, with him distant, you've taken it up again."

"That's not true—"

"It is true. I'm not sure what it means," Diana continued. "Unless Tom being around distracts you the same way Free Cell does. Of course, Mike's gone, too, so maybe it's him."

She waited for me to argue.

I resisted.

"And you just lost that game."

I shifted my focus to the screen. The game had ended. I'd lost.

She chuckled softly. "I'm going to load footage on drives for you to bribe organizers to talk, then I'm out of here."

When she came back, I was hard at work. Not playing Free Cell.

As she plunked the drives on my desk, I said, "Aha."

"If I don't ask *aha what?* are you going to keep whatever you found to yourself?"

"Absolutely."

She exhaled through her nose. "Aha what?"

"I found a reference to Sears starting to use the Roebucks name on jeans for men in 1949. And remember, Shelton didn't say jeans from Sears, the way most people would, but specifically Sears Roebuck, like he might have seen that name on the label."

"Or he was simply using the more old-fashioned name. I remember my grandmother referring to it always as the Sears Roebuck catalog, never just Sears."

"You and Aunt Gee. Spoilsports."

"That's me. You know, I could join your call with Mike and Jennifer from home, tell you what else I've found out."

"You could tell me now. If it's more about an affair—"

"Not fair to Mike and Jennifer."

"Fine. Thanks for the drives."

"I suppose you want me to get the scoop on Willa Rennant."

"It's not what I want that matters," I said sanctimoniously, "it's what you want."

She snorted. "What about you? What are you doing between now and when they call?"

It struck me in that moment—as it should have struck me earlier—that Clara Atwood was likely at the museum.

It was open on Sundays during the summer, not to mention there was probably considerable work to clear up after the reenactment *not* happening yesterday.

"I'll swing by the museum, see if Clara's there, ask a few more questions."

Chapter Thirty

MY TRIP TO the Sherman Western Frontier Life Museum waited when I saw a figure pass the large window at the Nineteenth Century office building of the *Sherman Independence*.

Needham was also working on a Sunday.

I parked in front and knocked on the door.

"Nice job last night," he said, letting me in. "Especially fending off Thurston."

I sighed, my musings from first thing this morning streaming back.

"What?" he asked.

"How do you keep yourself fresh, chasing after the next story?"

"By chasing after the next story. What's this sigh about?"

I hadn't realized I'd sighed again. I told him about telling Mike I didn't reciprocate the interest his Chicago station showed in me and my wonderings about becoming like Thurston and aging in place.

He slanted me an amused look. "Just because you're not chasing a big career doesn't mean you won't chase the story. Might mean that for some, not for you."

His amusement faded as he looked at me from under his bushy brows.

"You can't really be worried about that."

"Complacency is worth worrying about," I said. "I was always driving when I was building a career. But if I'm staying here what's to keep me from becoming Thurston Fine?"

"First, you have a brain. In fact, you have the *Wizard of Oz* trifecta—brain, heart, courage. You also have a personality. Although at the moment, you're not using the brain much. Look, when you work at a little paper like the *Independence* from first to last, you sort these things out early or you're in trouble.

"Career is an external way to assess how you're doing, convenient for keeping score, but an artificial construct. Plum story assignments, better beats, awards, working for a bigger outfit. Rinse and repeat. Salary, too. That's all somebody else telling you you're doing okay. It's not how you're *really* doing. That comes from inside."

"You're saying peel away the trappings of career and you have… What?"

"What matters. Elizabeth Margaret Danniher will always chase after the next story. It's the way some of us are built, including you."

"The Needham Bender Next Story Doctrine."

"Exactly. And right now, I'm working on the next story—for Tuesday's edition. And, no, I'm not telling you the exclusive info I have for it. Although if you want to tell me more about the body found in the cave… No, I can see you won't. Maybe later on, when each of us has used up what we have now and trading might help both of us."

"It's so relaxing to talk with you, Needham, since you cover both sides of the conversation." Actually, it was energizing. But he didn't need to know that.

He grunted. "Leave me alone now, but come to dinner—Thelma would love to have you—and we'll gossip about what's not fit to print or put on-air."

After insisting he check with Thelma—his wife not only said she'd love to have me come for dinner but insisted I bring Shadow—I accepted, left him to his work, and got on with my own.

YES, OF COURSE, I stopped in the museum shop first for a brownie.

Vicky Upton and I exchanged please, thank you, and you're welcome almost like normal acquaintances.

This time I merely waved to Sandy—letting her think I had an appointment without giving Clara a chance to say she didn't want to see me.

Clara and Nadine were, once more, in Clara's pod at the back of the office.

I knocked on the pod wall before entering—serving as something between requesting permission and announcing arrival.

The women looked up simultaneously, strengthening the impression of identical expressions of strain, worry, and lack of sleep. They had multiple computer screens displaying spreadsheets, plus stacks of sorted papers, and a yellow legal pad with a long list and only a few things crossed off.

"How's it going?" Might seem like an odd question when it was obvious, but sometimes giving people a chance to unburden themselves of their troubles brought unexpected dividends.

"Just great." Clara's sarcasm added bite to the words.

"Oh. Elizabeth," Nadine said. Moisture sheened her eyes.

"Don't start again." Clara's tone was as unsympathetic as her words. But she did pass a box of tissues to Nadine. "Refunding tickets is not my idea of fun."

Nadine emerged from behind a tissue.

"We'd sold more tickets than ever to the Miners' Camp Fight." Pride pushed through her other emotions for a moment, then subsided under them. "At least the camp was completed and we don't have to reimburse those fees. And some people are saying to keep the money from the reenactment."

All business, Clara said, "Not enough. We're assessing the damage."

I grimaced my empathy. "Good thing you have that insurance."

"Yes, thank heavens," Nadine said fervently.

"Not enough," Clara repeated.

Hard to tell if things were really that grim or if she was determined to see them that way.

"I only stopped by to see how you two are doing and say it's a shame the reenactment was ruined."

Clara narrowed her eyes. "No, you didn't."

I returned her look. "No, I didn't. I *did* stop by for those things, but also to ask if either of you knows if anyone—staff members or kids or simply someone you saw—was up by the butte where the body was found on Thursday or Friday."

"Not the whole week?" Sarcasm seemed to be Clara's go-to stress reliever. "The deputies wanted to know about the whole week."

"That was before someone reported seeing him Thursday morning."

"Who?" Nadine asked, eyes wide.

"Last person to see him," Clara snapped.

"Not necessarily. Don't be surprised if that last-time seen changes. They'll keep trying to pin down later sightings."

Nadine repeated her question. "Who was it?"

I shrugged, as if I didn't know. "Just be glad it cuts your questioning down from Thursday morning to Saturday morning."

"But we've already been questioned," Nadine protested.

Clara half rolled her eyes. "Tell her, Elizabeth."

Chapter Thirty-One

"YOU'LL BE QUESTIONED again. And again. The more time passes without the sheriff's department pulling in the killer, the more the *agains* will pile up."

"And that, Elizabeth will tell us," Clara said, "is why we should answer her questions. Because she and her friends at KWMT will figure this out faster than the sheriff's department and that will prevent our misery from being prolonged."

"True." I said it as if Clara had sincerely endorsed us. "Starting with what I already asked—see anybody up where the body was found before the riders went up?"

"No. As I told Sergeant Shelton, when I was out there, I was too busy to even look in that direction until the reenactors rode up. I didn't realize something was wrong until someone else pointed out that O.D. Everett had started up that way with Mrs. Parens in the utility vehicle. Was that you, Nadine? I couldn't remember."

The other woman shook her head. "Wasn't me. It was either Anna Price-Fox or that young reenactor's mother. I don't remember her name."

"In other words, we're no help at all. What are your other questions, Elizabeth, because we need to get back to this." Clara flipped her hand at the screens and papers.

"I understand you dated Palmer Rennant last year, Clara."

"Seriously, you're asking about my romantic life again?"

What did she expect when the guy showed up dead? But I was being tactful.

I tipped my head at her reference to our first meeting. "Would you call your time dating Thurston Fine romantic?"

I figured that period in her life was far enough in the rearview mirror that she'd see the humor, allowing me to take that approach. Besides, we'd first bonded over mutual disdain for Thurston. He had done some good in the world.

She laughed. Short and harsh. "Fair point. Not romantic. Call it my dating life."

"Then, yeah, I am asking you again." I watched her closely. The amusement faded, but didn't disappear, so I kept going. "True you dated Palmer Rennant for a while late last summer?"

"True. And not a big secret. Not a secret of any size. He told me I was the first person he asked out after the divorce. No reason to think that wasn't true." A skeptic after my own heart. "We went to some movies, had a few dinners. That was it."

I pulled my phone out and showed them each a version of my photo of the watch. If they recognized it from last year, Mrs. P and O.D. Everett and even Aunt Gee claiming they didn't might lead ... somewhere.

"Recognize the watch?"

"No," Clara said.

To her *no*, Nadine added, "Not one a young woman would wear."

"Palmer Rennant didn't wear it while you dated?"

Clara shook her head.

"At those meetings you had with him?"

Both shook their heads.

Maybe the others truly hadn't recognized it. Though I still thought they knew more than they were telling me.

"Any insight into what kind of divorce it was from Palmer's point of view?"

Clara paused. "He didn't badmouth his ex. More like they got bored with each other." Uncharacteristically, her voice rose at the end as if asking a question. She shook her head. "Really, I had no sense of deep animosity between them. On the other hand, we didn't date long."

"Why was that?"

Her mouth stretched in a smile I wouldn't want directed at me. "He was a pleasant enough guy about most things, but he was a jackass about the reenactors in general, and the Miners' Camp Fight reenactment in particular, as well as, by extension, the Two Rivers Camp. Kicking us—them—off his property because he could. He actually bragged to me, saying it was his first move as a sole operator after the divorce papers were final. He'd looked for loopholes in the contract that would have let him block the events right after he bought, but his wife insisted he live up to the contract.

"But the sales contract offered no protection after that one time. He thought he was hot stuff for having the power to shut us down— that's what he said. He *shut us down* and he was proud of it. That's when I stopped accepting invitations from him. And he acted like my decision came out of nowhere. I mean, yeah, I'm not directly in charge, but the museum backs the reenactment and is involved with it and the camp. And he had a few things to say about the museum, too."

"Did he fail to see what it meant to you? Or didn't he care?"

"Didn't care." The words shot out of her, then her expression changed. "Maybe a mix. I mean, we ran into each other on the street right after Nadine and I signed the papers for the new site and I was quite pleased about it. I told him, not rubbing it in—at least not blatantly—but letting him know he hadn't defeated us. And he *still* didn't get it. Started back in about reenactors and spurious history and how he was saving the world from these horrors. And I got quite sharp with him that he hadn't done anything except shake up the event for the good and make himself look like a mean-spirited prick.

"And that's where the fail to see comes in. He was surprised—I think genuinely surprised that anyone wouldn't agree with him. Including me. Despite what I do and what I'd told him multiple times. But once you pushed back against his failure to see, I do think there was also a level of not caring."

Nadine was shaking her head.

"What is it, Nadine?" I asked.

"Some people are so ... close-minded. Living history is like everything else. It can be done well or not. You don't say close down Broadway forever because someone puts on a bad play in their basement. And it doesn't have to be Broadway to be good, to grab people's attention, to expand their interests. It's so... so ignorant to dismiss all reenactments, all living history."

"What do you say to those people who dismiss reenactments or living history as leaving history in the hands of non-professionals?"

Clara took up the job of answering. "Nadine's being tactful. The self-appointed critics say far harsher things than that. Which is interesting, because they proclaim there are inaccuracies especially arising out of broad-brush approaches, yet then these same critics use the broadest of brushes and often decry reenactors as racists, rednecks, and a number of other derogatory terms, as if it's obvious just from the fact that they are reenactors.

"Here's what I say to those people: We could all sit in museums waiting for people to come to us. Or, perhaps, writing scholarly papers for the historical quarterly of our specialty. Or even mount a display for fellow historians on the changes in military tents in the last quarter of the Nineteenth Century. But none of that reaches the people who are not already interested or already experts in a narrow, narrow slice of history.

"Not only that, but it misses out on serving—in fact, actively re-cruiting—those who learn best by seeing, smelling, touching, hearing, and doing, rather than reading."

Nadine smiled wanly. "What she said."

Clara presented a much sharper portrait of Palmer Rennant and his views on history than Willa had. Did his ex-wife sidestep to protect him, his memory?

"I take it you and Palmer didn't agree on that."

"You could say that." The edge to Clara's voice softened. "The strange thing is he wasn't like that when I first met him. That was about five years ago when he came in looking for some ancestor. Didn't have anything direct for him, but gave him resources to follow here, at the library. Didn't he talk to you, Nadine, about the Miners' Camp Fight?"

"He did. I pointed him to the copies of the survivors' accounts at the library. Never heard from him again."

That didn't seem promising. I tried another angle. "How did you come up with the new site?"

Clara shot me a quick, assessing look with an odd edge of … sympathy? That was a guess, never having seen an expression from her before that I'd describe that way.

"The owner wanted to stay anonymous, but approached Tom Burrell, who brought the idea to us. That paved the way. James Longbaugh drew up an agreement that protected the owner and us, and donated his time doing it."

"Great. I'll get with them for whatever background you can't answer."

I did that well. Lots of experience not showing personal reactions to sources.

"There's really nothing more to tell you. Nadine?"

She shook her head.

"How about the owner of the property you moved the events to?"

Nadine smiled. "A lifesaver."

"No idea who it was?"

Two head shakes. Nadine echoed Clara's earlier words. "Wanted to stay anonymous."

"I've never heard of that before. How did—"

"You'd have to talk to the lawyers," Clara said. "They handled that. Now, we really have to get back to work."

That sound you heard was the door slamming on me, since Clara knew as well as I did that one of the things lawyers did best was not talking.

Didn't mean I wouldn't try.

Chapter Thirty-Two

I LET THE neighbor girl know she could stand down from dog duty. I fed Shadow, gave him a walk, then loaded both of us in the SUV for the drive to the Benders' house.

With a minor detour on the way.

Any detour is minor in Sherman, but this one truly was only a block out of my way. The block it took to get from the front of Courthouse Square to the back, where the Cottonwood County Sheriff's Department had its offices, along with the fire department and the tiny Sherman Police Department.

In case something was happening there, something like a suspect taking the perp walk inside.

Nope.

Instead, I saw Deputy Lloyd Sampson walking out of the building, looking like he'd been rode hard and put up wet—a vivid phrase I learned from Tamantha and have been waiting to use.

I rolled to a stop at the curb and lowered the driver's window as he reached the main sidewalk.

"You look tired, Lloyd. Rough day?"

He gusted out a breath. At the same time, he rubbed both wrists against the side of his uniform pants, then twisted them around to rub the backs.

"Sitting in front of a computer for hours and hours. Wasn't what I expected when I got into law enforcement. Plus, this dam—darned rash."

Below the unbuttoned cuff of his uniform sleeve, I saw raised, red bumps that ran together to form welts on his wrists and lower forearm.

"Checking out the records of desperados?"

"Truck keys." Either his literalness urged him to set me straight or he wanted to assure me there were no desperadoes in Sherman. "General Motors used to have different designs for keys. I mean before the electronic kind we use now. But even the old-fashioned flat metal keys changed up."

Truck keys?

Old-fashioned truck keys?

My mind jumped to Shelton. So uncharacteristically telling me about the wallet in the back pocket of the cave body, yet I'd known— absolutely *known*—he was holding something back.

Something like vehicle keys also being found?

I said, barely on the polite side of bored, "Is that so?"

"Yeah. Even before the flat keys with a rectangular or half-moon cutout for putting them on a ring—kind my Dad had—that open area looked sort of like a two-ball snowman that mostly melted. Never had seen them before, but when I kept looking, back and back, there they were." He ducked his head. "Not that you'd be interested in that. Sorry."

"Not really," I fibbed. But he'd not only clam up completely if I asked any of the questions buzzing in my mind, he'd know he'd given something away. The flip side, though, was he wouldn't believe it if I gave up too easily. "But I would like to know if the department's made progress on when Palmer Rennant was last seen alive?"

"Can't tell you that. Can't talk about it. Sheriff's department business. Can't talk."

I exhaled deeply, a thwarted journalist. "Okay, Lloyd. You have a good night."

"You, too, see you later, Elizabeth." He left with the vaguely guilty expression he often seemed to have around me.

And this time I hadn't even dragged anything out of him. All I'd done was say hello and ask about his day.

I would *not* feel guilty about making him feel guilty. Especially since I had research to do—soon—on General Motors vehicle keys.

But I would do him a favor.

I called out, "Lloyd."

He stopped and waited for me to let the SUV roll forward to put the driver's seat even with him again, looking even more preemptively guilty.

"Lloyd, you better have that rash on your wrists checked out."

He glared at his wrists suspiciously. "Poison ivy. Should've known. So busy today, I didn't pay attention to the itching. Where in blazes—?"

"Since you don't have it on your hands. I'd say you got it when you were wearing gloves. Best guess would be from the bush by the opening to the cave when you wrapped police tape around it. It did have three leaves. Have you had poison ivy before?"

"Yeah." He groaned. "I'm real sensitive to it. Usually watch for it like a hawk, but..."

Under the excitement of a dead body and the pressure of Shelton's exacting eye, he hadn't paid attention to the triple leaves of that bush.

He thanked me glumly.

As I tapped the accelerator, he took out his phone and connected with someone. "We still have any of that cream from when I had poison ivy last time?"

✧ ✧ ✧ ✧

ONCE MORE PROVING you could buy anything you didn't want on eBay, I found entire collections of "vintage" keys for sale, though most of them looked just plain old.

And I couldn't see detail well enough on my phone, as I discovered when I pulled over on a random street between the sheriff's department and the Benders' house. I'd have to wait until after dinner, when I got home to a larger screen to explore the keys thoroughly.

Still, I was inclined to look kindly on the crumbly old things and that put me in a particularly cheerful mood ... which immediately aroused Needham's suspicions.

I assuaged those suspicions by expressing delight that Shadow's first wariness of a new place passed when he recognized Needham and Thelma as established friends. His universe of trusted places kept expanding.

We had a lovely dinner of roast beef, fresh vegetables, and fresh peach cobbler, with a side order of thrust and parry between Needham and me.

Thelma scolded us while slipping treats to Shadow.

In other words, a good time was had by all.

I FUDGED THE time of the scheduled call with Mike and Jennifer to leave the Benders' without exacerbating Needham's newshound instincts.

That gave me just enough time on my laptop, using Lloyd's descriptions and Internet search tools, to find the pre-electronic keys with the half-moon and rectangular openings he described. They were listed as being used from the mid-1960s well into the mid-1980s.

I went farther back in search of his melted snowman description, and there they were, meeting the newer type in the mid-'60s and extending back into the '30s at least.

WITH MIKE AND Jennifer on the video call from Chicago, and Diana connected from her ranch, they pounced on me, proclaiming they could tell I'd found out something.

I explained the trail from Lloyd to the Internet to my conclusion: "Shelton saw a key with the body in the cave that must have had that melted snowman kind of opening."

"Why?" Jennifer quickly added, "Oh. Because Lloyd wouldn't have kept searching farther back if the rectangular and half-moon keys were what Shelton had him looking for."

I pointed at her on-screen image in acknowledgement. "Exactly."

"That's good, Jennifer," Diana said, "but still leaves us with thirty or so years."

"That's better than the hundred and fifty I thought we were looking at when I left Mrs. P and Aunt Gee. Plus, it makes it less likely our mystery corpse is connected to Palmer Rennant. Unless—"

"Want me to check if he had relatives or connections here from that period, when I get back?"

"That would be great. Also see what you can find out about local people missing from the Thirties into the Sixties. And Lloyd said truck keys, so anything connected with a truck in particular. I know," I said in response to her groan. "That's a long period, but there weren't as many people in Wyoming then, so that should help."

Before she told me it wouldn't, Mike asked, "Couldn't it be some poor guy passing through?"

"Possible, not likely. Not if I'm right about Shelton having an idea of who it is." I added, "I also think Mrs. P is holding out on us."

Chapter Thirty-Three

"**YOU THINK MRS.** P suspects who the cave body is?" Jennifer asked.

"Good luck tackling her if she's decided not to tell you," Diana said.

I ignored that spurious encouragement and told them about her mini-reaction to the studded belt. That led to a complete report of the lunch, plus the news on Sally.

"That's too bad about Sally. Going to keep Mrs. P and my aunt so occupied we won't have much access to them—not that that's the only reason it's too bad," Mike added hurriedly.

"Yeah, we know *your* priorities," Diana said.

"He does have a point." I sighed. "I'd hoped to soften up Mrs. P to give me contact info for the reenactor they said is training to be a paramedic. No time—"

"Aleek?" Jennifer asked.

"Yes. How did you know—?"

"I know Aleek. How many people could have been planning to ride in the reenactment and training to be a paramedic? He's already passed some of that stuff. I'll send you his contact info."

"That's great. Still, Mrs. P being unavailable means we're stymied to some extent on the cave body, unless Jennifer comes up with a viable missing person from the right period. But there's lots we can do about Palmer Rennant's death, starting with recapping what we've each learned today."

"All I've learned is that the Cubs are weak in left-handed pitching, but so far the fielding is offsetting it."

"Thanks, Mike. I'll be sure to tell my dad. I saw Clara and Nadine again today."

That was a short report.

"You consider them suspects?" Jennifer asked.

I exhaled. "They'd have a lot better motive if this were a year ago or anytime in the year before that, because of Palmer Rennant kicking their events off his property. But once they found this better location with the cooperative secret landowner, their motive evaporated. Successful camp this year, more tickets sold for the reenactment than ever before? Why kill Rennant now?"

"Especially since they had to refund tickets," Mike said.

Diana shifted our focus with a question. "What do you make of the information about the paint, Elizabeth?"

"I don't know that I make anything of it meaningful at this point. But it's interesting."

"The red and yellow paint was there in the staging area overnight, so anybody could have used it," Jennifer said.

"They'd have to know it was there," objected Mike. "Would someone who was moving a dead body around stop and root in the supplies on the off chance there was paint there? More likely somebody who knew the stuff was there. Knew exactly where to go and how to put it back."

"The reenactors? The organizers? Camp kids? Why would any of them kill this guy?" Jennifer asked.

"Another interesting point," I said, "is the marks were little more than blobs. Nowhere near the symbols the reenactors had."

Mike jumped on that. "If the painter made little effort to make the marks accurate, that points away from the reenactors."

"Or someone wanted it to point away from them," I said. "A reenactor could have deliberately made the marks vague and unlike their usual symbols. Or someone else could have wanted to not implicate them."

He *huh*'d. "That would be clever."

"Or," said Diana, "the time exposed to the rain and air overnight could have turned originally sharp marks into blobs."

"I won't say no completely, but I don't think so, because the ones up by Rennant's shoulders were blobby, too, and those would have been at least somewhat protected under the overhang, so why would they blob?"

"The verb to blob?" she murmured at me.

"But if it was a reenactor, why use paint at all?" Jennifer asked. "Why call attention to themselves in the first place?"

"Excellent question. Same goes for someone who didn't want to implicate them. No paint at all implicates them even less."

"So far, you guys seem to be eliminating possible suspects. What about the wife—the ex?" Mike asked.

"Elizabeth talked to her," Diana said, "but before she reports, let me tell you guys what I picked up. General impressions are that she's a pleasant woman who's extremely smart, which makes a few people uncomfortable.

"I talked with Shelby Wattelka—you know she's got her real estate license now—who helped her find a new house. Palmer kept the one at the ranch. Willa wanted to live closer to town. Shelby said the settlement must be good, because Willa Rennant wasn't worrying about money. Got a real nice house in that new area this side of the country club."

I felt my eyebrows rise. I'd heard about that development. Specifically, I'd heard it was making Thurston Fine and other residents of the established area around the country club pea green.

"A friend of mine from school is on a committee with Willa Rennant at the country club," Diana continued. "And she says that in the past year Willa has been working out, changed her hair style, and started getting regular facials, and manicures."

"Ah," I said.

"Ah, what?" Mike demanded.

"Post-divorce rehab."

"Exactly. My friend says she's never looked better *and* she's jumped in volunteering at the library, working as a voting judge, and on the board for her new development, as well as the country club."

"Is she seeing anybody?"

"Word is she's playing the field. Not anybody special."

Good for her.

"I've got something else," Diana said, "but, first, tell them about your conversation with Willa Rennant before we switch topics."

When I finished, Diana said, "The Jolie that Willa mentioned must be the same person I picked up rumors about today. Jolie Graf."

She filled in Mike and Jennifer on that aspect.

I was trying to follow a jangle in my memory. "Why is that name so familiar...?"

"Which—?"

I held up a shushing finger to the screen. It was there... right on the edge of my mind... Got it. "*Jolie Graf.* She was one of the women who had a fling with that guy with the thing for rodeo queens, Keith Landry."

"That's right, she was. I'd forgotten that. Good for you, Elizabeth," Diana said.

"Not sure it has any connection, though. Sure would be interesting to know more about her. I'll see what Penny has to say on that and several other topics tomorrow."

"You can't possibly be out of sea salt caramel pie," Diana protested.

"I'm not." There were at least two slices left—for tomorrow's breakfast. "I'm going to the supermarket for the good of our inquiries."

"Wish I could sacrifice like that," Mike lamented.

"How much did you eat at Wrigley today?" I asked.

"That's not the point—"

He was hooted down.

"I miss Tom," he said. "At least I had one on my side."

A lull hit. Diana stepped in.

"You want to share what you've found, Jennifer?"

"Not yet. Finish what else you got."

"A motive that's not from a year ago and wiped out by subsequent events," Diana looked around her screen, saw she had all our attention. "Palmer Rennant ran down Otto Chaney's dog. Remember him?" The last was directed at me.

"He didn't have a dog."

"I wasn't asking if you remembered a dog. I meant, do you remember Otto Chaney?"

"I do," I said with great dignity. "Met him while we were looking into the deaths at Red Sail Ranch. So, is Rennant on the Red Sail Ditch with Connie Walterston, the Chaneys, and the rest of them?"

I'd learned a lot about the politics and intricate interpersonal relationships of the enforced community that grows out of sharing water from the same irrigation system.

"Rennant's property is on Red Sail Ditch, but he rents most out and wasn't involved with the ditch. To get to his place, you go past the little road that dead-ends into Otto Chaney's for about another mile. But the houses are much closer together than that. Imagine something like this." She held up her hands, like she was framing a shot—fingers straight up, thumbs at right angles to the fingers and pointing at each other, then she tipped her forefingers toward each other, not quite closing to form a triangle. "Rennant said the dog was always on his property."

"He didn't have a dog when we went to his place," I protested again.

"Must have been a rare time between dogs for Otto, because he always has a couple," Mike said. "Usually sad cases. Always rescues."

If I'd known the crusty older man had that particular soft side to his personality, I would have warmed to him more.

"Was this an accident with the dog?" Mike asked.

"Otto doesn't think so," Diana said, "and that's what matters."

Chapter Thirty-Four

DIANA RETURNED TO the point of her narrative. "He adopted this dog not long ago. It was mostly lame and was dumped by somebody before Otto took him in. Apparently, he barks. A lot. And loudly. He also chases cars. Not a whole lot of cars out there, but when Palmer Rennant drove along the road, the dog chased his car part of the way, then cut through the brush and beat Rennant to his own front door, then he'd bark and bay and howl at him.

"Also, the dog would make a racket when Otto let him out when he got up. Which is considerably earlier than Palmer Rennant got up. Rennant called and complained. Otto lectured him about lazy people who were still in bed when the sky started to lighten. It went downhill from there, including a call to the sheriff's department. Apparently, Shelton told Rennant to get earplugs and said it was an old dog who wouldn't be around much longer.

"According to Otto, Palmer Rennant wasn't willing to wait for nature to take its course. Otto found the dog hit over on the road to Rennant's ten days ago. Shelton found evidence on Palmer Rennant's vehicle. Rennant said it was an accident, that the dog ran out in front of him."

"He didn't call anybody?"

I shared Jennifer's indignation.

"Said he thought it was a coyote until the sheriff's department showed up. Shelton told Otto there wasn't enough evidence to prove it was deliberate, but Otto had no doubt. Also, no forgiveness, even when Rennant paid the vet bill."

"The dog survived?" I was glad Jennifer asked. I hadn't because I wasn't ready to hear the answer.

Diana's mouth listed. "He did. Had surgery and he's even more lame than before, but he gets around."

"How'd you hear all this?" I asked her.

"Connie. Also, some from Hannah Chaney." Hannah's husband was Otto's nephew.

"Even if Otto proved it wasn't an accident, is that enough of a motive for murder?" Mike mused.

"Yes," the rest of us said together.

"Palmer Rennant lost a whole lot of sympathy from me." Jennifer's mouth and eyes tightened. "I know. We can't let not liking the victim stop us from finding murderers because it's wrong no matter what, and I'll keep working, too, but really. Somebody who'd run over a dog? Especially an old, lame dog who'd finally found his forever home? That stinks. And," she added defiantly, "I don't mind anymore that Rennant was run over by the horses. Kind of poetic justice."

"As long as you're thinking like that, let me tell you what I found out about rigor mortis this morning."

Jennifer made no noises during my account of my conversations with Dex, then with Aleek, Paytah, and O.D. But when I finished, she asked, "Why are you so interested in this stuff?"

"Trying to get to the time of death," Mike said.

"Some. But it's also the gaps."

"Gaps?" Jennifer repeated.

"Intersections, really."

Mike snorted. "Oh, that explains it."

"Okay, listen. Try backtracking. Because Palmer Rennant's body maintained that tipped-on-its head fetal position when it was found, it makes twelve-thirty Saturday afternoon about twenty-four to thirty-six hours after he was killed. Although that's rough because cold slows the process and it was definitely chilly Thursday night, all day Friday, and Friday night."

"But it wasn't freezing. Would *chilly* be enough to slow it?"

"It sure didn't speed up the process. Didn't get warmer until late morning Saturday. And even then, the body was under the overhang so the sun didn't reach it.

"Say death happened late Thursday night or the early hours of Friday. The body could have been moved shortly after death, but otherwise it had to be in that near-fetal position while rigor set in—and I don't think it could have been a short period with Wyoming having a patch of November in August."

"Okay," Mike said slowly, "but what does that tell us?"

"It tells us approximately when Rennant was killed. That's first. The next thing it tells us is that he almost surely died while in that fetal position. Because the alternative is that someone posed him in that position shortly after he died. Which is possible, but why?"

"Ritual? Special meaning? There are murderers who pose their victims?"

"Religious or funereal poses, sexual poses, exposed poses—all those, yeah. But I have never heard of anyone posing their victim on their side in a fetal position. On the other hand, dying in the fetal position? Absolutely. Trying to protect themselves, or drawn up by pain, or the muscles pulling them into that position as they died... Okay, Jennifer, I promise, no more. You all get the point, right?"

"If we take that as read, where does it get us?" Diana asked.

"I'm afraid that where it gets us is to a couple big, fat questions. Where was the body that it was in a fetal position long enough as rigor set in to maintain that position, yet it wasn't found?"

"His house," Jennifer said immediately. "Nobody went there as far as we can tell and you said his ex-wife said that wasn't unusual."

"Nobody except Otto Chaney's dog," Mike muttered. "Maybe the dog did it. Motive, revenge."

"Then how did the dog move the body to the butte? And the *really* big question—why? Because, putting aside the dog as a suspect, someone went to some trouble to get the body up there. Almost certainly in the dark."

"Why in the dark?" Diana asked.

"First, because of the time needed for rigor to fully set, which it had to be for the body to be in that position Saturday. Second, because there were people there until sunset Friday, then back in the morning Saturday. Third, they couldn't have dumped the body Saturday morning because it had stopped raining and tracks would have shown. So—"

"Wait, wait," Jennifer ordered, starting to type into her device. "Let me figure this out. Killed at, say, twelve-thirty a.m. Friday with lots of question marks after that. Left somewhere—more question marks for that—where he was in the fetal position and nobody found him. Then, sometime Friday night or early Saturday morning, the body's moved to the butte."

"Good recap. We might be able to narrow the move time down a bit more, by finding out what time the rain ended, closing the opportunity to get him up there without leaving tracks," I said.

"The rain ended about five Saturday morning. But I'm not sure it helps. Won't most say they were home in bed at that hour? Even if someone else vouches for them, it would be a significant other, who might lie for them."

I grimaced at Diana's image on the screen. "Thanks for that bit of sunshine."

"Okay, I understand all that," Mike said. "But it makes your question about *why* even bigger, right? They have the body somewhere that it's not found all day Friday, so why move it? And especially why move it to where it was found."

"I can think of three reasons. Because it wasn't safe where they'd left it Friday, but they didn't have a choice, so as soon as they had an opportunity, they—the killer—moved the body."

"That's one." Jennifer had her head down, typing.

"Because they wanted the body in that particular place to point to the body in the cave."

"That's two."

"Because they wanted the body found and knew there'd be activity there."

"Three."

"I don't know about three," Mike said. "If you want a body found, why not drop it in front of the Courthouse—okay, not the Courthouse, because you could be spotted. But there are a lot of other places where it would be pretty dead—no pun intended—and you could drop off the body without being seen but it would be found in the morning. And that wouldn't involve a trip up to the butte."

"All good points. So, if three is the reason, yet the murderer picked the butte, that comes back to the significance we talked about yesterday. As we keep inquiring, we should be on the lookout for pointers to those reasons."

Diana said, "Two is the one that bothers me. It was such a long shot that you found the body."

"Maybe that I found it, but not such a long shot that it was found. You think Shelton would have left that scene without the cave being thoroughly searched, not just that first scan?" Unanimous head shakes. "Once they turned the lights on in there, it was a sure thing to find the cave body. But even without that, somebody who was on the scene stumbles into the cave pretending to be distraught, leans a hand on a rock, and... *voilà*. Amazing discovery."

"That's so sneaky. I love it," Jennifer said.

My brief grin faded. "Number one is the one I don't like. Because when I think of all the places where that body could have been all day Friday without being found, my head wants to explode."

"How could we start tracking them down?"

I grimaced at Mike's face on the screen. "Safe for you to ask, since you're in Chicago. Honestly, I don't think we do. Not unless we're absolutely desperate. For now, we keep it in mind—really, all three possibilities and any others we come up with about why move the body—and wait for something to snag our attention."

Chapter Thirty-Five

"OKAY, JENNIFER, NO more drawing out the suspense. Spill," Mike ordered. "Did you get the postmortem? Is that why you're about to burst?"

She maintained her dignity in the face of that characterization.

"No success on the postmortem yet. However, there are three things—well four. The first part is boring. Nothing on his background check raises a single red flag. Solid financially, no legal issues, never in trouble with anybody that I can find. He did have allergies, but nothing major physically.

"The second thing is sort of related, because it says why his finances are so good."

"We know that. From the companies he started and sold, like Elizabeth told us," Mike said.

"That's some of it, but the important thing is he's part of this FIRE thing. Have you heard of it?"

"Yeah, I have heard of fire. Cooks my meat." Mike's crack spared Diana and me admitting Aunt Gee told us about Rennant's involvement and ruining Jennifer's moment.

She exhaled an impatient *Old Folks* breath. "Not fire like flames. FIRE like the letters that stand for Financial Independence, Retire Early. It's a ... movement, I guess you'd call it. People save their money like crazy and invest it, saving instead of vacations or buying stuff or getting new cars and all that. When they get enough—they call it their number—to support them for the rest of their lives, they retire."

"Hard to believe people really do that." Diana sighed. "Real people. With kids and a regular job."

"Yeah, that's what they say. I suppose they could be lying, but... nah, at least some of them have to be telling the truth. But some start off making a lot of money, so that's easier and a lot of them live really, really cheap, before and after they quit working. They call it frugal, but some of them... Really, they're cheap."

"I can do that," Diana said.

"Can your kids? *Would* your kids? Besides, you can't retire. Not as long as I'm at KWMT," I said. "Can't lose our best shooter."

"That's the other big thing," Jennifer said. "A fair number of them don't actually retire."

"They have enough money to support them the rest of their lives and don't retire?" Diana's disbelief rose with each word.

"Yeah. A bunch post that it removes the stress from their jobs and they like it again. Or they'll work part-time or do something else that doesn't pay as well but they like better."

"I don't care what you say, Elizabeth, I am checking this out."

"I'll send you the links I found, Diana. They support each other." Jennifer paused. "Sometimes they nag each other."

"Maybe they'll nag my kids, too. I can hope, right? Okay, back to Palmer Rennant. He was doing this FIRE stuff?"

"Yes and no. I found his online handle and tracked back a bunch of his posts on five of these communities—two primarily. He had done the FI part by selling that company for a bunch. Then he started another company, his *play project*, he called it. And then he sold *that* company. That's when the Rennants moved here. And then he started really posting, giving advice, talking about theories, and stuff."

"Anybody angry about his advice? Investments gone bad, anything like that?" I asked.

"Not that I saw. The groups he was in don't go for hot stock tips or stuff like that. It's really pretty boring. Make a plan, keep doing it, keep expenses down including for investing, little amounts add up, don't panic, don't stray."

"I'm liking this more and more." Diana held up a hand to me. "I know, I know, back to Palmer Rennant. So, he didn't make any enemies with this FI or FIRE stuff?"

"Wouldn't say that. Sounds like his wife didn't like some of it. He'd get on there and complain about her complaining."

"Not the path to marital harmony."

"Nope. And a fair number of them agreed with her. Said there was being frugal and then there was re-re-reusing used tissues. Which they used as an example, but I had a teacher who really did that and she'd stick it in the cuff of her sweater. *Yuck.* I tried to avoid letting her touch me, especially with that hand, but I couldn't always get away. She was *fast.*"

"And it didn't kill you," Diana said. "I think I'll tell my kids that when they use a roll of paper towels to wipe up a drop."

"At least they're wiping up," I said.

"You have a point. I'll see what else I can find out from the rumor mill about Palmer and Willa, what was going on before the divorce, and since. That was what you were about to ask, wasn't it, Elizabeth?"

"Absolutely. I'll wait to tackle Willa again until you report back. Might give me more entry points to get details. Jennifer, anything else from these online communities?"

"Not really. Unless you want me to go way, way back. I read what he'd written right up until this week."

"Let's save the backtracking for if we can't find anything in the more recent past."

She did not acknowledge that largesse. "The recent past's what else I was going to tell you about."

"Items three and four," Diana murmured.

"I found posts on a couple of those online financial groups where he was bragging about kicking the reenactors and camp off his property. Really proud of himself."

"He named the groups? Gave details?"

"No," she admitted, "but from knowing what happened and the dates, it was clear that's what he was talking about. In one of his early posts about it, he *said* it was about insurance—not wanting the liability of the groups on his property. But later on, he loosened up and said stuff about history and academics telling a pack of lies, changing history for their own purposes to make a name for themselves and write papers and get tenure and stuff like that. And that reenactors were way, way worse. He said the only real history was tangible stuff. And that was being saved by a handful of people who were after the real history, not interpretive junk. He went on and on. Really didn't like reenactors. That started a couple disputes—wouldn't call them flaming—these people are awfully polite compared to the tech guys, who do *not* hold back. Anyway, when that was going, he let out some stuff that made it clear his wife—newly ex-wife—agreed with his critics. And didn't they jump on that? Including telling him that showed he was wrong because it led to his worst financial mistake—getting divorced. And how he'd paid a lot for doing that."

She sounded amused.

That faded, but her eyes brightened.

She had something more. Something good.

Diana, likely spotting the same sign, said, "The fourth thing?"

"Russell Teague."

Chapter Thirty-Six

NOT WHAT I expected.

Which was interesting... What *had* I expected? More about the ex-wife? Something about another woman?

"What does Russell Teague have to do with Palmer Rennant?"

"A lot. Rennant said stuff in his posts about a rich guy, though he never named him. But he did mention hot air balloons and this guy collecting *real* history. He also said he'd sold his second company to this guy's family business *and* that the guy influenced Rennant's move to Wyoming."

Diana and I simultaneously made a *huh* sound. There are coincidences and then there are not coincidences.

"So, I got one of my guys who likes business stuff and knows about company sales, so he can spot who did well in the deal, and how it was *structured*, though why they call it that I don't know. He found it right away and it turns out, Palmer Rennant sold his second company to a subsidiary of Teague's maternal grandfather's company—remember that's where all the money came from, while he got the ranch after his father died. *Plus*, he found juicy stuff about Palmer Rennant hitting it off with Russell Teague and one article said that was because they were weird in the same ways and it was a good thing they each had good lawyers to work through the necessary legal and financial issues."

She sat back, looking satisfied. "What do you think of that?"

"I think you hit the jackpot—though it was because of hard work, not luck. I also think it's really interesting. Don't know what it means in the scheme of things with Teague being sick…"

"About to die," Mike said. "I have a source—somebody who knows the inside baseball on what's going on with Teague. And I might have gotten the source into a suite at Wrigley Field for each game of the series starting tomorrow."

Working that source became his assignment. Each of the rest of us would continue digging where we'd already started.

"I'll tackle Willa again, see if I can get more. I can wait until later in the day, Diana, if you can pump the rumor mill about Palmer and Willa, what was going on before the divorce, and since. Might give me more entry points."

"Sure. I'll see what else I can find out."

"Great. I'll also go out and talk to Otto Chaney about a dog."

"He's mostly harmless, but you are not going there alone, Elizabeth," Diana said. "I'll meet you. But we'll have to work around my assignments."

"We don't want two vehicles sweeping in like it's an FBI raid. That tends to put people off, cuts their inclination to talk right down to nothing."

"We'll rendezvous by the entrance to Red Sail Ranch. Connie won't mind. We'll take your SUV to his place, so it doesn't look like official KWMT business, either. I'll call when I see an opening."

AFTER WE WISHED Jennifer success and fun with her interview—"It's just a talk"—at Northwestern the next day, she and Mike signed off. But, seeing Diana didn't leave my screen immediately, neither did I.

"Why are you frowning?" she asked.

"I'm having a hard time reading Jennifer's feelings about visiting Northwestern and what might come out of that."

"That's because she's afraid of how much she wants it and how disappointed she'll be when—that's how she's thinking—she doesn't get it. So, she's protecting herself by not saying much."

"Magical thinking." I answered her raised eyebrows, "Believing that how she thinks about it will affect the outcome."

"Oh, yeah. My daughter practices that, too."

I waited.

She said nothing.

There was only so much waiting I could do.

"Is something going on with Jess? Is that what's worrying you?"

"God, is it that obvious?"

"No. I'm that good."

She laughed. Her real, full-out laugh. But when it ended, she didn't look like she had much to laugh about.

"I didn't want to talk to you about it."

I felt an unexpected stab of hurt, but said, "Then don't. Talk to somebody else, but you need to talk."

"If not you, nobody."

Miracle cure for this kind of stab wound. And then—because who couldn't use a little extra salve on a stab wound—I asked, "Not even Russ Conrad?"

"Maybe especially not Russ." She exhaled sharply. "I think that's part of the underlying issue, along with being a teenage girl. But what's visible above the waterline is… Well, have you talked to your brother and sister-in-law since they left?"

That was the question she asked, but it wasn't the question she meant.

"J.R.?" My nephew and Jessica hit it off in the first two days my brother's family was here, along with my parents. Mom and Dad then took Bill's whole family to Yellowstone—repeating a trip they'd taken only six weeks earlier—before they all came back to Sherman. In those final four days, the connection between the teenagers was apparent to all. Including J.R.'s younger brother, Justin, who talked about googly-eyes and fake-gagged until his father made dire threats about cleaning the garage when they got home.

"Yes. He's a great kid," she added hurriedly. "It's nothing against him, but—"

"They're twelve-hundred miles apart."

"Which mostly I'm grateful for, because they're kids. Not that you'd know it to hear Jess. She's building elaborate plans based on him and I can't entirely blame her because they're messaging hundreds—easily hundreds—of times a day."

"Yikes."

"Exactly. But if I say anything logical or reasonable or try to reel her back in nearer reality, she flies off the handle at me."

Jessica Stendahl was a good kid. Smart and funny and generally well-grounded. On the other hand, she had that hideous cocktail of hormones flowing through her that nature inflicted on teens. Usually, if the brew bubbled over, it produced sharp words between her and her younger brother, Gary Junior, with their mother the mediator, not the target.

Gary Stendahl had died in a ranching accident when Gary Junior wasn't much beyond a toddler and Jessica not all that much older. Diana should have earned every motherhood medal in the world for the way she'd gone to work to provide for her kids to keep the ranch that was their inheritance and their heritage together, and—most of all—created a strong, stable family of the three of them.

"It's her first major ... whatever this is."

"J.R., too. His mom told me that when they were here." She'd been glad it was a nice girl, though she might feel differently now with the two-way message blitz.

Diana released a deep sigh. "Gary's more overtly emotional, his feelings closer to the surface, but Jess can be harder to interpret, harder to reach... She remembers her father better and she misses him."

Ah. We'd detoured from J.R. to someone a foot taller and a couple decades older. The sheriff of Cottonwood County. "How does she feel about Russ?"

Diana cut me a look. "About the way you'd expect. Doesn't help that he's law enforcement—the sheriff, for heaven's sake. Talk about an authority figure. He's been really good about not sticking his oar in, but sometimes it's clear he wants to. And, no matter what, he's not Gary. I don't know if she can ever forgive him for that."

DAY FIVE

MONDAY

Chapter Thirty-Seven

"**I FOUND A** person in Wyoming. Here is the phone number at the University of Wyoming you want to talk to—307-555-0176."

Dex's phone call caught me still asleep. But I'd learned to take notes with my eyes closed decades ago. "Is there a name, Dex?"

"Radford Hickam."

"Dex, you are a diamond of the first order." Perhaps with my earlier thoughts about KWMT-TV's non-gem status rolling around and my brain still snoozing, I added, "No matter how long it took, waiting for coal to turn into diamonds was worth it in your case."

"Coal is not the source of diamonds. Diamonds are created from carbon under exacting requirements of heat and pressure."

"But coal is carb—"

"The carbon in coal is not the carbon that formed diamonds. Furthermore, diamonds are found in vertical formations, while coal is horizontal."

"But..." I didn't even try to finish the *I always heard/Everybody knows* excuse. I didn't like it as a journalist. Dex hated it as a scientist.

"The single largest source for diamonds we see commercially is believed to be from the formation of the Earth's mantle, with volcanic eruptions bringing them to where diamond prospectors find them. The other sources together account for a small minority. Impacts of asteroids, plate tectonic subduction processes, and meteorites are those other sources."

Impacts from asteroids didn't sound like the best plan for getting diamonds, what with the downsides. That middle one made my head hurt. And meteorites, which had less severe downsides than asteroids, still had downsides, along with being unreliable.

"In addition, the diamonds from those other sources are small— nanodiamonds in the case of meteorites."

And then there was that.

"Okay, Dex. Thanks for the contact, the lesson, and—"

He hung up.

RADFORD HICKAM WOULD be teaching and in meetings all today, according to the message on his machine. I could text and he'd get back to me at his first opportunity.

I skipped that offer. For this kind of first contact, I preferred a phone call. It let me feel out the source ... and be more persuasive.

I'd keep trying.

Somewhat better luck with my second effort, when I used the number Jennifer sent me for Aleek, the paramedic-in-training.

The young, female voice that answered the phone said Aleek wasn't home. But she clearly wanted to chat. So, we did. She had to be Tamantha's age or younger.

The thought of Tamantha triggered a question. "Did you go to the Two Rivers Camp last week?"

She did. And we were off to the races.

By the time I heard what surely must have been everything she'd learned at camp, my asking if she knew where Aleek was naturally led to her reading off his Cottonwood County Community College class schedule on the fridge.

The class that particularly caught my attention ended in about ninety minutes and was taught by O.D. Everett.

THE GAP BEFORE Aleek would be out of class left a perfect chunk of time to stop at the Sherman Supermarket for a chat with Penny.

More accurately, to listen to Penny.

A couple blocks from my destination, Mike called.

"It's not directly related to either dead body, but I thought you'd be interested in some info—well, rumor—on Russell Teague's will."

"How did you get anything on his will?"

"One of our reporters overheard a loose-lipped lawyer in the hospital hallway talking to his office. Did I tell you they've got folks at the hospital for a deathwatch? Business reporters rolling in from all over."

"I wouldn't say no to a rumor about his will."

"I figured." I swear I heard Mike grinning. "It's divided in two parts. The corporate and other stuff from his maternal side is one part, and that's what the business reporters are hot about. The Wyoming stuff is entirely separate. And, apparently, different lawyers drew up the two parts and then a coordinating lawyer made the two sides play nice. None of the lawyers were happy with Russell's many weird touches."

"That's great stuff, Mike. Do you know any of the specific terms?" What a juicy story that would be for some of my connections (or their connections) and thus prime trading material.

"Not yet. Working on it. Now that I know about the will, I think I can get more out of the guy I got in the Wrigley Field suite."

"Keep at it. I've got to go now. I'm at the supermarket."

His sigh held wistfulness. "You don't have to hang up. I don't have to be anywhere for a while and I can listen in while you talk to Penny. Nobody does it better. I might pick up pointers."

"Like you'll need to get things out of Penny any time soon. Besides, I have to shop first." But I didn't end the call as I parked and got out.

Chapter Thirty-Eight

I **PICKED UP** a lunch salad for me, fresh fruit for Mrs. P's vigil, and flowers for Sally while I listened to Mike talking about reconnecting with former Bears teammates and friends in the Chicago area. I was glad for him. Truly glad.

"Okay, I'm almost to checkout. I'm taking the earbuds out and putting the phone in my pocket. Don't talk."

"Got it."

"Well, hi there, Elizabeth." To her usual greeting, Penny added, "You're in on another mess, eh? Two this time. Murder and—"

"I didn't—" Why did I even try? I had no hope of stemming her flow. Besides, I had nothing to be defensive about. Nothing.

"—mayhem wherever you go. Dead before he ever got there—"

So much for KWMT-TV having an exclusive on *that* bit of news.

"—of course. Butte's a strange place to take him. And with the camp kids there the day before and everyone looking forward to seeing how they did the reenactment this time with racing down the butte and all. Not like trying to pretend nobody saw them behind some skinny trees a few yards down the creek bed, when every soul did see. Didn't like to say anything then but it made them seem not real bright. New place, new opportunities, I say, and so did she, and not all talk. Money where her mouth was with how hard she worked, that's for sure. All she'd done on the camp and reenactment for months and months and months, then the Ferguson house job the month before for her. Well, with—"

"Ferguson. That name's famili—"

Mistake. My curiosity might pivot Penny's talk about Nadine away from the reenactment and toward her other job, preparing for estate sales, as Paige and Verona told me Saturday.

"—her. Not got the hang yet of being boss. Lucky, because she works like crazy. Handles all the details, because she's nice, when her problems with details can look like—"

She had to be switching back and forth between Paige and Nadine. No way would I interrupt to sort it, not after my Ferguson mistake.

"—she's not on the up and up, but it's really just not keeping up. The business is about all she can handle. Comet's why. Mary kept everything and when she died, Bill kept her, too. Least a while. Took some explaining to get Reverend Boone to see what it meant that Bill didn't buy Comet, three weeks in a row."

That struck a memory. Penny told me about that after Mary Ferguson died.

Natural causes for a woman nearing ninety. *Not* one of our inquiries, thank heavens. We had more than enough with two bodies and Mrs. Parens acting strange.

"That's interesting, but—"

"Knew she wasn't breathin' anymore when he did that. No way he'd go home without Comet if she were. He went, too, end of June. Poor old soul, never the same after. Some get along better after they're apart than when they're together, but not them."

A quick sideways look from Penny made me wonder if that last line slipped in because she was thinking of another couple who, unlike the Fergusons, got along better apart. Willa and Palmer Rennant? Just how much apartness improved their relationship? The permanent kind?

I mentally scurried to catch up with Penny, whose dispensing of news and gossip waited for no person's cogitations.

"House went even faster. Not easy with the way she kept every last thing. Give her credit, she kept it all clean. Comet. Everywhere, everything, even though it took some of those labels right off, not to mention expiration dates, but she didn't hold with them at all. Expiration dates conspiring to make you give up what you'd bought at a lower price and buy new at a higher price. Not to mention companies not making what she liked anymore. Supposed to turn things in, she never—"

"Palmer Rennant," I threw in.

"—would. Never let go of anything. Kept 'em and kept on using 'em until all used up, others she was still taking and said they worked great, despite it being decades. *T'ch*. Probably sent her to her final sleep. She got forgetful toward the end. Even before the end, nearly killed her once. Told her—both of them—to be careful. Cures aren't always cures when—"

"Cocaine for toothaches," I murmured.

"—they get down—"

"Is that true?" came from my phone.

I held it against my hip while I tried to lower the volume one-fingered, without looking at it.

Neither that nor Mike's interruption slowed Penny any.

"—to the bottom of things. Getting to the bottom of things is what's needed, even when it's not wanted. Wife's the last to know, they say, and that's the truth, even when it's plain as plain could be, especially when she didn't want to see it, wouldn't see it. Pure—"

That didn't match what other sources said about Willa, though I'd stack Penny's reliability—if not her clarity—up against anybody. Still, didn't hurt to check…

"Willa Rennant said Palmer dated—"

Slipping in a comment to Penny worked like an old-fashioned jukebox. No immediate response because other items were lined up ahead of it, but sometimes getting there eventually.

Trouble was, you couldn't tell when one ended and the next began.

"—stubbornness. Eyes squeezed shut and crazy idea on top of it. Not all at once. Drop him over it, start up with him over it, the reenactment's in the middle. Brownies caught him, but already a parent to two nice kids, why take her on? Easter parade's not enough. Widow with three nearly grown boys—too good a head on her shoulders. It's like teaching a man to fish. Same—"

"Which one's Jolie Graf. Is there anything—"

"Fish?" my phone said. "You mean—"

"—principle. Took that on from the start, fought off—"

"—once you teach him, he'll remember forever, like riding a bike?" Mike asked.

I tried for the volume again with no success.

"—efforts to put in all sorts of things that aren't true because they thought it would be a better story. When—"

I think I might have followed the S-curve logic of that transition—going from *principle* to *principal,* which made her think of Mrs. P, which brought her back to the reenactment and the camp. Or one of them. Probably the reenactment, because of the reference to a better story.

The last of my items slid into a bag.

Penny totaled out the sale, waited for me to deal with the credit card, then handed over the receipt.

But with no one behind me, she showed no inclination to hurry me along.

"—the original's plenty good. And as for telling stories, some don't even bother and maybe that's better. Because otherwise you got one side one-upping the other, building up fairytales that only those Grimm brothers could like, much less keep track of. When what they need to do is remember about fishing. What Proverbs says about teaching a man to fish—"

"Proverbs? In the Bible?" Mike asked, louder. Darn, I'd toggled the volume the wrong way.

"—because if you give a man a fish that gives him a meal, but give him a fishing pole and he can get his own meal. Though some men want—"

"There's nothing about a fishing pole or—" came from the phone.

I took the phone out of my pocket and hit mute.

"—a lot more than a fishing pole. They want the fanciest outfit and a motorboat and the whole kit and caboodle. And they go after it—"

Mike's interruption hadn't derailed Penny, but it left me scrambling to piece together fragments. "Rennant? Do you know when he was last seen alive?"

"—no matter what. Good for the goose, good for the gander, in theory, that is. And the gander might not agree. Can't say, except in here wanting Halloween candy Thursday afternoon."

Someone else came into the checkout chute. I curbed my inclination to scream *No*.

"Bye, Elizabeth."

Then Penny Czylinski did something remarkable.

She didn't look away from me to the next person in her line. Instead, she kept her eyes locked on mine as she said, "Well, hi there, Jolie."

With a display of discipline I didn't know I was capable of, I did not look at the person behind me. I met Penny's eyes to let her know I'd received her message.

Then I took my purchases and moved to a bulletin board displaying *For Sale* and *Help Wanted* notices.

Standing at an angle to the board, I skewed my eyes to the side for a view of Jolie Graf.

She could kindly be described as thin. Bones protruded from the low neckline of her tank top—not only her collarbone, but the rippled ones below it.

Her bones were tanned. Very tanned. The kind of tan that looks like the skin's been rolled in dust.

While she'd been among a list of women from an earlier inquiry of hit-upons by a rodeo producer, I had never met her before.

But I had seen her before. Here, in Penny's line.

Penny's memorable greeting to her then included having not seen Jolie since she'd *had work done*.

The fact that the work was still obvious a year later did not speak highly of the result.

I remembered the occasion, I remembered the woman, but until this moment, I had not connected the Jolie of that earlier encounter in Penny's line with the one reported to have been dating Palmer Rennant.

I sneezed. Three times, hard and fast.

Dust.

For half a second, I wondered if Jolie Graf's tan ... But then I saw a coating of the stuff on the yellowing pieces of paper tacked to the board. Evidence the Internet had thoroughly penetrated even Cotton-wood County.

Having purchased a head of lettuce and an orange, Jolie Graf passed me and I followed.

Chapter Thirty-Nine

"HELLO, JOLIE." I approached her just outside the door. "I'm Elizabeth Margaret Dan—"

"TV? I... I can't talk to you."

As if I had a camera smack in her face.

"This is for background. About events in the life of Palmer Rennant."

"No, no, no." Her mouth appeared too wide for her jaw. No way of knowing if that was from the work she'd had done or part of her emaciated look. Was she ill?

"I understand you're upset. That's natural. It's upsetting for everyone when there's a murder like this. And when you know the victim and care about him..."

She looked frightened. Or maybe not. It was hard to read her expression.

I suggested, "We can go somewhere private to talk and—"

"Oh, no. I couldn't. Couldn't."

"You did know Palmer Rennant, didn't you?"

"Know him? Yes, but—"

I wasn't letting her take back that positive answer. "That's why it's so important I talk with you. It might help lead to the person who killed him. I know you'd want that—"

"I don't know anything. Nothing."

If I could break through her resistance... I pulled out my phone with the cropped photo of the watch.

"Did you ever see Palmer Rennant wear this watch?"

Her eyes darted around before finally landing on the screen. "Oh. He wore it in the water. At the pool."

"That was while you two were seeing each other?"

This time her mouth just formed the *Oh*.

"You *were* seeing Palmer?"

"I don't think I should answer—No, no."

"Jolie—"

"I can't." She hurried away with her flaccid shopping bag.

JOURNALISTS CAN SPEND a lot of time in parking lots, on the phone or messaging. Some lots are better than others, depending on ambience, amenities, convenience, central location. The Sherman Supermarket's lot was one of my favorites because there was plenty of elbow room. Also cookies and pie nearby if cravings became urgent.

I toggled off the phone's mute button.

"Hey, you had me on mute," Mike accused.

"I'm seeing advantages to this remote detecting."

"You did that on purpose."

"I did. Because you don't interrupt a source who's saying something important."

"I wasn't aware Penny was saying anything important—or Jolie Graf. Did she say *oh* or *no* more often?"

"You don't interrupt a source who's saying something not important."

"What about when she's wrong? Saying something's in Proverbs when it's not."

"Not then, either. But how do you know it's wrong?"

"I'd remember."

"You know the whole Book of Proverbs?"

"We had to memorize a certain number of verses from one of the books of the Bible for Sunday school. An older friend told me, uh, Proverbs was easiest so I picked that."

"That doesn't explain how you would think you knew the stuff about teaching someone to fish wasn't in there."

"Okay, the older guy didn't say Proverbs was easiest."

I eyed his face on the screen. He looked off to the side. I deduced, "He said something else that made you read all of Proverbs."

"He might've said there was sex in there. I was a kid—a boy—and I read the whole thing—carefully—looking for sexy parts. Go ahead, laugh."

I probably would have if he hadn't invited me to.

Besides I knew when I told Diana and Jennifer, their laughter would make up for me restraining mine now.

"I gotta go. Need to call Diana."

We hung up with him looking skeptical.

But I made good on my excuse by calling her, right after I laughed.

"Diana, if you insist on going with me to Otto's—"

"I do. Has to be later in the afternoon. If I can finish my assignments and get the footage logged in, say, five at Connie's? I'll keep you posted. What have you gotten so far?"

I gave her what Penny and Jolie said.

Diana did laugh about Mike and his reason for reading Proverbs. We'd have to wait to test Jennifer's reaction.

"What do you think about Penny's rundown of the women Palmer Rennant dated in the past year?" I asked.

"The one who dropped him over the reenactment was Clara Atwood."

"Agreed."

"Brownies and the parent—Vicky Upton from the museum gift shop?

"Makes sense. And the widow with three nearly grown boys?"

There was a pause. I suspected we had the same person in mind, but neither wanted to broach it. I cleared my throat and offered, "Connie Walterston?"

"Well, if it is, good for her. It is almost a year since Brian's death."

"We have to talk to her."

"I suppose. But who is the Easter parade?"

"No idea. Maybe Connie will know. I sure hope she's more forthcoming than Jolie Graf."

She sighed for me. "Although you can look at it as confirmation that she was involved with him or she wouldn't have been so scared to talk to you. What else do you have on tap?"

"The community college next. Then the hospital to see how Sally's doing. Might see Mrs. P there. I'm hoping for several call backs and thought I'd show up at Willa Rennant's house this time."

"Getting a gauge on the suspect by her surroundings, huh? By the way, nothing on Palmer fooling around pre-divorce. Nothing negative on Willa. And not tales about blowups between them, pre- or post-. I did pick up one item on Willa today. Last year, after Palmer locked the door, so to speak, on his property, Willa made a substantial donation to the committee that runs the camp and reenactment. It was felt to be an apology—unnecessary, but much appreciated. She's well-regarded."

"And Palmer?"

"Persona non grata. Well, not entirely. He did remain in the country club and had a regular foursome. But otherwise, definitely not part of the in crowd. It did not appear to bother him in the least. Gotta go now. At my next assignment."

Chapter Forty

THE COTTONWOOD COUNTY Community College has one main building, which is less than impressive.

It's a long, low structure dwarfed by the nature around it.

A lot of buildings I've seen in Wyoming are long, low and unimpressive.

That might be an expression of common sense. Not only the practicality of the structures, but the recognition that they cannot compete with the mountains, the distances, and the sky.

I found the directory, looked for the room number my excellent source gave me. As I walked down the hall toward it, I realized the classrooms on one side had their doors open.

When I slipped into the back of the room where O.D. Everett taught, I realized why. The hall's air-conditioning was significantly more effective than in the rooms, where it competed with the sun-warmed windows, even with blinds partially drawn.

But the students appeared fully engaged, despite the warmth and, by my reckoning, this being the last few minutes of class.

O.D. was talking. "—those who devote themselves to trying to right the wrongs of the past are on a fool's errand. The past is not to be forgotten. It teaches us. We carry those lessons in us into the present and future to prevent the ills of the past being repeated. We bring the good of the past, also. But we do not remain in the past."

He paused, looking over the class members.

"The past that is not to be forgotten, includes the lessons of this course. You certainly will carry those with you into the future when you submit your final papers in one week. That is all for today."

As the students stirred, gathering their belongings, I left. I didn't want to pounce on Aleek as soon as he walked out.

When I saw him heading for the main doors, I retreated more and waited outside.

Paytah Everett walked out with him.

"Hi, Aleek, Paytah. Remember me? Elizabeth Margaret Danniher from KWMT-TV."

They stopped, displaying no obvious enthusiasm for my presence.

"I hoped to benefit from your paramedic expertise, Aleek."

That thawed a couple layers of frost.

"I'm not a paramedic," he said. Which I knew, but if it gave him the opportunity to explain, showing his knowledge, that was good. "I'm an EMT—Emergency Medical Technician—and taking the training for Advanced EMT."

"He's already moved up one step and he'll go for full paramedic." Pride for his friend came through in Paytah's words.

"It'll be a while," Aleek warned.

"That's hard work," I said. "And very admirable. It was clear you knew your stuff when you checked for a pulse."

He looked slightly wary.

Rather than let him wonder what I might be getting at, I spit it out. "Could you tell if he was stiff?" He didn't react, but I heard Paytah draw in a breath. "Could you tell what stage rigor mortis was at? It seemed to me the large muscles were in full rigor, but couldn't tell about small muscles. But if the small muscles weren't as stiff…"

"They weren't. Rigor mortis was starting to pass off. Early in that stage."

"The skin was cool?"

"Yes. Something else. I couldn't see well because of the angle, but I thought I saw marks on his shoulder, under the paint. Dark marks, then light marks below on his upper arm, like it pressed against something and stayed that way."

"Lividity."

"That's what I figured."

His wariness had fled with the technical talk. One side of his mouth lifted as he looked at his companion. "Just some of what I've gotta know. And deal with. Still think it's so glamorous?"

That clearly settled some old discussion in his favor.

Paytah avoided acknowledging that by saying to me, "You never said why you did not think Jeremiah's horse killed Palmer Rennant."

"Not Jeremiah's horse, not any of yours. Because we both came to the same conclusion. He was already dead." I squinted, studying him. "Though from different reasons. Why did you think he was already dead?"

He thought he was going to stay quiet.

"The horses," I said.

"They would have acted differently. My horse would have acted differently. He did not strike the man, but he would have acted differently."

"Yeah, you and that horse of yours would have levitated over a live body," Aleek mocked.

Forestalling Paytah's response, I stuck in quickly, "Do you know if any of the horses landed on the body with their full weight? Your own, or Jeremiah's, or if someone else mentioned it…"

"Everybody said their horse cleared the body. All of them couldn't have or there wouldn't have been those marks."

"No," Aleek said thoughtfully, "but I believe them that nobody's horse landed full on. Jeremiah was first and he said his horse went sideways, almost cleared. Then all the horses that followed were alerted, along with the riders. We turned wider than Jeremiah did, so not right over the body."

"That's right. We all tried to miss him. Like a boulder sticking up from the ground."

Aleek shot me a look.

I'd bet he was thinking that *boulder* could have collapsed from a direct, full-weight stomp.

Addressing Aleek, I asked, "You know why I thought he was dead before any of you rode in there?"

"No blood."

While Paytah exhaled recognition of that observation, I hit Aleek with another question. "Did you have any idea of what might have killed him?"

"Couldn't tell with the position he was in. Can pretty much rule out he was shot or stabbed in the back. Other than that, couldn't see well enough."

"What would the possibilities be?"

One shoulder lifting an inch indicated nearly infinity.

"Like?" I pushed.

"Stabbed. Heart attack. Shot with no exit wound. Stroke. Poisoned. Asphyxiated any of multiple ways, including his own vomit. Not there..."

"He probably wasn't killed there, anyway."

He met my gaze again. "Yeah. Really, cause of death could have been a whole lot of things."

Paytah said a word I didn't know, but recognized the tenor of it as a curse. "You're really into this stuff?"

O.D. emerged from the main doors. His slow, casual gaze took in everything as he joined us.

"Thinking about going into forensics," Aleek said. "Medical examiner and doing autopsies, except I don't know about the med school stuff."

"Good for you. Another question, did either of you or people you know go up to the buttes recently to hang out?"

"No." Paytah's tone conveyed that such a thing was impossible.

In the instant my gaze met O.D.'s I thought of Mike and Jennifer saying they and their friends went up there. Was this a divide between tribes and not-tribes that Two Rivers Camp had not bridged?

Then Aleek said, with the same note of impossibility, "Younger kids."

So, at least this particular divide was age.

I said to him, "If you're really interested in pursuing beyond paramedic, you should talk to Deputy Alvaro. Tell him I said to call him. One of his sisters works for a guy in Montana. Could give you the rundown. And thank you very much. If you think of anything else, give me a call."

I gave him my card after writing Alvaro's number on the back.

"I will."

We smiled at each other. It's not everybody you can connect with over a mutual interest in dead bodies.

The two young men said good-bye to me and O.D.

I lingered. "They must be disappointed at the reenactment not taking place."

He gave a short, soft grunt.

Thinking of his classroom comments on the past, I asked, "What's your opinion of that event?"

"It is natural for the young men to want to remember and bring these specific events back to life. There is no harm in that. As long as they also remember those events are ripples in the stream of history— disturbances in water that continued to flow against us."

A wry twinkle came into his eyes.

"I said something similar to Palmer Rennant the last time we talked."

"Oh, when was that?"

"After the meeting when he finally confirmed he would not allow the reenactment and camp on the property he bought."

"How did you get along with him?"

"Other times, well enough. At that meeting not. He rode off in odd directions. For example, when I said similar to what I said to you, he replied that he wished people who participated in Civil War reenactments as Confederates remembered about the major stream of history and didn't keep acting like the South won." The wryness of the twinkle deepened. "He added numerous adjectives that I have not repeated."

"What did he have against reenactments?"

"That I do not know. Perhaps Clara Atwood knows."

If I asked directly, he'd back away. Instead, I asked something I'd guessed at, and invited him to agree, "Oh, right. Because they argued about that when they were dating."

"Yes."

"Do you know of any connection between Palmer and Russell Teague?"

"No."

But he didn't seem surprised by my question.

Chapter Forty-One

A CALL CAME in as I drove toward Cottonwood County Hospital.

Matt Lester's voice greeted me. "Hey, Danny. How's it going in the Wild West?"

"Fine. When are you and Bonnie coming to visit?"

"We wanted to leave the field clear for the Dannihers thundering through town. Bonnie said your folks were there twice this summer?"

I understood his surprise. I'd fended off my parents visiting me until recently. When I moved to Wyoming, they drove with me from Illinois, where I'd spent time with them post-divorce. Their first impression of Cottonwood County had not been favorable.

"This time, they liked it so much they came back, with my brother, his wife, and their four kids in tow. Mind you, a lot of what they liked was Yellowstone Park, but Sherman's growing on them."

"Hey, with that kind of recommendation, can the Lesters be far behind?"

"I hope not. It would be great to have you and Bonnie here. I do recommend doing it soon, or waiting until next June."

"Heck, no. We want to cross-country ski at Yellowstone. We should get you out, too."

"I'll wait for you by the fire in the lodge. With a hot toddy."

He scoffed at my priorities. "Speaking of hot toddies, you owe me one or something comparable. I promised to take the biz reporter out for a drink and word is he's a cognac fancier. But I don't think you'll complain about the price of this information."

My journalist antennae tingled. "Oh, yeah?"

"Yeah. There were three more levels of successively bigger companies owning the ones you left in your message, but this cognac-swilling guy eventually got back to a name you'll recognize. Russell Teague."

I whistled. Then I whistled again.

"Does it fit what you're digging into?" he asked.

"I have no idea. But the guy who sold the company at the front of that line of Russian nesting dolls moved here after the sale."

"Small world coincidence? Or something more?"

"Wait. There's more. Same guy turned up dead Saturday."

"Why do I have the feeling it's not natural causes when you're involved?"

"I am *not* involved." Indignation faded as I added, "Natural causes aren't officially ruled out yet, but I'm betting the other direction."

"Connection to Russell Teague?"

"That's an interesting question. There's no sign they've done business together since that sale." Even as I said it, I wondered if there was some connection through Old West history, with Russell Teague scooping up and moving historical, semi-historical, and downright decrepit buildings around the region for his personal playground, while Palmer Rennant shooed away a local history reenactment.

But even if I had something firm, that wouldn't interest Matt's Philadelphia area readers—or, more accurately, the cognac-fancying business writer's readers. Something else might, however.

"So, what I found's no help?" he asked.

"Matt Lester, I'm disappointed in you. You know you never know about info until you know."

"Wow. You're a regular journalistic sage."

"Just to prove it, I'll give you something that should please your cognac-loving biz writer friend. Russell Teague is in a hospital in Chicago. Most likely dying. Multiple-organ failure. The *Chicago Tribune* had the story."

"Well. Well, well, well." That didn't obscure the sound of his typing. "I do believe he will be interested. Thanks, Danny. Give me a call any time you want some info that ends up helping me."

I laughed. "Will do."

Chapter Forty-Two

I ATE MY lunch in the hospital parking lot, thinking about what I'd heard so far today, and trying to not sigh that it wasn't more.

A search on my phone didn't produce anything new on Jolie Graf. I did see a picture of her husband, Kamden. A bulky guy with a wide smile.

Another call to Radford Hickam got the same message. Once again, I declined to leave my information.

I brought the flowers and a bag carrying the fruit in a basket inside, where I found Aunt Gee in the hallway outside the closed door to Sally Tipton's room.

"The doctors are in with Sally right now. Emmaline's in the ladies' room. How nice of you to bring Sally flowers. They will brighten her room."

"How is Sally?"

"Not good. Not good at all. The stroke's damaged her heart even worse and it wasn't good before. She can survive the stroke, but her heart's not going to last much longer." Gee Decker didn't mince facts, but her voice was heavy. She shifted to her more familiar business tone. "Mike says you're hoping to get cause of death."

I didn't want to risk saying the wrong thing, so I concentrated on looking hopeful, but not desperate.

"Far too early for a final determination," she said. My hopes ebbed. "They're hoping toxicology might provide answers. Obvious trauma—gunshots, stabbing, blunt force, strangulation—are highly unlikely."

"Thank you. That's—"

"I should tell you, Sally's asked to see you."

She knew how to cut short a thank-you.

"*Me?*"

"Yes. Though when I say she asked… She can't really talk. There's paralysis in the muscles in her throat and some around her mouth. When you see her, you'll see it's drooping on one side."

"The condition is dysarthria." Mrs. Parens arrived in time to edit her friend and rival's comments.

Aunt Gee shot her a look that should have withered her. On the other hand, if Aunt Gee's looks could wither her next-door neighbor, it would have happened decades ago.

"It is part of the reason that you shall not see Sally today or likely anytime soon, Elizabeth. Gisella and I limit our time in the room and further visitors are strictly forbidden. The doctor has agreed with me about that. Even if what Gisella interpreted as a request to communicate with you is accurate, Sally does not have the strength for such attempts."

"Doctors said her mind seems to be working fine, but she's got paralysis on her right side." Gee dared Mrs. P to interrupt with that scientific term, then resumed. "She's right-handed and what with trying to write with her left hand, much less the effects of the stroke… She's struggling."

Both of these stalwart women looked worn. They had, after all, known Sally Tipton for most or all of their lives. Plus, the daunting factor of being reminded of mortality—especially your own—that most hospitals induced.

"How about if I take you both to the cafeteria for a cup of tea?"

There was also an outdoor patio I recalled. Fresh air might do them good.

We left the fruit and flowers with a kind aide, who promised to put them in Sally's room. Then we headed to the cafeteria.

Tea, seats outdoors, and fresh air all accounted for, I searched for a topic to distract them without sparking disagreement.

Complete and total blank.

So, I shifted strategies and hoped distracting one directly would distract the other indirectly.

I lobbed the first hand-grenade by saying, "Despite everything that's happened, I can't help but feel it's a shame the reenactment didn't—couldn't—happen Saturday. You know they sold more tickets than ever?"

They murmured, not wildly interested.

"I was looking forward to learning more about the Miners' Camp Fight and how it fit in with the Montana Road. I heard someone saying the Miners' Camp Fight was a side issue and it didn't matter if it scared people off from the west-of-the-Bighorns route, because the Army knew what it was doing staying east of the mountains."

Mrs. Parens' erect backbone turned to steel. "Nonsense."

It *was* nonsense. I'd made it up, patching together pieces of what she'd told me for a theory I hoped she'd dislike.

"If the Army had enforced the 1851 treaty, there would have been no Montana Road. Miners and others would have been forced to take routes to Bozeman that would have taken longer to travel but would have not infringed on territories accorded to the tribes by treaties, with a result of much less loss of life."

Mission accomplished—so far.

"Gold fever," I murmured knowingly.

"Indeed, that malady prompted many to be foolhardy. They frequently paid a price for it. It is unfortunate that many others besides the gold seekers paid a horrible price, including soldiers ordered to build and occupy those forts along the Montana Road.

"They were sent there with instructions to protect the travelers on the Montana Road, but there were few of those. Quite soon it became apparent the soldiers themselves needed the protection, which is why the three forts were constructed, requiring log stockades a dozen and more feet tall. Further, the support from the Army was insufficient. Among other things, the soldiers went without pay for extended periods, including six months at one point.

"In addition, the combined boredom and sudden outbursts of hostilities resulted in madness—as they called it—among the troops.

There are documented cases of soldiers taken to St. Elizabeths Insane Asylum in Washington, D.C. Each, of course, only after they ascertained they were not feigning the symptoms."

"My," Aunt Gee said. "I knew there were a good number killed, especially when that Fetterman led a bunch of them into an ambush. And, of course, the desertions. But I didn't know about the poor souls going insane."

"Fetterman?" I asked.

Both of the older women looked at me as if I'd asked who Abraham Lincoln was.

In that moment, I particularly missed Mike and the others. Mike, because he had a knack for saying or remembering the wrong thing and drawing attention away from my ignorance on Wyoming topics. Diana, Jennifer, and others because they often remembered pieces of whatever Mrs. P was talking about, filling me in without betraying my ignorance.

This time it was on full display.

"Captain William Fetterman led a contingent of about eighty men—some barely boys and others civilians—into an ambush executed by the tribes and every member of his force was killed."

Mrs. Parens looked around, as if expecting her packed bookcases to be nearby. Making do with a sheet from a pad withdrawn from her voluminous bag, she wrote quickly.

Aunt Gee clicked her tongue. "He was a Civil War veteran, but didn't know about fighting out here. It was reported he said to give him eighty men and he could ride through the Sioux nation. They proved him wrong that day. Fell into the trap and others died for it. And then the Army named a fort after him."

Mrs. P handed me the sheet of paper. Three book titles, authors, and dates of publication, written off the top of her head. "You will need to read these for a fuller understanding of the circumstances of that incident and the Montana Road."

At least she didn't assign book reports. Yet.

"Many soldiers suffered and died in the two years—only two years—they were tasked with protecting the Montana Road. After that short time, those forts were abandoned. Another treaty was written, this time acknowledging the reality that tribes controlled territory recognized as Native American in the 1851 treaty."

"The tribes beat them," Aunt Gee said.

"That is a fair assessment," Mrs. P said. "It might be of interest to you, Elizabeth, that there was another element in the timeline of that period in this region."

"Oh?" I tried to keep it neutral. I wasn't about to deny interest in something Mrs. P expected me to be interested in.

On the other hand, how interested was I? Especially with two dead bodies from significantly more recent times begging for my attention.

"This was the same period as the construction of the transcontinental railroad. Those constructing the railroad were understandably concerned about safety amid attacks by the tribes. That meant financial backers were, perforce, eventually concerned, which created political support for protection to complete the railroad.

"The construction coming from the east had reached as far as eastern Nevada in 1866, when troops were sent to protect the Montana Road, resulting in the building of the three forts. By the time the forts were abandoned and the new treaty was made in 1868, the railroad had reached western Wyoming, well past the southern terminus of the Montana Road, having suffered many fewer attacks than had been feared."

"Gold miners and the others didn't need the Montana Road anymore," Aunt Gee said. "They could take the railroad. Though, they still needed to get up north to Bozeman."

I'd been watching Mrs. Parens closely. "You don't think it was ever about the miners. You think it was misdirection. Conspiracy, too?"

"I merely note the timelines."

"But you suspect the forts were a decoy to let the railroad be completed with fewer attacks. That there was far less interference from the tribes because they were well occupied with their campaigns against the Montana Road and its forts. That those soldiers were sacrificed—"

"I did not say anything of the sort," she said severely, "nor have I drawn such a conclusion, because I have not found research that sheds direct light on any connection, much less confirms one. As with your work, one can form a hypothesis, but as long as certain facts remain out of your grasp, it remains a hypothesis, not a conclusion, nor a demonstrable fact."

Somewhere in that statement, we had left the 1860s, the Montana Road, and the transcontinental railroad.

For now, it would remain one of those hypotheses—based on impressions I'd gathered—that she was talking about the identity and the story surrounding our mystery cave body. Although I wasn't prepared to rule out Rennant completely.

Either way, Emmaline Parens wasn't telling me until she was ready.

Both women looked brighter as we parted, so that ploy succeeded. I left with even more questions.

Chapter Forty-Three

I HAD A message to call Wardell Yardley at my earliest convenience.

I did. From my SUV, still in the hospital parking lot—see why journalists have favorite parking lots?

"Wardell Yardley," answered the crisp, professional voice.

"Hey, Dell. It's Elizabeth Danniher."

"Danny," he said in a different voice, one that had taken off the suit, tie, and dress shirt that cost a boatload of money each and put on his jeans and jacket—they'd still cost a boatload, but he'd look slightly more like a man of the people. "How are you?"

"Good. And you? Keeping busy?"

"Busy, but bored. You know how D.C. is in August."

I did. Hazy, hot, and humid. Yet, in the years I'd lived there, there always seemed to be a day or two when the weather broke. When it was cloudy and cool. A promise that the steam bath of a Washington, D.C., summer would end someday, with the faintest threat that the longed-for end would also be the beginning of something unwanted.

Winter.

In Wyoming, the reference to winter was all threat, no promise.

But knowing Wardell Yardley, he was not talking about meteorological issues.

"All the pols escaped to more hospitable environs?" I said.

"And all their satellites gone with them, leaving only the people who do actual work, which means this town is nearly empty."

"Such a cynic, Yardley."

"Such a veteran of D.C., Danniher."

I chuckled. "And did this wily veteran get anything for me?"

"Not a thing." He packed it with disgust, yet sounded a lot more cheerful than he would have if it had been the other way around.

"Well, get out your ledger book, because I have something for you, which means you go even deeper in debt to me."

"Me in debt to you? After all I've gotten for you since you moved out where your sources are sagebrush and cows? No way."

"Put together anything you've shared in the past year and half and it's a drop in the bucket of what you owed me before I came here. Now, do you want to hear what I've got or do you want to do a line-by-line accounting?"

He sputtered a bit, then said, "Spill."

"Russell Teague is dying in a hospital in Chicago."

"*What?*"

"You heard me. *Tribune* had a story and AP picked it up." I did not mention my original source, because Dell was entirely capable of trying to co-opt Mike as his personal Chicago correspondent.

He cursed fluently in four languages I recognized and another I didn't. "How can that be when I had an alert on his name and gold coins?"

"The stories didn't mention the gold coins. No interest in them in Chicago or most of the country. You should have had the alert on his name alone."

"All those dreary business stories, every time some stock he's associated with went up or down a penny. How close to dying is he?"

"They're not releasing a timeline," I said dryly. "But word is that he has multiple organs failing—that is not for reporting."

"Like I'd report that. I'm the White House correspondent, not the weird rich people beat reporter." He dropped from that lofty tone to add, "Not anymore."

"Not to share with your business coverage team, either."

He didn't even employ words to scoff at that.

"How will this affect the gold coins story?"

He'd come out here last fall to report on a stash of coins found and their disputed ownership. It had been his bosses' idea to put him in touch with flyover territory. It nearly ended in disaster—but that was another story.

"I have no idea."

"Stay on that angle. Will his estate pursue the legal case? Who's inheriting? Get those answers for me—"

"I am not your stringer, Yardley. I have stories of my own to pursue."

"Like what?"

"Never mind like what. I'm—"

"Hah!" he crowed. "Small town nothings."

"I'm hanging up now, Dell. You're welcome for the update—and don't forget to add it to my side of the ledger."

Chapter Forty-Four

UNLIKE THE HOUSE Palmer Rennant kept in the divorce, Willa Rennant's new one was not a timber behemoth making an overt nod to western heritage. No, rather than a modern take on the Ponderosa ranch house from old *Bonanza* shows, this was a restrained modern glass, timber, and rock structure.

Its neighbors used the same materials, yet each was individual.

The development definitely put the original country club area in the shade.

Willa Rennant opened the door to my bell-ringing. She looked unsurprised to see me, but not particularly pleased.

She also looked more like someone who'd had a shock. Yesterday she'd still been running on organizational adrenaline. Today it was gone.

"More questions?

"Yes. Is this a bad time?"

"No worse than any other." She exhaled sharply. "Come in. I'm just tired of answering questions about my ex-husband. Including where to bury him. It doesn't seem right that this falls on an ex-wife."

"No, it doesn't."

I said that with sufficient fervor—brought on by empathy while imagining taking on those duties for my ex—that she gave me a sharp look and led me inside.

The interior displayed similar good taste to the other house with a less traditional feel. She hadn't gone all sharp edges and cold surfaces, either. It was polished, but a home.

"I'd understood you still have horses." I tipped my head toward photos of her and her kids on horseback.

"We do, the kids and I. We board them, where they have plenty of room."

She waved me to a chair, but paced to French doors to look out on a patio.

"Have you made progress? The sheriff's department doesn't seem to have. Or else they are telling me nothing because I'm a suspect." Her lip curled on the last word.

"It's very early. These inquiries are complicated and take time and often they seem to be leading nowhere."

That was the perfect introduction to showing her the photo of the watch.

"Do you recognize this?"

She exhaled heavily, then came back to where I was and sat in a chair opposite, looking at the photo. "No."

"Palmer never wore one like it?"

"Oh."

She was silent long enough that I nudged her. "Willa?"

"I was trying to remember if I'd actually seen the watch. If I did, it didn't register." She handed the phone back. "Two or three months after the divorce, Palmer and I crossed paths at the country club. He was bursting about something. Didn't tell me what it was and I didn't ask. But he did say Russell Teague had given him a watch just like one Teague had to *celebrate*. Before you ask, I did not ask what they were celebrating or anything else. I didn't want to know. Anyway, I wonder if that was the watch."

Okay, maybe I needed to let go of the idea that whatever Mrs. P was hiding had anything to do with the watch.

She looked at me hard. "Was he wearing it … when he was found?"

"Yes."

Then she surprised me by saying, "You asked about the horses. I've been thinking about them. More precisely thinking that I took the horses in the divorce, I could also have taken that land. I should have.

He wouldn't have fought me on it. We would have traded something else.

"He bought it, so it seemed right—No, in all honesty, I never thought about it. I let it go. I just... I was tired. I was so tired. I should have recognized he would indulge his feelings on the subject and upset our community. Anyway, I should have fought to claim that property. I would have been happy to let the event continue."

"I wouldn't worry. I interviewed organizers and they were positive about the change."

"Until Palmer's murder canceled it."

As if searching for a more tactful subject, I looked around the room.

"He must have done very well to be financially independent, to afford the ranch, and—" I tipped a hand to our surroundings.

"So I shouldn't have complained?" she asked with a snap.

I said nothing.

"I'll have you know that without my income—dwarfed as it was by his—he would not have been able to walk away from his career when he did. My income, my making a home for him as well as the kids, and, yes, my handling the finances. All vital. He loved the theory, but I did the work. He went off and played, I was the grownup."

After two slow breaths, she was back to calm.

"As you no doubt have recognized, that was a source of friction in our marriage. He never devoted the time to the family that I or our children hoped for. It wasn't that his work demanded time away from us, he *enjoyed* the time away. He preferred that to his family. Once here, he added on to the work and subtracted from the family. I said we would have continued to be connected by our children, but that tie endured only to the extent that I nurtured—no, nagged him about it."

Her exhalation gusted.

"Yes, he provided extremely well for us, and we didn't need half of it. I will say, in fairness, that his decision to move us here—and it was his decision—turned out to be excellent for the three of us."

When she seemed inclined to stop there, I nudged her along, like my entry in a turtle race. "What about for Palmer?"

"He was not as happy here as the rest of us. Not until—" She smiled dryly. "—I told him I wanted a divorce. Though I do not believe that was the direct cause of his change in attitude. He'd tried several new ventures in the years we were here and they failed or he lost interest or both. But something caught and held his interest about six months before I asked for the divorce. He didn't share what it was. He never did. With the kids gone... I chose not to be alone in a marriage. Better to have my solitary state be official."

Chapter Forty-Five

I REACHED DIANA'S appointed rendezvous spot outside the Walterstons' Red Sail Ranch just as Connie Walterston and her youngest son, Austin, braked to a stop at the end of the ranch road.

I hadn't blocked them in, because I was parked off to the side, where turning vehicles packed the dirt solid. A matching spot awaited Diana on the far side of the ranch road.

They'd stopped to say hello, Connie in the passenger seat and Austin driving the pickup.

"Hope you don't mind," I said. "Diana's coming. We thought we'd leave the Newsmobile here for an hour or so, if that's okay."

"Sure thing. Or drive up to the house if you want."

"This is perfect. I was hoping to talk to you sometime soon, Connie."

"I thought you might." Her wryness confirmed that Penny's reference to the widow with three nearly grown sons and a good head on her shoulders fit Connie. "I'll be at the trailer all morning."

The trailer was where she ran the office for a road paving company Tom Burrell took over when his father retired, along with the ranch.

"Great. Hey, Austin, I had a question for you, too. When you and your friends go up to the buttes, you go into the cave, right? Did you ever see the body there?"

"No. Must've been a slide afterward." Lost in his disgust at that rotten luck, it took him an extra beat to catch his mother's look. "I mean—"

"Don't add a lie to it, Austin," she said.

He swallowed.

I swooped right in, taking advantage of his chastened state. "When was the last time you or your friends were up there?"

"A week ago last Friday night." Careful not to look at his mother, he added, "We knew about the practice for the reenactment the next day and all the stuff last week. Didn't want to take a chance at being caught."

"Did you go in the cave?"

"Yeah. But we didn't see anything. And we had good lights."

"Do you know Paytah Everett and a friend of his named Aleek?"

He looked puzzled, but said, "Yeah. They're older."

It reinforced Paytah and Aleek's reaction.

"Were they there the last time you and your friends were?"

"No."

"Ever seen them there?"

"No. Except—well, saw them from a distance Saturday when we were waiting for the reenactment to start."

"If you had seen a body in the cave, what would you have done?"

He thought about it a moment. "Probably let a bunch of them pretend they hadn't been there, but a couple of us would've told Sergeant Shelton. Can't hide something like that."

I knew exactly how he felt.

"Thanks. Didn't mean to hold you guys up."

Austin gratefully reapplied himself to driving. Connie waved as they departed.

With no sign of Diana, I tried another call to Dex's connection.

This time Radford Hickam answered.

"Hi, I'm Elizabeth Margaret Danniher from KWMT-TV—"

The voice chuckled. "He said you'd be calling."

"Did he?" That didn't sound at all like Dex.

"Also said not to tell you anything."

Not Dex.

"Shelton," I concluded.

"Yep. Wayne Shelton from the Cottonwood County Sheriff's Department."

"Ah, but I'm calling because a mutual friend gave me your name. A mutual friend from back east?"

In a different voice, one filled with respect, he said, "He said Danny would call me."

"That's me. Danniher. Danny."

"Well, this is awkward, considering my promise to Sergeant Shelton. Although…"

"Although," I prompted.

"Come to think of it, actually, what Sergeant Shelton said was to not share anything I told him with you. If you ask questions that don't have the same answers as his… Further, we have done only the most preliminary of examinations. Much, much more to come. It's up to you if you want to try questions."

Dex might have been able to give me another recommendation, but this was his first choice. And now the guy had challenged me to come up with questions that drew answers that Shelton hadn't already scooped up.

You bet I was going to try.

"Could you tell from the photographs how recently the rock slide that revealed the belt and the skull might have happened?"

"Ah, excellent. Not only not a question the Sergeant asked, but one I wondered about. I'm not an expert on rocks, but I would say quite recent."

Before the breath I drew came out as words, he continued.

"No, I wasn't satisfied with that answer, either. I checked with a colleague who is an expert on rocks and she went even further. First, she said likely within a week, two at most, of the photograph being taken. Then, she noted there had been mild seismic activity centered on that area. Mild to us, but to precariously piled rocks, potentially significant. That was on the Tuesday before the photograph was taken."

When Palmer Rennant was certainly still alive. Significant?

Could he have seen the body? Said something about it to the wrong person—? But why would someone wanting to keep the cave body a secret take Rennant's body there? That made no sense.

Still, we had likely narrowed the time when the body was exposed. And that significantly cut the chances anyone spotted it before I did.

Which made it more likely—at least to my thinking—that the cave body was not related to the reason Palmer Rennant was taken to the buttes.

"Was the belt previously protected by rocks while the shirt and jeans above and below it were previously exposed?"

"Well-observed, Ms. Danniher. Or may I call you Danny?"

"Please do."

"That is exactly what appears to have happened. Although that previous exposure does not mean those items were visible, but rather that more oxygen reached them than the belt. From what I saw, I suspect there were repeated shiftings that covered up, then exposed different areas at different times as a result of shifts in those rocks."

That confirmed what I'd thought, though I wasn't sure how it advanced anything.

"Did the missing piece of the skull indicate a blow? An attack?"

"Alas, that is a question Sergeant Shelton asked."

Darn him. Of course, he did.

"Can you confirm that the cause of death was natural causes?"

"No, we cannot."

"Is that based on the difficulty of establishing the cause of death or from the physical evidence of the body? Or likely associated with the body?" I tacked on, thinking how rock slides could have moved around evidence.

"Hah. Adroit. We cannot confirm the cause of death was natural causes based on physical evidence. As I have yet another meeting I am now late for, I'm afraid…"

"Just a couple more."

Physical evidence ruling out natural causes must point to an accident or foul play.

Asking about foul play would track too closely to Shelton's forbidden territory.

I asked, "Does the physical evidence point to an accident?"

He paused a moment. "It does not point solely to an accident as a cause."

A fatal blow on the head could come from a falling rock... A bullet could still mean an accident. Or not.

Radford Hickam said, "Your final question for now—"

"Is there anything you can answer that I haven't asked that is likely to be of interest to me?"

He laughed. "Superb, Danny. Absolutely superb. I will need to think about that to give you a complete answer. I will call you back, but I should warn you it might be some time for the examination and final report."

Just as well he couldn't answer now, because the dust trail approaching promised to be Diana.

We said friendly good-byes and I immediately messaged him all my contact info.

Chapter Forty-Six

FIRST THING DIANA said when she got in my SUV was, "As a cameraperson, I'm telling you to quit pushing your sunglasses on the top of your head, your bangs look like spikes of tumbleweed."

"Just for that, I won't tell you what I've learned today. And I don't have bangs."

She looked at the shorter hair around my face. "Not halfway up your forehead like Elizabeth Taylor in *Cleopatra* or Claudette Colbert in *It Happened One Night*, no, but—"

"I do *not* have bangs."

She regarded me for a moment. "Childhood bang trauma? Tell your sad story to Diana, dearie."

"My mother claimed I wouldn't hold still and she had to keep cutting to—"

"Even them out," we said together.

"How short?" she asked with a measure of brisk sympathy.

"Guys with a two-day beard had longer hair than my bangs."

"Photographic evidence?"

"Kept in a vault by my brothers for blackmail."

"Okay, no bangs. But put down your sunglasses anyway so that short hair doesn't permanently spike, then tell me all."

Sometimes a friend can be a body brace, too, taking the wobble out of even old traumas.

I told her most rather than all because it wasn't a long drive to Otto Chaney's place.

The green paint on the compact house had gotten duller since I'd seen it last. And I either hadn't noticed the screened door before or it had acquired several punched-in areas that seemed designed to funnel bugs into the house, rather than keep them out.

Otto, sitting in an old metal kitchen chair, and two old dogs occupied the porch.

Otto held onto one barking dog by his collar, while a second trotted amiably down the steps to greet us.

Turning off the SUV engine made no impression on the barking dog, but when Diana and I emerged, it quieted.

Otto, however, did not release the dog. Probably because it wore a cast on one back leg and a brace on the other, as well as having a patch of fur shaved from one front shoulder.

"What do you want?" Otto demanded.

"Hi. Do you remember me? Elizabeth Margaret Danniher from KWMT-TV and this is my colleague, Diana Stendahl." Who had stopped to rub the ears of the amiable dog at the bottom of the stairs.

I kept climbing them. "We met—"

"I remember. Don't have any call for TV reporters being here asking—"

"Oh, poor baby."

I said that to the injured dog. Not Otto Chaney.

The animal was a white-muzzled cross section of dogdom, with crafty eyes and a roguish side-lolling tongue. He glanced at Otto, then me, standing on the second step, my arm stretched out with something in my hand.

With one deft twist, he escaped Otto's hold and came to me, taking the treat neatly from my palm. Shadow would never know one of his supply went to a stranger.

I rubbed under the dog's chin, which was passable with him. Then found that spot on his good shoulder and just behind it where his braced leg couldn't reach to scratch. I applied my nails and he melted into a puddle of dog bliss.

"Huh. Never seen him like that. Not even when I rub there."

"You need fingernails."

"Fingernails," Otto scoffed.

This dog was too long to have made the scratch marks on Rennant's front door. He would have scratched a good five or six inches higher.

"What's his name?"

"Devil."

My spurt of laughter seemed to please the old man.

Surprisingly good cooking smells came through the porous screen door to us.

I sat on the porch beside the dog, still applying my nails. Diana and the other dog joined us.

"And that's Max."

"Hello, Max." Diana punctuated the formal introductions with more petting.

"What do you want?" Otto asked.

"Ask a few questions."

"Suppose it's about that Palmer Rennant getting himself killed. I'll tell you this, free of charge—I didn't kill the evil-hearted yuppie."

I couldn't remember the last time I'd heard someone called a yuppie. "Someone did. It's not good for the neighborhood to have murderers loose," I pointed out.

"Especially not with your great-niece around."

Score one for Diana.

"Suppose."

"When was the last time you saw Palmer Rennant?"

"Saw him inching down the road in that red truck of his Thursday afternoon, like he'd reformed for good. Only to hear the truck driving crazy fast middle of the night, like he hadn't nearly killed Devil on Tuesday. But if you're asking when I talked to him, that was Tuesday at the vet's office when I near took his head off, apology or no apology. Paul shoved me into where Devil was and wouldn't let me out. Hannah took care of letting that piece of crap ease his conscience with money. They can say all they want about him being sincere, but if he was, he wouldn't't've been driving that way in the wee hours, days later."

"Tell us what happened with Devil."

Even from his highly colored account, it was possible it had been an accident. Seemed safe to say Rennant had been going too fast. Also safe to say Devil chased the car.

In fact, Otto said, chasing and being hit by a car was how he was hurt earlier. Vehicle-chasing was the reason he was adopted out to someone on a ranch.

"Only got one truck to chase here and Rennant doesn't leave every day. Just Devil's luck the man drives like a maniac." Abruptly, he said, "I'll tell you one thing. If you're trying to figure out when that guy was dead, it was by Friday morning."

Startled, I flicked a look toward Diana. Couldn't tell if Otto's time-line matching with what we'd figured for the rigor surprised her as much as me.

"Fool dog woke me like he had to go out during the dark hours. With me not moving as fast as I used to, he slipped out before I closed the gate, and went right to Rennant's place. Barking his fool head off. Rennant would've raised a fuss if he'd been around to raise one."

"How do you know that?"

"He called and complained and whined to the sheriff's department every other time, didn't he?"

"I meant how do you know the dog—"

"I can tell when my dog got out, can't I?"

Without betraying the patience I called on, I asked, "How do you know he went right to Rennant's place?"

"Well, can't say for sure he went *right* there, but he was there. When he got back, had leaves in his fur from the plant Rennant said he picked on purpose for by his porch because it's called dogbane. I know that stuff. Gets in hay and can kill horses, too. Damned white-collar idiot, trying to kill our animals."

"Came back with something else, too, but his wife—ex, now—won't make a big deal over a few scratches in that truck of his, specially not with him dead and all."

He sounded quite satisfied with that state of affairs.

"Scratches? How do you know there were scratches on Rennant's truck?" A vision of scratches in the red front door came to mind. "Did you see it?"

"Didn't need to. Devil came back with red flecks in his paws. Not a lot, but with him getting out like that and needing to change him to a clean bandage, I was working close with his paws and saw it. Both front paws. None on the back. I knew that color. Color of that killer truck."

Same color as the front door. But there was that problem with where the scratches were...

"Did you go to Rennant's house to check?"

"Hell no. Seemed like justice to me—Devil scratching up the paint after Rennant nearly killed him with that truck."

"Did you hear or see anybody at Rennant's house Friday, Friday night, or Saturday morning?"

"Not a sound. And don't go over there, so didn't see anything, either."

A buzzer sounded from inside. "I've got supper to fix. These dogs don't feed themselves."

The good smells from inside were for the dogs.

We thanked him and went to the SUV, while he leashed Devil to the porch railing and went inside, leaving the dogs outside the decrepit screened door.

"Be careful Devil doesn't chase the vehicle," Diana warned me.

Devil was otherwise occupied. Lured by those good smells, he and Max stood right in front of the door. Max jumped up, resting his front paws on the crossbar set handle-height on the door.

Then Devil rose up, too.

I'd been mistaken.

With the cast on one back leg and the brace on the other, Devil couldn't do the full stretched-out reach with his front paws that Max accomplished. Instead, he squatted in back and stretched up his front legs. Reaching right where I'd seen those scratches on Palmer Rennant's front door.

I started the SUV and Devil's head pivoted toward us. He barked rapidly, lunged toward the steps, realized he was tethered. Still barking, he returned to the smells coming through the door, jumping up again, scratching at the door.

Chapter Forty-Seven

BACK AT CONNIE'S, we called Mike from the SUV. Jennifer was still at Northwestern, now having dinner there. He was awaiting her call to pick her up. He pledged to share everything we said with her.

He repeated his news on Teague's will for Diana's benefit, then we gave him today's highlights, ending with Otto.

"*Planting* dogbane? That should be criminal."

"That's the headline you take out of our visit with Otto Chaney?" I asked. "Rennant hit Devil with a truck, Otto might have killed Rennant, and you're focused on a plant? Even if it is called dogbane—"

Diana said, "Dogbane is a problem for livestock and other animals. But plants in the same family are decorative. Rennant might have been talking about that. He might not have been aiming to kill Otto's dog."

"Better not be dogbane," Mike grumbled. "Still, if Rennant nearly killed Otto's dog with the truck Tuesday, why wait to kill him until—what did we say with the rigor?—very end of Thursday or early hours of Friday?"

"Because he heard Rennant driving fast again that night. Rennant had been careful earlier in the day, returning from town, where he was seen at the pharmacy, then the supermarket. But Otto heard him tearing down the road during the small hours. Made him furious again and he acted. That's a theory, anyway." Diana's finish indicated she didn't particularly want that theory to be true.

"Or maybe Rennant went after Devil for scratching his truck," I said.

"The dog? Scratched the truck? That's no big deal to fix."

"Otto said Devil had red paint on his paws," Diana pointed out.

I added, "But Rennant's front door is red, too, and there were scratches at the right level."

"Much more likely," Mike said. "Scratches from dog nails on vehicles can mostly be buffed out. An old dog like you described, especially only a few days after being hit and hurt... I'd really doubt it could do major damage. All you have to do is..."

Only half-listening, I missed when he finished.

"Elizabeth? You there?" he asked.

"Yeah, yeah. Thinking."

"What are you thinking?"

"That we actually have three mysteries going on—Palmer Rennant, the cave body, and Mrs. P acting weird."

"Really, you're putting Mrs. P in the same category?" Mike asked.

"Your aunt does. In fact, I'd say she ranks it as more important, since that's the reason she gave me the ID on Palmer Rennant."

"How are they connected?" Mike asked.

"Aha," Diana said. "That's the whole question, isn't it?"

"It's sure a large part. And I'll admit, knowing there are three doesn't help us much. Because all three might be woven together or all three might be separate or any combination of two."

"You're right. Not real helpful," Mike said.

"Knowing what we don't know is always a place to start."

"It's not as good as knowing what we do know," he persisted.

"Can't argue with that."

I told them my thinking about the narrow window when the cave body was visible pointing toward the two bodies being unrelated.

"So, one murderer chose the buttes to hide a body and another chose the place to be sure a body was found? Weird," Mike said.

"Weird, maybe, but that's a good synopsis. And, if you think about it, it worked out for each of them. The cave body was there for decades without anybody finding it, while Rennant's body was there twenty-four to thirty-six hours before it was found. Each murderer got what he or she wanted."

✧ ✧ ✧ ✧

I MADE A detour on the way home to the part of town with big, old houses mixed in with more pedestrian structures.

My destination was one of the latter, but I parked in front of one of the former, its yard decorated with a sign advertising an estate sale the next month. This must be the Ferguson house Paige Schmidt and Nadine worked on.

I'd had no idea it was next door to Jolie and Kamden Graf.

Jolie Graf went white under that dusty tan again when she saw me at her front door.

It rarely bothered me when I had that effect on people. I wouldn't let it this time, either.

"No, no. Go away," she whispered immediately.

"Who is it?" called a man's voice. From this angle, I saw, reflected in the hallway mirror, a match for the photo of Kamden Graf. He looked taller and broader in the mirror. "Are we ever going to eat? You can live on air, but I can't."

I told Jolie, "I will go away now if you'll talk to me later. I'll meet you in the supermarket parking lot at eight-thirty."

"I can't—"

"I said, who is it? If I can't get dinner at home, I'll get it somewhere else. Told you I have to be out of here soon."

"No, no. I'll be right there, darling." To me she whispered, "Please—"

"Meet me," I repeated as the door closed on me.

Chapter Forty-Eight

SHADOW SNIFFED INDUSTRIOUSLY and a bit indignantly at my hands, shirt cuffs, and jeans when I got home. He was far more interested in where I'd been than in me. That was how jealousy worked.

I thought about that.

Could that sort of dynamic be operating between Willa and Palmer Rennant? She hadn't been all that interested in him, but she was jealous of the other women? And she took Penny's thinking to heart about disposing of the man, rather than the other woman.

Or in this case, other women.

But why wait until there was a string of them? Why hadn't the first two, three, four triggered the reaction?

Or could it be one of the other women who responded that way? If, so that pointed at Connie Walterston, being replaced by Jolie Graf, which I simply didn't believe. *She'd never do that* wasn't evidence, but it sure as heck satisfied me for the foreseeable future.

Oh, wait, Connie thought there'd been another woman. And Penny hinted at it. One between Connie and Jolie. We needed to track her down.

If there was, that didn't leave Jolie Graf out, especially if Palmer Rennant dumped her. Could that be what she was hiding?

And then there was Otto's revenge motive. Didn't seem strong to me, but I might be prejudiced based on dog ownership.

And it sure beat Clara's would-have-had-a-motive-a-year-ago.

Heck, at this point, Palmer Rennant should still be alive based on the weakness of known motives.

Time for my supermarket parking lot rendezvous.

I WAS THERE first.

Twilight remained. And with the store open until ten it was far from deserted. I chose a spot near a light but well away from any other vehicles.

Five minutes after the appointed time, here came an old four-wheel-drive with a wraith-thin driver ... and vanity plates that included J-O-L-I-E.

I blinked my lights. Twice. Then I tooted. Finally, she spotted me, parked alongside me, and got out. I gestured for her to get in the passenger seat.

She really wasn't good at this. She should have insisted I get in her vehicle, where I'd more likely need to be wearing a wire to record her. In my own vehicle, I could have set up enough listening devices to please the Russians.

I didn't start with questions immediately, because waiting made her anxious, and I hoped that would make her more pliable.

"You... You can't come to my house again."

"I won't have to if you tell me what I need to know."

"I don't know anything."

"You know Palmer Rennant."

Her chin sank lower.

I prodded. "How long have you dated?"

"A few weeks—only a few weeks."

"Are you afraid your husband will find out?" What I really wanted to ask was if she was afraid of her husband.

She swallowed. "Are you going to tell him?"

"That's not my job, Jolie. My job is to try to find out who killed Palmer Rennant."

"But I don't know," she wailed. A wail without much behind it, but a wail nonetheless.

"Did he ever talk about being afraid of someone?"

"No."

"Having a dispute with anyone?"

"No."

"His ex-wife?"

"Oh, no. Not her."

"Did anyone threaten him?"

"No."

"What did you two do together?"

"*What?*"

I'd thrown that in to break up the monotony. She seemed to think I wanted a step-by-step on their sexual exploits.

"You must have done activities together. Movies? Dinners?"

"We couldn't go *out*." She sounded appalled.

I was half tempted to say that from what I'd heard her husband hadn't been nearly as discreet.

"Was he working on projects? In business with anyone?"

"Well…"

"Yes?"

"He and my husband were doing something together. But he wouldn't talk about it," she said hurriedly.

"Still, you must know about it from your husband."

She wilted a bit. "No. He doesn't talk about it to me. I just know it's not his insurance business. It's something else." And then she seemed to rally. "Something he—Palmer, Palmer Rennant—was excited about."

That was the cream of the evening's very poor crop.

I didn't know which of us was happier to have it over when I told her she could get back in her vehicle and leave.

I was too dispirited to even go inside. A totally wasted trip to the Sherman Supermarket—and that didn't happen often.

I spent the rest of the evening watching *Dial M for Murder* while I read information on dogbane, the little available on Russell Teague's condition, financial independence links Jennifer had sent me, and wondering if Jolie could be trying to protect—or frame—her husband.

DAY SIX

TUESDAY

Chapter Forty-Nine

JOURNALISTS CAN OFTEN feel something big coming. Most likely it's industrious brain elves putting together bits and pieces swimming around in our heads into something semi-coherent, but still below the conscious level.

A few revel in that sense. The rest of us don't, because what makes a big story rarely means butterflies and cupcakes. More like that bad moon rising feeling.

Except it was the sun rising. And I was awake to see it.

Not a good omen.

✧ ✧ ✧ ✧

I KNOCKED ON the open trailer door and accepted the invitation to come in.

Under Connie Walterston's hand, the inside of the trailer west of Sherman looked clean, organized, and neat, with no evidence of spiders in sight. Quite different from my first visit.

"Looks like business is booming," I said.

She gestured me toward a visitor's chair across the desk from her. "This season has been a vast improvement and next year promises to be even better, which I wish was enough to make my boss happy."

Not a direct poke into my personal affairs, but close.

"That's what you get for working for a grump," I said cheerfully.

"Was really glad to run into you yesterday. And thanks for letting me ask Austin those questions."

"As the beneficiary of your question-asking abilities, I have a lot of confidence in them, Elizabeth. How did you know Austin and his friends had been up to the buttes?"

"Mike Paycik went up there in his high school days. Jennifer Lawton, too. It seemed unlikely that suddenly stopped in the past few years."

"I'm his mother, but I would say he was being entirely truthful with you. Especially about telling someone if he'd seen—or heard that others had seen—a body up there."

I suspected Brian Walterston's death and the circumstances surrounding it had sensitized his family and a number of other people to the impact of people going missing.

"I think so, too. As a matter of fact, I have information that the body most likely wasn't revealed until rocks shifted a week ago."

"Oh." That syllable of interest rested on a foundation of relief. Austin had told the truth and I had information that verified it beyond a mother's belief. But I also saw her considering further implications. "Do you think Palmer Rennant saw the body?"

"I have no idea. He was certainly alive until Thursday afternoon, so it's possible."

"Right. Penny." There was no sense even being surprised she knew.

"Yup. Last sighting I've heard about was Thursday afternoon at the supermarket. Connie, do you have any idea why he would be up there at the butte?"

"None."

"You dated him, didn't you." I didn't make that a question, so she didn't have to say yes or no. "When was that?"

"From the end of May into June. It was ... pleasant." Her gaze came up. "And so strange. I mean, there truly wasn't much to it. Movies, dinners, a couple events in Cody. We talked, but it was nothing like... Well, I suppose that wasn't fair to him. I couldn't expect it to be. One the love of your life you were married to for all those years, the other a near stranger.

"But I was grateful to him and real sad to hear about his death. He didn't rush me. He sort of let me get my sea legs again, if you know what I mean, without any big drama."

"That's interesting. I heard he wasn't real tuned in to ... nuances."

"Oh, he wasn't. I found that rather refreshing. So many people have tiptoed around me the past year. He didn't. It also meant I could be real blunt, too."

I hadn't thought of that upside.

"When you were seeing each other, did he wear one of those watches that looked like a cockpit gauge?"

She chuckled. "He did. Very proud of it, too, even though he never used it for anything—used his phone, even for checking the time."

"Did he ever talk to you about his ancestors or family tree?"

"Not that I recall. I guess if he did, it didn't make an impression on me."

"What about history?"

Her brows drew down. "There were a few things about *so-called* historic sites and museums and such. Said one time they should all be shut down. I got a little sharp. Said they were important, including for letting the newcomers know what happened before they set foot in town." She grinned ruefully. "He got under my skin, what with knowing all Tom does to keep the local history and such going."

"Any more about that?"

"No. Oh, wait. I did suggest a trip over to Buffalo and he started in about not wanting to have anything to do with the place ever again and somebody had told him a pack of lies."

Fort Phil Kearny was near Buffalo. Then, again, so were other things. Including Buffalo itself.

"Do you know who else he dated?"

She laughed. "In this county? I couldn't help but know, especially after a couple people saw us together a time or two. Then I heard *everything.*"

Willa's comment about people informing the ex repeated in my head. Did she know it wasn't just ex-wives?

"But I'm not sure about repeating..."

"Let's do it this way, Connie. I know he dated Clara Atwood short-ly after his divorce a year ago. And there was something about a woman connected to brownies and why would Rennant get deeply involved when he already had two nice kids, which I took to be Vicky Upton, and why would Rennant take on her daughter, the inimitable Heather Upton."

She spluttered in an effort to stifle laughter. "That is wicked. Accu-rate, but wicked. Not you, Elizabeth, but ... Penny?"

"Absolutely. Had you heard he dated Vicky?"

"Yes. And that Heather broke them up. Then the girl goes off to college and Vicky's left alone again." She shook her head. "A shame. Vicky's been lonely a long time."

"Then there was someone Penny referred to as the Easter Parade woman."

"Oh dear. I suppose I might as well tell you."

"Please."

"Rosalee Short."

"Any relation to Ivy from the library?"

"Her half-sister. She does wear hats. A lot. And not sensible ones. Any time she's at an outdoor event everyone spends half the time chasing down her hat. But I think you can forget her, Elizabeth. She's been gone since mid-June, taking care of her maternal grandmother in Rhode Island. She died over the weekend—the grandmother, not Rosalee."

"Clara, Vicky, Rosalee ... these are in chronological order?"

"I believe so. Then me."

"After you?"

Connie paused a moment then plunged ahead. "I heard talk about Jolie Graf. Oh, there was word about someone else before Jolie, but I never heard who that was—or might have been. Then the rumors about Jolie."

"What did you think of those rumors?"

"In a way it was hard to believe and, in another way, not. If I'd been asked before then to list the ten women in the county least likely to cheat on a husband, Jolie would've made the list. At the same time, if I'd listed the ten men in the county least faithful to their wives,

Kamden would be on that, right up toward the top." She paused. "Or bottom, if you looked at it the right way."

"Rumor? Or more?"

"I saw him with the maid of honor in the bathroom at his wedding reception."

"Well. Okay."

"I'm not telling any secrets because other people did, too, and talked about it. I witnessed another incident and Brian saw one, too—despite our best efforts not to. A number of the women talked about it right out in the open. And then the rumors… Honestly, I don't know how Jolie *couldn't* know.

"Always seemed she was gaga over Kamden. The kind of gaga that's never certain of their partner, always trying, straining for the security of being loved."

Sadness and sympathy softened her face. She'd had that security of being loved with Brian and she felt sorry for those who didn't.

A truly nice woman.

"That must be what the diets and cosmetic surgeries are about, poor soul," she added.

"She's not sick?"

"No. She did that to herself." She looked even sadder. She continued in a far more pointed way. "Hard to believe people—especially intelligent, good people could be so blind about what they do to themselves. Beyond the sort of physical things Jolie Graf has done into missing out on the opportunity for a good love. So hard for others who care about them to watch it happen."

"I hear you're staying in touch with Mike Paycik in Chicago," she added. "We'd sure hate to lose you from KWMT—and Cottonwood County."

This chair was really not comfortable. Or maybe it was the look she sent me.

I stood.

"Well, thanks for all your help, Connie. Good to see you."

And even better to get out of the trailer suddenly dense with meanings.

Chapter Fifty

ONE OF THE bits—or possibly pieces—that floated up from the nighttime churn into my daytime consciousness was a desire to see Palmer Rennant's pickup and the dog scratches. That's where I headed next.

It being on the other side of the county and far from Connie's—or anyone else's—hints didn't hurt.

I drove. Alone. With the music up. Letting the bits and pieces out to play in the sunlight.

I detoured when, on the last leg to Palmer Rennant's house, I spotted an unlikely vehicle in front of Otto Chaney's little house. A pale blue SUV.

And Otto Chaney's front porch held a most unexpected occupant.

Willa Rennant. Sitting on the metal kitchen chair, with a grocery bag by her side.

No sign of Otto. But there was a clue to his whereabouts, since the rusting ranch pickup usually parked to the side of his barn was gone.

She smiled at me as I took a seat on the porch floor, with my feet down a couple steps.

"I suppose you're here to ask Otto questions. Can't imagine he takes well to that," she said.

"He doesn't. And you?"

"To offer apologies. I asked around. Apparently, many people heard about Palmer hitting Otto's dog last week, but nobody told me. Not until I asked after what you said. They'd share every detail of his dating life but not about his hitting a dog. I can't believe—Or maybe I can."

Half-tempted to say she needed to change her sources of information—if Thurston was an example of the country club set's priorities and reporting skills, she was in trouble—I withstood temptation. Partly because I realized that what she couldn't believe might have nothing to do with people telling her things but rather with her ex hitting a dog with his truck.

And if it was the latter, her last phrase raised another question.

Focusing on the dog issue, I asked, "Could you imagine Palmer trying to hit the dog?"

"Deliberately trying to? No. Not being careful out of impatience or being oblivious to other creatures in this world? Yes."

"While you were living there, you never had trouble with Otto's dogs chasing your vehicle or showing up on your front porch?"

"No."

"Did Palmer mention that happening to him?"

The frown lifted, but her eyes narrowed. "No, but he likely wouldn't. He had no tolerance for such things and he would not have invited my telling him to not be a jerk, to slow down. As for being on our front porch... What if they were?"

"Did you happen to go to Palmer's house on Thursday or Friday?"

"No. I told you when I last saw him."

That reminded me she'd been an executive. And knew how to remind subordinates that they were subordinates. Sure glad I wasn't one, or I might have been intimidated.

"Would it have been unusual for no one to go by his house for a day or two?"

"No. Last I knew, he had cleaners out Tuesday and Saturday. By the state of the house—and comments from the sheriff's department Sunday, the cleaners kept their regular schedule last week. Other than that, visitors to his house would have been..."

When she tailed off, I let the silence grow so she could process whatever was churning in her mind.

"No, even with the women he saw, I don't imagine he had them to his house regularly. He wouldn't have been rigid or extreme about it, but he'd go to their places far, far more often than they went to his house.

"In every house we lived in together, he had a room that was all his own. It's where he spent most of his time. No one else was ever allowed in when he was there and rarely when he wasn't."

"Was that where his computer was?"

"Yes. Are you thinking it was taken? It wasn't. Not until the sheriff's department took it. They hope to get into it, but I wouldn't be at all surprised if they never succeed."

I'd be surprised if they *never* got in it. But for right now, I wasn't broken up to hear it presented them with a frustrating obstacle.

"Was his private room where he accessed the forums where he wrote about his financial independence efforts?"

Her face cleared. "You *have* done your homework. And I suppose you've also uncovered his posts on those forums, not that it would be much of a challenge. He didn't hide his personal information—or mine—particularly well. Which I pointed out to him numerous times. But he never was particularly good at seeing anyone else's point of view. His was right. Everyone else was simply not as smart as he was."

"You sound remarkably at peace about that."

"Oh, it used to make me angry. Very angry. I learned to live with it until I couldn't anymore." She shook her head, apparently at herself.

"It was better for both of us. While we were married, I looked at what the marriage wasn't and what he wasn't. He wasn't a partner. He spent time in the marriage only when it suited him. He wasn't much of a father for the same reasons.

"After the divorce, I saw more of what he was. He was a superb sperm donor." Her mouth quirked. "I got great kids out of that marriage and that included the genes he donated. And he never interfered in my raising of the kids. Early on—I almost said in our family life, but he really wasn't ever part of that, so I'll simply say early on—I tried everything I could think of to involve him. He simply wasn't interested in participating except when the mood hit him, which wasn't frequently.

"Gradually, I gained the perspective to see the benefits of that. As

I said, he also was an excellent provider."

"In connection with Palmer not allowing the reenactment and camp to be held on that property any longer, you said Monday that you should have recognized Palmer would indulge his feelings on *the subject* by upsetting your new community—what subject?"

She said nothing.

I nudged. "He seemed to have strong feelings about reenactments."

She laughed, a sour edge to its lightness. "His whole family's like that. Say the word—or get in the neighborhood of the topic—and they'd go off. A tirade by one feeding the next, then the next, then the next, in an escalating spiral. And not one of them recognizing how crazy it was. In fact, it outraged Palmer that his kids not only didn't share the Rennant hobby horse, but were inclined to laugh off the whole matter. My influence, I'm proud to say. That, too, outraged him."

"His whole family?" Prejudice could run in families, but prejudice against historic reenactments? That I'd never encountered before. "It seems an odd thing for a family to be so, uh, vehement about."

"Ah."

She paused after that single syllable.

I didn't push. Not immediately, anyway. See where silence got us first.

After a moment she made a wry grimace. "I must have caught some of the Rennant sensitivity on the topic over the years or I wouldn't be hesitating now. But it's silly, really. As I told my children all their lives."

She drew in a long breath. "A Rennant ancestor is generally described by historians as being responsible for the loss of a battle in the War of 1812." She produced that grimace again. "Most people couldn't name three events from the War of 1812 and this battle would not be among the top ten. The Rennants have been refighting the battle—and the historians—ever since. But that was only the beginning.

"That Rennant's grandson was determined to bring glory to the name during the Civil War. Instead, he made another blunder, leading troops into a trap sprung by the Confederates in Northern Virginia. It became known as Rennant's bridge, which became a town called Rennant's Bridge. It became a favorite of Confederate reenactors— after all, they won that one. As fate would have it, Palmer's grandparents settled in the next town over and that became the hub for Palmer's branch of the Rennant family.

"I suppose at some point the connection was made of the family name to the bridge, the blunder, and the annual reenacting of it. Instead of accepting it as *history*, they bridled. By the time I came into the family, it was established that the rest of the world was wrong and had it out for the Rennants, especially historians and reenactors."

"That must have made quite an impression on Palmer growing up."

"Yes. He was never one to give up. Over anything, no matter how trivial, and even when it was the only sane thing to do." After that one-breath statement, she pulled in oxygen. "Well, I suppose it stood him in good stead with his businesses. Although it wasn't comfortable going through our married life next to a man who could be triggered by words like history or historic or reenactment. Not that I can say I didn't have warning.

"The first time he took me to his family home, his paternal grandparents were there as well as his parents. His grandfather told this story about Palmer at about eleven years old riding his bike miles and miles and miles to a reenactment—not that the Rennants ever conceded it was a reenactment, because they disputed the original account. It was an *event*, in Rennant vernacular. Anyway, he bicycles all the way there— without permission—and proceeds to make stump speeches about how inaccurate the presentation is. He gets into a scuffle when they asked him to leave. Leading to the police escorting him away—still shouting about how wrong the historians were. The police bring him home, where his mother is frantic, but his father and grandfather couldn't be prouder of this scion of the Rennants taking the fight to the enemy."

She shook her head.

"Inside the family, it's seen as such a righteous cause. I saw some in-laws get caught up in it, too. But when you step away and look at it from a distance…" She shook her head.

"What about a connection to the Miners' Camp Fight reenactment?"

An ancient ranch truck puttered toward us from a field, catching Willa's attention.

"You mean other than the land? Not that I know of."

"Did he go over to Buffalo a lot?"

Her faint frown cleared. "Oh. You mean that Fort Phil, uh—"

"Kearny."

"Right. Fort Phil Kearny. He started in on that several years ago. I knew he'd been doing research—I think that's why he moved us all here. First few years, he was more interested in starting another company. That company didn't pan out and he switched a lot of his interest to genealogy. Family, but not the live one in front of him."

She stood with her last words to address her host.

"Hello, Otto, I brought some treats for your dogs. And a pie from the supermarket for you. Penny recommended it."

"Miz Rennant. Nice to see you."

"I'm so sorry, Otto."

"Not your fault," he said gruffly. "Appreciate the treats and all. Like to meet my current roommates?"

"I would."

Chapter Fifty-One

WHEN WILLA RENNANT got into her baby blue SUV, Devil barked and strained against Otto's hold.

"You here for more questions, because I've got work to do," Otto said loudly over the barking.

"One question—or about one topic. You said Devil went to Palmer Rennant's house late Thursday or early Friday morning."

"Yeah. Raised a ruckus. Heard him clear. Took him forever to come back to my whistling."

The SUV turned out of sight and Devil quieted.

"You also said Rennant drove away fast from his house that night. Was that before or after Devil went over there?"

"Had to be before, didn't it? Or, like I said, Rennant would've called the deputies."

"You were awakened twice that night?"

"Twice? No. Sleep like a log, except when Devil or Max—"

He stopped. Looked from me to the dogs, then back at me.

"You saying I heard the truck after Devil got me up and went over there? But then why didn't Rennant...?"

Why didn't Rennant complain as he always did?

Because he was dead.

And the person who drove away fast from his house had killed him.

❖ ❖ ❖ ❖

SURPRISING GOOD NEWS and unsurprising bad news awaited me at

Palmer Rennant's house.

The surprising good news was that one of the men at the bottom of the steps strung across with police tape was Kamden Graf.

The unsurprising bad news was that the other was Deputy Richard Alvaro.

I assessed the situation as I slowly rolled into the gravel area in front of the porch.

They were arguing. At least Graf was. Richard didn't look happy.

I eased the wheel to the left and coasted to a stop directly behind Rennant's truck, which was in the same spot as Sunday.

I got out and walked along the driver's side of the truck—no scratches—and had rounded the front and started up the passenger side when Alvaro strode over to meet me issuing a stern warning to Graf to not cross the police tape as he came.

"This is a police scene, Elizabeth. You can't—"

"Behind the tape, of course, is the scene under your control. But I have the widow's permission to be here." I reinforced the mild fib by gesturing to the gravel below my feet and reinforced his distraction by saying, "I have a question for—"

"I'm not answering any questions."

"It's a small one and it can't possibly hurt to hear it."

I'd spotted scratches on the passenger door. The same height as the ones on the front door ... and the same height as Devil's paw-reach on Otto's door.

"Not going to answer."

"Fine. Just listen." Also scratches beside the truck door, as if the animal tried to open it. "Did you or any of the sheriff's department's people move this truck? I mean before you impounded it."

He opened his mouth then snapped it closed ...

"You did impound it, didn't you? It's just back here now because you've processed it?"

"I told you. I'm not answering questions."

I held up pacifying hands. "Okay, okay."

Slowly, I circled him as if heading back to my SUV.

He paused, then strode past the front of Rennant's truck, his back to me and putting space between us as he pulled out his phone.

I immediately detoured toward Kamden Graf, who'd remained at the bottom of the steps.

His angry face changed when he saw me approaching. He assumed an expression he probably thought of as charming and I considered smarmy.

I put on an expression that said at this moment I craved smarmy above all else.

"You must be Kamden Graf. I've heard so much about you. I'm Elizabeth Margaret Danniher with KWMT-TV." I rushed through me and got back to him. "Just the other day I heard how wonderful you are with insurance. Now, who was it...? Oh, dear, it's just *gone*." From my itty-bitty air-filled head. "But I'm sure they were telling me about Nadine Hulte getting a great deal on insurance from you or was it someone else who—?"

"Must've been someone else, because I don't recall that name." He'd jumped the gun out of fear I'd dredge up a memory that someone else was responsible for the great deal on insurance. Then he realized he'd implied it himself and rushed in with, "I can surely give you the best deal on insurance in northwest Wyoming. No question there. You come by my office. Any time. I'm conveniently south of town off the highway."

"Oh, by the Kicking Cowboy?"

His demeanor shifted to something even less charming than smarm at mention of the bar that teetered on the edge of seedy.

"Very near. Very near. Any time you want to meet there instead of the stuffy old office, that would suit me fine. Day or night."

I giggled.

In that instant, I really hoped he'd murdered Palmer Rennant so this performance proved to be worthwhile.

I felt no guilt at wishing that on him because he clearly had never watched a segment of "Helping Out!" or he'd know this was an act.

"I heard you know the poor man who was murdered, too. You were a friend of his? Or was it your wife...?"

He slid right by the mention of Jolie and said, "Business associate."

"Oh. Only business. Not personal."

I glanced away from his face for the first time.

That accomplished several things.

I double-checked the height of the scratches in the red paint of the front door—just Devil's jumped up-height.

I scanned both his wrists for a watch similar to Rennant's and Teague's.

It put Kamden on his smarmy mettle.

He immediately chased after my flagging interest. "Business can be personal, too. We worked closely together on a groundbreaking exposé of the wrongs so-called history has done to people. Going to prove they were accused of all sorts of things that weren't true and discredit the organizations perpetuating the injustices. First of a series. Starting here in Wyoming, moving back to the Civil War, then further back to the War of 1812."

Jolie had kept her mouth shut better than he did. Did Kamden not tell his wife what he'd just spilled to a stranger? Did Palmer tell her anything?

Kamden's words echoed with the tenor of Willa's accounts of her ex's obsession.

But how did Russell Teague fit in? He hadn't loved the way local history viewed his family. Was his the Wyoming history? Or was there something with Palmer?

"That's fascinating. Starting in Wyoming?"

"Our major, major backer wants to start local. Once we grab them by the throat with that one, the others will follow and we'll turn the peddling of so-called history on its head. Discredit the purveyors of the misinformation like that little museum in town and their whole house of cards comes down."

Now, *that* smacked of a Russell Teague quote.

I widened my eyes. "Wow. They've told a lie about local history?"

"Not just one. Trying to undermine our most prominent family—"

Teague had to be the source of that.

"—and impugn a good man with allegations his ancestor deserted when it was no such thing." His head tipped toward the front door, leaving me no doubt who he meant without his saying the name.

Desertion? That didn't figure into Willa's accounts.

"What will happen now with this poor man dead?" No mention of Russell Teague, because I didn't want him to think I was aware enough of events or connections to raise his guard.

"That's what I'm trying to find out. There's material in there that, by rights, belongs to me, but will this deputy listen? No. Too busy—"

"Elizabeth."

Deputy Alvaro wasn't happy with me.

I raised my shoulders and looked up at Graf. "Oh, dear, now I'm in trouble, but I just couldn't resist talking to you."

He reached out and squeezed my upper arm, clearly limiting himself to that because of the deputy on hand. "We'll talk again."

"Can't wait."

As I passed Richard, he gave me a puzzled look, but said nothing.

Just as well, because in a couple more steps, my phone rang.

Shelton, according to caller ID.

I waited until I was in the SUV, Richard watching me all the while.

"Hi, Sergeant."

"What's this about Rennant's truck?"

"Yes, I *am* having a nice day, and you?"

I was learning to distinguish his growls. This one said *no, not a nice day*, and he blamed me, the picture of innocence. It also told me no one in law enforcement had moved the truck. If they had, he wouldn't have bothered to growl.

"You've impounded it, right? Processed it already? Found anything yet that doesn't match Rennant?"

"What do you know?"

"Me? *Know?* For sure? Not a thing. Yet."

He hung up on me.

And not the way Dex did.

Chapter Fifty-Two

THE ENDING OF that conversation with Shelton put me in such a good mood that I lived dangerously and bought two brownies from Vicky Upton on the way into the Sherman Western Frontier Life Museum.

With brownies in hand, I asked, "Vicky, you dated Palmer Rennant, what did you think of him?"

"I'm not talking to you about him."

Darn. And I thought we'd made such progress.

"You could have insight that might catch his killer."

That didn't work any better on her than it had on Jolie. "It was months and months ago. Has nothing to do with who killed him now. And I'm not talking to you."

Which is why I bought the brownies first.

"Did he wear an expensive watch when you were dating? One of those that can go underwater. Complicated stuff on the face."

I saw an answer forming on her lips.

She pressed them closed and turned away from me.

If I'd been forced to bet, I'd say the answer was *yes*, he'd worn such a watch. But guesses made insecure building blocks for investigations.

Still, my good mood endured. Even when Clara took one look at me standing at the entrance of her pod and said, "Oh, God."

Nadine was there again, too. She smiled—tired and strained, but a smile—and said hello.

"I come bearing gifts," I said.

Clara narrowed her eyes at me. "What?"

I plunked a KWMT-TV envelope on her desk. "Don't lose that. It has a thumb drive of extra footage Diana Stendahl took Friday and Saturday, plus a release form so you folks can use it to promote the events in two years."

"What makes you think we'll still have them in two years."

"Oh, now, Clara, don't go back to being pessimistic." Nadine turned to me. "Thank you. Truly. This will be wonderful, especially if... Well, if we can expand the programs, try to draw in more kids, for example."

Clara scowled at her. Incredulous? Or warning her? "That would be great. Not realistic, but great."

"If the museum gets the gold coins—"

"We can't *spend* them. They'd draw in more visitors, but if you think that will be enough..."

"Will be?" I asked. "Counting your gold coins before they're adjudicated? Do you have a reason to be more optimistic about the museum's claim now?"

She scoffed. "Like what?"

Like with Rennant out of the way he couldn't carry on Teague's fight to secure the coins.

"When did you last talk to Palmer Rennant, Clara?"

"There's no reason for me to tell you that."

"Is there a reason for you not to?"

"Really? You're questioning me as a suspect in his murder? Why not the body in the cave, too?"

"Died before you were born, or I would."

"Just tell her. She needs to ask these questions," Nadine sounded muffled—not by something physical, but her own emotions.

"No, she doesn't. The sheriff's department, maybe, but not her. And if you question us, you might as well question Emmaline Parens and Gee Decker, too. Oh—" Clara turned to me with an unpleasant intensity. "—and Tom Burrell, since they're on the committee and have as much reason to dislike Rennant as we do. They were as angry at him last year as we were."

"You mean when you found out he wouldn't let you use his land for the reenactment and camp. Because you found that out before he told the committee officially, didn't you?"

"What if I did? That was a year ago. And not exactly a big secret, since everyone on the committee—and probably well beyond it—knew I was the source for that information."

"How did you find out?"

"It didn't take any feat of espionage, if that's what you're thinking. He just started talking about it. Delighted with himself. Absolutely delighted at planning to destroy—"

Her hand jerked toward the papers and spreadsheets on the screens.

She pulled in a breath through her nose.

She was back to cold calm when she spoke.

"Leave, Elizabeth. We have work to do. To see if we can save this, much less achieve Nadine's roseate view of expansion. And leave Palmer's death to the sheriff's department."

I did not leave her a brownie.

AS I DROVE toward the station, my phone rang.

"Paycik? Could you ask your aunt a couple things? But first—don't tell me you didn't get Jennifer to her flight on time—her parents will have your hide."

"Got her there. Plane took off on time. And they should be picking her up soon in Billings. Now be quiet and listen, because I have an exclusive you'll want to hear. Teague is dead."

"Exclusive? The wires will—"

"The wires won't have this next part—next two parts. Guess who's the executor for the Wyoming part of his will."

"Guessing games? Do you know how many murders are caused by guessing games gone wro—?"

He saved both of us by interrupting. "Tom. Thomas David Burrell."

"*What?*"

It was a good thing I was on a deserted stretch of road—in other words in Wyoming—because I reflexively clomped my foot on the brake.

"There's more."

Chapter Fifty-Three

"**OH, YOU ARE** going to like this, Elizabeth."

I pulled off the road. "No more teasing. Tell me now."

"In the Wyoming part of Teague's will, the provision about the ranch said that if Palmer Rennant predeceased Teague—which he did—the ranch goes to the Sherman Western Frontier Life Museum."

"*What?*" I might have broken a sound barrier with that word. "Why? He hated the museum. He and Clara Atwood were knives-drawn over the gold coins."

"And that's the second shoe to drop. If Palmer Rennant predeceased Teague, then Teague ceded any and all claim to the gold coins to the museum."

I felt like the British at Yorktown, when the only possible song that fit was *The World Turned Upside Down.*

"This is crazy."

"Sure changes who had motive to kill Palmer Rennant, right? If his ex wanted her kids to inherit a bundle—a bigger bundle, since he was pretty well off already—she wouldn't have killed him before he inherited from Teague."

"It all depends on what she knew about Teague's will. That goes for all of them."

"What they knew and when they knew it," he paraphrased from the famous Watergate-era question.

"Exactly. I wonder if I can get any better feel about this from James Longbaugh."

"He won't spill confidential information," Mike warned.

"All I want is background on how things work in Cottonwood County," I said innocently. "Speaking of Cottonwood County, see if you can find out from your aunt if the sheriff's department has been looking at Rennant's place as a possible death scene and if they have a cause of death."

JAMES LONGBAUGH SAID to come by his law office at one-fifteen and he could make time for me for a few background questions. That left time for a Hamburger Heaven pit stop on my way.

Longbaugh was at least a fourth-generation lawyer in Cottonwood County. As far as I could tell, he covered every aspect of law short of international and constitutional. I wouldn't count him out of those areas either. I just hadn't seen him at work on them.

His law office was also fourth-generation, originally built as a combination home and office, now all office. I liked that he and most of his neighbors had kept the history in the small, square houses with touches of woodworking whimsy, all located a couple of blocks from the courthouse.

Apparently, his making time for me included rushing his lunch, because, when the twenty-something receptionist ushered me into the conference room that clearly started life as a dining room, James was finishing a steak salad at the table.

He started to clear it away, but I protested. "Please, James, finish your lunch. How about if I tell you what I'm wondering about while you take your time."

He glanced at the clock. "That's a good idea."

I started my questions about how the timing of wills and probate worked in Wyoming, especially in connection with when the provisions of a will might become public.

After a swallow, he asked, "Russell Teague's? After the report on TV that he was sick, I checked online. Sounds like it's close to the end for him."

Which told me James hadn't written the will. If he had, he wouldn't have asked. And he sure wouldn't have speculated on the state of Teague's health.

"Yes. Do you know if it was drawn up in Wyoming or—?"

"Only know it wasn't drawn up in this office." He took a final bite and chewed thoughtfully, with another glance toward the clock. "I did hear talk that he'd written a new will about a year ago, superseding one he'd had from back East."

"Any details or—?"

"No details. Now, regarding the timing… If it's going through probate, the first thing is to get the death certificate and then—if the family's pushing things along—it's about another two weeks before it starts probate. And even then, the court can put all of it or some of it under seal, so it might never be a matter of public record."

"Ah." That probably sounded like a tire deflating. "The upshot is that there'd almost certainly not be any public record of his will now."

"That's right."

With Teague dead, the chance of more loose-lipped lawyers plummeted. Even the East Coast ones would keep quiet about Wyoming provisions now.

I slung the strap of my bag over my shoulder. "Thank you, James. I appreciate your—"

"Not so fast, Elizabeth. Because the other factor in this is the kind of setup I'd expect Russell Teague to have—whether drawn up in Wyoming or elsewhere—would not go through probate at all. It would be designed to avoid probate, along with minimizing taxes."

I frowned, "That sounds like it's even less likely people would know the terms of the will."

"Maybe. But you can't ignore the human element. Some people tell everyone they meet about their will and estate planning. Sometimes it's just having a naturally sharing nature. Sometimes it's to hold something over the head of somebody—or somebodies—in their life."

Russell Teague, naturally sharing? No.

Holding something over somebody's head, telling Palmer Rennant, if you don't do what I want, I'll leave it all to the museum? That I could see.

But telling the museum—in the person of Clara Atwood—that if

Rennant predeceased him, they'd be very happy? No, I didn't see that.

So, as a process for word about the will to get back to Cottonwood County, we were back to the likes of a lawyer overheard blabbing on the phone in a hospital corridor.

Unless… Unless Russell Teague told Palmer Rennant the terms and *he* told someone.

And I could imagine the man who'd bragged to Clara about kicking the camp and reenactment off his property also bragging that he would inherit what otherwise could have been a windfall for the museum and all its programs.

Another element remained. It felt tangential at this point, but…

"What about the landowner of the buttes land letting the camp and reenactment use that site?"

"Anonymous."

"Surely not to you, since you work out the legalities to protect the events."

"There were protections in place for anonymity."

That didn't mean he didn't know who the person was.

"James, if Emmaline Parens is the anonymous owner, would you tell me?"

I hadn't realized that at some level I'd thought that was the answer to that small mystery as well as her behavior until the words popped out. Though why she'd keep it a secret…

"No." He cleared his throat. "I should have said, no, I wouldn't tell you."

I sucked in a breath, held it a beat, then expelled it in laughter.

"I deserved that. I can't believe I asked that question."

"I didn't mean—"

"It's all right. I truly did deserve it. Well, thank you, James—"

A knock sounded on the conference room door.

"—you've been very helpful."

The receptionist opened the door. "Your one-thirty is here."

"Be right there." He wiped his hand on a napkin as I came around the table and joined him at the door. "Any time, Elizabeth."

He opened the door and said, "Serena, will you come in here and help me clean this up. I'll be right with you, Tom."

He said that last part to his one-thirty.

Thomas David Burrell.

Tom turned toward the door, starting on *No problem*.

The door closed with James and the receptionist on the far side of it before the words emerged. Leaving Tom and me, alone in the tiny waiting room.

Maybe I was overly suspicious—it is a tendency in my profession—but James Longbaugh's clock-watching took on a whole new meaning. As did jamming me in during his lunchtime. He had set this up.

Without Tom's cooperation or knowledge, as was obvious from his expression.

"Tom," I said neutrally.

"Elizabeth."

Clearly not a happy accident to his mind, our meeting this way, one-on-one for the first time since he'd declared us friends only and decidedly without possibility of benefits.

He'd made the declaration for the sake of Tamantha. To keep from confusing her about a relationship that confused the heck out of me— and I suspected him—as well as the intertwining and lingering confusion about my relationship with Mike.

"How are you, Elizabeth?" Tom's low voice turned the question into something ... personal.

"I'm good. And you?" I tried for spritely. No idea if I achieved it.

"Good. Tamantha said she enjoyed talking to you Friday."

"Yes. Heard all about Sheepherder bread. Fry bread, too." I smiled. That was a mistake. Because he smiled. And ... Yeah, a mistake.

"I do have a question for you." My brisk professionalism wiped out his smile.

"Ask." No promise he'd answer.

"Who is the landowner of the property where the reenactment and camp moved to? I know you were the liaison who persuaded him to it."

"He wanted to remain anonymous."

I *hadn't* known Tom was involved, but had guessed. Now he'd confirmed it.

He was rattled, too.

"Does he still want to be anonymous? Or doesn't it matter anymore?"

He gave me the cool, level stare I'd encountered when we first met. "Why wouldn't it matter anymore?"

"Because he's dead. Russell Teague."

He tipped his head forward. He must have forgotten he'd taken his hat off when he walked in, because without the brim it didn't completely mask his reaction. Or else he thought his saying we weren't going to explore whatever it was between us had wiped away the past fifteen months of my getting to know how to read him.

Then he showed he knew me better after the past fifteen months, because he conceded. "How'd you know?"

"Why? After all his animosity toward the museum…"

He shrugged. Abruptly his efforts at being unreadable shifted to concern. "What are you doing here? Problem you need James' help with?"

"No. What about you?"

"Routine. But—"

Before he could finish, the conference room door cracked open.

"Looks like your appointment's about to begin." I think I did reach spritely that time. "See you later."

Chapter Fifty-Four

JENNIFER WAS BACK.

After her parents picked her up at the Billings airport, the family had lunch at the Haber House Hotel.

Now she'd joined Diana and me at my house, waiting for Mike to arrive cyberly.

"I'm exhausted from talking." She'd declined a share of a brownie, leaving one each for Diana and me. "There's still so much to tell them—I promised to be home for dinner, too. Did you know we went to the theater? It's like ... it's not even the same thing as at the high school. I mean, they're both plays, but... *Wow.*

"And did you know the whole city of Chicago burned down? *Not* because of a cow—and they had to start *all* over and lots of people died."

"A large part burned, not all. A fire in Wisconsin the same day killed many more—"

"We saw an amazing painting at the Art Institute that's really big and it's tiny dots of color—"

"*A Sunday Afternoon on the Island of La Grande Jatte* by Georges Seurat."

She frowned. "The name was about a park."

"*La Grande Jatte* is an island and it has a park. The painting shows people by water with—"

"That's it. But the cool thing was all the dots—all over this *really* big painting. Up close, they looked random, but when you backed up, they came together to make people and dogs and sailboats and sky and grass and trees. Just like pixels. Only that guy did it by *hand* with *paint*. *Hundreds* of years ago."

The word pixel sparked tales of her technical adventures at the museum, library, and workshop, mostly in a foreign language.

"I've got to go tell the guys I'm back. There was hardly time to get online while I was there." She zoomed out the back door.

Diana patted my arm. "That's okay, Elizabeth, I'm interested in hearing about the fire in Wisconsin...?"

"The Peshtigo Fire. It killed as many as twenty-five hundred—the largest recorded fire casualty in the country. But few heard about it at the time because telegraph wires burned. There'd been a drought that summer and there were also lots of fires in Michigan in early October."

"My." She regarded me with a twinkle. "Better now?"

"Unless you want to hear competing theories on the fires, including a meteor or chunks of a comet to account for all the fires? Except scientists are skeptical."

"No. I'm good."

"Are you humoring me?" Notice I didn't ask until I'd partially unloaded.

"Yes."

Jennifer returned. "Thanks for the name of that guy, Elizabeth. I sent links to everybody, though I don't know if it will be as cool online."

Diana and I exchanged a look. Online coming in second with Jennifer? Talk about *wow*.

"Before Mike calls," I said, "tell us how talking to the Northwestern folks went."

"Fine, I guess."

"What did they ask?"

"Lots of stuff."

"Who did you talk with?"

"Three—no, four professors, a dean, and a couple students."

"How long were you there?" Diana asked.

"Ten until about nine-thirty."

"Jennifer, that wasn't an interview, it was a courtship," I said.

"What did they say about you going there?"

"Nothing. Do you want me to search more about Palmer Rennant now that I'm home, where I belong, and with my own system?"

I opened my mouth, but used the indrawn breath meant for words to ease out pain after Diana kicked my bare little toe.

"We'll talk about the murder when Mike calls." Diana's words covered my agonized sound. "Ah, and I bet that's Mike now."

It wasn't.

It was Audrey.

"Thurston's doing a newsbreak at the top of the hour. Russell Teague's death."

"But that broke hours ago."

"He just found out. Elizabeth, he's going on live. And he's writing it himself. He keeps muttering about how you're not the only newsperson. He won't listen to anything I say. I tried to call Les, even though…"

Even though he hated being called and seldom helped anyway.

I looked at the clock. Our enemy and our friend.

"Audrey, you have great instincts not wanting him to screw this up. But you have to put your efforts where they will do the most good. How many people will see a live newsbreak? Let him win this. Save your ammunition and your time for the Five and Ten, when more people are watching."

More still being not many for KWMT-TV.

"Thank you, Elizabeth," she said fervently. "I will. I—" Shouting came from the background. "Gotta go."

We had the TV on when Thurston came on screen, still adjusting his tie.

HE PRESSED HIS lips together then said, "It is with deep regret that I inform you of the passing of a leading member of Cottonwood County, Wyoming. Russell Teague died this hour—"

"Wrong."

"—in Chicago Hospital."

"No such place."

"My sources—deep and well-informed sources have told me that among the beneficiaries of Russell Teague's will is Palmer Rennant, who so tragically died recently. Specifically, he inherits property owned by Russell in Cottonwood County.

"It is a testament to their friendship and meeting of minds on intellectual matters that the acreage here in Cottonwood County will pass from one friend to another."

"No, it won't."

"Shh," Diana ordered.

But it didn't matter. Thurston wrapped up with a promise of the complete story at five o'clock.

"Less than a minute on the air and three major errors. That has to be a record. Even for—That's got to be Mike."

"Sorry I'm late," he said. "The darned video's not working. Are you all there? What are you talking about?"

"All here. We listened to Thurston report that Russell left his ranch to Palmer Rennant."

"That's wrong," Mike said.

"Exactly what I said, but I didn't tell Diana and Jennifer more so you could reveal your scoop."

He told them about the split will, Tom being executor for the Wyoming holdings, the provisions about Palmer Rennant, the museum being the backup beneficiary.

"But that's what Thurston said. Rennant inherits all Teague's Wyoming stuff," Jennifer said. "That's a big motive for Willa to kill Palmer."

"They're divorced. Besides—" Mike objected.

"Then her kids. Close enough for—"

"Not them, either. Teague died *after* Palmer Rennant. Rennant couldn't inherit because you can't inherit when you're dead. He didn't get Teague's stuff, so he can't leave it to his heirs. Thurston was totally wrong. The museum gets it instead."

"Wow," Jennifer said.

"What if she didn't know?" Diana asked.

"Great point. In fact, the question of who knew is vital for several of them." I repeated what James said, concluding, "Meaning there's no public-record way for people to have known the will's provisions."

"More questions without answers?" Diana muttered. "This leaves out Rennant's heirs, too, right?"

"It cuts out *that* motive," I agreed. "But there could be personal motives."

"Like Willa decided a divorce wasn't enough," Mike said.

Jennifer added, "Or Otto and the dog. Or did we rule him out because of *why wait to kill the guy Thursday when he hit the dog Tuesday?*"

"That doesn't rule him out. He didn't have opportunity Tuesday because his nephew kept them apart at the vet's office. Didn't kill Rennant before Thursday afternoon, because Penny saw Rennant then. After that..." I shrugged.

"But what about what he heard Thursday night or early Friday morning? And you worked out that Otto heard the vehicle driving away after Devil's noisemaking, which should have triggered Rennant calling the sheriff's department and therefore he was dead and the fast driver was the killer?" Diana asked.

"Pretty neat reasoning," Mike said.

"That's easy. Otto lied. Devil went over there—the scratches prove the dog was there at some point—Rennant called Otto to complain, Otto went over there and killed him, then lied about the vehicle driving away fast in the middle of the night."

"How?" Diana asked. "How did Otto kill him?"

"That goes for anybody. We don't—"

"Wait. I talked to Aunt Gee. She was cagey, but the short answer is no, the sheriff's department doesn't know a cause of death. She talked about how long toxicology can take, so I'd say that rules out the obvious—shooting, stabbing, strangling, and blunt force trauma.

"Also, Elizabeth, she would not say if the sheriff's department views Rennant's house a potential murder scene, but they have pulled in his truck, but it will take a while to be gone over."

Before they could ask what that was about, I caught up Diana and Jennifer about my trip to Rennant's house and meeting Kamden Graf.

Then I brought us back to where we'd been.

"Along with the sheriff's department, we don't know the means. What we do know is the approximate gap between time of death and when he was found, that he stayed in that particular position until rigor was established, and that he wasn't discovered during that time." I reconsidered. "*Probably* he wasn't discovered. Let's say no one reported discovering him."

"You think somebody saw him and didn't mention it?" Diana did not like that idea.

"Possible."

"But Clara Atwood has to be the Number One suspect now," Mike said. "All that stuff going to the museum? Bet she gives herself a raise."

"It depends."

"Of course it does," Mike grumbled. "And here I thought I missed that phrase. Okay, Elizabeth, what does it depend on?"

"The obvious, for starters—did Clara Atwood know the museum was the backup beneficiary?" Then, I took another angle. "Remember your objection to my third possible reason for moving the body? That there were easier places to dump it and still have it found quickly? How about picking the buttes because you wanted to know when the body was found—so it was clear Palmer predeceased Teague—but you didn't want to be the finder yourself."

"Not bad."

Diana added, "The buttes would be familiar to Clara. Comfort level."

"Always wise for dumping a body." More prosaically, I added, "The roads to and from were almost certain to be deserted."

"She'd know immediately when the body was found," Diana said.

I pointed to her, signifying *you got it*. "Although, on the flip side, somebody like Otto could have wanted to get the body *away* from his place—and his dog. Chose the butte because the body would be found and he wouldn't be associated with it."

"That goes for several of the others." Mike said.

"Like who?" Jennifer challenged Mike.

"Willa," he responded immediately. "Jolie."

"You guys haven't seen Jolie, but the issue with her would be how she got Palmer's body there—or anywhere. She's emaciated."

"An accomplice?" Jennifer proposed. "Maybe she and her husband were in on it together?"

"What about Kamden Graf on his own?" Mike said.

"The business association stuff?"

"I have something—"

"Kamden?" Diana repeated doubtfully. Something was bugging her to have interrupted Jennifer that way. "Jolie has the motive, if Palmer dumped her or—"

I inserted, "Which we don't know."

"—something went wrong in the relationship."

But Diana's frown deepened as she spoke.

Chapter Fifty-Five

"**WHAT'S BOTHERING YOU?**" I asked her.

"What I hear keeps getting muddled."

"Muddled how?"

"First, there is nothing—I mean nothing—about Palmer Rennant having affairs before the divorce. He's been connected with a few people since, mostly in public dating situations, all the ones we know about. Pretty darned innocuous—movies in Cody, dinners at the country club, that sort of thing. Clara Atwood is generally considered a rebound situation, because it didn't last long."

And the end of their dating lined up timewise with the committee learning Rennant was kicking the camp and reenactment off his property.

"You said first, what's second?"

"Everyone I talked to heard rumors that Jolie Graf and Palmer Rennant were having an affair. They surfaced about three weeks ago. Starting at the country club. They seem to have spread from the pool set to the golf set, then beyond.

"But maybe half are inclined to dismiss it as a rumor with no grounding in reality. Including some folks who usually grab onto any rumor with both hands."

"That doesn't mean it's not true," Jennifer said.

"No," Diana agreed slowly. "But it is weird. And everybody I talked with *did* believe Kamden was having affairs—people who doubted Jolie was having an affair, were sure he was."

"Does Jolie know about them?" I asked.

"The general feeling is she's tried really hard not to, but even she couldn't miss them lately."

"Could that have started the rumors about an affair with Rennant? People felt like she *should* have an affair, and here was this recently divorced guy, the right age, the right social circle, and someone put one and one together for twenty-five?"

"I suppose." Diana's heart wasn't in it.

"Still, it gives Kamden a motive—jealousy."

Jennifer scoffed at Mike's suggestion. "If Kamden Graf was having all these affairs, he couldn't be mad at Jolie for having one."

Diana and I looked at each other, then her.

"*Au contraire, mon ami.*"

"What does that mean, Elizabeth?" she asked suspiciously.

"Literally, it means, to the contrary, my friend. What it means in this case is there are plenty of men and not a few women who think they're entitled to have an affair, but not their spouse. There was a news article about a woman who shot her boyfriend when he broke into their home and caught her doing the deed with someone else. She said she shot him because she hadn't given him *permission* to catch her."

Diana snorted.

"People are crazy. I like my research better." Jennifer paused. "Most of the time. Beside the early background on Palmer Rennant, I don't have much. But I put the guys on Russell Teague to cover the bases. They found a recent application for an LLC—Limited Liability Company—but it's really vague. One interesting thing is it used his address at the ranch, like it's something local, when his others don't. Wondered about that with Kamden and the business association stuff.

"I've had no success getting the postmortem. We've kicked around ideas, but…"

A three-way chorus of, "No hacking."

"Stay on that LLC," I told Jennifer. "Especially for any connection with Rennant or Graf. It sounds like they weren't going to limit themselves to going after the reenactment and Three Rivers Camp, but spreading out to broader history.

"I'll follow up with Willa, but Jennifer, if you could see about Fort

Phil Kearny—check if there was ever a Rennant there." I stared off for a moment. "Also see if you can access the first-hand accounts of the Miners' Camp Fight at the library. If you can send me copies, that would be great."

"Sure. You think there's a connection?"

"I have no idea. But I do have one more thing." I shared the Rennant family history, as told to me by Willa.

Jennifer reacted first. "Weird to get worked up about stuff like that."

"You'd be worked up if it were about your parents or grandparents."

"Because I *know* them."

"Some people feel strongly for more generations."

"Still weird. First, there's a lot less of some ancestor in you for each generation you go back. Four grandparents, eight grandparents, then sixteen, thirty-two, sixty-four, a hundred and twenty-eight, two hundred and fifty-six, five hundred and twelve ... And there's less and less chance you're related to the person with each generation."

We all looked at her. "How do you figure that?"

"Don't you watch those shows where celebrities find their ancestors and they do the DNA and find something completely off the wall—something that shouldn't be there if the people who were supposed to be related really were, so then you figure somewhere along the line, somebody had a baby who wasn't fathered by the husband, or somebody else was swapped at birth or *something*. So, chances are, Palmer Rennant wasn't even related to the guy who screwed up in the Civil War, must less the one who screwed up in the War of 1812."

That was certainly an interesting way to look at ancestry and family pride.

"It might be weird, Jennifer, but it seems to be Rennant's pattern," Diana said. "We have that from other people than his ex-wife—like Clara and Nadine—as well as his actions."

His pattern...

"There's that face," Diana said, as if from a distance.

"What face?" Mike demanded.

"The one that says something just clicked in Elizabeth's brain."

"Darn this broken video. I love that face."

And then I gave a little shiver and I was back in my living room and the voices were regular volume.

"What were you thinking about?" Jennifer asked.

"Palmer's patterns and scratch marks on Palmer's truck. Willa said Palmer always parked in front of the middle of the steps to his porch, because it was convenient for him and he didn't care it wasn't convenient for others."

"That fits what we've heard about him," Diana said.

"It does—it fits his pattern. But the truck *wasn't* parked there the day after he was found. It was parked thoughtfully off to the side."

After half a beat, Mike said, "Sheriff's department moved it so they could get in and out."

"They say they didn't. Then there were the scratches I told you about on the truck."

"I knew it—the dog did it."

I interrupted Diana. "Devil's not a suspect, but might be a witness."

She asked, "How do you figure that?"

"Devil's pattern. He doesn't just chase moving vehicles, he reacts when someone is *in* a vehicle, even if it's still. Remember when we went there and he was going nuts on the porch after we'd parked? But as soon as we got out of the SUV, he stopped. I saw the same thing with Willa. Devil was fine, then she got in her SUV and he barked and carried on immediately.

"When Otto let Devil out Thursday night or early Friday morning, he said the dog went to Rennant's house and made such a fuss he was sure Rennant would call and complain."

"Right. We figured that was because Rennant died before he could complain," Mike said.

"Yes, but why did Devil raise such a fuss?"

Diana got it first. "Because someone was in a vehicle at Rennant's house."

"Exactly. Someone curled up into a fetal position against the side of the passenger door, where Devil scratched. A position that explains the marks Aleek saw on the shoulder—under the attempts to paint his back and shoulders—and fits with the position set by rigor."

"Then why did the dog scratch at the front door? Rennant was in there first?"

"Or another person. Someone Devil wanted to follow, as he tried to at Otto's house. And that's the person Otto heard driving away fast. He'd thought it was before Devil raised his fuss, but when we went back over it, he realized it had to be after."

"Someone who?" Jennifer asked. "Willa?"

"That's the question, isn't it? But we know more than we did.

"That's if Otto didn't lie," Mike reminded us.

Chapter Fifty-Six

JENNIFER MESSAGED THAT she'd check with Fort Phil Kearny tomorrow and sent the link for accessing first-hand accounts by the Miners' Camp Fight survivors. They weren't long, but they were photos of handwritten pieces.

My eyes and my head ached. And no mention anywhere of a Rennant. Unless the handwriting was even worse than I thought.

By ten-thirty, I was tired of my own thoughts and no old movie was satisfying my itch.

Diana had gone home to her kids.

Jennifer was spending the evening with her family—so unreasonable of them to monopolize her.

Mike had done two sportscasts, then gone out with co-workers.

I called Diana.

"I know it's late, but I hoped you'd help me untangle my thoughts."

"I can't. And I have to get off the phone."

"Diana—?"

"Jess is an hour late and she's not answering her phone or messages. I have no idea where she is. She was upset about—She was upset, but she seemed better and I thought going out with her friends would help—But they're home now and she's not."

"I'm getting off the line. Message me if there's news or I can do anything—"

But I already had an idea of what I might be able to do.

As soon as we disconnected, I hit speed dial.

"Mom? It's Elizabeth. I know it's late and I hope I didn't wake you—"

"You didn't. I'm putting you on speaker. Jimmy, it's Elizabeth."

"Maggie Liz, great to hear from you. How's Sherman and Cottonwood County?"

"Hi Dad. It's fine."

"Except for another murder—or two," my mother said. I hadn't adjusted to my parents getting a personal stream of KWMT-TV, thanks to Jennifer. "But you're not calling about that."

"No. I was, uh, wondering how Bill, Anna, and the kids are since their return?"

A beat of silence came from Illinois. "I told you, Jimmy."

"So you did."

"Told him what?"

She didn't answer directly. "It's about J.R. and Jessica, isn't it?"

"Jessica?" Dad asked.

Mom clicked her tongue. "I told you that, too, Jimmy. The lovely girl in Wyoming. Diana's daughter."

That wiped out my wondering if Jessica had dumped J.R. Mom wouldn't have called her lovely if she'd dared to break a Danniher heart. If J.R. broke Jessica's heart, Mom would be sympathetic, but not as warm.

"What makes you think that, Mom?"

"Well, first, because you're calling." Score one for Mom. "Second, because J.R. was trying to take his brother's head off earlier this evening."

"Which brother?" I asked out of curiosity.

"Justin."

"What did Just do?"

"He took J.R.'s phone. They didn't know that at the start. They only knew J.R. was turning the house upside down because he couldn't find his phone. Justin disabled the find feature, which they didn't know until Bill thought to go to the neighbors where Justin was on a sleepover. He is truly gifted with electronics," said the proud grandmother. "Even with the phone back, J.R. was beside himself. Justin did something else to it that's causing a problem—temporary, I'm sure. Bill and Anna sat J.R. down and tried to talk sense to him."

Lots of luck talking sense to a teenager who thought he was in love. Especially for the first time.

Mom scoffed. "Sense. With a teenager."

Good heavens, my mother was becoming me.

"What kind of sense?"

"To look up from his phone once in a while," Dad said. "He's been physically present and not with us ever since we got back from Wyoming—great visit, by the way. You should have seen those kids at Yellowstone. And you made it possible by getting us out there to Wyoming."

"You thanked me multiple times already, Dad."

Mom got us back on track. "J.R. was frantic that Jessica would think he was ignoring her. He tried to use his mother's phone, but didn't know Jessica's contact information. It's all programmed into his phone. That made him more upset."

"Ah."

"Elizabeth? Is something wrong? Is it Jessica?" Had to be Mom radar.

"I don't know exactly. But you've helped. I'll call—"

"You'll tell us what you can tell us when you can tell us," Dad said.

Mom didn't commit to that restraint.

✧ ✧ ✧ ✧

I HELD MY phone looking at it.

I could call—but my call would jolt the fear adrenaline in Diana's system.

A message? Not the best medium to convey nuance.

Oh, hell.

I drove to Diana's ranch, with Shadow as shotgun.

Well, not shotgun. Fine for humans, too dangerous for my dog.

✧ ✧ ✧ ✧

I KNOCKED ON the door to Diana's ranch house, opened it, and called, "It's me, Elizabeth," all at once.

Diana spun around from the sink. I also spotted Gary in the darkness of the hallway that led to the bedrooms.

"Elizabeth, what are you doing here? Have you heard something—?"

"No. I came to wait with you."

Shadow passed me and went to Gary, who dropped down next to him.

With him taken care of, I went to Diana. A look from her held me off from hugging, but she squeezed my arm briefly before letting go abruptly.

"She's always been home by her curfew. She's an hour past. And she's alone. She dropped off the two girls she was with and they said they had no idea where she went. She didn't say anything to them."

Anxiety had set her mouth going. Better to let it run or pull her up short? I had no idea. I experienced an unexpected longing to call Mom.

"I don't know if that's girlfriend solidarity against the parent or it's true, because she can keep things to herself, but—"

"Diana, is Jessica upset about J.R.? I have it from an excellent source that he's been upset most of the day because Justin hid his phone, disabled the find function, then messed up something else. They only found out a short while ago and Justin was read the riot act ... at the same time they're talking to J.R. about being less obsessive."

"He hasn't broken up with her?"

"Good heavens, no. He's beside himself about being out of contact. In fact, it's a little crazy—"

"It's a *lot* crazy. But I must be weak, because I can only be grateful he didn't break up. She wouldn't tell me what happened. She was trying to be so cool and unfazed. I thought letting her go with the girls might make that pose become real." She scraped her hair back from her forehead with one hand. "I should have known—"

She broke off and jabbed at her ringing phone with far more strength than it needed.

"Hello? Yes. ... Yes. ... Yes. ... Okay."

She ended the call, sucked in a breath, then filled a glass with water and drank it down. She filled one for me, then refilled hers.

This one she drank more slowly.

Then, her head tipped slightly.

Her gaze came to me, but she pitched her voice to the hallway. "She's okay. Russ—Sheriff Conrad—has her. They're on their way. Should be here soon."

"That's great." I spoke loudly, as if that would cover the ragged breath from the back hall we all heard and pretended not to.

"You should be in bed, Gary." Diana's voice had regained its mother certainty.

"I don't get to hear you yell at her?"

"Now."

Gary peered at me from the hallway. "Can Shadow stay with me?"

I wasn't nearly as good as Diana at laying down the law. "Until I leave."

"Overnight and he can sleep in my bed."

Shadow looked at me, too. He never got to sleep in the bed at home.

"Until I leave, but I won't pay attention to where he is until it's time to leave."

"Deal. C'mon, Shadow."

The guys left, six feet patting away into the deeper dark.

"Thanks," Diana said dryly. "Dog hair. Just the thing to top off an adolescent boy's sheets."

I shrugged. "He wore me down."

"Yeah. You put up a valiant fight."

"I thought so."

"Speaking of a valiant fight, are Bill and Anna doing any better with keeping J.R. in touch with reality than I am with Jessica?"

"Doesn't sound like it. Maybe you guys should talk? If the parents at both end of the messaging orgy are united..."

"You think they'd be open to that."

"I do, but I'll check."

"This blew up so fast and so strong... I don't even know what's normal for teenagers messaging each other when they're across the country."

We talked about that. And her worries about parenting a teenager in the throes of first love. I said that as far as I could tell there were no right answers, though there were some awful ones and avoiding those was the primary goal. In the midst of telling her she was the best person I knew for avoiding awful answers, I broke off.

We'd both heard a vehicle outside.

Jessica came in first, nearly levitating with rage. I suppose that was better than misery.

Sheriff Russ Conrad followed with stolid neutrality.

"You can thank *him* for your truck not being here." Not looking at her mother, Jessica rattled out words like bullets. "He wouldn't let me drive back. He made me just *leave* the truck out there. It'll probably be *stolen*. I just needed to *think*. And it's all too *stupid*."

"You are not allowed to drive after 11 p.m." Conrad's voice still had the cop calm, but he'd had a good look at Diana by now and stolid was gone, along with neutrality. A muscle jumped in his jaw.

I heard Gary's—and Shadow's—stealthy return to the listening post in the dark hallway.

"That's just *stupid*—"

"The top two time periods for teen driver fatal crashes are six to nine p.m. and nine to midnight. You're also not supposed to drive with more than one non-family member under eighteen. But you had two girlfriends with you earlier."

"One's eighteen," Diana said quietly. "She was sick as a girl and missed more than a year of school. I wouldn't let Jessica break the rules."

Conrad heard her, but I doubted Jess did. She was focused on the sheriff.

Gary crept forward, his face now visible. Shadow's head rested on his thigh while my dog's worried brown eyes went from face to face.

"You wouldn't understand, because you're not human—"

"*Jessica*."

"—but I needed my friends. Besides, I dropped them both off."

Jessica's tone flounced with disdain.

"You didn't need them more than you need to stay alive. Teens are ten times more likely to be in a fatal car crash than adults."

"You're not my father."

As an outside observer, I wanted to take points off that accusation for lack of originality. On the other hand, it was a classic because it drove the point of the knife in deep.

"No. I'm the sheriff. And I've been out on too many calls when a kid like you thinks the laws of physics and reason don't apply to them and they end up as blood and guts and bones on the highway."

Color ebbed from Jessica's face, but not as much as from Diana's face.

"Too many times I've had to go and tell the parents that's all that's left of their son or daughter and the kid isn't coming home ever again. The last thing on this great earth I want to do is bring that kind of news to your mother because she loves you and I love her."

My focus popped around like a pinball.

Jessica's color rushing back so fast I thought she might keel over. Gary's face twisting into a silent *Ewww* at the display of adult emotions. Diana's eyes widening with shock, while her hand went to her throat. Conrad's intensity receding against the realization of what he'd said, when he'd said it, and to whom he'd said it.

But grim determination quickly shored up Conrad's intensity. Grim determination would take the glow off a declaration of love for most women, but Diana's mile-wide stripe of practicality took it in stride.

I wondered what my expression showed as I realized that not only was this the first time Jessica and Gary were hearing that Sheriff Russ Conrad loved their mother, but it was the first time Diana had heard it. Possibly the first time he'd realized it.

Gary finally emitted the "Ewww" he'd been working up to.

It unfroze the tableau.

Jessica spun around and ran past him toward her room.

Diana gave Conrad a look that both bestowed and asked for patience, then followed her.

Gary followed up—in case we hadn't understood his earlier sentiment—with, "Gross." Then he, too, headed for the hallway to his bedroom and Jessica's, with Shadow behind him so as not to miss out on any in-the-bed time.

"Don't say it," Conrad ordered without looking at me.

"Don't say what? Great timing? Deft touch?" He growled after each question. "Or that if you hurt her—or them—I'll hunt you down and destroy you with a clear conscience and, even if Shelton makes the arrest, I won't have a single regret. On the other hand, if you make her happy, I'll continue to tolerate you."

"Might be the nicest thing you've ever said to me." The driest of smiles accompanied that.

"More than you deserve. But I go the extra mile for Diana."

"Better watch it. At this rate, we'll become friends. Friendly," he amended immediately.

"I'd never rule out miracles. Especially if you get your head on straight and get smart about Jessica and Gary."

He shifted his gaze toward me without moving his head. "What would be smart?"

"How about instead of spouting statistics at them, have them dig up the statistics themselves. Have them teach each other, essentially."

Now he faced me. "Sort of like you do when you report those stories that keep you out of my hair, when consumers warn other consumers about scams, not just the officials issuing the same old warnings."

His interest and enthusiasm scared the bejabbers out of me. Cautiously, I said, "Yes, sort of like that."

"Hmmm."

Only partly because his reaction kicked in my atavistic instinct for self-preservation, I gathered up my things.

"Tell Diana I'm leaving Shadow tonight for his healing properties, we can arrange a handoff tomorrow, and none of them should overindulge him with treats. Got that?"

"Maybe I better go, too."

"No way, Conrad. First, you relay my instructions. Second, you said it and now you wait for Diana to straighten as much as she can with her daughter tonight before you say it again, like it should be said."

DAY SEVEN

WEDNESDAY

Chapter Fifty-Seven

AFTER YESTERDAY'S WAY too early rising, last night's drama at Diana's, and a restless effort to sleep that I was not prepared to admit might have been from not having Shadow around, I rolled over and went back to sleep after my eyes opened the first time with the bird-chirping penetrating my consciousness in a way it rarely did.

The phone had a different idea.

It rang less than a minute after reclosing my eyes.

I could have waited it out, but caller ID said Audrey Adams, KWMT-TV.

"Elizabeth, the sheriff's department's called a news conference."

"What about?" They'd already solved—?

"Only said an ongoing case. Thirty-five minutes in the sheriff's office."

Thoughts about the potential topic of the news conference sank beneath the jolt of the timing. "Thirty-five minutes? I'll barely get there in time. What about—?"

"He's on his way. Not happy because it's early. He's probably already planning an extra nap this afternoon. If you don't want to go... At least the story will get on-air with him covering it. Diana's on another assignment, but I'm sending Jenks," Audrey said.

"Good." The veteran cameraman had become my second-favorite. "I'm going, but Thurston will insist on doing the story."

"I know."

"I'll send you bullet points to check his story."

"Thank you," she said fervently.

Glad somebody's day had improved.

MY PHONE RANG again—probably a good thing, because I'd closed my eyes again. The call came fast enough to be an I-forgot-something-callback. I answered only with hello.

"Elizabeth?"

Not Audrey. A male voice, familiar.

"Yes, this is Elizabeth Margaret Danniher of KWMT-TV."

"James Longbaugh here. There's going to be an announcement about the disposition of Russell Teague's Wyoming holdings. It will be held at the Teague Ranch. You're welcome to come."

"A news conference?"

"Wouldn't call it that."

"But you're inviting the media?"

"Inviting you. And a few other selected people."

"Okay, what time?"

"I'm asking you to meet at a, uh, staging location rather than going directly to Teague Ranch. If you'd be at the Circle B in two hours, please."

Tom Burrell's ranch.

Not a choice based solely on geography, even though Teague's was the next ranch north of the Circle B. Executor duties? I felt my forehead crinkling as my eyebrows rose.

But all I said was, "I'll be there."

And hoped the Cottonwood County Sheriff's Department was succinct.

SHERIFF RUSS CONRAD stood behind his desk—swept clear of its usual papers, the computer screen turned off, and no keyboard in sight.

He looked tired. Others might think it was from working hard on whatever led to this announcement. I knew better.

Shelton was on one side of him. Alvaro, Sampson, and the main desk officer named Ferrante on the other. I had the impression Ferrante slipped in front of the other two at the last second.

Jenks was there and set up.

Not straight in front, which would produce a boring and flat shot, but slightly at an angle to Conrad, with the potential to shift to Shelton and the trio.

He winked at me.

He'd taken the best position, leaving a crew from Cody a less advantageous spot. We were hitting the big-time to draw crews from out of town.

It also meant the sheriff's department called Cody well before notifying KWMT-TV of the news conference. Unless Thurston had turned off notifications again.

Needham and Cagen came in, both nodding to me. Needham eyed Jenks' set-up and sat in the one chair that would ruin it.

Jenks said, "Hey."

Needham feigned innocence, the old devil. He did move, though.

Sheriff Conrad gathered attention with a slight shift.

"I won't stand on ceremony. You all know who I am. I'm here today to let you know about fine policing done by the Cottonwood County Sheriff's Department in identifying the body found Saturday in a cave in the buttes. That successful effort was led by Sergeant Wayne Shelton. He will give you the information. Sergeant Shelton."

The two men swapped spots, with the sheriff stepping behind Shelton, an unexpected gesture of modesty or generosity.

Or cleverness.

Especially since his self-introduction minimized the way it could be used in packages.

Conrad took over as sheriff less than a year ago and, in a few more years, he'd face an election. He had a reputation for toughness. That might not get him support in the department. But ensuring the credit went to Shelton, who was popular with the deputies for unfathomable reasons, would.

Shelton looked at each of the members of the media as if we were suspects.

"The body found Saturday in a cave in our county was that of a long-time Cottonwood County resident last seen alive sixty-one years ago, by the name of Luther Tipton."

Chapter Fifty-Eight

I SURE GOT my wish for succinct.

Though not my wish for much information. At least they confirmed he was Sally's father.

I was messaging Jennifer—and cc'ing the others—to call off the hunt for missing people in Cottonwood County, when Thurston Fine stood to leave with an aggrieved sniff.

"A waste of my time," he grumbled as he walked to the door, cutting off other people trying to exit. "Nobody cares about a nobody missing for decades."

I couldn't totally disagree with the first part, since Shelton and Conrad clamped the lid down on any information past the identification and information from the original report that Tipton had been involved in a bar fight. Arriving law enforcement found the other participant badly hurt and no sign of Tipton.

The next day, the other man died. Tipton's truck was found not far away from the bar, out of gas. The official conclusion at the time was he'd wandered off and died somewhere.

As for now, officials decreed no *speculating* on the cause of death, how or why Luther Tipton was found in a cave in the buttes, or anything else.

Their refrain was that the investigation awaited results from scientific experts looking at the remains.

Echoing my earlier question to Radford Hickam, I asked if there was any reason to rule out natural causes. That got a "that would be speculation at this time" and twin scowls.

The second half of Thurston's plaint—that nobody cared—was laughable, unless you worked for the same station he did, which drained the humor.

As Jenks passed, I said quietly, "Audrey knows it's a good story. You'll get plenty of footage in."

He winked and kept going.

As I messaged Audrey suggesting she put together a package for the network with today's announcement supplemented by Diana's best footage from the weekend, the Cody crew left, chattering about how viewers would love this up and they sure wished they could get into the cave. If only there hadn't been another murder outside it.

I stifled my victorious grin. Wait until they saw Diana's stuff.

Needham patted my shoulder, then leaned down to say close to my ear, "Some stories shouldn't be chased."

I looked up in surprise, but he'd already moved on.

I remained seated.

What was bugging me about this?

We now knew who the body in the cave was. He'd been missing more than sixty years, declared dead more than fifty years ago. Hickam had basically said he couldn't rule out foul play, but couldn't rule out an accident, either.

"You going to sit there all day?"

I looked up and saw Shelton and I were the only ones left in the sheriff's office. Even Russ Conrad had left.

"Maybe. Unless you answer some questions—No, not the ones you already said you wouldn't answer. New ones. You suspected it was Luther Tipton from the start, didn't you?"

He almost grinned, replacing the urge with his more habitual scowl. But he pulled around a chair and sat facing me.

"Kept it in mind as a possibility. Only man in the county who went missing that period."

"How'd you know what period before UW got the body?"

"Vehicle keys. Right period. Right kind for what he drove."

"There were keys by the body and you didn't tell me?" I hoped my indignation sufficiently covered Lloyd Sampson's derriere from any exposure.

His information hadn't helped much, but that wasn't his fault and I wanted to keep him in a position to be a source—unwitting, but still a source.

Another part of my mind, though, noted that Mrs. Parens hadn't had those advantages, yet I'd swear—

"Not my job to tell you. As for the wallet, wasn't surprised Luther Tipton's wallet survived all these years. He didn't ever pull it out voluntarily."

"You said he went missing nearly sixty-one years ago. You couldn't have known—"

"Glad you can do that much math, anyway. I wasn't even thought of then. But my father and I used to go over the county's cold cases, from the time I was a kid. Different one each weekend."

"Some families play board games or cards, maybe put together a puzzle. Figures the Sheltons combed over cold cases."

He didn't deign to respond. "My father always said Luther Tipton kept his money in an iron grip."

"And what did your mother say? Was there any rhubarb pie involved with Luther Tipton?"

Rhubarb pie had figured into his parents' interactions with another old-time Cottonwood County resident and with their courtship.

He *tch'ed*. "She was a teenager when he disappeared. Dad not much older."

"Disappeared, huh?"

"There one day, gone the next—or one night. After the fight outside the bar. Other guy died, Luther disappeared, presumed dead. The county didn't go into mourning over either one."

I'd heard him tell the story about the bar fight from the original reports. Just wasn't sure I believed it. "Not well liked?"

I remembered Mrs. Parens saying her father worked for Luther Tipton for a brief time, leaving over his employer's treatment of animals and people.

"Doesn't mean anything. Most folks stayed away from him. And he wasn't the kind to go toe-to-toe. More a sidewinder."

"*Sidewinder*? Who are you? Gabby Hayes?"

"Gabby Hayes? Who are you? A hundred-year-old cowboy?"

"I might have watched a few old movies lately. Nothing wrong with that. It expands our horizons and puts us in touch with our cultural past. But what about the people who couldn't stay away from Luther Tipton? Like his family. Like Sally."

He lifted one shoulder. "Sally was a kid."

"You and I both know that doesn't mean she couldn't have killed him. Especially if…"

"Never any rumors about him messing with her."

But he and his Dad had considered it during their cold case roundtables, or he wouldn't have answered so quickly. "What about Sally's mother?"

"Long dead. Driven into an early grave, according to most of the county."

"Just him and Sally, living alone?"

"Not for long. He married a woman from South Dakota about six months after they buried Sally's mother."

"Ah."

"No *ah*." He exhaled shortly. "They looked into that. Looked into it plenty. The stepmother and Sally were both on the place when he disappeared. Came into town to report it together. Sheriff tried to get one to say they'd seen the other do something suspicious, or had been away for a while to open an opportunity. They said they were together the whole time."

"Mutual alibis? Really? Nobody considered they could be accomplices?"

"Problem with that is everybody said Sally and the stepmother hated each other—neighbors, the school, the preacher, even the band of despicables Luther played cards and drank with. No outward conflict, because Luther would whale away on both if either of them disrupted his peace … or for other reasons if the spirit moved him. But never spent a second with each other they didn't have to. Didn't have a good word to say about each other."

"Misdirection? Conspiracy?" I'd used those same words with Mrs.

P in a discussion of a hypotheses about the Montana Road and the building of the railroad ... when the discussion wasn't about that at all.

"Then it was a conspiracy they started the day Luther brought his second wife back to Cottonwood County and it continued every day before and after his disappearance. Everybody said, those two females did not like each other."

He looked at me without moving his head.

"Including Emmaline Parens. As soon as the Tipton place sold and they split the proceeds in front of an old judge—who declared Luther gone for good, if not dead until the seven years were up—the stepmother packed up and went back to South Dakota. Barely waited long enough to put Sally with a local family. That's where she stayed until she finished school. Her share from the sale of the property was enough for that little house of hers. Right out of school, she started working at the high school cafeteria and stayed there until she retired."

"But if Luther Tipton left his vehicle on the highway, how did he get to—?"

He stood. "No more buts. No more questions. Get your foot out of the door, Danniher. Metaphorically speaking. Time for you to go. And that's not metaphorically speaking."

Chapter Fifty-Nine

BEFORE I WAS even out the sheriff's department door—not meta-phorically speaking—my phone rang.

The sheriff's department news conference.

James Longbaugh's call.

What next?

I kept walking to be clear of listening ears. It also gave me a chance to see I had a message from Jennifer.

It rang twice more before I answered.

Aunt Gee was what was next.

"You need to come to the hospital, Elizabeth. Sally wants to see you. Right now."

"You said that before, but—"

"You and Diana. She's on her way. We need you both."

DIANA APPEARED AT the open driver's window of my SUV in the hospital parking lot, startling only half of the life out of me.

"Putting off going inside?"

"I'm making phone calls," I said with dignity. I held up my phone. "Say hi to Mike and Jennifer."

Diana had circles under her eyes but seemed cheerful. I added those to Conrad's appearance and came up with a suspicion.

"Hi, Mike and Jennifer. Wait a second and I'll get in the passenger seat so I can hear better."

With her settled in beside me, Mike said, "Okay, enough build-up.

Who's the body in the cave? No fair keeping Jennifer and me in suspense."

"I already know," Jennifer said. "Elizabeth messaged me from the news conference. And it's my fault we didn't figure it out first. If I'd started searching missing people from my setup right away instead of being in Chicago—"

"Hey, it's not anybody's *fault* and the important thing is the body's identified," I said.

"Who *is* the body?" Mike asked plaintively. "Everybody knows but me."

"Luther Tipton. Sally's father."

"Sally Tipton's father? Why isn't he in the cemetery like everybody else?"

"He went missing when Sally was barely a teenager. Long presumed dead, but now the question is what was he doing in the cave."

"Oh, right, I do remember hearing something about that. Interesting. Has he been in the cave all along?"

"Looks like it. Shelton suspected it was Luther from the start. He was holding out on us and still is. News conference my derriere. It was a deliberate move to get the word out widely so we couldn't find it out ourselves, then leverage that information to force more information out of Shelton."

"When you put it that way, it was downright rude of them to disclose the ID," Diana said.

"Go ahead, be sarcastic, but it was."

"Elizabeth. The experts found enough identification in the man's wallet to make it official—"

"And that's another thing. Not waiting for the DNA? The final report from the forensic anthropologist?"

"You know the dental records matched."

"After sixty years? How is that even possible?"

"It's possible when the current Dr. Fortinel is the third generation in that practice and they don't throw anything out."

"How do you know all details, Diana?" Jennifer asked.

"Jenks sent me his footage."

"What's the big deal?" Mike asked. "Luther's been dead a long time, no matter what. Not like your other victim."

"Not *my* victim—"

"You know what I mean."

Jennifer spoke up. "About Palmer Rennant, did you make anything of those Miners' Camp Fight accounts?"

I groaned. "I read them. Not much."

"Me, either. Took me forever to decipher that handwriting. I kept trying to figure out why they were capitalizing *When* until I realized it was the name of one of the guys. I thought it was *the deserted When*, but it must have been *they deserted When* … and then the poor guy had his head split open. They must have felt guilty about it."

I hadn't gotten any sense of guilt from what I'd read, but I'd have to try the difficult handwriting again. I had gotten more than his head was split open.

"You know, one good thing about the sheriff's department's news conference," Mike said, "is it solves one of those three mysteries you said we had going. We can put more energy in this … and Mrs. P."

Unwilling to acknowledge Luther Tipton as wrapped up, I said. "We've gotta go. Sally Tipton asked to see us. Both of us."

Mike said. "She's up and talking? Good for her. I thought she wasn't doing well."

"She isn't."

✧ ✧ ✧ ✧

"HOW'D IT GO after I left last night?" I asked Diana as we walked into the hospital.

"First, thank you for coming. I might not have shown how much I appreciated the support. Shadow was a huge help. He was in with Gary. Then, when I was leaving Jessica's room, he slipped in and crawled in with her. He put each of my kids to bed last night."

This time I'd been able to be a body brace for her. Nice to be able to return the favor. Well, me and my dog.

She sighed. "It's going to be a process. I might have hugged Shadow a time or two, myself."

"That bad?"

She chuckled, then looked surprised at herself. "Russ was still there when I came out. He said you threatened him if he didn't stay."

"That's accurate."

"Thanks. We talked. A good talk."

"I sure hope that's not all you did."

"That's all I'm prepared to tell you about."

"Fair enough. When do I get my dog back?"

"I'm taking off work early, I'll pick him up and bring him over then. Both kids have activities until late."

Chapter Sixty

WITH DIFFICULTY AND using her left hand, Sally Tipton took up a fat pencil from the table that extended over her bed. She wrapped her fingers around the barrel with the point straight down.

"She wants the paper," Aunt Gee said.

When Mrs. P didn't move to fulfill that want, Aunt Gee clicked her tongue in impatience and moved up the left side of the bed.

Mrs. Parens had made her objections clear—even clearer than before—in the hallway, stating that Sally was in no state to see me or Diana.

When a nurse said Sally had been so agitated last night when the TV news came on and had worn herself out so completely with writing *see* and my initials that fulfilling her wish had to be better for her than not, Mrs. P gave her a look she usually reserved for Mike's worst Wyoming history gaffes.

The nurse withstood it better than the former NFL player. She even added that Sally's further agitation when Diana appeared for a moment on a station promo that was nine-tenths Thurston and one-tenth the rest of the staff from two years ago, persuaded her in consultation with Gee that Diana needed to be here, too.

"This is entirely against my best judgment. This is ill-advised," Mrs. Parens declared. "If you insist on this, however, you shall not mention the announcement made by the sheriff's department."

"How do you already know—?"

"Oh, it's all over the hospital," the nurse said.

Mrs. Parens ignored us. "Not under any circumstances shall it be mentioned. Do you understand?"

With that caveat, here we were, in Sally's room.

For the second time.

The first time we went in, Sally had grown agitated again, nodding and jabbing her left hand in the direction of Diana with an odd circling motion.

Diana got it first. "My camera?"

Sally stopped gesturing.

Diana returned with it, giving me an eyebrows-up look.

I lifted one shoulder half an inch.

Diana began filming.

As Gee told me Monday, one side of Sally's face drooped. She seemed shrunken, but more so on the right side, which did not move. But her eyes, devoid of her usual mask of coyness and silliness, were more direct and determined than I had seen them.

Now, Gee cleared a space on the table and put the pad under the erratic point of the pencil.

Sally focused on the paper, but her pencil didn't contact it.

After a pause, Mrs. Parens blew out a short breath. Impatience? Sorrow? I couldn't tell.

Sally's head came up slightly, as if she intended to look at Mrs. P, but the move wasn't enough to reach that destination. In the next instant, her head dropped back down and the pencil tip finally connected to the paper.

She drew one wavery line down the paper, started another, even more irregular. A second try at the initial line or another part of the design? Either way, it appeared destined to cross the first line, until her hand jerked and the pencil tore the paper.

Sally looked toward Gee.

"A fresh sheet? Just one moment." Gee pulled away the first sheet and arranged the second.

Sally panted with exertion, her hand shook more, and the pencil did not make contact.

It seemed she started to look toward Mrs. P, but if so, she changed her mind and directed her gaze to Gee again.

"What if I support your arm, Sally. Will that help?"

Sally gave no response. Her face had gone gray, but she seemed determined to convey something with that pencil.

Gee said, "Blink once if you want me to support your arm and twice if you do not want me to."

Without moving her head, Sally looked toward Gee and blinked once.

We waited. No second blink followed.

Gee cupped her hands under the older woman's forearm, then positioned Sally's fisted hand over the paper.

"Ouija board," Mrs. P muttered.

A new shaky line emerged down the sheet. After a few panting breaths, Sally began another line, this one intersected with the first more emphatically than her previous attempt. Sally sank back against the pillows of her raised bed, her eyes closed. She held onto the pencil as if the effort to release those muscles was too much.

Aunt Gee and I looked at the paper, though Mrs. Parens appeared to ignore it.

When Sally opened her eyes, she looked from Gee to Mrs. Parens to me, with an exhausted air of inquiry. Having arrived at me her gaze remained there.

"An X?" I asked.

Mrs. P gave me a peeved glance.

I ignored her.

Sally stared at me, then blinked twice.

"Okay, I can see that one tail is longer than the other, so not an X." I squinted at the marks. "Two creeks? Or rivers? Two Rivers Camp? Or—Sorry. I should only ask one thing at a time."

Sally blinked twice.

Trying to decide if that was no to creeks or rivers or the camp or my asking one thing at a time, I moved to the side table and poured water into the mug there with a straw. When I turned back, though, the notion of negotiating the logistics of giving the woman the water without usurping her autonomy yet without setting her up for failure swamped me.

Without a word, Mrs. Parens took the mug from my hand and moved with it to the top of the bed by Sally's head. She placed the end of the straw in Sally's slightly open mouth.

Mrs. P's move shunted me back, giving me a new angle on the paper.

"A cross?" I asked.

Above the mug, Sally blinked once.

"A cross." I heard a thread of triumph in my voice at getting it right.

That faded quickly. Because what did a cross signify?

"The hospital chaplain?" Aunt Gee asked. "You want for folks to pray for you?"

Two blinks for each.

"A Christian burial?" Aunt Gee tried again.

Sally blinked once.

"You shall receive one." Mrs. Parens spoke quickly. Almost as if she'd been prepared for that, yet she hadn't offered it as an interpretation. She hadn't offered any interpretation at all. In fact, she could be seen as trying to circumvent this entire line of communication.

Sally blinked twice.

"Yes, you shall," Mrs. Parens said in her sternest voice.

Sally blinked twice, waited, then blinked twice again, a pause, then two more blinks, a pause, then two more.

As she did, I thought about Mrs. P's reactions concerning Sally and today's hot news topic around Cottonwood County.

Mrs. P knew something I didn't.

That wasn't all that unusual.

But this something appeared to be also unknown by Aunt Gee, which was highly unusual, and to involve Sally Tipton.

Taking a leap, I asked the woman in the bed, "You're not concerned for yourself?"

One blink.

"Is your concern for the man they found?" I was aware of Mrs. P stirring beside me, but kept my gaze on Sally.

She blinked once.

"Do you know who it is?"

She blinked once. Then moved the pencil to the paper. Aunt Gee supported her arm. She created a stick figure with a lopsided head and shaky limbs, but identifiable. Then she moved the pencil next to this and created another one half the size of the first.

Breathing hard at the exertion, she looked up at me.

"Two people?" I didn't want to jump to conclusions or push her in any direction.

She blinked once. Then her hand and the pencil hovered over the smaller figure before bending her arm to bring it closer to her chest.

She looked up at me again.

"You? It's you?"

She expelled a breath that sort of whistled out of her mouth, and blinked once.

Then she jerked her hand from the smaller figure to the larger one and back. The pencil touched the paper, creating jagged lines between the two as she made two more passes.

"You're connected to this other person. You were a child and—"

"Your mother?" Aunt Gee asked.

"No." Mrs. Parens' tone made both Aunt Gee and me look at her. She pressed her lips tightly together. "We shall leave now. Clearly, we have tired Sally and that cannot be good for her. As well as likely making her mind wander."

I might have gaped at Mrs. P. My reaction inside was pure gape, I just don't know if my mouth muscles got with the program.

She was abrupt. She was almost rude. She certainly wasn't considerate of Sally's possible feeling about her abilities.

Gee did not gape. Instead, apparently seeing this as an opportunity to move ahead in an arena when Mrs. P was retiring from the lists, she said in a low tone, "She was reading Needham's article about Palmer Rennant and what you found in that cave at the butte when she had the stroke. She must have guessed... She must have."

"We will not—" Mrs. Parens started.

More loudly, Gee asked the woman in the bed, "Your father, Sally?"

She blinked once.

Frowning, I asked, "You want a Christian burial for your father?"

She blinked once.

Then she pointed at me.

Chapter Sixty-One

I PLACED A cup of tea in front of Emmaline Parens where she sat by the windows in the mostly empty hospital cafeteria.

"Sometimes," I said, "I feel I'm way behind on these inquiries because I'm not from here, don't know the layers of origin stories, don't know the ins and outs of the connections and eruptions of more recent events, don't know the intricacies of the land, don't even speak the language."

Mrs. Parens regarded me, possibly waiting to see if there were more cars on that freight train of self-pity. Or, possibly, of frustration.

"Sally wants a Christian burial for her father. Wanted Diana to tape her request. Oh-*kay*. But a request of *me* to see to it? And you didn't want her to communicate that to me? I don't get it."

I raised my hands and let them drop on a loud exhale.

"It occurs to me that in this situation, as in those you have resolved, not knowing the things you listed has given you a connection with and an understanding of others who have more recently come to Cottonwood County. In addition," Mrs. Parens continued, "what you have listed as absences of knowledge or skill have the effect of giving you a different, one might even say fresher, view of relationships, events, and personalities than might be drawn by those of us with the history, language, and knowledge."

"Great. Except now I'm tasked with seeing to a Christian burial for this guy, when…"

When I suspected the woman who'd given me that task of being involved in his murder.

And why not Mrs. Parens? She was the natural—Ah.

That sense I'd had Monday that Mrs. P hadn't been talking only about her stance on the Montana Road and the railroad crossing southern Wyoming clicked.

She'd been talking about Sally, her stepmother, and Luther.

I have not found research that sheds direct light on any connection, much less confirms one. ... As long as certain facts remain out of your grasp, it remains a hypothesis, not a conclusion, nor a demonstrable fact.

She'd suspected—strongly suspected—but never had the facts to... What?

She'd been a teenager herself when Luther was killed. Not sure of her own suspicions or simply knowing they couldn't be substantiated? But over the years, had she watched Sally closely?

Had she drawn me into Sally's orbit in an earlier investigation not to protect Sally nor to prove her innocent, but to make sure she was looked at closely in case she had killed again?

I didn't have answers. Only more questions: What would I have done in those circumstances? What was I going to do now?

"You have looked at your watch twice in the past minute, Elizabeth. If you have an appointment, do not let me make you late."

Actually, I planned to be late.

"Saturday, up at the butte, when I showed you a photo of Palmer Rennant's watch, you said you were no expert in men's watches. That was not an answer to my question."

She met my gaze squarely. "It was the only answer I was prepared to give until I talked with the authorities. As it turned out, the authorities knew his identity before I was called upon to offer my suspicion."

That was the only reason? To give Shelton first dibs on her information?

"To your knowledge, does Palmer Rennant's death and finding Luther Tipton's body in that cave intersect in any way?" At a glimmer in her eyes, I added, "Beyond geography."

"No."

We looked at each other for a long moment.

Mrs. Parens wasn't lying.

She also wasn't telling me everything.

I SHOVED MY sunglasses to the top of my head as I took in the reality that I was first to arrive at the Circle B Ranch.

How on earth had that happened, when I was twelve minutes after the time James Longbaugh set?

Tamantha sat on the porch steps, alone.

I parked and went to sit next to her, exchanging hellos.

"We couldn't *really* talk at the camp with all those kids around." Before I fully processed that warning, she said, "Mike's gone. Why aren't you Daddy's girlfriend again?"

I pulled in a breath. "I'm going to tell you something hard, Tamantha."

She turned to better aim her direct gaze at me.

"That's not your business. That's between your father and me. But I'll tell you something else. What's between you and me is strong on its own and it doesn't need me dating your father."

Under her open, intelligent examination I felt her doubt. "I don't want you to go away."

I swallowed. Had we left not dating her father and arrived at the death of her mother?

I put my hand on her back. "I could tell you I won't ever go away, but you know I don't control *ever*. What I do promise is I'll always be your friend. Remember, you and I knew each other first."

She blinked, clearly struck by that. "We were friends first."

More like she gave me orders, but this wasn't the time for such nuances. "Yes."

She put her hand on my knee. "Okay."

Behind us, the front door opened and Tom came down the porch steps.

"Mrs. George is waiting for you to decide what flavor cupcakes you're making, Tamantha."

She hopped up. "Gotta go. See you, Elizabeth."

"Bye, Tamantha." I stood, too. To face her father.

"You're early." He sounded justifiably surprised.

I took the sunglasses off the top of my head. Something to hold onto might come in handy.

"I suspect you can thank James for that."

Our gazes met and filled in the blanks that it was just like at the law office.

He hitched one shoulder. "Gives me a chance to say this could be a bit tricky. Not entirely sure what reception we'll get at Teague Ranch."

After his daughter, armed guards should be a snap.

"We plan to go in groups," he continued. "You'll ride with me."

"I don't—"

"Also, Mrs. Parens and Gee Decker. If we single out them and a couple others to not drive solo, we'll never get there…"

He was right. "But I don't have to—"

He reached up to push back the short hair around my face. Or maybe to straighten it, considering what my sunglasses had probably done to it.

I backed away.

His hand remained extended with nothing to brush away for a moment before he dropped it. At the same time, the brim of his hat tipped down, shadowing his eyes.

"We're not doing this, Tom."

"Sorry. You're right." His head came up. "But that doesn't mean I'm not going to care about you and watch out for you. Won't let any friend walk into a bad situation, sure not going to let you."

"You don't *let* me do anything."

"Elizabeth—"

"I'm not stupid enough to do something just because you said not to or to prove how independent I am even if… Anyway, I make those decisions."

After a pause, he gave a deliberate, single nod. "Okay. When you're making those decisions, though, would you factor in what Tamantha would do to me if something happened to you?"

I couldn't stop the twitch at the corner of my mouth, but subdued it. "I will factor that in."

The sound of another vehicle approaching reached us.

Chapter Sixty-Two

THE GUARD LOOKED through the windshield as Tom's truck rolled slowly to a stop. It seemed to me he stared at me.

Ahead of us, James Longbaugh had gone in with Clara Atwood and Nadine Hulte. Behind us came O.D. Everett, with Anna Price-Fox and Ivy Short. I'd recognized a light blue SUV with a single occupant that approached the gate before our group and there were more vehicles behind our group.

Tom, looking around our surroundings as if casually, lowered the driver's window and identified himself. If he was looking for an exit strategy, I didn't see one. We had a rock ridge on our right, which also masked the entry from the highway. On the left was a little building beside the gate, then a strong fence through rough country.

The gatekeeper—not carrying a shotgun as he had previous times I'd arrived at Teague Ranch—gave Tom a cursory look, scanned the two older women in the backseat, then shifted his attention to me.

"You're that Danniher woman."

"I'm Elizabeth Margaret Danniher from KWMT-TV."

"Thought so. Mr. Teague hated you."

"I've been invited."

"Really, really hated you."

I looked at Tom. Apparently relaxed, but not relaxed at all, he looked at the guard.

The man's mouth widened in a grin. "The jackass is dead, so go on in. Glad to have you. Only hope he knows. Go right on in."

He straightened and grandly waved us ahead.

✧ ✧ ✧ ✧

WE DROVE PAST the collection of Old West buildings jostled together along an ersatz Main Street. I counted three dozen—an increase since my previous trip—before they went out of sight and we dropped into underground parking.

"All those buildings," Gee said. "I had no idea he had so many."

Mrs. P looked grim.

A man in the Teague Ranch uniform of ironed jeans, shiny tooled cowboy boots, a shirt with a bolo tie directed us to an elevator and pressed the button for the main floor.

My first visit took me higher, to where Teague had secure displays of many of his acquisitions. This main floor area was more Las Vegas Presents the Old West.

A business-suited man greeted James and Tom and led them away. The rest of us were escorted to a room I'd swear was modeled after the Ponderosa from *Bonanza*. Forget a nod toward western roots, this dug up the whole tree and plunked it in front of you.

A lectern stood at one end, a table with cookies, coffee, tea, and water stood at the opposite.

I found a spot with a good view of both without being in the middle.

O.D. Everett, Anna Price-Fox, and Ivy Short joined Mrs. P and Gee. Clara and Nadine went to a window that gave a view of the Old West town and stayed there, talking in low voices.

I spotted Willa Rennant, drinking coffee, appearing self-contained, and watching everything.

More filtered into the room. By their dress, employees.

The biggest surprise was the arrival of Kamden Graf. It took a second to notice Jolie Graf, masked by his bulk and clinging to his arm with both hands.

Willa's presence was also a surprise. Unless Teague wrote in some remembrance for the Rennant family in the event Palmer predeceased him?

"Still the thousand-mile stare?"

I hadn't even seen Needham approach. I jumped on him.

"Needham, what did you mean, not every story needs to be chased?"

"Just what you thought I meant. Luther Tipton. He's dead and from everything I ever heard he was a man who needed killing. Some men do, you know."

He spoke so mildly it took half a beat for his words' sharpness to hit. And leave a shimmer of shock in their wake.

Perhaps recognizing my response, he smiled slightly. "Wouldn't act on it personally, mind—woman or man—but I can think it. And I can think of the alternative when such people live on."

His face changed.

Less of the smart, noticing journalist. More of the man who said some men needed killing.

The alternative...

If Luther Tipton hadn't died. What would life have been like for Sally? Her stepmother?

Yet she wanted a decent burial for the man. What did that say about—?

"Ladies and gentlemen. If I may have your attention, please. I'm James Longbaugh."

He spoke from the lectern at the front of the room. Tom stood next to him, with the business-suited man in the background.

The noise didn't cease immediately, especially as some jockeyed for better views.

Kamden Graf moved through the crowd as if he didn't have a human limpet on his arm, saying hello and smiling at women. Only a few greeted Jolie. I stayed out of his line of sight.

I did see Willa Rennant make eye contact with her. Jolie shrank closer to Kamden. Willa's gaze moved on.

Once James had everyone's attention, he continued, "I have been asked by the executor to share information with all of you on behalf of the Russell Teague estate."

✧　✧　✧　✧

THE GOOD THING about knowing ahead of time what a dramatic announcement was about was you got to watch how others received the news. At least as many of them as you could watch at once.

"—and both those properties are to be sold, with the proceeds to be divided among the current employees by percentages listed in a document each of you will receive."

"The Cottonwood County Library receives Mr. Teague's personal library from this property, as well as all research and materials pertaining to his Teague lineage, with a trust account to maintain the collection."

Ivy Short looked pleased, concerned, and slightly confused.

"In addition, the property known as The Buttes is given to the Sherman Western Frontier Life Museum—"

Sucked-in gasps came from several directions. "*He* owned it?" came from someone far to my right, though I couldn't spot the speaker.

"—with the understanding that it is not to be sold for at least one hundred years, is to be used for Two Rivers Camp and the Miners' Camp Fight reenactment and to be renamed the Russell Teague property."

"We can live with that, we can live with that." Nadine patted Clara's arm and smiled broadly.

"With the exception of two additional bequests, all Russell Teague's holdings of real estate, property, and cash in Wyoming go to the Sherman Western Frontier Life Museum."

For two long beats, the room went silent.

Then Clara sucked in air as if she'd just come up from underwater, O.D. Everett slapped one fist into the other palm, and the guard from the gate started laughing.

"Are you sure?" someone in back asked. A few more joined the guard's laughter.

James reined it in with three words.

"There are stipulations."

As he read requirements that boiled down to the historic buildings collected on the property being opened—for a fee—to the public and the whole enterprise run by the museum, I studied faces.

I missed the beginning of Clara's reaction because Kamden Graf's broad back was in the way. I moved for a better angle and caught a glimpse of red, but when I looked toward it, all I saw was Nadine's blue shirt and Clara's white as they hugged.

As they released each other, I concentrated on their faces. Clara radiated joy. Beside her, Nadine mouthed over and over what looked like *It's a miracle, it's a miracle.*

Mrs. Parens looked pleased, but a little gray. The strain of being at Sally's bedside? Surprise and wary happiness suffused Gee's face. Needham was as busy watching people as I was.

Other than a tinge of grimness, Tom remained expressionless. His dark eyes surveyed the group. Then landed on Willa Rennant as she spoke.

"Palmer Rennant's children get nothing?"

"Not from the main bequest, ma'am, but—"

Executive brusque, she cut off James. "Then why am I here?"

"Yeah, me, too," Kamden Graf said. "Did you bring us out here just to cut us off at the knees?"

James focused on Willa. "As your children's representative, you need to be aware of the final two bequests. The first is outright. A watch matching one your ex-husband had goes to either your daughter or your son, whichever did not receive their father's watch, so each child has one.

"The conditional bequest is that if either or both of Palmer Rennant's children, as well as Mr. Graf, choose to see through to publication the, uh, project titled 'The Manipulation of So-Called History,' a sum—"

A sound came from the direction of Mrs. P and Aunt Gee, but since I could guess their opinion of that opus, I continued watching Willa Rennant and Kamden Graf.

"—of five-thousand dollars will be divided amongst however many of the three participate. That—"

"Five thousand? Divided three ways?" Graf's loud voice quieted all other sound and seemed to shrink his wife. "Why, they were talking tens of thousands just for me from the royalties. That's what I was promised. I've got a contract. I get all the royalties. Not some piddling—"

"This is an addition to that agreement, which remains in place, Mr. Graf. If the piece is published, you receive whatever royalties there might be."

"Well. Okay, then," the man said, clearly not picking up from James Longbaugh's even words that the lawyer did not believe there would be royalties.

"Copies of the documents and the employees' schedule of payment are available on the table on that side of the room."

James' announcement started a surge in that direction.

Nadine floated near me, caught on a wave of bodies moving toward the table.

"It's a miracle," she said—audibly this time.

As she shifted away, I spotted the source of the red I'd glimpsed.

Raised marks on the inside of her left wrist. Poison ivy?

I shifted, trying to see her right wrist. From this angle, I saw nothing.

I'd taken half a step after her, when Tom said from behind me, "You're not surprised."

I turned to him, not prepared to reveal Mike's role in my lack of surprise.

"What would be interesting to know is if everybody else is truly surprised."

His gaze sharpened on me for half a beat, then he casually scoped out the rest of the room's occupants again.

"Huh." That's all he offered.

"Why did he name you as executor of this part of his will?"

"Revenge. Spite."

"You think he thought the ranch and the rest would go to Palmer Rennant, which would make the backers of the museum crazy, both because it would be all in an enemy's hands and they'd know how close they'd come to getting it."

"Yep. Then toss in that I'd be forced to implement it as executor."

"He had to know you could decline to be executor."

"Could," he repeated.

I huffed out a short laugh. "He knew you wouldn't decline because you'd try to protect the community as much as you could while still doing your legal duty. That way, he'd torment you from beyond the grave."

"Could look at it that way or that he'd've given me an opportunity to make his choices not quite as painful for the county as they'd be with someone else as executor."

"Pollyanna," I muttered. Deeper indentations at the corners of his eyes were his only response. "But even with this happy ending for the museum—not so happy for Palmer Rennant—I thought you'd hate having this ranch open to the public, people swarming into the place next to yours. Why *don't* you hate it?"

He took his hat off and rubbed the back of his neck with his other hand. It was an excuse to lower his head so I didn't see his face.

"You see tourists swarming to Cottonwood County?" I didn't have to see his face. I heard the amusement low in his voice. "Much less to that collection of old buildings—heavy on the saloons? Clara and the museum will improve it, especially with the cash, but still… Swarms?"

"You have a point."

"And a plan. A new road into here. Not as close to my place. Not close to entrances into other places, either. Better approach to the old buildings. Won't see any of the modern the way you do now."

"And I suppose the kids' camp and reenactment will be fully supported. Going to hold them every year?"

"Raised making the camp annual with James."

"What is his role? He claimed he had nothing to do with the will."

"He didn't. He's strictly my representative. Wanted someone to steer me clear of any legal cliffs."

"And be the public face."

"That, too. As for the reenactment's future, we'll get with the tribal leaders. It's a big project. Not sure they'd want to commit to every year. Plus, there could be an opportunity for an event around the historic buildings—"

"A whiskey festival to celebrate the saloons?""

"—to alternate with the reenactment," he finished solemnly, though one corner of his mouth quirked.

"That all sounds lovely for the future. I'm interested in the past. The immediate past. Specifically, a murder. Who knew about this?"

He tipped his head and lifted one shoulder, dismissing my question.

"Burrell, do you really think that's a satisfactory answer? More important, do you think *I* will think it's a satisfactory answer?"

He looked me straight in the eyes and said, "Can't get no satisfaction."

We were no longer talking murder.

Then, right next to us, I hear James' voice saying, "What you do with it afterward is your decision, but the watch will be delivered to your children, Mrs. Ren—"

She interrupted him.

But they'd lost me with the broken-off syllable.

Ren.

Not *When.*

Wren.

Chapter Sixty-Three

EAGER TO TELL the others of that small mystery solved, I hustled my ride toward the exit.

"Mrs. Parens, Gee, Tom," a voice called as we reached Tom's truck. "Oh, and Elizabeth. You, too. Clara asked me to tell you, we're having a little impromptu gathering at the museum tonight. You're all invited to come. Seven o'clock."

"I'm not sure this evening…" Gee started with a look toward Mrs. P's strained face.

Tom helped Mrs. P into the truck.

Nadine backed up a step, preparatory to turning away. "No need to tell us ahead of time. Come if you can. We'll talk more about the future later. This is social. As Clara said, to be with people who understand what this means."

"Thank you. I—" I interrupted myself. "Gee, Nadine, that's a nasty rash on your wrist."

"I know. You'd think if I were going to get a rash it would have happened last week when I was out with the kids, not from the past few days in the office with Clara." She lifted one shoulder. "I have no idea where it came from."

I might. But I wasn't sharing.

She smiled. "The marvelous thing is no more trying to figure out how to support the events next time around. The museum will be able to up its support for sure."

Her smile dimmed and she rubbed at the rash on her left wrist with her right hand. "It itches like crazy."

"Looks like poison ivy to me. I'm sensitive and I've seen some around."

She jerked her scratching hand away. "Poison ivy?"

"Absolutely. Last time I had it, I had good success with an antidote the pharmacy—the one downtown—had. I don't remember the name, but I'm sure they will. But you have to get it on fast once the rash shows. Well, bye now."

She released a pained growl, then renewed scratching, though with her cuff between her arm and fingernails. "Yeah, yeah. Bye."

As we drove out, Gee asked, "Was that poison ivy? I didn't get a good look at it."

"Pretty sure."

I felt sharp looks from Tom and Mrs. Parens, but my focus was on what I'd swear were two unmarked sheriff's department vehicles pulled off the side of the road down the highway from Teague Ranch.

At the Circle B, I said short good-byes.

Once in my SUV, headed to town, I called Jennifer. "Can you get away from work?"

"Important?"

"Yes. Nadine knows Diana and me, but she hasn't seen you." Yet another reason to miss Mike … yes, and Tom. They provided additional options for subterfuge. "Go to the pharmacy. Hang around close enough when Nadine talks to the pharmacist to hear if she really has poison ivy."

"That's all?"

"That's all. Oh, except keep your eyes open for unmarked sheriff's department vehicles."

"Tailing her?"

"Possibly her. Possibly someone else. Possibly several someone elses. Also, that account by the survivor of the Miners' Camp Fight, what if he wasn't writing *the deserted When*, but *the deserter Wren*—W-R-E-N?"

"The bird? That kind of wren?"

"Or a nickname or alias for someone named Rennant."

"*Rennant.* Oh. One of his ancestors was at the Miners' Camp Fight?

But—"

"What if he was at the Miners' Camp Fight because he deserted from the Army? Family members kept joining up to expiate that 1812 blunder. What if one came West? Fort Phil Kearny—all the Bozeman Trail forts—had desertions. If he hooked up with that group of gold miners who left the fort to try the route that brought them here—"

"I'll call the guy at the fort again on the way to the pharmacy. Where will you be?"

"My house, but if you need to finish your shift, call or message instead of coming."

"You kidding? I hear that tone in your voice. I'm coming."

"**WAITING FOR JENNIFER** is driving me crazy," Mike said from the screen of my propped-up device. "We could start going over everything now, let her catch up."

"It hasn't been long," Diana soothed.

She and Shadow had been waiting for me when I got home, Mike called soon after. The house felt better with Shadow in it.

Diana added now, "What are you thinking about, Elizabeth?"

I didn't look up from Free Cell, playing on my laptop while Mike occupied the other device. "Insurance. I was trying to remember something Verona Fuller said."

Diana chuckled. "If it was Verona Fuller, it was definitely about insurance."

"Event insurance? Wonder if it covered canceling the reenactment because of a murder," Mike said.

Diana shook her head. "Doesn't matter now. Assuming the will holds up, the museum will get the ranch, the butte land, and enough money to fund them for a long, long time."

"Not to mention the gold coins," Mike said.

I looked up. "I was thinking about an exchange I'm not sure I told you about." I repeated the conversation at the museum Friday morning, when Nadine suggested including Rennant in the coverage and Clara decisively rejected the idea.

"Does that mean Clara knew he was already dead or—" Mike broke off and looked past me. "Jennifer. At last."

I twisted around to see my front door opening.

"What happened at the pharmacy? Did you get ahold of someone at Fort Phil Kearny about—?"

She broke in. "There's bigger news than that. Jolie Graf and her husband are at the sheriff's department. I saw them going in."

On the screen Mike flopped back on his couch. "They got there before us."

"Had to happen sometime." Diana had the solace that it would make her honey happy. For the rest of us, this was all downside.

"Twice in a row. Luther Tipton and now this." Jennifer patted Shadow on her way to a seat. "It stinks."

"Don't give up yet." Only peripherally aware of it, I started a new Free Cell game.

"You have something in mind?" Mike lifted his head and peered through the screen.

"Nothing concrete. I just... I keep thinking about what Penny said about teaching a man to fish."

Mike straightened. "Hey, I looked that up. Did you know it's not from the Bible? Some people say it's an old Native American saying or an old Chinese saying or an old somewhere else saying, but there's no evidence. Articles said the concept had been around, but the actual saying, with fish and teaching, is traced to an author—the daughter of William Thackeray—in the 1800s."

"What does teaching a man to fish have to do with any of this?" Jennifer demanded. "Isn't it pretty darned clear the sheriff's department thinks Palmer was messing around with Jolie, Kamden found out, and killed him."

"Unless Willa found out and wanted revenge even though they're divorced." Mike said.

"I would never murder a woman who was my romantic rival. What's the point?" Diana said.

"In general, it's considered that the point is to remove the competition." I won the Free Cell game and started another.

"That's stupid. A woman who shoots the other woman is simply making more work for herself."

Jennifer said, "Explain that, Diana."

"It's the Penny Czylinski school of he-done-me-wrong. If you shoot the woman, the guy's hungry the next day, just like a man you give a fish. But if you shoot the guy, you get to the root of the problem, like teaching a man to fish."

She appeared to conclude we hadn't followed her explanation. I thought we were all trying to process Diana—*Diana*—saying this.

"A man who cheats will cheat again. A woman who determines that shooting the other woman is her solution to a serial cheating man, will need to shoot the next woman and the next and the next. It becomes monotonous. Better to fix the problem permanently."

I muttered, "Can't wait to tell Russ Conrad this theory of yours."

"Mine and Penny's. He's heard it from me already."

"In relation to this case?"

"No."

Mike whistled. "Way to warn the sheriff he better treat you right."

"Yeah, but can we get back to this thing?" Jennifer keeping us on the straight and narrow—or trying to get us onto it. Impressive. "The Grafs are at the sheriff's department. Does that mean everything's over or doesn't it?"

"It doesn't." I forestalled three open mouths by saying, "First, Jennifer, did you get anything from Fort Phil Kearny?"

"Yes. There was a guy on the roster, roll call, whatever spelled R-E-N-E-N-T. He's listed as a deserter."

"What? What's this about?" Mike asked.

After explaining to him and Diana about the Miners' Camp Fight survivors account referring to *the deserter Wren*—"Or Ren, short for Rennant," Jennifer said—I added, "Yet another Rennant ancestor not showering himself with glory. This explains Palmer's attitude about the reenactment."

"And meshes with Russell Teague hating how his ancestors are viewed. Two of a kind."

"Yup. Now, Jennifer, what happened at the pharmacy?"

"Nothing thrilling. Nadine Hulte came in—the guy behind the counter called her Nadine, so no great detective work there. She asked about poison ivy. He looked at her wrist, said she had it, sold her some goop, she left.

"She went into the liquor store nearby. I stayed in my car in case she'd seen me in the pharmacy. Guy came out and put a box in the truck for her and she had a couple bags. Then she went to the museum.

"You said to see if she was being followed—I mean by someone more than me. She was. That new deputy just down from O'Hara Hill. Stayed in the car—unmarked, like you said. He never noticed me. When she went to the museum, he peeled off. I figured we knew where she was for a while, so I followed him.

"Went right to the sheriff's department. That's when I saw Jolie and Kamden Graf going inside with Richard and Shelton."

"Nice work." We all praised her.

"Okay, Elizabeth, talk," Diana ordered. "We know you figured out what was bothering you because you stopped playing Free Cell, so share."

I looked down, and she was right—I'd turned off my laptop.

She was also right that what was bugging me had surfaced up to the level of forming words.

"For starters, I don't think Rennant's possible cheating is a strong motive for Willa. A really good divorce settlement, a new house, good relationship with her kids, sprucing herself up, doing social things, getting involved in the community. That all sounds like a woman moving on with her life. Not one angsting over her ex."

Diana tipped her head, staring at the top of a picture frame, before bringing her gaze slowly down to me. "I agree."

"Plus, why be upset over Jolie when she wasn't about Clara or Vicky or Rosalee or Connie before them?" Jennifer asked.

I heard Vicky's voice saying it had been months and months since she'd dated Rennant. Which made some sense for why she wouldn't talk to me.

Jolie Graf didn't have that reason. Why was she so scared to talk?

"Willa's not out completely, right?" Mike asked.

"Nobody is. But there's something else. Why didn't Penny tell us Palmer was having an affair with Jolie?"

"Penny rarely *tells* us anything."

"I don't agree, Mike. She tells us lots. She just masks it amid a lot of other stuff we're not interested in." I reconsidered that. "Not at the top of our current interest, anyway. But she—"

"Elizabeth? You're frowning."

It took me a couple beats to respond to Diana.

I started slowly. "Penny didn't tell us or hint or toss in pieces about Jolie and Palmer." My word train picked up. "She didn't include *anything*—I'm sure Mike and I didn't miss it—about them having an affair." I jerked upright. "Because they didn't have one." Into the silence, I repeated, "No affair between Jolie and Palmer. Never happened."

"But there was so much talk. All the rumors…" Diana stopped her own words.

I nodded at her. "What you said about the rumors being weird, people not believing them. Rumors can be wrong. And I think Penny actually *did* tell us. Mike, remember what she said about good for the goose, good for the gander?"

"How could I? You had me muted."

"You could hear, you dope. I just didn't want you talking."

"I'm a highly paid professional. What I have to say is—"

"I want to hear Elizabeth," Jennifer interrupted.

"All right, all right. Yes, I remember the goose and the gander."

"But then she added *in theory, that is.*"

"What does that mean? Is this more to do with fishing?" Jennifer asked.

"Sort of. Maybe. If Penny was talking about Jolie and Kamden as the goose and gander, that would mean Jolie was fooling around on him, the way he fools around on her. But add *in theory* and what do you have?"

"That she wasn't fooling around," Diana said.

"Exactly. Also, when Penny listed the women Palmer dated, she never mentioned Jolie. Not once."

"But the rumors. They came from somewhere," Jennifer protested.

"What if they came from Jolie. To try to make her husband jealous?"

It was so clear to me. I looked from the two faces in the room to the one on the screen.

"The woman has practically starved herself to death trying to get his attention. You should have seen her today at Teague's ranch, clinging to him. And think of all the rumors circulating about him cheating on her—at their wedding, for heaven's sake. She had to know. She had to.

"She finally tried to do something about it by spreading rumors to make him jealous. *What's good for the goose is good for the gander.* Rennant dated a number of women, one after the other. That made it more believable—though all the others were single. But Jolie probably didn't recognize that in his pattern."

Diana nodded. "It explains the contradictory vibes I picked up."

"With Penny never including her, I'll buy it," Mike said.

"So, now what?" Jennifer asked.

"We go to the sheriff's department. Because now," I said with a bit of triumph, "we've got something to get our foot in the door."

Chapter Sixty-Four

I WAS TRYING to not listen to Jennifer, on the phone in the back seat, schmooze with a hacker pal when a familiar figure came out the back of the sheriff's department building.

I swatted the air toward the back seat, not taking my gaze off our quarry. "Shelton."

"Gotta go, Dirt." Yes, Dirt was the guy's nickname. I did not want to know why.

Diana, in the front passenger seat, was already on alert.

I stopped Jennifer from opening her door with a gesture. "Let him get closer. So he can't duck back in."

"Ah," she breathed.

"Now."

Shelton swore as we emerged simultaneously. "You three. Go to the front desk where the rest of your kind are supposed to be."

"We're not here to learn what you've found out, Sergeant. We're here to share something we've found out."

And get our foot in the door.

IT TOOK CONSIDERABLY more finagling to get from a foot in the door to our entire selves in the observation room.

The sheriff's department had gone high tech under Sheriff Conrad, with video in the two interview rooms and screens for each in this cubbyhole. One screen showed Kamden Graf looking peeved. The other showed Jolie weeping.

I was holding out to be in on the interview before I told Shelton my blinding insight. I hadn't made much headway when Diana gave me her *be reasonable* look and I decided to try that.

"Get them in one room together," I said.

Shelton scowled.

"They're dancing around, not giving you anything, right?"

The scowl intensified.

"Jolie thinks her husband has a motive, is terrified he did it, and is determined to protect him to the end.

"Kamden, on the other hand, knows he *doesn't* have a motive and he can't figure out why on earth you'd think he might, so he's bobbing and weaving trying to figure out what's going on, while you're not telling him because you're trying to worm a confession out of him that he'll never give."

"You're saying because he didn't do it?"

"No. I don't know if he did it. What I'm saying is he wouldn't have done it for the reason Jolie thinks he might have and has you thinking he might have."

The scowl brought his brows even lower and his face darkened, at the same time light gleamed in his eyes, like a sunset just at the horizon with a universe of boiling black clouds above it.

What he said was, "You saying you don't know who did it. I like that."

I ignored that, thanks to Diana's elbow in my side. "Put them in one room together. Tell her husband in front of her that she thinks he killed Palmer Rennant because Jolie was having an affair with Rennant and see what happens. What do you have to lose?"

Shelton and his scowl left the room with no indication if the clouds or the line of sunshine would prevail.

Diana, Jennifer, and I looked at each other to see if one of us had a blinding insight into what Shelton would do. Heck, we even resorted to looking at Lloyd Sampson, who looked back blankly.

It was three minutes before Richard Alvaro escorted Jolie out of her room.

At almost the same time, the other screen showed the door to

Kamden's room open and Shelton walk in with a hold on Jolie Grafs arm. Alvaro entered behind them, closing the door and taking up a stance on the opposite side of the table.

"Oh, Kamden. Oh, darling—"

Jolie dove toward her husband, but Shelton retained his hold on her one arm. Her feet still near Shelton, she tipped against his hold, her free arm reaching, imploringly, toward Kamden. They looked like the beginning of the clunkiest pairs skating death spiral ever.

Kamden shrank away.

Safe in the separate room, Jennifer and I chuckled. Diana sucked in her cheeks. Sampson made a sound.

Shelton never broke. He did glare toward the camera, which stopped Sampson's sound.

"Jolie, stand up." He accompanied the order by drawing back her arm, tipping her upright. "Kamden, move your chair down."

The man complied with an enthusiasm that left him almost against the far wall. One-handed, Shelton set a chair for Jolie on the same side, but nearer the door.

Presumably, Alvaro could get across the table to get between them if necessary. Just in case, Shelton sat at the end of the table, with a clear shot at Jolie.

"Okay. It's time we get things straight here," Shelton started. "There's talk around town that could give you two motives for killing Palmer Rennant."

"*Me?* I don't—" Kamden got in first.

"That's—"

"Quiet." Shelton's word carried the day. "We're clearing that up right now." He looked down the table at Kamden. "You have a motive because Jolie was having an affair with Palmer."

"But—" Jolie started.

Shelton's stop-sign hand nearly clipped her in the nose.

Kamden looked like he was having a hard time comprehending the words.

"You think I—*Me?* You think I did that? No way. I didn't kill him. Why on earth would you think that?"

"Like I said. Talk about him and your wife."

"Because she was having an affair with him? I wouldn't—"

Jolie burst out, "But I *wasn't* Kamden—I wasn't. There was nothing between Palmer and me. I'm so sorry. So desperately, desperately sorry. It was a terrible idea to make you jealous. I know I shouldn't have. I should have trusted you. I was so miserable, so unsure and I thought if you saw that you could lose me... But I never thought you'd react this way or I swear—I *swear* I wouldn't have let people think Palmer and I were... you know. I never meant the rumors to drive you to such desperate action. I never thought you'd kill Palmer."

"I *didn't*. Had no reason on earth to kill the man."

"But—But—"

Over Jolie's protests, Shelton addressed Kamden. "Did you hear those rumors about Jolie and Palmer?"

"I heard a little. Didn't think it was true. Seemed too good to be true, you know? Get—"

"What? *What?*" Jolie screeched.

"—her off my hands, like. Give her something else to think about."

"You scum-sucking, stinking pile of—"

She had more energy than I'd expected.

"Quiet." Shelton cracked his whip again. "I want yes or no answers from you two. Jolie did you start the rumors that you were having an affair with Palmer Rennant."

"Well, an *affair*..."

"Yes or no?"

"Yes."

"Were you having an affair with him?"

"No."

"Less than an affair, but still having relations with him?"

"No."

"Okay. Now, Kamden, did you hear the rumors?"

"Yeah. I guess. Didn't—"

"Did you act on those rumors?"

"Uh, did I... Huh?"

"Did you kill Palmer Rennant?"

"No. I been telling you and telling you that. *No.* And if you've been thinking I would have because of rumors him and her were doing the dirty, I'm here to tell you, no way."

Chapter Sixty-Five

"YOU SHOULD HAVE seen it, Mike." Jennifer was exultant, trying to tell him everything at once about Jolie and Kamden Graf. "Elizabeth and Diana were like this one-two punch right to Shelton's chin. And it went exactly the way Elizabeth told him, but better. It was as good as the play in Chicago."

"But those are real people," Diana reminded her quietly.

Mike asked, "But did Kamden *know* she wasn't having an affair? If not, if he thought she was, even though she wasn't, he had a motive."

"He didn't *care*. So he had no motive." With a glance toward Diana, Jennifer added. "That's sad for her. But she'll be better off without him. She has to be."

"No motive for Jolie, either," Diana said. "She wanted Palmer alive to try to make her husband jealous."

"Two suspects down. Where does that leave us?"

Mike sure knew how to deflate a mood.

Like chemicals sitting next to each other with no problem until a catalyst starts a chain reaction, those bits and pieces were back cascading through my brain. Facts, observations, and snatches of conversation jostling each other. I grabbed some as they floated by.

Otto's dog Devil scratching the passenger door and the front door.
Connie didn't know who came after her.
The watch.
Rennant's truck parked at the side of the porch instead of in front.
Poison ivy.

Why the butte and when.
Pillow talk with a different pillow.
Mary Ferguson.

"Mary Ferguson," I said aloud. "And a catalyst."

"What does that mean?" Jennifer asked.

"It means I'm going to the Sherman Supermarket."

"Of course. More pie?"

I did not dignify Diana's question with a direct response. Instead, I asked, "Anyone want to go with?"

THEY ALL CAME. Jennifer and Diana in person, Mike in Diana's pocket with her finger on mute.

Okay, we did buy pie, but that was because we needed something to get into Penny's line.

Diana and Jennifer followed me, forming a human buffer against anyone overhearing what I asked.

"Well, hi there, Elizabeth. Quite a turn up we've got with that strange fella dyin' and his even stranger will. Came right—"

I leaned forward and spoke directly to her. "Penny, the old pills Mary Ferguson kept that were taken off the market, were they sleeping pills?"

"—out of the blue to most, though he knew. Kid with a secret, 'cept it was a secret about how he'd use a bomb to blow things up. Can't say he shoulda been killed, but sometimes things work out in the end. Could've been topsy-turvy around here. Told her those pills could be dangerous. They'd—"

"Sleeping pills?" I pressed.

"—done it before, killing, when they were supposed to be helping. Supposed to sleep. But you get stung, all right, like handling hornets. Though Mary had a constitution of an—"

Like handling hornets...

Diana cleared her throat, letting me know someone had come into line behind us.

"Yellow jackets?" I asked urgently.

"—ox. Always him with health issues. But she goes first. Isn't that the way? That's the name. Hornets, yellow jackets. All bees to me. Bye now."

"**YELLOW JACKETS? HOW** did you know that? And what does it mean?" Mike asked from Diana's pocket, once we were back in my SUV.

"That was the nickname for a barbiturate that's supposed to have killed Marilyn Monroe. Long off the market after too many people died, but that didn't bother Mary Ferguson. Even with her constitution like an ox, Penny told us last time she'd nearly killed herself accidentally with those pills a few years back, yet she kept them around. There they were, waiting."

"Waiting for what?" Jennifer asked.

"Or who?" Diana added.

"Hold on. I need to make a phone call. But I don't want to do it while I'm driving."

"But—"

"Shh. Don't distract me."

I had too many distractions already with the pieces swirling through my head.

I kept hushing them at the house, too.

Diana made that easier by serving slices of pie to the three of us actually here. I did my best to tune out Mike's griping.

That was easier when I called a number and said, "Willa?"

That quieted everything but the chewing.

"It's Elizabeth Margaret Danniher. I have a question I hope you can answer. You said Palmer *switched to seeing a woman named Jolie.* Switched from whom? Who was he seeing before her?"

After a slight pause, she said, "Funny you should ask. My son told me his father mentioned the last time they talked that a woman from the museum broke off with him and twice was two times too many and he'd never date another woman who thought so-called history was important.

"I was debating calling the sheriff's department. Palmer didn't use Clara Atwood's name and I'd hate for Palmer Junior to be drawn into this, especially if it's not necessary…"

I should go directly to heaven for not telling her to skip calling the sheriff's department.

I didn't tell her *to* call, either. There's such a thing as *too* saintly.

MY COHORTS DID not nominate me for sainthood, not even when I related the conversation word for word.

"That's it—it's Clara Atwood," Mike said.

"No." I softened that rejection of a possible solution with, "Not yet, anyway. I have this list going through my head. But it's still missing pieces."

"Share."

"It might not make sense…"

"Share," Diana repeated.

I did. With Jennifer typing it into her device.

Otto's dog Devil scratching the passenger door and the front door.
Connie didn't know who came after her.
The watch.
Rennant's truck parked at the side of the porch instead of in front.
Poison ivy.
Why the butte and when.
Pillow talk with a different pillow.
Mary Ferguson.

At the end, I said, "Add *a catalyst*. And write down the fight at the Ferguson house."

Jennifer did, then sent it to all of us. But I didn't want to see the list—it already took up too much space in my head.

"The fight was the catalyst?" she asked.

"I think… I think it was *about* the catalyst. I know they don't line up or form a pattern."

"That's okay." Diana looked over Jennifer's shoulder at the list. "We know how your mind works on these things."

"We've got some of those," Mike said. "Otto's dog, the truck, why the butte and when, Mary Ferguson, and we're down to two with who came after Connie—Clara or Nadine. The pillow talk could apply to them. I don't get the watch, but poison—"

I jerked up. "The watch."

"Is that the catalyst?" Jennifer raised her fingers, ready to type.

"No."

"Why *are* you obsessed with that watch?" Mike asked.

"The timeline and something else. But first, the timeline. Clara says she didn't see it. Vicky won't say, though I think she really, really wanted to say yes. Connie said he wore it. Then a gap—our missing woman. And, finally, Jolie says he wore it."

"But Jolie didn't have an affair with him. What—?"

"No, but she saw him wear it in the pool—which must be where she spends a lot of time—"

"It is," Diana slipped in.

"—to do that to her skin. Palmer told Willa last fall that Teague gave it to him to *celebrate*. Clara could have broken up with him before he got it, so never saw it. So that all fits. But celebrate what?"

"Their effort to discredit history," Jennifer said.

"I don't think so. Kamden said that started this spring and you said the LLC was recent. But Rennant already had the watch. James Longbaugh said there was word about Teague drawing up a new will a year ago. The will that mentions the exact replica of Palmer's watch and leaves it to either his son or his daughter."

I looked at them expectantly.

They looked back at me.

"*Not one a young woman would wear,*" I quoted. "Why would Nadine associate that watch with a young woman? Why would anyone? Unless ... unless they knew Russell Teague's will included the provision that his matching watch would go to whichever of Rennant's children hadn't inherited Palmer's. Which meant Palmer's twenty-something daughter would have one of those watches.

"To know that, Nadine had to know about the will."

I nodded to myself. "And not just that Rennant was the first beneficiary, but what happened if he predeceased Teague. Because if the deaths happened the other way around, and Rennant inherited everything—including the watch—there was no need for that bequest.

"So, when he told her about *that* provision, is there any chance in Palmer Rennant's universe that he *didn't* tell her he would inherit everything and trash the programs she felt so strongly about? And, having told her that, would he not also rub it in about the museum being the secondary beneficiary that missed out because he got it all?"

I looked around at my friends, who'd kept silent while I followed that thread, inch by inch.

Diana expelled a long breath. "If he didn't, it goes against what we've heard about him being oblivious and not having a filter."

"Nadine?" Mike said. "*Nadine?* But how?"

"She's the missing woman?" Jennifer asked. "Willa said it was Clara."

"She did. But that's not what Palmer told his son. He said *he'd never date another woman who thought so-called history was important*—that certainly applies to Nadine. And *a woman from the museum broke off with him and twice was two times too many*—he could easily lump Nadine in as a woman from the museum and be talking about two women, not the same woman twice."

"Even if Nadine is the missing woman, why tell her about the will if Rennant didn't tell the others?" Diana asked.

"Because she was interested in the same things he was—on opposite sides, but the same interests. Can't you just hear this man saying, *Guess what? I'm inheriting all this stuff, use it to smash the local history elements you've spent your adult life working on and—ha, ha, ha, listen to this—if I weren't around, your precious museum would've gotten it all.*"

They absorbed that for a moment.

Then Jennifer asked, "Now what?"

"Now we go to the museum. They're having a celebration tonight."

✧ ✧ ✧ ✧

THE CELEBRATION HAD wound down by the time I got there.

If the others hadn't insisted on so much planning... But maybe this was better.

"Hi. Did you hear the great news?" Sandy, the front desk receptionist, picked up empty glasses and plates from the otherwise deserted entry area.

"I heard."

We'd agreed I'd go in alone.

Well, they'd agreed with my plan to go in alone after we'd spotted three unmarked sheriff's department vehicles near the museum. They considered that backup.

I thought Jennifer and Diana following me in separate cars, supplemented by them and Mike listening was plenty. Especially, since Jennifer put a recording device in a cupholder in my SUV's console, another on the ceiling side of the visor, a third in my other sweater pocket—all in addition to my phone.

"You're too late." Vicky Upton wrapped up leftover snacks from a buffet table. A platter at the center must have held her brownies. Empty, darn it. "All the guests are gone."

"What about staff? Just the two of you left?"

"No, Clara and Nadine are in Clara's office. Go on back," Sandy invited.

I heard muffled voices from the sweater pocket where I had my phone.

"Thanks, I will."

In the back hallway, I pulled the phone up and said urgently. "Be quiet. I *will* mute."

"What if you're wrong? Don't go back there alo—"

I muted.

Chapter Sixty-Six

CLARA WAS ALONE.

Misdirection? Conspiracy?

My heart thudded with the mental syllables.

I'd thought of them in connection with Mrs. P's view of the timing of the Bozeman Trail forts and the railroads. Then, about Sally and her stepmother possibly killing Luther Tipton.

Now I wondered...

What if I had the wrong one? Or only half the answer?

Could all the things that applied to Nadine apply to Clara?

There were other possible causes of death. The poison ivy could have come another way.

"Hi. Where's Nadine?"

Clara looked up. "Oh, hi, Elizabeth. She went home, said she's going to bed. Just left. No, wait. Something about ice cream from the supermarket. I'm going home, too. But I'm going to have more to drink. Lots more to drink."

"Somebody driving you?"

"Vicky. Said I wasn't fit to drive. But you can catch Nadine at the supermarket if you hurry." Her voice followed me out. "Hope you like ice cream."

I DREW MY SUV up in front of the figure trudging away from the supermarket, missing her toes by plenty, but putting the passenger door right in front of her face.

"Hi, Nadine," I said cheerily. "Hop in."

She looked from me to her vehicle beyond me. "This isn't a good time. I have ice cream."

"I want to talk to you about your poison ivy. Won't take a minute," I fibbed, leaning across and pushing open the door.

"Okay. A minute. You were right about the poison ivy. I do have it. What are you doing? Where are you going?"

The last two anxious questions came when the SUV moved. "Just over here, so we're out of the way of traffic."

I parked in the middle of a patch of empty parking lot, quietly locked the doors from the inside, shut off the engine, spotted two unmarked sheriff's department vehicles, plus Diana and Jennifer, and turned to her.

Her earlier joy from the announcement was gone. Ripples of lines showed under her eyes, her skin sagged, drawing down lines from the corners of her mouth to her chin. She looked like an age progression rendering come to life.

"The no-itch lotion they recommended at the pharmacy is helping. Thanks for suggesting that." Her voice was drained of all energy.

Looking at her, I changed my approach.

Questions—the things I loved best in language—could let her rebuild her defenses, answer by answer. But right now, she had no defenses.

Time for statements, leaving no escape.

"What I don't understand is how you got the poison ivy, Nadine. There wasn't any near the camp. Only place there was poison ivy was up on the butte. You said you weren't there during the week or when Palmer Rennant's body was found."

"I wasn't."

"How did you get that poison ivy on your arm? It's the same place Deputy Lloyd Sampson got it—above a pair of gloves. Except his was on both arms from wrapping police tape around the bush by the cave entrance, while yours is only on your left wrist. Where it touched the poison ivy bush near Palmer's body when you used your left hand to brace yourself as you painted red and yellow marks on him."

"I didn't. I wasn't."

"The rash on your wrist, the rash the pharmacy confirmed is poison ivy before selling you a remedy, says otherwise. It takes longer to develop in people who haven't had poison ivy. Deputy Sampson has had it before. He had a rash twenty-four hours after contact. But you'd never had it before."

Her lips parted. I cut her off.

"You didn't recognize the rash. You didn't recognize the *itch*. You never had it before."

She didn't argue.

I backed off slightly on the accusatory tone but presented the statements as unassailable facts.

"But the painting on his back… That's what I don't understand. That pointed the finger at the reenactors from the tribes."

"Oh, *no*. I would never do that. I've studied the symbols and techniques. I never would have tried to duplicate them because that would be so disrespectful of their meaning to… to try to cover up… Him— His shirt was off."

How do you know that, Nadine?

She was there when he was found. That fact wasn't on-air or in the *Independence*. I didn't see Mrs. P or O.D. Everett gossiping about what they saw. Could Nadine have talked to one of the reenactors?

I held my bottom lip between my teeth to hold in the questions.

"Tell me about the insurance."

The silence stretched long, especially because I was holding my breath.

"I didn't intend to *not* get insurance this year." She sounded peeved. "I've done it every other year. I always do it. It's routine. It's basic. It's needed, like I told you…"

I fought to not gulp in air. "But this year you didn't get it."

She didn't respond. I'd made it a statement, but had I pushed too hard?

I softened my tone, my words. "You needed the money for something else."

Her head jerked up. "You think I—You think I *stole* it? I'd never—"

"Not steal it. But it went to something else and the funds became confused, so you couldn't tell what money was used for what…"

"I could tell. Precisely." She seemed more insulted at the idea she'd been a poor record-keeper than she'd stolen the money. Or killed a man.

The first time I talked to her…

Wherever we can save a penny to spend it on the events instead, that's a win.

"The money went to something important," I said.

"Supplies for the camp. We'd scrimped so much last time, with two pairings having to share ingredients for making sheepherder's bread and for fruit stew. This year each pairing made their own loaf and their own portion of fruit stew. That's vital for their bonding, for their pride, for their sense of ownership of the event.

"But he wouldn't listen to any of that. He was awful, just awful. I don't know how he found out."

It wouldn't help her misery any to speculate Verona Fuller's loose lips unknowingly sunk her ship.

"He was … triumphant when he told me that afternoon at the Ferguson house, right before that other man called him into the house next door. He said right out he'd use what he knew." She looked at her hands, twisting the handle of the shopping bag. "I had to try. Even knowing how he was, I had to try. I went to his place to beg him not to say anything. One more day of the camp and then the reenact-ment—the most tickets sold ever—and we'd be fine.

"But he said he'd be out first thing in the morning and stop the last day of camp, make sure there was no reenactment and that would end us. Refunding the last day of the camp would have ruined us, much less refunding reenactment tickets. He had so much, was going to get more. And we were so close, then to lose everything."

That came close to saying she knew about the inheritance, but not close enough.

"It wasn't fair. And while he was planning all this … this *evil*, gloat-ing over it, he acted like I was there to start things up again.

"I told him to put his shirt back on. I told him I couldn't be with him if he closed the camp and reenactment. I *begged* him. I said it wasn't for me, it was for all of Cottonwood County and beyond, for everybody to experience history and he got ..." Surprise, even shock showed in her eyes. "He got so angry. In a rage. Screaming. He wasn't making sense, talking about a bridge and 1812 and desertion. It made no sense. His face got red and the veins stuck out on his forehead and neck and I thought..."

She let it drift long enough that I risked a question, "You thought what?"

"I thought maybe he'd die. Right then and that would solve everything. But after a while, he started screaming less and then he was sort of gulping. He got past the gulping, breathing slower and slower..."

"I asked if he wanted water. Sort of automatic, you know? He said yes. I went to the back of my SUV and there it was ... beside bottled waters for camp, the box with things from the Ferguson house that couldn't go in the trash or recycling or get sold, because they were medications. Even without expiration dates you could they tell were old. Really, really old. And there was one Mary Ferguson used a marker on that said..."

"Sleeping pills," I supplied.

"Yes. I put ... a few in a water bottle. I had no idea what it would do, if it was enough to... I just wanted him to sleep. To be quiet."

Or for that breathing to get slower and slower until it stopped.

"He sat there drinking that water and he talked and talked and talked about how he'd crush the reenactment and the camp and then he'd take on Clara and the museum and make it tell history the way he wanted. When he finished—the water, not the talking—I asked if he wanted more. He said yes. This time I put more pills in. He said it tasted odd, but he drank it anyway. Only now he was getting sleepy. Really, really sleepy. And I started thinking how wonderful it would be if he slept until after the reenactment. I'd have to quit when he woke up and told people, but the events would be safe...

"But I couldn't have him in my SUV. I mean, what would I do with him?"

Chapter Sixty-Seven

"Getting him out was a nightmare. I opened the door on his side, ran around to get back in, braced my back against the driver's door, then pushed him with my feet. In the end, he popped out so suddenly, I slid out after him. He sort of staggered around. I thought I could get him into the house, but he wanted to curl up and sleep. If he'd gone down, I'd never have gotten him up. Truly a nightmare."

Not the best for Palmer Rennant, either.

"His truck was right there in front of the steps, closer than the front door and I didn't have to get him up the steps. I was so grateful it wasn't locked. I tried to get him in the driver's side, but he stumbled around and I couldn't steer him. When he went close to the passenger door, it was like a miracle. I opened it and sort of guided and supported him. I had to really push to get him up in the seat. I thought, I really thought he'd fall out on top of me and I'd have to leave him on the drive—sleeping—"

Sleeping.

Did I hear the beginning of a defense forming?

"—and I didn't know if anyone would find him and that didn't seem … right. I barely got him in and then he curled up, with his knees drawn in and his side against the door—"

A near fetal position against the side of the car door. That explained the rigor mortis position and the lividity Aleek saw.

"—and it wasn't closed all the way and then that damned dog showed up, barking and barking and jumping on the side of the truck and I had to shove the dog away, then shove *him* back in and reclose the door—three times before it latched right."

She panted—from talking fast, but possibly also from the remembered exertion.

"I thought... I thought he'd just sleep there. Sleep off the pills. It wasn't hot or real cold, and he was in the truck. Lots of people sleep in their trucks."

Definitely a defense.

"That dog wouldn't leave me alone. He kept jumping up. On me. On the truck. On my vehicle. On everything."

"The dog tried to follow you when you went in the house to look for the keys to the truck." Not a question.

"I thought ... I might need them. I didn't break in. The house was open. I was hardly inside and the dog was scratching and scratching. Thank heavens, I found keys on a peg in the kitchen. When I came out, the dog was still there. It kept barking and barking as I backed out my SUV. It's a miracle I didn't hit him."

Leaving Palmer Rennant dead or dying in the passenger seat of his own truck. No wonder she focused on the dog.

"I got out of there as fast as I could. But then there wasn't a word. I was tense about it all day Friday. He'd wake up and he'd be screaming from the rooftops or someone would find him and I had to be calm. Totally calm. To show I wasn't crazy. That he was the one. *He* was the one."

Except he hadn't fed himself sleeping pills. Pills she kept from a house she'd cleaned.

"But when I went back Friday night, he... he wasn't ... awake. We drove to the butte. I'd seen teenagers do it. It wasn't hard.

"He was curled up against the door and he wouldn't ... move. I didn't know how I'd get him out. Then I remembered how I'd gotten him out of my SUV the night before. So I did that."

She'd used her feet to push him out. She did the same to get him out of his truck and left him where he landed. With rigor mortis not yet past, he stayed in the curled-up position.

"But there he was with his shirt off and you didn't like that," I said.

"I didn't. As if—After I'd told him no. But he took it off anyway.

And tried to grab me and kiss me, while he was telling me how he'd ruin *everything*. Then, later… He looked so bare and I tried to put his shirt on but I couldn't and I thought of the paint and it seemed like a way to cover him. But I didn't make them real symbols, I'd *never* do that. Never."

To cover his bareness or to cover the lividity that signaled his position in the truck? Either way, she wore gloves. Consciousness of wrongdoing—as if dumping him weren't enough. And then she leaned her left hand on the rock and the three-leaved plant that grew against it to steady herself.

"You knew he'd be found at the butte." And when.

"I … I acted on instinct. It didn't seem right, his not being found. His family wondering…"

Not concern for his family. Palmer had to be found before Teague died so there'd be no question of who inherited.

I spoke quietly, but with no doubt. "The museum, your programs, all that good was so close, so very close to what actually happened today, when they got everything. But as long as he was living, they'd lose everything. He'd ruin the programs you built, ruin you, ruin the museum, ruin history itself. You knew because he told you about the will. And how the museum could inherit. He did that … talked about things without thinking how it would make others feel."

"No. No."

I wanted to push. Oh, how I wanted to push.

I pulled in a slow breath through my nose, and backed up. "You dated during the summer, but you said you'd met him before."

"Years ago, when he was looking for ancestors. He was married, so nothing happened. Plus, he got really angry about what he found in the local archives. Wouldn't ever talk about that. Then I saw him the day Paige and I did the estimate on the Ferguson house and he was next door to see Kamden Graf. After that, he called me and I thought, why not? Clara never handled him right or he wouldn't have refused to let us use the property. If it had been me—But that didn't matter anymore. We found someplace better. So why shouldn't I go out with him? Why shouldn't I have … romance?

"After a couple weeks he was really excited one night and told me Russell Teague was sick, maybe dying. I couldn't imagine why he reacted that way."

I held my breath.

She was at the precipice again. So close...

"He said he would use all Teague's money to shut us down and go against the museum. I couldn't believe it at first, but the more he talked, the more I could tell he meant every word. It wasn't fair."

Then she added, far more prosaically, "I couldn't go out with him after that."

I could keep at her to connect the final dot that she'd known that Rennant dying would make the museum the major beneficiary.

But that defense-building bothered me. A lot.

I did not want to be called as a witness to say I'd tried everything I could to get her to confess, but she stood by her denial.

It sucked, but better, in the interests of justice, to let Shelton have his inning.

"Nadine, it will come out that you didn't get insurance this year."

"It was a mistake. That's all. With the inheritance, the museum can make up the difference."

"You need to tell everything to the sheriff's department."

"I... I can't. It's been so awful. Telling you... It's helped. But now, now I have to go."

She opened the SUV door and got out. Something white dripped from her grocery bag. Ice cream.

"Nadine, did you know Palmer had cleaners come to his house?"

She turned to face me. "Yeah. A couple times a week."

"Do you know which days?"

"Not Friday," she said with bitterness and started away.

Lights and sounds froze her after three steps.

She was going to talk to the sheriff's department very soon.

Chapter Sixty-Eight

"...THINK SHE'D KNOWN about the inheritance for a couple weeks. Long enough for the injustice to fester."

"Why tell her and not other women he dated? Or did he?" Diana asked.

"No way did he tell those other women, or it would have gotten out. Besides, the reason he told Nadine was Teague was so sick. Plus, she cared as passionately about the topic as he did—just on opposite sides."

It was odd recapping this with each of us being a face on the screen, but by the time Shelton decided he'd rather talk to the suspect than the witness and released me, Diana had gone home to her children, Jennifer to her parents, and Mike, of course, was in Chicago.

Actually, my chat with Shelton came after he'd let me loose to do a live breaking news segment on the arrest on the Ten—accompanied by predictable Thurston Fine apoplexy—before I returned to the sheriff's department, as I'd promised.

The old softy didn't even insist I wear an ankle monitor to the station.

"What about Vicky Upton? She works at the museum shop," Jennifer said.

Mike shook his head. "She's not interested in history. As I bet she let him know first time he expounded his theories."

"Right," I said. "But Nadine was perfect. It's like someone finding a rare stamp. Who better to understand the achievement than a fellow stamp collector even if—maybe especially if—that person's a rival? Far more satisfying than telling someone who says, *Oh, yeah. Weird stamp.*"

"But she didn't admit to you she knew about the will. How do you prove he told her when it was the two of them and he's dead?"

"She did admit it in a way," Diana said.

"No, Mike's right. She didn't completely confess to that. Maybe Shelton can get her to say it. Otherwise, the sheriff's department will have to make do with all the other evidence, including her stopping for the paint at the camp, using gloves, and all the forensics they'll get from his truck, her SUV."

"Why'd you ask her about the cleaners' schedule?" Jennifer asked.

"If she'd known they were coming Saturday, she could have left Rennant at his place—actually he would have been found earlier, because they came in the morning.

"But to her view, they failed her Friday. I failed her Friday by not going there to interview him. She wasn't about to wait any longer, so she took him to the butte to be sure he was found Saturday and she'd see it—from a safe distance."

"I get that the answer to *why take him to the buttes?* is her need for him to be found before Russell Teague died," Mike said. "But there's poison ivy other places around the county. That doesn't say she's guilty."

"Her confession doesn't persuade you?" Diana asked.

"I'm persuaded. Just trying to figure out how Elizabeth figured it out."

"The poison ivy? She spent last week at the camp almost from early morning until sunset. Except when she came into town Thursday to go to the Ferguson house and the committee dinner, then Friday, to try to persuade me to go to Rennant's house. From Sunday on she was in the office with Clara. No opportunities for poison ivy in any of that."

"You think she really killed him because of the insurance? As you pointed out it was coming out, no matter what."

"Yeah, but with him alive she's caught over the insurance *and* he kills the camp and reenactment. With him dead, they keep going, the museum gets bundles, and maybe she survives not getting insurance.

But more than anything, I think the insurance was the catalyst after she'd festered about the inheritance and what Rennant would do with it."

"Explain the insurance from the start," Jennifer requested.

"Nadine failed to get insurance for the events this year, redirecting that money to the kids. Verona mentioned Saturday not seeing Nadine when she expected to. But then Paige said she'd seen Nadine with Kamden Graf and that led me—and probably Verona—to think Nadine got insurance from him.

"Except, he told me he didn't know Nadine. Not only was there no reason for him to lie about that, but there was no sign of recognition between them today at Teague Ranch. That meant he hadn't sold her insurance."

"Paige was just wrong? If she hadn't screwed up, you could have figured this out days ago?"

"I don't think she was entirely wrong and no way could I have figured it out days ago. What she said was she'd seen Nadine with Kamden—*or was it with your new client?* The new client Verona said came in about damage to his truck from hitting an animal."

"Devil," Diana said. "Her new client was Palmer Rennant. He hit Devil on Tuesday and went to check with his insurance agent when he was in town Thursday, running errands like the pharmacy and supermarket."

"Exactly. Verona gets chatting with him and unknowingly gives him enough to figure out Nadine didn't get the insurance. He knew Kamden, so easily could have checked with him, too.

"That same day at the Ferguson house, Paige saw them together, with Kamden, which is why she mixed up which man she saw Nadine with. Nadine was there to pick up things she was supposed to dispose of, including the old sleeping pills Penny told us Mary Ferguson kept—and kept using—even though they were off the market for decades. Your Aunt Gee saw them in the back of Nadine's SUV that night," I said to Mike in an aside. "Palmer and Kamden were at the Grafs' house, no doubt working on their big literary project, cutting its teeth on proving history wrong about the Rennants, then taking on the

Teagues.

"Where was I? Oh, yes, so Palmer sees Nadine and lets her know he knows about the lack of insurance and what he plans to do with his knowledge. He was completely engrossed in his own viewpoint and tuned out her devastation.

"She goes to his place that night to try to reason with him. He thinks she's there for sex ... all the while boasting about what he's going to do to the programs she's devoted so much of her life to and getting more and more worked up. According to her, the pills were an impulse to calm him down and make him stop talking."

"You don't believe it?"

"I have my doubts. Though even she might not know what was in her mind, especially with the second round."

"So that's our three mysteries," Mike said. "Nadine says she killed Palmer so he wouldn't ruin the events—though we think she knew about the inheritance—Luther Tipton died in the cave after a barroom fight, and Mrs. P was worried about Sally and Nadine, because she'd figured out the first two way before us."

My mind stuck on Mrs. P.

Had she suspected Luther was in the cave? Had she sent me up to view the reenactment thinking or hoping I'd somehow find the body?

After draining a glass of water, I decided she hadn't.

Not that she *wouldn't*, but hadn't. Because it left far too much to chance.

Although... What if she planted a thought about the cave in the ear of Paytah or another reenactor? I was sent as backup? And Rennant being left there was a fluke?

Unless she'd suspected Nadine and—

No.

I was getting as paranoid as Shelton.

My phone rang.

"I'm almost afraid to answer it," I told my friends' faces on the larger screen.

"Who is it?"

"Local number. Don't recognize it."

"Answer," Jennifer urged me.

I probably couldn't have withstood the curiosity anyway.

It was the strong-minded nurse from the hospital.

"Sally Tipton died a few minutes ago. I believe Mrs. Parens would like to see you."

"I DO NOT know what that nurse based her assumption on that I wanted to see you, Elizabeth. Sally has died. Gisella and I shall deal with the practical matters here, then she will kindly drive me home. It is a shame you were brought out to the hospital at this hour of the night for nothing."

I didn't tell her that her *hour of the night* was my prime old-movie watching time, but tonight I'd spent it, uh, chatting with Wayne Shelton, then debriefing with my friends.

Especially since Aunt Gee said, tartly, "That nurse is astute enough to think you might tell the truth now and get that load off your back. Since you won't tell me, she thought of Elizabeth."

"Nonsense. There is nothing—"

"The truth can't hurt her anymore, Mrs. P."

That brought her up short. I didn't know if it was the wisdom of the words or my calling her Mrs. P to her face.

She glanced toward Gee, released a sharp breath, then said, "Perhaps you are right, Elizabeth. I have been so accustomed to protecting that woman from potential consequences... I'm not at all sure I did the right thing all those years ago, nor through the years that have followed. If she'd been forced to own up..."

Two incomplete sentences nearly back-to-back. Mrs. Parens was beside herself.

"I don't agree," Aunt Gee said briskly. "In these times, perhaps Sally would have had justice, because people understand more about abuse—physical, mental, and emotional. They know what a man like Luther Tipton truly is. Although they get it wrong sometimes. Still, in these times, perhaps. Back then? No.

"If you'd made her face the consequences, you would have consigned her to a far greater hell than she deserved or than her silliness led her into during her life."

"Thank you, Gisella." Mrs. Parens' solemnity was a tribute to the solace of Gee's logic, as was the moisture in her eyes. She blinked it away and stood even straighter. "But I will not alter my stance that if ever a man did *not* deserve a proper burial, Christian or otherwise, it was Luther Tipton."

I heard Needham's voice again.

If ever a man deserved getting killed...

"That's okay, Mrs. Parens, Sally gave me that job."

"No, Elizabeth, that is not your duty. Sally did what she did to force my hand, with you as an impartial witness, even going as far as being recorded by Diana."

Unspoken was that Gee wouldn't have forced her hand. In a choice between fulfilling Sally's wish and accepting Mrs. P's decision, she'd have backed Mrs. P.

Body braces came in all configurations. Mrs. P for Sally Tipton, Gee for Mrs. P ... and vice versa, as I knew.

"Are you going to see to it he gets one?" I asked.

"Yes."

Aunt Gee put an arm around her neighbor's shoulders. As if that contact renewed her resources, Mrs. P added with her usual decisiveness, "But I will not see that man in their family plot. He'll be as far from Sally and her mother as possible."

DAY NINE

FRIDAY

Chapter Sixty-Nine

ANOTHER PHONE CALL.

After these past few days, I needed therapy to overcome phone call aversion.

This one was Mrs. Parens, asking me to come to her house at my earliest convenience.

Diana, Audrey, and Jennifer—all working with me on a special report for KWMT—and I translated that as immediately.

Mrs. Parens welcomed me in and directed me to a chair in a small sitting room.

She sat as upright as ever. And it wasn't that she'd added white hair or wrinkles overnight. She'd had both as long as I'd known her. But the white and the wrinkles had altered with the subtlety of observing the passage from one day to the next. Until one day it's not late summer anymore.

"I received a letter in yesterday's mail. The envelope came from James Longbaugh's office with an enclosure addressed to me from Sally."

I felt my eyebrows climbing.

"James included a brief note saying that by sending me the letter, he was fulfilling a commission from Sally."

She held out an envelope with faded pink flowers around the edges. Handwriting filled a sheet with the same flowers splashed diagonally across the top left and bottom right corners.

Saw the news last night with that smart lady reporter on TV and then read it in the paper just now, so I suppose it's true.

They found Pa.

My stepmother and I never did care for each other. That was entirely true. Didn't ever love her and she didn't ever love me. And people knew it. Didn't try to hide it, neither one of us, from the start. Wasn't with a plan or anything. Just was.

I remember my mama and she did love me. I still remember what that felt like. Never anything like that with my Pa or my stepmother or anyone else.

I'll give my stepmother this, she never whipped me. Never hit me at all. And she'd let me eat when I was hungry. Pa didn't always. Depended how he was feeling. Oftentimes, he wasn't feeling generous to other folks, including his family.

He hit my mama and he hit my stepmother.

One night he hit me, too. And he grabbed me where he shouldn't have and said something. I don't remember what it was precisely, but he made himself clear. My stepmother and me looked at each other, just for a second. Guess there was a lot in that look, because when she came up behind him with the cast iron pan, I was ready with the next size down on the other side of him and hit him back to her. We each hit him a couple times with the edge of the skillet and then he crumbled down out of his chair, taking a good plate with him, and we waited a bit, getting our breath back and to see if he'd get up, but he was dead.

After a spell, I said the Butte Cave, just like that. She nodded, even though I don't think she could have known where it was. But she was trusting me. We didn't have any choice except to trust each other then.

Neither of us said a word other than the name of that cave the whole time. Not when we heaved him up into the back of the wagon, not while we took that long, slow trip. It was even harder getting him out of the wagon and into the cave. I suppose we were both real tired by then.

Never could recall the trip back to the house. I suppose our old horse Pearl did the navigating.

Back at the house, we had to rouse up to scrub real good. Wouldn't have done any good with the kind of things they show on TV these days, but back then it was plenty. It started raining during the night and went well into next morning, so we used that as we cleaned out the wagon. And it wiped out our wagon tracks good enough from the night before.

She did say a few words then, that we were going into town to the sheriff and to say as little as possible to him. Took us a while with Pearl and the wagon, because Pa wouldn't let her, let alone me, drive his truck. Not to mention it wasn't there.

Sheriff didn't seem the least bit worried about it when we came in and my stepmother said Pa was missing, and neither of us had seen him, and with me backing up her story when everybody knew we didn't like each other, nobody gave a thought to it being other than we said.

Turns out his truck was found on the highway and there was blood in it from a fight with another man hurt so bad they weren't sure he'd live. He didn't, not beyond a week, anyway. With Pa nowhere to be found, they figured he and the other man tried to kill each other, and if Pa wasn't dead, he was long gone.

That let them hurry things through in the court, making the property half mine and half hers, and the money the same after the place was sold.

Couldn't come fast enough for my stepmother. Don't think she could look at me after. With things settled, she packed up and left real fast. Not a word.

I didn't mind her leaving. Not at all. But I didn't feel the same. Not entirely. Maybe if I had, I wouldn't have let other people see as much—that let them know or guess.

I looked up at Mrs. P. "Mildred and Avis?" I said of two contemporaries of Sally's.

She declined her head in a single nod of confirmation.

I said, "Wormed it out of her and used it as leverage."

Another single nod of confirmation.

I resumed reading.

Some that guessed have kept their guesses and their thoughts to themselves, which I do appreciate, no matter what they might think.

Now it's over. He's found. It will all come out.

I can't say it's a relief. I could have gone on along without him ever being found, without it ever coming out. But can't change what is.

I wrote this all out, so it was clear. Sometimes I get off track with talking. If the truth doesn't come out and the sheriff's department doesn't come to arrest me, I might need this to set things straight later on.

It was signed and dated Sunday, the day she'd had the stroke, while reading the *Independence*'s special edition on the discoveries of Palmer Rennant's body and the body in the cave.

"You told me a studded belt didn't mean anything to you," I said abruptly.

"I do believe what I said was that I could not say and I could not, for Sally's sake as well as to not involve you more deeply. He hit her and her stepmother with it, as you no doubt gathered. I once saw him do so, until my father stopped him."

Which was why she took on the burden of Sally.

I refolded the letter. "She never named you as one of the people who guessed."

"That is an unexpected display of discretion on Sally's part. She leaves no instructions for or wishes concerning the disposition of this document or the knowledge it contains. I shall determine what to do in that regard as events unfold."

She straightened, took the pages from me and returned them to the envelope.

If Shelton and Company got a wild hair someplace it didn't belong and decided someone other than Sally and her presumably long-dead stepmother were responsible for Luther Tipton's murder, Emmaline Parens would not sit idly by.

"I'm sorry, Mrs. Parens."

"There is nothing for you to be sorry about, Elizabeth."

"I know Sally was a friend of a kind and—"

"She was not a friend, not of any kind. She was a responsibility. I took it on willingly long, long ago, without recognizing all that it entailed or that it inevitably involved moral and ethical uncertainties. Once taken on, it could not be put down until the end."

"I was also thinking of Nadine Hulte."

She held silent a moment. "I have been fond of her for some years and that has not changed. She remains important to me for the good she achieved in the past." She turned toward me. "But I do not, in any way, condone her actions. I am sorry for what she has done, including what she has done to herself. I am not sorry that you have proven instrumental in bringing her crimes to light. I respect your actions, and I thank you for them."

Hot tears pinched at the bridge of my nose. I blinked hard.

She reached over and put her hand on top of mine.

"Doing the right thing is often not easy. It is, however, always right."

✧ ✧ ✧ ✧

MY TIME IN O'Hara Hill meant working late on the special report.

When I reached my middle of the night quiet street, a familiar pickup was parked in front of my house. A tall figure sat on my front porch.

He rose as I approached and gestured me to the chair. He sat on the top step, turned sideways so his back rested against the post and we could face each other. Or not.

"Good piece tonight," Tom said.

"Thanks. The special will be tomorrow night. Saturday night's not great for airing it but Sunday's worse, and didn't want to push it to Monday."

We spoke quietly, not intruding on the hush.

"You—you and the rest—make us viewers feel it's the most important story you've ever told. That's a real talent."

"Needham said something similar. About chasing the next story for its own sake, not as a step to the next job."

"Not exactly what I said." He studied me. I held still under the survey, but didn't open up. "You've done that—what Needham said—as long as you've been here."

I thought about him on his ranch. I thought about Needham. I thought about Diana. I thought about Mrs. Parens, Aunt Gee, Sergeant Shelton... Not aiming for *careers* in the sense so many used it in the TV news business, but doing the work. For its own sake.

I thought, too, about news people I'd known at numerous stations. The ones not looking to go anywhere else, who'd found their home. Yet they weren't shellacked, not even lightly. Because career wasn't their motivator. The work was.

It was about the work.

Satisfying.

I examined the word. It fit.

Because I was good at it?

Yes, partly. But if that were the complete answer, I'd play Free Cell all day.

I thought back through the investigations we'd done.

And Mrs. P's words on doing the right thing.

I heard my exhale.

So did Tom, judging by his, "Worked out all the puzzles?"

"No. There's still why Teague made the museum the backup beneficiary."

"Suppose there is."

"As well as why he agreed to let them use the butte property."

"That, too."

"Don't give me that. You know all about it. And the strange behavior of Emmaline Parens. You two are thick as thieves. Plus, you being at James' office right after Teague's death and right after I learned you were his Wyoming executor."

"Somebody talked out of turn."

"Not here. Mike dug it up in Chicago from people on the non-Wyoming side."

"Hear Mike's doing real well in Chicago. Hear you could be, too."

"He's doing great, as expected. As for me, I'm still here. And still waiting for answers. C'mon, Burrell. How did you get Teague to make the museum his backup beneficiary? Why did he go along with it? You know I'll find out. It will be easier on you if you tell me."

"Threat?"

"Truth."

"Wasn't me. Mrs. Parens went to him. Said she'd leave her entire historical collection to him instead of the museum if she died before he did, if he'd make the museum the beneficiary to his Cottonwood County possessions if he died first. Also, he'd agree to the camp and reenactment using the butte property until one of them died and settled the matter for good."

"She… *Why?* And the museum was only his backup beneficiary. If he was her first ben—"

"He said he had more at stake. He slid in Palmer Rennant and pushed the museum second. She adjusted her will, too, excluded prime articles, including some on the Teague family. The haggling between those two…"

"But why? Why would she? Why would *he*? It's like those old tontines. A gamble you never know the outcome of because you're dead."

"I'd say she thought it was a chance to rescue his ranch while getting a home for the reenactment and camp. He thought he'd outlive her and scoop up her collection at nearly no inconvenience to himself."

"How did she know he wouldn't outlive her? I mean in the ordinary turn of events…"

The lines at the corners of his eyes deepened. "You're not thinking Emmaline Parens had anything to do with Teague's death."

"No, of course not." Not even Mrs. Parens could manage a hereditary disease that caused multi-organ failure, even if she'd wanted to.

"She didn't know she would outlive him. But I'd say she thought she had a decent chance, knowing her family history of longevity and his of not. Plus, her collection would be—will be—a terrific addition to the museum, but what she's won with her gamble sets up the museum for a long, stable future."

"But when word came Teague was seriously ill—terminally ill—she became uncomfortable," I theorized. "And, knowing the consequences of Rennant predeceasing Teague and Teague predeceasing her, she worried that someone who cared about the same things she did murdered Palmer Rennant to benefit the museum."

"She was at least partly right."

She was.

Another question rose. "Tom, do you think she did the deal with Teague because she knew Luther Tipton was up there?"

"No."

"Because she had an inkling he was up there?"

He paused, looking toward the dark treetops against the sky. "No."

"But you wonder."

His eyes came back to me. "I can live without knowing."

Was he telling me I should do the same?

And then he said something more.

"I'm getting better at living without knowing."

Epilogue

MONDAY MORNING, I walked into the KWMT-TV newsroom feeling drained but satisfied.

Without Mike around, Diana and I drew in Audrey to help with our in-depth report on the murder of Palmer Rennant. Jennifer took on expanded duties, too. Including learning more about structure and editing.

KWMT had a limited time to benefit from her advancing skills.

She'd decided to start at Northwestern after the first of the year.

Outwardly, I was gung-ho. Inwardly, contradictory reactions butted heads.

Then I encountered Jennifer's mom, Faith, at the supermarket and her expression reflected exactly what I felt. She must have felt the same about my expression, because right there in the laundry detergent aisle and smiling the whole time, we hugged and teared up.

Audrey was good and getting better, but she hadn't been along for the whole ride as Mike had for our earlier reports. Plus, we taught her as we went, not to mention a new member of the team slows things down.

Also, we just plain missed Mike.

Even though we continued to talk to him a lot. We made him the first viewer of the rough-cut and he had good thoughts about clarifying for anyone who hadn't followed the story as it developed.

Radford Hickam contacted me, saying he might have answers to my all-encompassing question in a year.

Forensic anthropology does not work at TV news speed.

In the report, we dealt with the case of Luther Tipton by reporting the Cottonwood County Sheriff's Department's official position that he perished after wandering off while inebriated and possibly concussed following a barroom fight.

Nobody said anything about how long a wander it was from his truck to the butte.

The special report aired Saturday night.

One of my first tasks after wrapping was to sign up for a course being taught by O.D. Everett on contributions and inventions of Native Americans. Seemed like good things from the past to bring with me to the present and future.

I'd spent the rest of the weekend on high glamor necessities like laundry, cleaning, and giving my dog two extra-long walks.

I also consumed baked goods, now that Iris and Zeb Undlin were home and the flow of those calories had resumed. The flow of calories from the Sherman Supermarket continued, along with Penny's Delphic annunciation that something was coming that would open my eyes wide.

But I'd already seen Sally Tipton's letter, so that was covered.

Sally's funeral was scheduled for this afternoon.

Mrs. Parens handled most of the arrangements, with Aunt Gee helping as she could around her job.

With Russell Teague dead, the museum's lawyers moved for a summary judgment in its favor in the disposition of the gold coins.

I alerted Wardell Yardley to that. He talked about coming out here for the final decision for a wrap-up story.

He didn't mention the museum curator, but I suspected she, too, was on his agenda. Again.

Clara was deep in preparations for the changes ahead, including looking for a replacement for Nadine. I heard Paige was in despair over finding anyone as good for her estate sale business, but Verona Fuller had taken her in hand.

Tamantha recruited me for an upcoming "girls' trip" overnight to see Fort Phil Kearny—her, Mrs. Parens, and me. I think Mrs. P got to her.

I had not talked to or seen Tom.

That thought was not the reason I was slow to absorb the mood in the newsroom.

After all, there were a number of other people I hadn't talked to or seen. Sheriff Conrad, Sergeant Shelton, Deputies Alvaro and Sampson, for instance. Wasn't like that affected the speed of my uptake.

No, it was solely because of that drained feeling I mentioned.

But after I put my bag into the bottom drawer of my desk and looked around the newsroom, I realized something was up.

Something big.

Audrey and Jennifer rushed me from different directions.

Audrey asked, "Have you heard? Do you know about it?"

Those questions slowed her down, letting Jennifer come in with the headline.

"Thurston's the prime suspect in a murder."

For news about upcoming Caught Dead in Wyoming books, as well as other titles and news, join Patricia McLinn's Readers List and receive her twice-monthly free newsletter.
https://www.patriciamclinn.com/readers-list

Thank you for reading Elizabeth, Diana, Mrs. Parens and Aunt Gee's latest adventure!

Changes are afoot at KWMT as the team of amateur sleuths adapts to life without Mike, a shift in Jennifer's focus and a more looped-in Audrey. Meanwhile, supermarket cashier Penny Czylinski, who bags all the town's best gossip, perceives dark clouds on the horizon not only in Sherman, but also in the KWMT newsroom itself. Because something big is coming, it involves murder, and it's closing in on KWMT.

Cross Talk

Enjoy **Body Brace**? (Hope so)

Elizabeth and friends ask if you'll help spread the word about them and the Caught Dead in Wyoming series. You have the power to do that in two quick ways:

Recommend the book and the series to your friends and/or the whole wide world on social media. Shouting from rooftops is particularly appreciated.

Review the book. Take a few minutes to write an honest review and it can make a huge difference. As you likely know, it's the single best way for your fellow readers to find books they'll enjoy, too.

To me—as an author and a reader—the goal is always to find a good author-reader match. By sharing your reading experience through recommendations and reviews, you become a vital matchmaker. ☺

Other Caught Dead in Wyoming mysteries

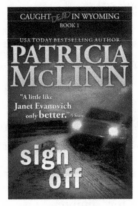

SIGN OFF

Divorce a husband, disrupt a career …
grapple with a murder.

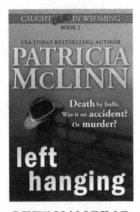

LEFT HANGING

Trampled by bulls—an accident? Elizabeth, Mike and friends dig into
the world of rodeo.

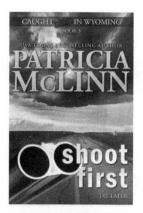

SHOOT FIRST

For Elizabeth, death hits close to home. She and friends delve into old Wyoming treasures and secrets to save lives.

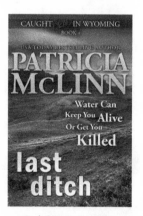

LAST DITCH

Elizabeth and Mike search after a man in a wheelchair goes missing in dangerous, desolate country.

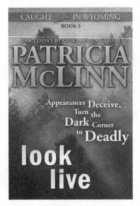

LOOK LIVE

Elizabeth and friends take on misleading murder with help—and hindrance—from intriguing out-of-towners.

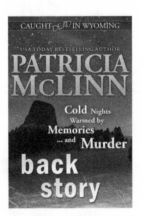

BACK STORY

Murder never dies, but comes back to threaten Elizabeth and team of investigators.

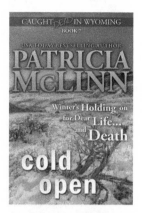

COLD OPEN

Elizabeth's search for a place of her own becomes an
open house for murder.

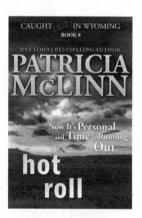

HOT ROLL

One of their own becomes a target—and time is running out.

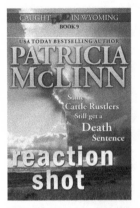

REACTION SHOT

Sometimes cattle rustlers still get
a death sentence.

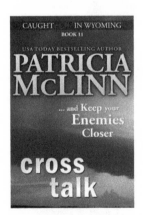

CROSS TALK

Breaking news: Storm clouds
at the station.

Secret Sleuth series

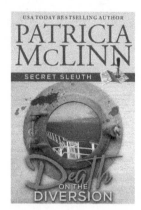

DEATH ON THE DIVERSION

Final resting place? Deck chair.

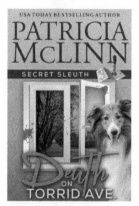

DEATH ON TORRID AVENUE

A new love (canine), an ex-cop and a dog park discovery.

DEATH ON BEGUILING WAY

No zen in sight as Sheila untangles a yoga instructor's murder.

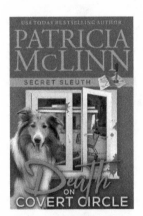

DEATH ON COVERT CIRCLE

Sheila and Clara are on the scene as a supermarket CEO meets his expiration date.

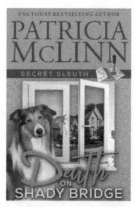

DEATH ON SHADY BRIDGE

A homicide cold case heats up.

DEATH ON CARRION LANE

More murder is brewing in Haines Tavern.

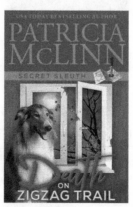

DEATH ON ZIGZAG TRAIL

Mystery With Romance

The Innocence Trilogy

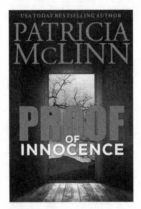

PROOF OF INNOCENCE

She's a prosecutor chasing demons. He's wrestling them.
Will they find proof of innocence?

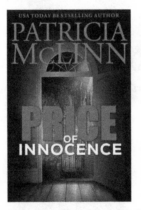

PRICE OF INNOCENCE

To solve this murder Detective Belichek will risk everything—his
friendships, his reputation, his career, his heart … and his life.

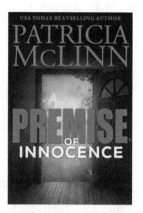

PREMISE OF INNOCENCE

The last woman Detective Landis is prepared to see is the one he must save.

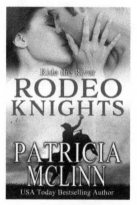

RIDE THE RIVER: RODEO KNIGHTS

Her rodeo cowboy ex is back … as her prime suspect.

BARDVILLE, WYOMING series

A Stranger in the Family

A Stranger to Love

The Rancher Meets His Match

Explore a complete list of all Patricia's books

https://www.patriciamclinn.com/patricias-books

Or get a printable booklist

https://www.patriciamclinn.com/patricias-books/printable-booklist

Patricia's eBookstore (buy digital books online directly from Patricia)

https://www.patriciamclinn.com/patricias-books/ebookstore

About the Author

Patricia McLinn is the USA Today bestselling author of nearly 60 published novels cited by readers and reviewers for wit and vivid characterization. Her books include mysteries, romantic suspense, contemporary romance, historical romance and women's fiction. They have topped bestseller lists and won numerous awards.

She has spoken about writing from London to Melbourne, Australia, to Washington, D.C., including being a guest speaker at the Smithsonian.

McLinn spent more than 20 years as an editor at The Washington Post after stints as a sports writer (Rockford, Ill.) and assistant sports editor (Charlotte, N.C.). She received BA and MSJ degrees from Northwestern University.

Now living in Northern Kentucky, McLinn loves to hear from readers through her website and social media.

Visit with Patricia:

Website: patriciamclinn.com

Facebook: facebook.com/PatriciaMcLinn

Twitter: @PatriciaMcLinn

Pinterest: pinterest.com/patriciamclinn

Instagram: instagram.com/patriciamclinnauthor